# THE LAST GOODBYE

# THE LAST GOODBYE

## H. Michael Frase

CARROLL & GRAF PUBLISHERS, INC.
NEW YORK

Carroll & Graf Publishers, Inc.
19 West 21st Street
New York, NY 10010

ISBN: 0-7867-0514-0

Manufactured in the United States of America

For Herbert Paul Rooney—


*When I was most malleable,*
*your unquestioning acceptance of all of me*
*allowed a young boy to become more as a man*
*than he would have otherwise become . . .*


*. . . thank you, Grandpa*

# THE LAST GOODBYE

Ah, when to the heart of man
Was it ever less than a treason
To go with the drift of things
To yield with a grace to reason
And bow and accept at the end
Of a love or a season.

—Robert Frost (1874-1963)

# 1

Josh Mitchell studied the small envelope, tapping it rhythmically against his open palm as he considered whether or not to slip it through the mail slot. Allowing his thoughts about a woman he'd just met to spill out in the privacy of his hotel room was not the same thing as letting her actually read those words. As he reconsidered his decision and turned to leave, Pamela Morrow's face materialized before him in the warm Carmel air, just beyond his reach, as it had a hundred times since she'd left his room in the early morning hours.

A smile easily formed as he heard his envelope strike the letters and postcards already collecting at the bottom of the antique mailbox. A mild wind from the sea rustled the fronds of a fat sago palm nearby and the familiar smell of salt spray stimulated his senses. It was going to be a glorious spring day, a welcome change from the hard Manhattan winter he'd left only a day ago.

Or had it been a lifetime ago? The thought broadened his smile.

With an enthusiastic pat on top of the mailbox—nestled in quiet harmony between a particularly resplendent pair of bougainvillea in front of the San Antonio House—Josh headed west on Ocean Avenue toward the water. He was only nine blocks from the bed-and-breakfast where he was staying, having wandered through the rows of shops and art galleries as he pondered the dilemma of whether or not to mail the letter he'd hastily written after Pamela failed to meet him for breakfast on the garden patio. Content that he had chosen wisely, he now looked forward to a slow and contemplative stroll along the enchanting shore that would return him to within a hundred yards of the Sandpiper Inn.

Carmel-by-the-Sea had always been one of Josh Mitchell's favorite places to visit and unwind, with its restaurants, inns, and incredible stretch of unspoiled oceanfront, but now romance would forever be part of the magic that defined this picturesque hideaway in his mind.

And in his heart.

Eighteen hours—he marveled at how his life had changed so dramatically in so little time.

Maybe, he thought with amusement as he walked, "Lucky" wasn't such a bad nickname after all.

When he reached the point where the hard black asphalt of Ocean Avenue gave way to the soft sands of Carmel Beach, Josh slipped off his loafers and carried one loosely in each hand like a child might do, a grin on his face.

It had been six months since his feet had pressed against these white sands, and, like a junkie in need of a fix, he'd longed for the familiar feel throughout the dreary winter in New York. The warm, pliable grains beneath his feet would itself have been enough to warrant a smile under ordinary circumstances, but today he had the added pleasures of Pamela's scent and feel filling his mind.

As he stepped onto the open beach, the water still a hundred and fifty yards ahead, his eyes beheld a familiar sight: the chair, easel, and glass frame of a sand painter.

Standing respectfully at the rear of the vacant folding cane-back chair, his shoes crossed behind his back, Josh bent at the waist and studied the artist's creation, a patiently crafted rendition of the bay and north point that framed Pebble Beach. The work was nearly completed, with layer upon layer of colored sands creating a two-dimensional likeness of the western horizon, surprisingly faithful in tone and detail. Josh marveled at the artist's palette: a dozen Jell-O pudding cups, formerly filled with the sweet chocolate and vanilla confection but now holding powdered silica in a variety of hues.

"This is beautiful," he said aloud, amazed by anything artistic. Despite being blessed with numerous talents, Josh Mitchell's gifts came from another part of the cosmos, the technological extreme, where analytical thought and emotional expression seldom met. Expecting a response of some sort—though he'd not actually seen the artist—Josh turned around, thinking the man or woman responsible for the work must be resting in the shade of the broad Monterey cypress that grew ten or twelve feet behind the chair. Though not hot by August standards, it was nevertheless quite warm this morning, more the result of a tepid desert wind rolling in from the mountains to the east than the temperate breeze wafting off the sea. A steel-blue sky as devoid of clouds as if they had never been created kept the temperature pleasant even for mid-March.

There was no one behind him. For that matter, there was not a soul within shouting distance.

Odd, he thought.

Josh looked up the beach to his right and saw only a lone man with a metal detector walking away from him, perhaps two hundred yards to the north. The man, dressed in dark slacks and a tan corduroy sport coat, was oblivious to the world around him, the cryptic voice of the hidden beach coming at him through a pair of full-coverage earphones, the electronic extension of his curiosity moving back and forth in a gentle arc as he patiently listened for the reflecting echo of metal—hopefully a tourist's lost diamond ring or an old silver piece of eight—buried beneath the sand.

He was certainly not the artist.

When he turned to his left and looked some distance to the south, toward his inn, Josh discovered where the rest of the people on the beach had gone. Parked ominously in the midst of perhaps thirty men, women, and children—the children mostly of pre-school age with the academic year still having more than two months before summer break—was the most unwelcome sight on any beach: an ambulance, this one belonging to the Carmel Fire Department, its rear doors hungrily open, its crimson warning lights spinning in silent and eerie testament to a tragedy unfolding nearby.

Josh wandered toward the crowd, half filled with a natural, though not morbid, curiosity and half with a dull sadness that anyone could die on a day as splendid as this, a majestic day, a day when he could believe in the promise of love for the first time in his life.

Eighteen hours. His mind toyed with the number as he ambled south.

He soon passed a man he'd missed at first scan, previously invisible within the broken shadows of a cluster of Monterey Bay pines: a white-legged tourist in baggie shorts and wingtips with black nylon socks, fiddling with his 35mm camera, its ridiculous-looking telephoto lens nearly as big as the man's calf. The white-legged man turned away when Josh looked in his direction.

When Josh had gotten within forty yards of the throng, a middle-aged man in a bright Hawaiian-print shirt, khaki shorts, and leather Teva sandals passed him, mumbling under his breath, his eyes on the beach before him. "Shame, real shame. Such a waste," he said to no one but the deaf ears of the universe, apparently never noticing Josh's presence. The man sported a new wide-brimmed Panama hat, his clothes were well-pressed, and the fresh scent of English Leather lingered close behind his deliberate footsteps. His plump, sunbaked face was partially hidden behind what were likely prescription sunglasses judging by their thickness—bifocals, Josh guessed—and while the man's face hadn't seen a razor in many years, his beard, no longer the full, dark mane of his youth but now a thinner ruff the color of the sand with which he worked, was long but neatly trimmed.

The artist, Josh felt certain.

Before Josh had walked another twenty yards, a pleasant-looking woman in a bikini top and white denim shorts popped from the crowd hurrying her two small children away from the frantic activity surrounding the rescue vehicle, a tiny trembling hand held tightly in each of hers. Her husband followed close behind, obviously not pleased that she was chastising him resoundingly for having taken their children to see a dead body at their tender age. "Men!" she grumbled loudly.

Though Josh didn't disagree with the woman, he couldn't help feeling sorry for the man who obviously hadn't regarded the situation with the malice of intent for which he was now being charged.

The two men exchanged brief glances as they passed, but the husband cut his eyes away and followed his wife, feeling no apparent need to respond to her ire merely for some stranger's sake. He would, after all, have to live with the woman long after they'd left the beach.

*God, don't let it be a child,* Josh thought. He felt a sudden shame that it would have been okay for the deceased to be a homeless derelict with no family and no one to mourn the loss. He sensed his heart thumping as he neared the vehicle.

He considered returning to Scenic Road which ran along the edge of the beach and skirting the unpleasant scene, but noted that the sea wall was now over six feet high and he was in no mood to scale the rocky bulwark.

In emotional self-defense, he conjured up Pamela's vibrant image, so full of life—so life-giving, he noted with a sense of hope he'd not felt since the end of high school, the smile returning to his face—and moved irresolutely toward the group, hoping to pass at the back of the gathering and move on to his inn. He wanted to go about his business without so much as a glance, not wishing to lose the feeling that warmed him like a ray of August sunlight.

*Eighteen hours.* He pulled the image around him like a shield.

On the passenger's side of the ambulance, Josh saw a 4WD Ford Expedition belonging to the Monterey County Coroner's Office and a Chevy Blazer with the markings of the Carmel Police Department, both previously hidden by the ambulance and the crowd. These two vehicles, far more than the ambulance—which always held out a hope for life—caused a chill to wash over Josh.

*Eighteen hours,* he repeated again. *Remember the way she felt.*

He took a deep breath and exhaled it noisily.

As Josh passed a small break in the crowd, at a point near the driver's side of the rescue vehicle, he was inadvertently afforded an unobstructed view of the activities at its rear.

Two men, both dressed in dark blue Nomex trousers and dark blue T-shirts bearing the Carmel Fire Department logo, stood over a single figure, quietly sharing some amusing twaddle; the coroner's investigator and a patrolman knelt opposite them, dispassionately discussing the fact that there were no apparent wounds on the extremities, no ligature marks, no fractured vertebrae, no unexpected punctures.

Drowning was the likely cause of death, they concurred.

A sheet which had previously draped the body had been pulled back while a fifth man, in boots, black jeans, and a white oxford shirt, hurriedly snapped photos with a Canon auto-focus camera and speedlight.

The photographer, who worked for the Coroner's Office, straddled the body's bare feet, which still pointed silently toward the water from which it had been dragged. The depressions caused by its heels, clearly visible in the sand, disappeared beneath the sneakers and sandals of the curious who'd formed a three-quarter circle around the firemen. The only break in the wall of onlookers lay squarely before Josh.

Human nature stopped him before he realized the subconscious act had occurred.

Though the lifeless corpse was still a full twenty feet away, and no clear view of the face could be seen from Josh's position—he was able to tell that it was a woman's body—the uneasy feeling from moments earlier became full-fledged anxiety. His mouth dried as if it had been filled with the sand between his toes.

He dropped his shoes and leaned on the front fender of the truck for support, his head bowed. No one noticed; each was in his own mind, grateful that he or she was merely watching the horror and not the one whose lungs were filled with sea water and whose skin was now the lifeless color of chalk.

Josh had never harbored a desire to derive cathartic release from another's misfortune, and had hoped to pass the tragedy on the beach without being confronted with the gruesome sight of a dead body. He had not imagined that the mere glimpse of it at twenty feet, however, would have caused such a reaction.

With his mind beginning to clear, like a punch in the face wearing off, his eyes returned to the still figure lying before him.


As Andy Wheeler, the coroner's investigator—a tall, burly man of forty or so with thick brown hair and penetrating blue eyes—and the patrolman finished their examination and the photographer snapped his last image, the two firemen began to cover the body once again. An image as cryptic as a ghost hammered painfully in Josh's memory, its intensity increasing with each beat of his heart.

He forced himself to look away.

What was he trying to remember? What could the corpse of a total stranger possibly be stirring in his mind?

His head snapped again toward the body, his eyes focusing on the right wrist that was just being covered by the shroud. *Oh, God, it can't be.*

It wasn't the sight of a person deceased that had brought him to his knees, but the sight of *this* person. Even without conscious intervention, his heart had held on to images as surely as a mother's face is imprinted upon an infant's mind.

The charm bracelet, that one-in-the-world trinket derived not merely from gold and silver but from a mélange of memories, without which Pamela, by her own proud admission, would have never left home, filled his eyes even as the glittering object disappeared beneath the sheet. It had been with her since her youth, earning its cheerful jangle as much from the gentle clash of baubles accumulated over two decades as from the collective echo of memories associated with them.

A feeling of nausea danced in his stomach.

The image of her skin, so warm against his body, being replaced by the pallid, swollen derma was too much to bear.

"*No!*" he shouted when his voice had been found again, then in a whimper, "It's not fair . . ."

The sudden emotional outburst drew everyone's attention, but none more than the patrolman's; the man stood and moved toward the front of the ambulance. "All right, folks, everybody's had more than enough show for one day. Break up this circus *now* and go on about your business. This is no way to spend a vacation."

The officer spoke with the hard, guttural voice of a drill instructor, his polite choice of words thinly masking his anger at a crowd that had failed to disperse after two previous requests.

Coroner's Investigator Wheeler directed the firemen to remove the body at once and deliver it to the Salinas morgue for the postmortem.

One of the firemen grabbed a backboard from the truck as the other began to tuck the sheet beneath the sides of the corpse. The crowd moved away, along the beach, each seeking the spot he had occupied before the excitement began.

Beneath the stand of Monterey Bay pines, deep within their shadows, the man with white legs missed nothing, the 1200mm lens providing as much magnification as a small telescope.

"You know this woman, sir?" the patrolman asked when he neared Josh.

Josh, standing erect now, saw the officer's mouth move but heard nothing, waiting anxiously for the woman beneath the sheet to begin coughing, to expel the brine from her lungs and complain vehemently about being mistaken for dead.

*You can do it,* Josh's mind screamed. *You can still get up . . . it's not too late. Please tell them that they've made a mistake, that they can't take you away. Please, Pamela . . .*

His silent prayer went unanswered.

"You listening to me?" the officer said abruptly.

Josh turned his head toward the unfamiliar voice, but his vision was on an image that could only be seen by the heart.

"Hey!" the patrolman barked.

It worked. The radiant memory which Josh had tried so hard to conjure up, free of the insanity at his feet, vanished before it could be fully found.

The patrolman, a serious-looking man of Asian descent, stood six-foot even with his two hundred pounds of tan, lean muscle distributed across a broad-shouldered frame. The bullet-proof vest added to the athletic appearance, exaggerating his chest and imparting an air of invincibility. His black hair was cut on the sides and back in a buzz with the top slightly longer: Marine Corps style.

"What did you say?" Josh asked, his voice sounding like he'd just been awakened.

"I asked if you knew the woman who drowned." He awaited an answer, his patience growing thin.

"What happened to her?" Josh asked weakly. "How did . . . she die?"

The officer wanted to shake him. In addition to a bloated, salt-bleached body less than an hour after breakfast, he apparently now had a loony on his hands, an empathet, one who can feel another's pain. He knew California attracted all manner of personalities like raccoons to a corn field, but Carmel was usually as free of such human aberrations as her golf courses were of crabgrass.

Wheeler backed his Expedition toward the wall lining the beach then put it in Drive and pulled even with the patrolman. "See you later, Ray," he said when his window had lowered. "I'll get you copies of the photos Mike took by tomorrow." With the Monterey County Coroner's Office being one of the finest forensics labs west of the Mississippi, the autopsy would be finished by then as well.

Patrolman Ray nodded only slightly, his lips tight. "You have some I.D. on you, sir?"

The Ford departed quietly.

Josh felt his back pockets—nothing, he'd left his room with his wallet still sitting on top of the dresser—then dug a hand in each front pocket. He had only a small silver room key from the Sandpiper Inn—for security reasons it bore only a box number—and one wrinkled business card with an unimportant phone number he'd scratched on the back of it yesterday. He offered the business card.

After a quick glance, the patrolman said, "You Joshua Thomas Mitchell?"

Josh nodded but flinched as the body was lifted and carried toward the truck, his attention still on the woman he'd met only hours before. He leaned against the fender once again for support.

*Why don't you just cry out, Pamela? Don't let them take you,* his heart shouted.

It wasn't fair that his boyhood dream should end this way.

"You on something, Mr. Mitchell? It's awful damned early in the day to be screwed up." The officer removed his dark glasses and took a close look into Josh's eyes—they were rimmed with water but appeared clearer than he would have guessed, the pupils normal size. He returned the glasses to his face. "You staying around here, sir?"

Josh produced the room key. "Yeah," he mumbled.

*It's not too late, Pamela. Tell them they're making a horrible mistake. Please tell them.*

"Well, if you've got something to offer here, Mr. Mitchell, let's have it, otherwise I think you should be heading back toward your hotel."

Josh took the key and the card and stuffed them back into his front pockets, then stooped to pick up his shoes. The ambulance driver took his seat behind the wheel and started the engine, his partner slamming the passenger's door. Josh jumped, then stepped away.

"Thanks for the help, Ray," the driver said. "Need anything?"

"Nothing I can think of at the moment, unless you want to do my paperwork for me."

"No thanks, got my own. Buy you a beer later."

"That'll work." The patrolman patted the side of the truck as it pulled away, then headed for his own vehicle.

As the ambulance passed, the driver gave Josh a hard look, then blew cigarette smoke out through his nostrils as the truck's tandem rear tires threw up a spray of sand. The firemen laughed heartily as the truck headed back toward Ocean Avenue.

*There's still time, Pamela. Just call out . . . I'll hear you.*

When the patrolman had left, and the area seemed deserted, Josh dropped his loafers and sat in the tire tracks the ambulance had made. He traced the ridges and valleys of the wide treads with his finger, careful not to disturb the sand. Though he did this for only a few minutes, later he could not have stated with certainty how long he'd been sitting like this. He was like a child locked in a dark closet, where ticks of the second hand passed like the pages of a calendar, his mind clinging to the images and scents of early morning.

It made him shiver to think how quickly love and hope could vanish.


"Lot of freaky shit going down this morning, huh? Too weird!" the unfamiliar voice announced behind him. Before Josh could look over his shoulder, the young man who had spoken plopped down on the sand beside him, planting his bright red rescue buoy vertically in the sand at his feet: a lifeguard.

Through blue mirrored lenses, he looked casually at the strangely quiet man to his left and said, "You catch the action a little while ago? Oh, man, real waste of good flesh, if you know what I mean. But, hey, breaks up the monotony of waiting for the Pacific to carry away California, huh? Wasn't like either of us knew the bitch, right?" The boy faced the water and wrapped his brown arms around his knees, his feet pulled close in a tuck position, chin resting on his forearms. A large, clear gemstone stuck squarely in the boy's left ear—Josh doubted it was the full-carat diamond it pretended to be— glinted brightly in the morning sun, its broad top facet occasionally directing a ray of sunlight into Josh's eyes, forcing a squint. It made him dislike the boy even beyond his crude manner.

"What do you know about what went on here?" Josh asked, containing his anger. He'd dealt with boorish clients for years and had become expert at allowing them to speak their minds on race, sex, religion, or politics while he maintained a position of stoic neutrality, no matter how difficult it had been at times. Such posture had made him comfortably wealthy and had not compromised his soul too badly in the process: It didn't mean he agreed with each cur he encountered just because he didn't punch out everyone who deserved it.

The boy glanced at the stranger then looked again toward the sea, speaking to the waves that lapped in majestic but disinterested rhythm against the shore. "You know about the great-looking chick that drowned, right?"

Josh nodded that he did.

"Well, I found her, dude, lapping against the shore like a piece of kelp." He looked to the stranger to see if he'd been duly impressed—he couldn't tell. Then he studied his watch, one of those large-faced stainless steel analog chronometers with countless subordinate dials and readouts that told you things few understood and no one really cared about. "It'll have been two hours ago in, let me see, six minutes and . . . fifteen seconds," he stated with atomic certainty. "You can still see her heel marks where I dragged her waterlogged ass out of the surf. Just did it because it's procedure—floaters kinda freak out the tourists, know what I mean—but it was a waste of time and energy. There wasn't no saving that bitch and I knew it flat out. I've seen a lot of floaters in my life, so I ought to know." He was sure the man would be impressed now.

"Do you always have to be such a crude bastard?" Josh said, surprised by the harshness in his voice. *Eighteen hours . . .* his mind fought for control, his emotions winning the battle. He stood and turned away, anxious to be as far from this cretin as possible.

"Man, what is *your* problem?" The boy stood as well, pulling his buoy out of the sand by the tow line and shouldering it like a soldier's weapon.

Josh turned quickly back and took two deliberate steps, putting his face within inches of the boy's. While Josh had ten years on the kid, and more than two inches in height, the boy stood firmly in place.

Josh's words were cold and hard, not for effect but because his heart had become a lump of ice, frozen by the loss of hope. "You want to know my problem? I knew the woman who died, knew her well, understand, and she was no *bitch*, she was a lady, the finest lady I've ever known. She didn't *want* to die, to have the last person on earth who touched her be some scumbag who doesn't give a rat's ass about anyone but himself." Josh's chin lowered slightly, lips tight, his eyes as narrow and unyielding as knife wounds. "Now, how fast can you say *lady*, asshole?"

"Lady," the boy mumbled quickly.

The pain in Josh's heart forced a tear from the corner of each eye. The hurt clearly visible in the stranger's expression was understood by the boy and his shoulders slumped a bit, but the boy had no way of understanding the depth of despair the man was feeling. All he could say was, "Sorry, man, I didn't mean nothing by it, just making talk, you know? Sorry."

He turned to continue his patrol along the beach.

"I have to know," Josh called out to him, his voice shaky. He half expected the boy to keep on walking.

Instead, he returned without bitterness to offer what he could. "What do you want to know that you haven't already heard?" He seemed older now, less sure. Josh remembered that one of the defining moments in his own life was when he realized he had slowly and without protest exchanged the certainty of youth for the doubt that accompanies maturity.

Josh didn't understand in his head the answers his heart was screaming for, and found the thoughts hard to construct. "I need to know . . . how she died. Exactly."

It was a clumsy start, but as good as he could do.

It wasn't one of his well-rehearsed sales pitches.

The answer seemed blatantly apparent to the kid: drowning was drowning. To his credit, he tried to find some response other than the obvious. "I guess she went into the water sometime after midnight, probably one or one-thirty, no later than two for sure. She had to have been in for at least six hours judging by the swelling around her eyes and lips . . . sorry," he offered sincerely, deciding it would be better to skip the details. "I don't know, maybe she had too much to drink or something . . . anyway, whatever the reason, she didn't make it. The surf can be pretty rough, especially late at night. Even an experienced swimmer can get more than he bargains for. Hell, you should see the bitch when she's really pissed off . . . the Pacific I mean."

Josh appreciated the boy's attempt to explain that the sea can claim anyone it wants anytime it chooses, regardless of skill or physical prowess. He tried to imagine Pamela Morrow fighting valiantly against a sudden riptide, against waves whipped into an unexpected frenzy by a desert wind howling down from the hills. *Why, Pamela?* his mind cried out. She hadn't been drinking, not more than a glass of wine or two at dinner. Why was she swimming fully dressed? What had she been thinking? He knew the boy had no answers.

He turned his attention to the ocean, which now seemed no longer a soothing place where brightly colored sails dotted the liquid landscape on Sunday afternoons, the stress of the work week replaced by the peaceful rhythm of Earth's bosom, but now as a predatory beast set only on regaining the strength it would need to claim its next victim.

The boy stuck his hands in the pockets of his trunks and spoke in a low voice, as if to himself: "But then, I guess that's what she had in mind all along, huh?"

"Had in mind!? Why in God's name would you say something like that?" Josh snapped, taking the boy's shoulder and turning him face to face. The old ire reared its head.

"But . . . I thought you knew . . . didn't they tell you?" the kid said defensively.

"Knew *what?*"

"About the letter."

"Letter? What letter?"

"The letter the lady left. I found it while I was waiting for the Fire Department to arrive. It was right there"—he pointed to a spot on the beach not ten feet away, a yard to the north of the heel gouges that still scarred the sand—"next to her shoes and purse."

"Where is this letter?" Josh asked. The blood pounded heavily in his ears.

"Cops took it, along with the rest of her stuff, I guess." The wind forced the kid's long, bleached hair into his face and he swept it back with both hands, his fingers acting as combs, his elbows held toward the sky, hands now locked behind his head. He was uncomfortable with the conversation and wanted to be on his way. "That's all I know, man. Sorry again for your loss."

"Did you read this letter?" Josh asked.

The kid dropped his arms and grew antsy. He readjusted his buoy. Josh knew he had.

"Nope, not me . . . wasn't none of my business what the lady was

up to. Just pointed her stuff out to the cops." The fidgeting continued. "I really gotta be going now."

When he took a step, Josh grabbed his arm. "That's a strange
choice of words, 'what the lady was up to.' I know you read the letter, man. Read it all. You had . . . what . . . ten minutes before the
EMT responded? Plenty of time to snoop around all you wanted, the
beach is empty at that hour. And, like you said, anything to break up
the monotony. You weren't exactly busy doing CPR, now were you?"

"Hey, anybody'll tell you CPR would have been useless in this—"

"I'll give you that much," Josh interrupted. "But you read the letter, didn't you?"

"I swear to you I didn't look through *any* of her shit, not her purse,
nothing."

"But you read the letter." It was now a statement.

"All right, listen, it was kinda unfolded already, you know, just
lying there, like the wind had blown it open, one of her shoes lying
on it. I didn't have to even touch it, just read what was there in plain
sight for anyone to see. You're not going to get my butt in trouble
with the cops for tampering with evidence, I didn't do anything—"

"Relax. Nobody's trying to get you into trouble. I knew this lady,
remember, and I have to understand what happened to her. You
gotta tell me."

The kid took a nervous breath. He felt caged. "You're not gonna
like it."

Josh braced himself, though for what he wasn't sure. His expression commanded the boy to continue.

"The way I figure it, like I told you, it's what she had in mind all
along. The letter said there was nothing else she could do under the
circumstances, no other way out. I'm sorry, man, but your lady-friend
committed suicide. She drowned herself right out there." He pointed
a shaky finger toward the surf.

Josh's eyes followed it like a road marker to Hell.

# 2

*Set thy foot down with distrust on
the crust of the world—it is thin.*

—Edna St. Vincent Millay (1892-1950)

An hour after the last of the official, the curious, and the morbid had left the beach, forty minutes after the lifeguard had punched a hole in Josh Mitchell's dreams, he sat again beside the tracks of the vehicle that had taken away Pamela Morrow's lifeless form. And along with it the hope that an old prayer had at last been answered.

Having not eaten breakfast—not a bite since dinner in Sausalito with Pamela fourteen hours earlier—his gut churned. As he fixated on a wave a hundred yards out that seemed to be advancing in dramatically slow motion, a frothy hitchhiker of whitecaps riding the crest of the aquamarine curve which bore it toward the land, his mind went back to their first meeting. It was on the plane from New York yesterday afternoon, when Pamela had interrupted a reverie about a simpler time in his life . . .

. . . It's late August 1987 and I'm sitting in the cab of my old black Chevy pickup, the one I've driven my last two years in high school.

My shoulders are against the driver's door, my head leaned back through the open window, a mild summer breeze in my hair, my bare feet in Samantha's lap. She is rubbing them gently and talking at length about her favorite subject: our life together after I finish college. I don't mind really, though I've heard it before, many times; there's little else to do in Selmer at this hour, though it is not late by big-city standards.

From a radio station in Jackson, playing softly in the background, the Statler Brothers are singing their latest hit, "I'll Be the One."

We made love an hour ago, by Twin Springs Lake, as we often do on Friday and Saturday nights, and Samantha is now in a particularly melancholy mood, filled with elaborate plans for not only the rest of her life, but for mine as well.

I listen, as always, contributing an occasional thought—well-placed and supportive since I've learned it's best not to disagree in such matters. I've come to realize that a woman, as I see it, views sex differently than a man, associating the physical act with commitment, undying devotion, and an idyllic future with her man.

I find it all confusing and a little scary: I don't know what I'm going to be feeling next week, much less in the future. Samantha seems so sure about it all.

It's not that I don't love Samantha; in fact, I'm as much in love as I can be . . . I guess. It's just that she and I don't share the same assuredness about tomorrow. It's hard to think about commitment to one person when I've only really *known* one person. This is where Samantha and I differ the most: She is so positive that I'm the one and only for her . . . while I just don't know.

I roll my head side to side and listen to the wind skittering across the water. It sounds more hollow here, spilling across the earthen dam on the south side of the lake, than it does when it lingers among the dense oaks and pines that have come to the water to drink.

Samantha rubs my feet lovingly and describes in great detail how the second story will be decorated in the redbrick house with the front porch swing that we *will* have in a few short years.

Restless Heart's "Why Does It Have to Be Wrong Or Right" is the last song of the hour, to be followed by the news. I'll turn the volume down in a minute.

I try hard to picture the room she is now walking me through, my mind more on the gentle curves of her firm breasts than the guest room furniture she is picking out of thin air. I like the way she looks, her feel, the soft tone of her voice, soothing, believable; perhaps this is all love is.

I must have been half asleep, with my eyes tightly shut and a stupid grin plastered across my face, because the first words I hear from Pamela Morrow are, "I'm sorry to awaken you from such a pleasant dream." They succeed, however, in recalling me from Samantha's loving touch in another world, another life.

She is standing in the aisle of the DC-10, at my left, patiently awaiting my return from Oz so she can take her window seat beside me. She is the most beautiful woman I've ever seen, ever imagined . . .


The wind had created a small sand devil at his feet—where the sea spray didn't reach and the sun had long since stolen the morning dew—blowing the hard dry dust toward his face.

Josh squeezed his eyes tightly together before the sand could reach its mark, though the lips he had just licked were coated like sugar cookies.

He spat out the gritty particles, rewetting his parched lips and brushing the sand from his shirt and pants as he stood. It had brought him back to a present from which he could see only a bleak future.

Josh recalled the lifeguard's words, "there was nothing else she could do under the circumstances," and his mind tortured him with the time they'd spent together, splitting eighteen hours of bliss into a thousand minutes of confusing conversation and fractured images, like the remnants of a trailer park after a tornado.

*Oh, God . . . Pamela . . . what could I have said that would have made a difference? Should I have seen the signs? Could I have known?*

The questions were as without answer as why the last wave had been shaped differently than the one prior. Josh took a ragged breath and tilted his head toward the heavens, the sun against his skin. On the horizon, to his back, dark clouds had begun to form, though they, like their predecessors for the last two months, would be burned away by the afternoon sun before they could bring the rain the Valley so desperately needed.

He knew it was time to return to the world, to his job. There was no getting Pamela back—life had taught him this much at least—and whether or not he would miss her for a month, a year, or longer, his life would still go on.

It would be longer, he knew.

He would miss, if not her contagious smile and her stately grace, then what she had represented to him, what she had rekindled in him.

He continued the walk toward his inn which had begun a lifetime earlier, the word "suicide" as impossible to swallow as soured milk.


The Sandpiper Inn sat along Bay View Avenue, like the familiar house of a friend. Its lushly landscaped front faced the teal waters of the Pacific, the meticulously maintained early California structure and the loving attention paid its diverse and colorful plantings had earned it the reputation as Carmel's most romantic country inn.

Whenever he made one of his hectic trips to the West Coast, Josh made it a point to allot a day or two at the quaint inn, always Room 5—a corner room with a pair of large windows and a king bed facing the sea—as a counterbalance to the frenetic life his job demanded the rest of the year.

As he reached the covered front porch, a fit, tanned, middle-aged couple in expensive beach attire hurried down the steps toward the ocean, their conversation excited and fragmented. They were late for their morning walk.

Josh could make out only two things with any certainty: There was a detective in the lobby asking questions of the guests, and the woman who'd died on the beach last night might have been murdered. The couple was hoping to see where her body had been found before the tourists eradicated all evidence of it.

While their morbid excursion both infuriated and sickened Josh, he leaned against the wall at the foot of the tile steps, knocking over one of the small terra-cotta pots filled with impatiens that lined the steps.

Murdered! The word was even harder to choke down than suicide.

Josh had long felt that the world was going to Hell—the values of the previous generations could now be seen only on the *History channel*—but while his seldom-voiced cynicism was for lost ideals, he'd always felt isolated from the harsh reality of death and violence that moved as effortlessly as a bird of prey through the lives of others.

Now his turn had come, a touch of cosmic fairness. No more observing death from the sidelines.

While the thought of Pamela's suicide had angered him, confused him, had caused him to examine their eighteen brief hours together, to wonder if he had contributed to her silent torment in any way, the thought of her life having been senselessly erased by a crack-crazed punk who wanted her money and possessions to buy dope, brought out in Josh Mitchell an anger he'd not experienced before in his twenty-nine years. It was an immediate and blinding rage.

Possessions . . . The oddly remembered word returned in haunting refrain. His ever-analytical mind ground up the letters and recomputed the meaning of the word, lending a sense of logic to a half-formed thought. *Why would a druggie leave a solid gold bracelet worth at least a thousand bucks in hock at any pawn shop in the Bay Area? Why would her purse have been left intact? And what about the letter . . . that damned letter?*

The frightened face of Pamela Morrow at the moment she realized suicide was her only escape began to replace the image of a murderous felon that had begun to form in Josh's mind.

"Only escape from what, Pamela?" Josh said aloud before he realized his voice had carried to the mailman who had suddenly materialized.

"Pardon me," the man said pleasantly from the landing, a small bundle of mail in his right hand, some magazines in his left. He was an athletic-looking man of perhaps forty, dark-skinned and clean-cut with a broad smile. He wore his spotless gray uniform well. "Did you say something, sir?"

The postman's words forced Josh to reenter the present. "No . . . sorry, just talking to myself again," he said with a forced smile, then quickly retraced his steps across the broad landscaped walkway, but not so rapidly as to attract unwanted attention. At the street again, he turned right down Bay View Avenue toward a coffee shop a block away. He realized he had to regain control before he stepped into the lobby and faced the detective he knew would be there for a while. He also knew that the man was likely standing between the desk and the fireplace, preventing Josh from reaching his room without an encounter. Sweat beaded on his brow, though the temperature was still mild.

His mind churned: If Pamela had died between midnight and two—in the lifeguard's estimation—then she would have been in Josh's room only minutes before her death, an hour at most. He remembered the clock by the bed after she'd left: 12:57 A.M.

A knot formed in his gut. If she had committed suicide, as her letter implied, then he was likely the last person to have seen her alive. If, on the other hand, she had been the victim of a violent act, then only the unknown assailant knew Josh had *not* been the last person to see her before she was murdered.

He selected a seat at a round glass table near the expansive front window which faced the street, away from the four other patrons at a booth along the wall, and ordered a cup of coffee when the waitress walked over. He took the paper napkin she'd left him and removed the yellow paper ring that bound it, set the utensils aside, then used it to wipe the sweat from his forehead. Damp and salty, he wadded it up and put it in the ashtray.

He couldn't remember a time in his life when he'd felt so many confusing feelings: from fear to despair, from anxiety to disbelief, from childlike sadness to animal rage. His mind was speeding and yet standing stone still, frozen in a moment on the beach.

When his coffee arrived, Josh took too large a swallow, burning his tongue and the roof of his mouth. "Perfect," he grumbled to the window. "My life just keeps getting better."

As he sipped more slowly from the heavy mug and watched the tourists on Martin Way browsing the specialty shops there, bags in hand, he tried to put the last twenty hours into perspective. Yesterday morning, before he boarded the DC-10 at Kennedy bound for San Francisco—as he'd done dozens of times before—he'd been just a salesman with a job he loved more than any other he could imagine; a guy with a girlfriend who wanted to get married but who saw no merit in being faithful.

Now, less than a full day later, his job was in serious jeopardy— Richard Hightower, the image-conscious CEO of Barnett Air would not tolerate any employee who became involved in a scandal that might reflect unfavorably upon the corporation (Josh was pretty certain being considered a murder suspect would qualify for Hightower's short list)—his girlfriend had become an ex-girlfriend, and he'd met and lost the most unforgettable woman of his life.

Pamela's face returned. Who was she? He'd seen her for the first time less than a day ago and couldn't get her out of his mind. It was crazy. He'd met lots of beautiful women in his travels. Many had expressed interest in spending time with him after only brief conversation. Some had attempted to get his unlisted home phone number from Barnett, enhancing his reputation as "Lucky" Mitchell. But this woman was different; she wasn't merely someone worth spending a little time with, someone to enjoy briefly and then move on— as he'd done too often to remember since high school—she was that one woman he'd waited all his life to meet, the one who had put him back in touch with everything he'd dreamed possible as a boy. He'd known it the first time he looked into her eyes—and saw the man he should have become staring back.

However, he made no apologies for the life he lived—it was an honorable existence with all the gadgets, trappings, and opportunities a person with his innate ability and dogged persistence deserved—yet it was *how* he had gotten there that often howled in his ear like the cold winds that blew across the fields of his childhood.

A knot gripped his throat and his mind was forced back to the situation before him; it was time to go. If he did the best selling job of his life, he would be able to explain to the detective that he had simply met a stranger named Pamela Morrow on the plane, they'd talked, had a pleasant dinner together in Sausalito, said goodbye, and went their separate ways. He'd almost convinced himself this was possible when his mind forced him to finish the mock interrogation: But then she showed up in Carmel, at *his* hotel with no fewer than forty-five other inns to choose from, had somehow gotten into his locked room around midnight with the intention of making love to him, had committed suicide or was murdered within an hour of leaving his room, and yet he knew absolutely nothing about her death until his walk on the beach at nine this morning.

He knew no one was that good a salesman. He couldn't expect his mother to believe a story like that, to say nothing of a detective. They'd heard every tale in the book. Hell, California cops were the book!

Josh stared into the tepid black liquid and asked for a miracle. He knew he'd need one as soon as the detective learned that a guest named Pamela Morrow had made up some wife-surprising-her-husband-on-his-birthday story for the resident housekeeper at midnight in order to obtain a key to Room 5—the one belonging to Joshua Thomas Mitchell. With less than two dozen rooms at the inn, it wouldn't take him long.

Though cynical about old-fashioned fidelity, Josh had always held a basic faith in the childhood postulate that if you did nothing wrong, you had nothing to fear. The mistrustful side of him knew that it was a naïve belief—right meant little anymore; power meant everything. His optimistic side, still the dominant force in his life, quickly challenged that he was an upper-middle-class white male: If the law didn't apply to *him*, to whom did it apply?

He stood, took a final sip from the mug, and headed back toward the Sandpiper Inn, ready to put his sales skills and that naïve faith to the ultimate test. He would tell the detective what little he knew about Pamela Morrow, answering only what he was directly asked, and hope for the best.

• • •

Detective Sergeant Louis Fachini was a fit man of fifty-two, with a barrel chest, square face, and piercing black eyes. At six-one, he was less than an inch shorter than the patrolman who stood quietly on his right, nearer the registration desk, but the same weight though the patrolman was half his age. His appearance was a source of pride for the detective. Fachini wore a white pinpoint cotton shirt with a brilliant red-and-green Jerry Garcia tie (he'd bought it because he liked the color scheme and not because he was a Grateful Dead fan). A black cashmere sport coat, a pair of pleated black silk and wool slacks with wide cuffs and an alligator belt, and black Ferragamo loafers completed the ensemble. He looked more like an expensive trial lawyer than a cop, a mien he cultivated.

He was finishing a ten-minute talk with a young couple near the lobby fireplace when Josh started up the front steps.

"That's the guy," the woman said so that she could be heard only by the two cops, "the one I told you about. When the waiter tried to take his order at breakfast, I heard him say that he was expecting to meet someone, though I never saw anyone join him, and we left after he did."

Fachini thanked the couple and they headed for the front door, passing Josh in the center of the lobby. He could sense their eyes on him but he ignored their stares, hoping yet to reach the stairwell leading to his second-story room without being stopped.

He knew it was a futile hope.

"Mr. Mitchell?" the detective called out.

Josh steered toward the man, rehearsing his answers in his mind. It was time to make a sale.

The uniformed patrolman flexed his shoulders and arms and moved casually to his right, putting himself between Josh and the front door, though he did it in such an effortless way, it would have appeared to someone less paranoid than Josh felt at this moment that he was merely easing the boredom of the morning.

"Yes?" Josh said pleasantly, hoping his voice sounded even. He stopped a comfortable distance from the detective, giving the man ample room. He'd learned early on that many a sale had been lost before it began by an overeager salesman stepping into a prospective client's "space."

"I'm Detective Sergeant Fachini. This is Officer Brettensen. Mind if I ask you a few questions, sir?" His pleasant manner implied that the intended interviewee could simply say yes and be on his way.

Josh knew better.

"No, I don't mind at all. I imagine this has something to do with the commotion on the beach this morning." He also knew a well-planned offense was better than the best defense. He studied the neatly dressed detective with a practiced eye, keeping his expressions and thoughts well hidden.

"You know about the drowning then?" The officer showed no surprise.

"I guess by now everyone in Carmel knows. I reached the ambulance just as they were loading the poor woman's body." The words burned in his throat but his inner voice warned him to keep cool.

"Taking a walk, were you?"

"Pardon me?"

"The reason you were on the beach this morning. So early, I mean." The eyes were doll's eyes.

"Yes. Got a busy day ahead and thought a bit of air and a walk would do me good. I'll be in stuffy offices for the rest of the week." The answer felt lame and contrived, though it had an air of truth to it. He pictured the letter he'd mailed, but before he could consider the words he'd written, Fachini snatched him back to reality.

"How well did you know Dianne Lane?" The black eyes narrowed.

"Who?" Josh asked honestly. The name was unfamiliar to him.

"The woman on the beach." He studied Josh's expression as a scientist studies cancerous cells under a microscope.

For a moment, Josh was sure he'd heard the man wrong. *Who the hell is Dianne Lane?* he wondered. He could only manage a dumbfounded expression as his mind tried to put the pieces into some reasonable order, though his genuine surprise served him well.

The detective produced a photo from his inside jacket pocket—actually an 8 1/2 x 11 color print from the master digital image in the California DMV database and transmitted electronically from the state capital to Fachini's office in Carmel an hour ago. He unfolded it and held it out for Josh to consider.

Though the woman's hair was longer in the photo, the image was clearly that of the woman he'd met on the plane yesterday, the woman he'd known for eighteen hours as Pamela Morrow. Yet the name beneath it said Dianne Marie Lane. *Why the hell would she give me someone else's name?* No wonder the desk told him, when he called down after Pamela missed breakfast, that there was no one registered under that name. Josh looked back at the detective. His mind, fixating only on the three words beneath the photo, managed a convincing: "I'm certain I've never seen this Lane woman."

"You sure, Mr. Mitchell?"

Josh was sure of one thing: Despite the name difference, Pamela Morrow and Dianne Lane were one and the same person. He didn't know why she had lied about her name—would probably never know now—but perhaps he'd just been handed the miracle he'd asked for: He had, in fact, never met anyone by the name of Dianne Lane in his life. He stood erect and confident. "I meet a lot of people while I'm traveling, detective, and I've got a pretty good memory if I do say so myself. I'm absolutely certain I have never met anyone by that name."

Josh had to know if the middle-aged couple he'd overheard earlier were reflecting an official position—that Pamela might have been murdered—or were simply letting their imaginations run wild. "I heard some people on the beach saying that this Lane woman committed suicide. There was supposedly a letter found." He tried to sound only mildly curious, as anyone under the circumstances would be.

Fachini bit his bottom lip for a second before answering. "Yeah, there was a letter. Too neat."

"I'm sorry?" Josh wondered, not understanding the response.

"Neat," the detective repeated. "Death isn't clean and orderly, Mr. Mitchell, it's chaotic and ugly, even in a bloodless suicide. Neat always means complicity. I'd bet my pension on there being someone else involved."

"You mean a killer?"

"I don't mean Jack Kavorkian, sir." Fachini turned to his notepad. Now Josh knew, though he wished he didn't. Somehow, if Pamela's death had been at her own hand, he would have eventually come to accept it. But *murder?* How could justice exist anywhere when such beauty and magic could perish at the hands of a nameless killer. The thought nauseated him and he wanted to go to his room, to pack, to put Carmel as far behind him as possible.

Now, if only he could escape the inevitable question about the guest who wandered into his room last night. He realized, just as his hope began to soar, that Fachini would have to be an idiot not to ask the night clerk if the guest named Dianne Lane had seen any of the other guests between the time she checked in—which couldn't have been before eleven at the earliest—and one o'clock in the morning.

"You're staying in Room 5, I believe," Fachini said, interrupting Josh's thoughts. As he spoke, he appeared to consult the small notepad, though Josh was not fooled by his ruse. If this man was unsure about anything in his life, it certainly wasn't Josh's room number.

He reminded himself to think before he spoke. *Remember, Josh, you knew her as Pamela Morrow.* "That's right. I checked in around ten forty-five last night. Drove down from San Francisco."

"You come here often, do you?" Again, Josh knew the information in question was already known. Apparently the detective was weighing the responses to known answers so he could better gauge the validity of other responses, those that really mattered.

"Every chance I get, though not as often as I'd like. You know how work can be." His nervous shaking had stopped as his confidence slowly began to come back to him, though he knew Fachini could not have noted the subliminal transformation. He was grateful to be in touch with some familiar feelings.

The cop merely nodded at the response, again looking to the notepad.

"I think the last time was January, if that's any help." Josh shifted his weight a bit.

"What do you do, Mr. Mitchell?"

"I'm a salesman for Barnett Air of Sacramento. Corporate jets." The personal pride usually associated with that response was harder than normal to summon.

The man was unimpressed and Josh began to dislike him for his curt single-mindedness. "You live in Sacramento?" he asked dryly.

"No, Greenwich Village. That's in . . ." Josh's voice tapered off. The man's eyes had told him it wasn't necessary to complete the unsolicited geography lesson.

"Mind giving me the phone numbers where you can be reached, you know, work, home, cell phone—any others I might need?" Fachini readied his pen. When Josh had done so, the detective clicked his pen and stuck it in his shirt pocket, saying politely, "Well, I think that's all for now. Thanks for your time, Mr. Mitchell. You've been most cooperative. Sorry to have kept you so long." He closed his pad, folded the photo, and stuck them both back inside his jacket.

Josh had reached the stairs leading to the second story before he realized he'd walked away, without another word, the release of having survived the inquisition triggering an automated survival response: Get as far from danger as you can as soon as possible. He wondered why Fachini hadn't asked him about Dianne Lane being in his room. He was certain the detective had to know she'd been there. Why was he playing this game? What was Fachini after?

Before Josh had climbed the first step, the detective spoke again. "By the way, Mr. Mitchell, just one more thing . . ."

Josh stopped abruptly. He knew it had been too good to be true. His mind went blank. He felt himself falling through the air with the ground rushing up at him and he struggled to keep the confidence of a moment before.

"Mind telling me about your guest this morning?" Fachini said.

Josh turned, his mind racing, his body plunging toward the ground, faster, faster. He fought to hold his expression as neutral as possible, though he was sure he would strike the ground at any moment and perish. As he was about to respond, the detective added: "The person who stood you up at breakfast at seven."

When a small portion of Josh's mind peered back into the present, where the danger had been seconds before, his response came from years of selling, of lying, with no forethought. "A rich, inconsiderate client. Been talking about one of our new carbon-fiber nine-seaters for two years and I'm still dancing with him. What's worse, it's not the first time he's stood me up. I guess having money allows you to be a jerk." *Don't embellish, you idiot, just answer the damn question. Which client? What if Fachini asks for a name? He'll know everyone with big money in the area. Think before you speak, fool!* Josh's heart pounded as he went through his entire West Coast client list, groping for the answer he knew he'd need any second.

Detective Sergeant Fachini chewed on the words for an agonizing eternity before speaking. "If I were you, I wouldn't waste my valuable time on a client like that," he said with frigid detachment, though lingering on the word "valuable."

"Gotta eat," Josh shrugged. The shakes had returned.

"Well thanks again, Mr. Mitchell. We'll be in touch if we need anything else."

And then the two cops were gone, and the room was as empty as if they'd been apparitions and the whole morning only a nightmare.


Josh Mitchell forced his legs up stairs as steep as the Rockies. In his room, he leaned against the closed door, exhausted, and stared out the window at the street below. The detective could not be seen but Josh knew he was there, waiting. Why the cop had chosen to play this game was beyond Josh's comprehension.

The one thing of which he was positive was that he knew less about Pamela Morrow—or more correctly, about Dianne Lane—than he needed to know.

His eyes turned to the king-sized bed. Pamela's body and smile, so warm and giving of life, beckoned to him.

He blinked the painful image away, knowing it would never again be, and threw his open suitcase on the bed.

When he'd checked out and was safely within the cocoon of his rented Volvo S70, its engine silent, he turned his gaze to the west, toward the sea that had claimed his dreams. Whether it had been the too willing participant in her suicide or the instrument of a murderer, he knew he would never see the ocean that had always brought him such calm the same way again.

He looked at the dash clock: nearly noon. He was due in Santa Cruz.

As Josh Mitchell pulled away from the curb, the white-legged man from the beach, well concealed in plain view amongst the other tourists strolling in chatty oblivion down Bay View Avenue, snapped a clear shot of the Volvo's license plate.

It would now be a simple matter for his people to learn all they wanted to know—all they needed to know—about the man who had been visited by Dianne Lane an hour before her unfortunate death.

# 3

Santa Cruz lies just forty-five miles north of Carmel, not more than an hour's drive up US1, the Pacific always on your left, its patient assassin, the relentless surf, shaping the beaches and jagged cliffs, tirelessly reclaiming the land it has sculpted since receding a hundred millennia ago. If Josh hadn't been late, he would have opted for an inland route, 68 and 101 through Salinas and Watsonville, putting the hated sea out of view—though not out of mind.

The tires of the NauticBlue S70 squealed against the smooth concrete of the parking garage, and when he'd taken the paper ticket thrust at him from the electronic attendant, Josh chose a parking space which didn't have a view of the sea.

His client's building rose high above East Cliff Drive, a tall, bronze glass obelisk that resembled a thousand other mirrored monstrosities blighting the coastline of northern California. It looked like money, a visage obviously intended by the architect and approved of by the tenant.

With the engine quiet for the first time in fifty minutes and a few placid moments to himself before meeting Mr. Paxton B. Thurgood III—founder (with his daddy's money), president, and CEO of Thurgood Hydro-Dynamics—Josh Mitchell let his mind wander again. He'd kept it tightly restrained since leaving the inn, filling it with the screeching, thundering sounds of an avant-garde music station. He disliked the racket such stations generally offered and seldom tuned to them, but on the drive up he wanted to stay as far away from familiar melodies as he could, ones that might stir emotions he wanted to repress.

It had only been four hours since he'd mailed Pamela's letter. The words he had written at eight this morning replayed in a frightening hodgepodge. He struggled to rearrange them as they had been written:

The secrets I have shared with you have never been revealed to another living soul. My life is what it is today because of the lies I have told, the lies I have lived. Now it's time to begin the life I was meant to be living all along. I have you to thank for this, Pamela.

He knew when the police read his letter, as they surely would with the cause of her death apparently in question, whatever his words had originally meant could be misconstrued and twisted to suit any purpose they required. If they wanted a killer with motive and opportunity, it would appear Joshua Thomas Mitchell of Barnett Air had both. They would grill him endlessly, probing the nature of the "secrets and lies" he alluded to in his letter, wanting to know if the reason he had killed her was to keep whatever he'd told her silent, having had second thoughts about his ill-conceived "confession" after she'd left his room. It wouldn't matter that he would tell them that the lies were merely about how he'd lived his life for the last decade—hurting no one but himself—how he'd created a façade that painted him as a sophisticated New Englander from old money when he was little more than a country bumpkin whose parents farmed the land and taught school. They would argue that those very admissions had given Dianne Lane the weapons by which she could expose him to his employer. With the loss of several hundred thousand dollars a year in sales commissions in the balance, it was quite believable her death—by a fabricated suicide—would have seemed an easy decision for him to make.

Josh felt shaky and his skin grew clammy. *Get a grip*, his mind cried out. *If you've done nothing wrong, you've got nothing to fear. You're thinking crazy. Nothing will come of it. . . . It was just a letter, for Christ's sake. Calm down.*

The words rang hollow.

"Who the hell am I kidding?" he said aloud. "This is not the Fifties, remember?"

As the paranoia grew deeper, the phone he'd laid on the seat beside him began to ring. At first it seemed like the sound was coming from another dimension, but he soon recognized the source of the annoying peal.

"Hello." His voice was flat, lifeless.

"Hey, old buddy, thought you were gonna call me." It was Kenny Kanazawa, Josh's best friend and head of software development for Barnett Air's stealth division.

In 1991, after Josh had graduated with honors from MIT with degrees in computer science and aeronautical engineering, he met Kenny on the West Coast while looking for a suitable location for the design company he had been planning on starting for four years. Kenny was a graduate student at Stanford, the youngest son of Japanese immigrants who, through tireless effort, had made a place in the new world for themselves and the six children they would eventually have. Kenny had been the technonerd of the family since sitting before his first computer at age eleven.

The pair hit it off immediately and were soon equal partners in Aero-Tech, a two-man company dedicated to developing a radar scanner capable of "seeing" the latest stealth fighters and bombers. They had both been fascinated by the events which had just unfolded during Desert Storm, the technology that had been so effectively demonstrated there, and realized that if they could "bust" the stealth aircraft of the United States, there would be a huge payoff for their success.

Fueled—and congressionally funded—by the decisive U.S. victory in the Mid-East, there were a number of corporations capable of making an airplane invisible to conventional radar. But few, if any, were working on the technology that would protect the United States in the event some foreign power came up with a stealth science of their own.

When, in 1993, at the point of personal and corporate bankruptcy, they reached a breakthrough in the algorithm—dubbed *Canterbury* after the medieval English ghost of the same name as an inside joke—and had "seen" for the first time in thirty long and lean months the military's best kept secrets flying invisibly in the midnight sky above the desert east of Los Angeles, they excitedly approached Barnett Air with their results, the company they had selected months prior for their first demonstration.

So impressed was Richard Hightower, newly appointed president of Barnett and a driven man determined to make a quick name for himself, that Aero-Tech—and Canterbury in particular—was purchased before either of the partners fully realized it had happened. Perhaps, if they had not been living in the same small Venice apartment, and hocked to the hilt to keep Aero-Tech afloat while they worked ninety-hour weeks, they would have held out for a better deal.

It's hard to be focused on the future when the rent is three months overdue.

By the time Aero-Tech had been absorbed into the parent corporation, and their technology was working well, both Kenny and Josh had Barnett stock worth a million dollars, their personal and company debts paid in full, long-term employment contracts worth six figures a year, and the car of their choice.

As they sat in their matching new Porsche Turbos, they smiled like they alone knew the secret of eternal life—not too bad for a couple of single guys three years out of college, they grinned. Only later, when they learned their hard-earned creation had been sold to the military for two hundred million dollars, did their shiny, new deal lose some of its gleam.

During the following year, as Hightower began to appreciate the natural sales ability of Josh Mitchell, he migrated him from development to corporate sales, then to jet sales, eventually giving him his pick of clients. In essence, Josh owned the continental U.S., and his rugged good looks, unmatched technical expertise, and skills at the controls of the company's most expensive aircraft had made him a great deal of money. But it was his jet pilot's license that meant more to him than all the money he'd earned.

With a passionate love of aircraft that went back to his childhood, where from his perch high in an oak tree he would watch crop dusters spraying the fields, skimming the tops of corn and cotton rows as effortlessly as an owl gliding in to pluck a mouse from a furrow, he was in heaven. Only on occasion did he miss the challenge of solving some programming dilemma, sitting across a desk from his best friend and arguing at length about the best method of arriving at a solution. But with Kenny constantly seeking advice, something which was taboo since Josh's clearance had not been updated in the last three years, he managed to keep closer to the development side of Barnett than he cared to anymore.

Kenny, on the other hand, lived for the technology. He had been expecting Josh's call at noon, an hour ago.

"Sorry, Kenny," Josh said sincerely, his thoughts far from such obligations. "Had a lot on my mind."

Kenny sensed something was wrong. "Hey, Josh, you all right? You sound like shit. You out all night chasing tail?" He chuckled out loud.

"Wish I had been. Nothing as exciting as that. Just . . ." He wanted desperately to tell his friend about the last twenty-four hours, to confide in someone, to get a fresh perspective on the whole crazy situation, but decided to wait until he could speak to him at Barnett headquarters in the morning, face to face. "It's nothing."

"Nothing, my ass. We go back too far for you to pull that old 'it's nothing' shit on me. What's up, buddy, Monica been hounding you again to slip a ring on her finger?"

Kenny and Josh had no secrets from each other, including their respective love lives over the years. There was nothing they couldn't—or wouldn't—say to one another. Kenny knew only too well about Josh's girlfriend of two years badgering him to marry her. While he felt sorry for Josh, he knew it was a situation his friend would handle when the time came. He also knew he wasn't crazy enough to marry Monica, no matter how much she nagged, or how great she was in the sack.

When Josh didn't respond, Kenny added, "Why not just tell her you consider sexual fidelity a prerequisite to marriage, as old-fashioned as it might sound?" He propped his tired feet on his desk, beside his Sun Ultraspark workstation, his Nikes on the floor beneath his chair. He knew there'd be a response shortly.

It was the first time Josh had thought about Monica in a full day. A wave of guilt had begun to wash over him, but was nullified by Kenny's last comment. "That was tacky, dickhead."

"Maybe so, but you know it needs to be said. What gets me, old buddy, is why you put up with her shit. We've known each other, what, six, seven years, and in all that time I've seen you with maybe thirty chicks, all of them real hot babes, some with lots of class and plenty of coin. Why Monica? Before you answer, remember I've got eyes. . . . I know she's great-looking and probably makes you claw the finish off the headboard while she's banging your brains out— what little you've got. But, Jesus, pal, if she was any freer with her goodies, you'd have to make an appointment to get laid."

"It's not as bad as that." Josh knew it was.

"Oh, bullshit! I've listened to you moan about it for two years. And even if you don't give a damn about her making a complete fool of you every time you leave your apartment for more than an hour, you apparently haven't watched much TV lately. AIDS is the gift that keeps on taking. Ever hear of it?" Kenny stood by his computer and stretched exaggeratedly, rolling his head side to side. He'd been in the same seated position for six hours. The phone he was talking on was hands-free and extremely small, a tiny earpiece in his left ear, the microphone at the corner of his mouth. It was a favorite among programmers who needed to work while they talked.

Josh wasn't emotionally prepared to debate the reasonableness of his choice in mates, or her lack of fidelity, despite having agreed with most of what Kenny had said. He decided to change the subject. "Why'd you call me? I know it wasn't to bust my chops about my girlfriend." Maybe Kenny would be happier if Josh told him she was, as of yesterday, his *ex*-girlfriend. Probably, but it would keep as well.

"You were supposed to call me at noon, remember?"

"Now that we're talking, what are we talking about?"

"We'll continue our little chat about Monica in the morning, you can be sure," Kenny warned playfully. "You are still planning on being here at eight, right?"

"Yep." He knew Kenny meant well, despite his insistent meddling.

"Great. In the meantime, be thinking about the problem we're having with Casper, the one I mentioned last week. Nothing we've tried has solved the recognition problem and I sure could use some help. Hightower has my butt over a tall flame because the Raytheon ST-18E scanner hasn't been able to spot the Navy's new stealth Cruise until it's practically up our—"

"Jesus! Kenny," Josh interrupted. "Why not take out a fucking ad in the Sunday *Times*. Maybe fewer people would know what you're working on that way." He couldn't believe his friend was discussing Top Secret technological development problems over the phone.

"Oh, get a life, Josh. You act like the world is still full of spies. This is the end of the century, the Berlin Wall came down years ago, remember? Nobody gives a shit about military secrets anymore. They all want to know whether Reeboks are gonna have blinking red lights in the heels next season or whether thongs will still be in at the beach. Personally, I hope they never go out of style."

"You're an idiot, you know it."

"Yep, complete idiot. That's why I need your help with the code on the new object bindings." Kenny dropped back into his chair.

Josh thought for a moment. "Have you checked the implementation repository?"

"Of course. All servers are up and running. The repository is completely up to date. Still no detection."

"How about the client server IDLs? Do they all match?"

"That's an idea. Now that you mention it, I'm not sure, I haven't personally checked them all yet. See, Josh, you're a genius. I'm gonna ask Hightower to reassign you to development for a few weeks," Kenny said. "You mind?"

"I wouldn't mind helping you for a while, you know that, but I've been out of the loop for three years. That's a lifetime in your field and you know it." Josh lowered the window on the Volvo. It had begun to get stale and claustrophobic inside the closed car.

"Our field," Kenny corrected. "Hell, it wouldn't take you a week to come up to speed. You may be nuts when it comes to women, but you have the best brain in the business when it comes to finding bugs in code."

"Had . . . perhaps. Now I'm Hightower's pet monkey."

"Ooh, is Barnett's big-dog salesman feeling sorry for himself today?" In truth, Kenny was puzzled and concerned by the odd and somber tone in his friend's voice.

Josh was surprised by his own words, too. He loved his job and thought his boss to be one of the fairest and most supportive he'd met in his work with dozens of the country's largest corporations and most powerful executives. He knew his emotional low wasn't a result of anything Hightower had done, quite the opposite, all his opportunity, his comfortable living, his bright future, were the direct result of Hightower's belief in him. What had his heart and mind in knots had begun at three o'clock yesterday in New York and had ended with Fachini's frigid stare as he listened to Josh lie about his absentee breakfast guest.

Lies. How much a part of his life they'd become, and with so little intent. All he ever wanted was to become a success, to make his family and friends proud—to be proud of himself. When was the last time he'd even spoken with his folks or the friends of his youth? When was the last time he'd felt pride in himself?

*Too* damn long, he knew.

He took a slow breath, trying to shake some of the melancholia from a brain that felt like it had been anesthetized. "Not feeling sorry for myself, just *feeling*. Something I haven't done much of lately. Too busy trying to knock the ball over the fence."

"I don't know anything about that stuff; computers suffer no such human infirmities. Listen, enough of this serious shit. If you haven't belted out a grand slam by now, being the most successful salesman in Barnett's history, I don't know what the hell you're after, Josh. See you at eight tomorrow."

After Kenny had hung up, Josh sat in the car staring blankly at the building across the street, as if it would speak to him and give him the answers he sought. "I don't know what the hell I'm after either, my friend," he mumbled at the silent cell phone. "I thought I knew . . . but now . . ."

The man with the white legs and big camera withdrew a small digital remote control from his baggy shorts and pressed the Unlock button once. From within the panel-type delivery van—its rear windows covered with a reflective silver foil that prevented unwanted eyes from peering inside, a thick curtain pulled tight between the front seats and rear cabin—a brief chirp signaled that the alarm had been canceled.

"It's me," he said to the van's lone occupant, a stocky, short black man seated before a vast array of monitors of various sizes, all mounted in a custom rack along the passenger's side of the vehicle. Few were in use at the moment: the surveillance operation in which they were engaged required little sophistication and less manpower, though other operations in which this van had participated had involved as many as six technicians interacting with various banks of computer and TV screens, monitoring suspect movement, audio, and video, as well as phone conversations and location data. One large monitor near the back doors was dedicated to a military-grade GPS tracking system which could receive constantly updated location and movement data from as many as four tagged vehicles at one time—providing an expensive but minute locator had been secreted somewhere on the vehicle to be tracked. It had not been done to Josh's car yet, though there were other ways of tracking anyone they wished. The other ways were simply less efficient.

Now that contact with Dianne Lane had occurred, they would shortly know all they needed to know about the man in the Volvo.

The white-legged man activated the alarm again and then took one of the empty chairs, in front of a quad Pentium-processor MMX workstation with enhanced graphics capability and a 21-inch digital monitor. He plugged a cable with a miniature DIN connector into the matching socket on the back of the camera he'd carried all morning. Within a minute, the fifty high-resolution digital images he'd taken since seven A.M. appeared in "tile" format on the monitor, each in a square frame 200 pixels on a side which allowed either horizontal or vertical composition. When he pointed to any of the miniature images (or "pixies" as they were affectionately referred to) with the mouse, it would instantly zoom to fill the screen, providing far greater visual information. The same level of detail that could be transmitted or printed.

He chose a clear full-frontal head shot of Josh Mitchell as he talked with the lifeguard and put the cursor over it.

"That the mark?" the black man asked.

"Would appear so, Tommy." The white-legged man selected another image.

"His car?" Tommy asked.

"Yep. Rented."

"Not your average Taurus, huh?" He moved closer for a better look.

"Must be a hot shot," the white-legged man said.

"What'd you expect, a school teacher?"

"Don't know. One was a school teacher."

"Oh, yeah, I remember, that dweeb from Ohio, right? You worked on that one too, didn't you?"

"Uh-huh," the white-legged man responded flatly, though he was justifiably proud of his contribution to that operation.

"How deep you figure he's in?" Tommy asked.

"Not my job."

"But you've got an opinion." The black man took the mouse and picked an image of Mitchell and Fachini talking, taken through the window of the Sandpiper Inn. His comment was about the man in the cashmere jacket; the uniformed patrolman was not in the picture. "Looks like a lawyer."

"Cop."

"Detective?"

"I imagine. We'll know in a few minutes."

"Probably thinks the mark had something to do with the Lane woman's death."

"Probably." The white-legged man had finished viewing the images he thought were the best, including the one showing the S70's license number. He assembled the eight pictures he wanted into an electronic folder and ran it through an encryption program, reducing its file size while simultaneously making it unusable to anyone outside the unit. When it had finished compressing, he transmitted the file to a secure number he'd chosen from his computer phonebook. "Get him on the phone for me, would you, Tommy?"

The man dialed a voice number at the same location to which the images were being transmitted. After two rings, it was answered. "He's on," Tommy said.

There was no need for formalities.

The white-legged man spoke first. "Sending you some pretty pictures. Need to know who the two men are, especially the younger one. He's the mark. The tag is from his rental."

"Where is he now?" the man at the other end asked. His computer indicated that a file had just been successfully received from Mobile Unit 7. With a click, he began the decryption process. He would have the images on his screen within the minute.

"Left a little while ago."

"We get a locator on the rental?"

"Nope. Didn't know what he had until he drove off."

"Dammit!" the other man said. Reacquiring him would be considerably more difficult now, unless . . . "He got a cell phone with him?"

"Didn't see one, but he smelled like a road warrior to me. He'll have a cell phone all right. Probably sleeps with it," the white-legged man said.

"Okay, we can put him in a particular cell anywhere in the country as soon as we get his number, assuming he's on."

"He'll be on. I know his type."

"A metallic blue Volvo shouldn't be too damn hard to spot. Any other activity there?"

"All quiet. Need to be moving on as soon as you give me a location and name."

"Have them both for you in fifteen minutes."

The white-legged man asked, "What do you want us to do with him once he's reacquired?"

The man on the other end thought for a moment, leaning back in his large leather chair. "Just watch him until I tell you otherwise. He'll make a move soon enough, now that Lane's dead. Get a locator on his rental when we spot it again."

"Will do." He hung up and looked at the black man for a long moment, his mind lost in thought. "You asked me how deep I thought the mark was in."

"Uh-huh." The man rocked back in his chair, his head against a metal cabinet containing a dozen automatic rifles. He folded his arms across his chest.

"I think he's so deep in this shit, his eyes are brown from it."

"Why haven't we spotted him before?"

"Doesn't matter. It's only important that we spotted him now."

"You think he did the Lane woman?" Tommy asked.

"Probably had to. I imagine she was about to rat him out, though why, I have no idea."

"Lover's spat?" The thought excited the other man.

"He was not her lover, at least not before last night. She only had the one. I have a gut feeling our mark hadn't seen Lane before yesterday, when she met him on the plane."

"Safe place to talk . . . thirty thousand feet." He got only a pensive nod in response. "What do you figure he's up to now?"

The white-legged man shrugged his shoulders and stared at Josh Mitchell's troubled image, still filling the screen. "We'll know soon enough, my friend. We'll know soon enough."

# 4

Thurgood Hydro-Dynamics and the rest of the Santa Cruz skyline had vanished in Josh Mitchell's rearview mirror two hours earlier. It had been a good sales call, ending in a signed contract for the June delivery of one of Barnett's new slender eight-passenger BA-35 twin turbofans. The option to lease had been declined by the chief financial officer, and the required purchase funds would be transferred into Barnett's account within ten business days. The client had expressed disappointment when Josh asked for a rain check for dinner and a night of celebratory drinking, but had not pressed the issue when Josh told him that if he didn't meet personally with the design team first thing in the morning—the order cutoff date—the founder's new toy wouldn't make his desired delivery date.

A lie. There was nothing timely about the order, though Paxton Thurgood III had been led to believe for nine months that he was the most memorable client Josh had ever enjoyed working with, a forward-thinking man among men, soon to be the envy of every other CEO in his field, and his new corporate jet would be one of a kind. Though they were only "sales lies," told by every man and woman who made a living hawking the wares of their employer, and therefore not considered lies in the moral sense of the word since they hurt no one and were actually expected by the customer, in Josh's current frame of mind, they felt as vile as lies that scarred the soul.

The unexpected bonus of the afternoon's lengthy and complex deliberations, besides the healthy sales commission, was to transport Josh out of his head and into his profession again, providing a surprising degree of relief from the trauma of the morning. So grateful was he for the release, that for over a hundred miles Josh had driven toward Sacramento in silence; no alternative music, no radio at all, only the wind through the sunroof. Now, with fifty miles remaining, as he stopped for gas just outside Cordelia Junction, on I-80, Monica's image filled his thoughts, the guilt that had tried to take root earlier now in full bloom.

He called home, hoping she'd changed her mind about leaving, though he knew it was not love but emotional isolation, the need to be with familiar faces, hear familiar voices, that had him dialing the number.

On the first ring, the answer phone picked up, its unexpected message a farewell gift from Monica: "Hello, you've reached 555-6482. Josh and I aren't here at the moment, but then, he never was here emotionally, which explains why I'm no longer here physically. You can leave a message for him if you want. Ciao, baby!"

Her sarcastic words and glacial tone were such a contrast to the warmth and tenderness he'd felt from Pamela. How he and Monica had parted yesterday afternoon played like he'd put a tape of the scene in the radio's cassette slot . . .


. . . I'm standing in front of the large living room window, in my duplex apartment in the Village, looking down at the traffic and people hurrying about in the rain on the streets below.

Monica is yelling at me as she moves around the room, just as she's been doing for the last hour and a half. My brain is full and I will soon be late for my flight to San Francisco. I know if I leave like this, she will not be here when I return. I'm not sure I care anymore. I know I should care, I just don't. Maybe I never did.

There is no way to put off my business trip—or the inevitable.

I watch the rain strike the window and form long streaks that refract the colored lights rising up from the street. Her voice is louder now, more intense. She gets angry easily, especially these days.

As the images blur, my mind wanders back to the summer after high school. Samantha and I are parked beside Twin Springs Lake. Samantha is a year behind me in school and constantly worries that our two-and-a-half-year relationship won't survive my going to college in Massachusetts—we need to get married now, tomorrow if possible.

I tell her what I've told her for a year: We need to wait until I finish college, so I can provide for us properly. I assure her that I love her and neither distance nor time will change that.

She tells me she feels the same and then talks about the house we'll have. I guess she knows not to push too hard; my mind is firm on this subject. She tells me we'll always be together.

Forever seems so long at eighteen.

I remember that her letters to me stopped before the end of my first semester at MIT, and that she was married to someone else—I'm sure I heard his name but I don't remember it—the day after she graduated from high school.

It's funny, I haven't seen Samantha since that August, in 1987, but I've begun to miss her more and more in recent months, or perhaps, what she represented. I'm sure of so few things lately.

My thoughts are yanked back to the present when Monica asks me if I'm even listening to her. I look directly into her eyes to assure her I'm hearing every angry word.

I long for the peace of the flight, but try one final time to console her and assure her of my feelings. It doesn't work any better than it has in the past month.

Though I'll be gone two weeks, I'm sent off without getting a kiss or a hug, just the sound of the door slamming behind me.

During the limo ride to the airport, I call home, hoping Monica has cooled off but, in truth, expecting more of the same venom I'd escaped twenty minutes earlier. She is strangely calm but then I understand why. She tells me that she will not be there when I return from California; she has found someone else and they seem to be in love; he's helping her move her stuff out later today.

It's juvenile, but I tell her to go fuck herself and hang up. It doesn't make me feel any better.

Maybe a little, I reconsider.

I stuff my cell phone back in my coat pocket and watch the miserable winter weather outside the car window, feeling neither relief nor sorrow. In fact, I feel almost nothing.

At Kennedy, I thank the driver, grab my laptop and my single bag, and head toward the American Airlines terminal. I make my way sluggishly through the busy concourse, toward Gate 49. My plane leaves at 3:40 P.M.—ten minutes. Boarding has already begun and I take my aisle seat in First-Class, order a cup of hot coffee with a shot of Bailey's, and put my mind on work, though it isn't as easy as I thought. Samantha's face forms involuntarily in my mind and I yield to the memory of making love to her by the lake. I'm soon in a light sleep.

I remember Pamela's first words to me: *I'm sorry to awaken you from such a pleasant dream* . . .

An eighteen-wheeler's horn screamed like a train at a crossing as the blue Volvo drifted across the center line. Startled from his daydream, Josh yanked the wheel to the right then hard left again when he realized his mistake. He quickly found the back half of his sedan on the highway's soft shoulder, gravel spraying from the car's rear tires as they slid in the loose surface. All at once, Josh was at a right angle to the flow of traffic, still traveling over seventy miles per hour, staring directly at the undercarriage of the huge, orange moving van six feet away.

In the cab of the truck, the driver could see the Volvo's predicament in his right mirror, but knew standing on his brakes would only involve himself and possibly others in the fray as his truck jack-knifed. He was sure that in a second, one of two things was going to occur: either the sedan would begin a barrel roll down the interstate, or the driver, in a panic, would slam on the antilock brakes, momentarily correcting the car's slide, and then whip the wheel to the left jamming it under the sixty-thousand-pound trailer.

Either would be fatal for the driver.

Both possibilities had run through Josh's mind as well.

He eased down on the brake, though fear was yelling for him to put his full weight on the pedal, and simultaneously cut the wheel to the right, not the left—just like he'd done many times on icy New York streets—putting the car back in its lane. He'd lost enough speed to be well behind the eighteen-wheeler now, and discovered that he had a pickup truck barreling down on him. The two missed by only a foot as the pickup shot into the passing lane, tires squealing. Four other cars that had been farther back passed him as well, and each had its own method of expressing the fear or anger of its occupants: horns blared, lights flashed, and passengers shouted profanities.

With the road momentarily clear behind him, Josh eased to the shoulder, pulling the Volvo fully off the pavement. He was shaking and his hands were wet with perspiration. It felt like a ball of fire had formed in his stomach. "Jesus . . . Pamela . . . what have you done to me?"


Forty minutes after nearly being crushed beneath an Allied Moving Van, the S70 pulled quietly into a guest space near the lobby of the La Quinta Inn on Jibboom Street in Sacramento, a block from the American River and three blocks from Barnett headquarters. It was the closest inn to work and not a bad place to lay his head, Josh had thought the first time he'd stayed there. He was exhausted from the two hundred miles he'd driven since noon, from the emotionally draining events of the morning, and from the inexcusable daydreaming on Interstate 80 which had almost cost him his life.

Physically and emotionally he needed rest, though he was sure sleep would come only after several hours, when his body was so exhausted that Pamela's lifeless image could no longer be summoned by his brain.

Without checking his watch first, Josh used the cell phone's speed dial function to call Kenny's direct line. Though most of Barnett's fifteen hundred workers had been home for two hours, he knew Kenny would still be at his desk. It was what he lived for, the true love in his life. Even when they had been practically starving, in the lean months before the deal with Hightower and Barnett, it was Kenny more than Josh who had worked the late hours. And while Josh respected his best friend's drive and dedication, he wished more for him from life than bits and bytes. Though Josh was still single because he'd never met the right woman, Kenny was unmarried at thirty because he simply didn't make time for such trivialities. He was busy saving the world from aggression and terrorism (in his mind, at least)—a mate could come when that daunting task was completed. Kenny answered on the first ring.

"Development, Kanazawa," he said in a weary voice. The problem he'd discussed with Josh earlier was no better and was beginning to take its toll on the entire development team, though none of the others put in his hours looking for a solution. He was alone in his office.

"Thought I'd find you hard at it," Josh said, feeling like the old days in Venice, where sleep always took a back seat to work.

"Where else would I be?"

"Out getting laid, I'd hoped."

"That's your job. Mine's keeping Hightower off my ass."

"Having any luck with the algorithm?" Josh switched the phone to his left ear as he reached down to the passenger's floorboard and pulled his laptop back onto the seat. It had been thrown there during the run-in with the semi-truck. He wasn't worried about it still functioning: the shock mounting in the carry case would have prevented any damage from such a mishap.

Kenny heard him grunt as he strained with the case. "Sounds like you're in the back seat right now. Want to call me back when you're through?"

Josh let it pass.

"Hey," Kenny said, "you stay last night at that old inn you always go to in Carmel? The Sandbox, right?" Kenny knew the name.

"Yeah."

"You catch all the action down at the beach this morning?" Before Josh could respond, he continued: "They pulled some rich Nob Hill chick out of the ocean—Dianne Lane, if I remember right. Had some kind of job collecting Chinese art. Been in the water all night, according to the cops. Seems she committed suicide, even left a letter. A real babe, too, judging by the pictures they've been showing on TV, though I'll bet she didn't look that good when they fished her out?"

A fist squeezed Josh's throat. He couldn't respond.

"I also saw where she'd flown American Airlines from Kennedy to San Francisco on Monday before ending up in Carmel. Isn't that the flight you always take?" Kenny wandered to the coffee pot that was never turned off in his glass-walled office, and refilled his cup.

Josh swallowed the lump. He knew Kenny meant nothing by his crude remarks, though the knowledge did nothing to lessen the severity of their impact. He was having a hard enough time thinking of her as dead without Kenny's vivid recollections. He managed a soft: "She was on the plane with me. We sat beside each other."

"No shit!" Kenny's fertile mind began to see the possibilities. "But I should have known 'Lucky' Mitchell would never have missed the opportunity to spend time with such a gorgeous babe." Kenny sat on the edge of his desk, sipping the brew in his cup. His 900MHz wireless headset telephone allowed him access to the entire development floor. "You have to switch seats to sit beside her?"

"Nope, luck of the draw."

"That's why they call you 'Lucky,' old buddy."

"You call me 'Lucky,' only you, and you know I hate it." Josh closed his eyes and leaned his head against the headrest. It wouldn't take much for him to fall asleep in the seat.

"If I remember correctly, that's how you introduced yourself to me when we met. I didn't know your name was Josh for a month." Kenny played with the clutter on his desk, neither reading the paperwork nor organizing the files as much as pushing it around into neater piles. His desk looked like an explosion at an Office Max.

"That was forever ago. Things change. People change."

"Yeah, perhaps, but there are a few constants in the universe, like matter never being destroyed, like the speed of light in a vacuum, like Lucky Mitchell chasing pussy whenever it crosses his path . . . you know—constants."

"You're such an ass. What about Monica and me being together for two years? That's not exactly jumping from one bed to the next at every opportunity." A headache began to form at the base of Josh's skull.

"She was the most unfaithful chick ever conceived. Don't give me that faithful—"

"She was, yes. Monica, not me," Josh interrupted. "I didn't cheat on her once in all the months we had a relationship."

Kenny's curiosity was piqued by his friend's last statement. "Did I detect the word 'had' in there?" He dropped into his chair and began to mouse through the e-mail he'd not read in two days.

Josh didn't want to go into this now, but he'd broached the subject and had little option now other than to hang up. "You heard right. We broke up Monday morning."

"For keeps? I mean, you two have—"

"Well, she and her new lover moved all her stuff out before my plane had left the ground. You decide."

"I'd say that sounds like for keeps. Sorry, anything I can do? You want to find a friendly bar and get royally shitfaced?"

"No thanks. I'm gonna hit the sack so I'll be worth a damn in the morning."

Kenny's mind was not to be silenced. His curiosity, driven by the afternoon news stories, forced it to forge ahead. "Okay, then, if you and Monica broke up before you made your plane, and therefore before you met Dianne Lane, it wouldn't have been cheating in your strangely puritanical mind to have jumped her bones, would it?"

"I didn't jump her bones, we just talked." The headache pounded painfully, now pressing against the backs of his eyes.

"Talked, my ass. Bullshit. This is your old buddy Kenny. I know

you better than your mama and it's physically impossible for you to
have passed up an opportunity to nail that babe."

"You're assuming I had the opportunity."

"Hell, you'd have made one for Dianne Lane."

"Kenny, listen to me, I did not 'nail that babe,' as you so crudely
put it. We talked on the plane, had dinner together, and then went
our separate ways."

*Why don't you just tell Kenny about Pamela coming to your room,
what she meant to you?* Josh knew Kenny would just ask who the hell
Pamela was. He rubbed his brow.

"Oh, dinner together, was it?" He chewed on the end of a pencil,
his mind running full tilt. "Where?"

"Jesus, you sound like a reporter for the fucking *Inquirer*. What's
the difference? We just had dinner, that's all."

"What's the difference? Listen to me, man, you ate dinner with
some babe hours before she tried to swim to Australia.
Unsuccessfully, I might remind you. The cops know about that?"

Josh wanted to be in bed. "Yes. I talked to them at the Sandpiper
Inn. I told them everything there was to tell, what little there was.
They're completely satisfied." If only that were true, he considered
painfully, the headache now expanding across his entire skull.

"Well, they may be satisfied, but Hightower's going to be considerably more difficult to please. Remember Gilliland," Kenny warned.
His curiosity had become genuine concern.

Josh knew Kenny spoke the truth. A few years earlier, one of the
junior vice presidents, a man named Daniel Gilliland, had been
arrested for possession of marijuana. He had one scrawny six-inch
plant barely thriving under a grow lamp he'd purchased a couple of
years earlier to keep a ficus from dying. The houseplant had not survived, and the cannabis had not been faring much better when a
neighbor spotted the illegal plant in the basement while borrowing
a garden hose. He felt it his civic duty to report such criminal behavior. In truth, it was little more than retribution for Gilliland having
misplaced the neighbor's favorite hedge trimmers several months
before. Even though the charge was quickly reduced to a misdemeanor and Gilliland had gotten off with only a warning, Hightower

had his office packed, the locks changed, and the boxes put in the parking lot while the junior vice president was still in court. There was no reprieve. Josh knew the same fate would immediately befall him if Hightower felt his actions could, in any way, reflect unfavorably upon Barnett Air.

"I remember Gilliland," Josh said defensively. "He broke the law and got himself busted for drug possession."

"Misdemeanor possession, Josh. I've had worse traffic tickets. You're mixed up in some wacko's death, for Christ's sake!"

"She was not a wacko, dammit, and I wasn't mixed up with her!" His words had not even convinced himself. They *were* mixed up together, linked, bound by fate, and no denial, no matter how loudly it was shouted, could change that fact. He took a calming breath. "Besides, there's no reason for Hightower to even know."

"Oh, that's great! You've got nothing to hide, so by all means, don't tell the boss. You know how illogical that sounds, Josh?"

"I don't care, Kenny. I've done nothing I'd be afraid to tell the old man, and I'm certainly no criminal, you know that."

"I wish my opinion was the only one that mattered."

"I did nothing wrong, Kenny." Josh's pulse raced.

"So why not tell Hightower?"

"Not yet!" Josh snapped. He knew he couldn't approach the company president, the man who held his career in his hand, without a full understanding of what had actually happened during those eighteen hours.

Kenny could feel the intensity in his friend's words. It alarmed him. "What's up, man? Talk to me. Seriously."

"Nothing's up. I've told you what there is to tell. I met Pamela on the plane yesterday afternoon, we had a simple, uncomplicated dinner in Sausalito, and then went our own ways. Nothing more."

"Who's Pamela?"

"What?"

"I asked you who Pamela was. A simple question, easy to answer."

"Sorry, I meant Dianne. You see, she meant so little to me I don't even remember her name. Satisfied?" The lie felt like a hot coal burning in his chest.

"Nope. How did she end up in Carmel if you went in opposite directions?"

"How the hell should I know? She wasn't with me. I never saw Dianne Lane in Carmel. I didn't even know about her death until the cops asked me about her just before I checked out." The story was getting so complex that Josh could no longer keep it straight. He'd told Fachini that he'd never met anyone named Dianne Lane. Now, he'd told Kenny that he'd had dinner with her.

He felt like a Judas, denying her like that.

Lies . . . God, how he hated them!

"I still say there's more going on here than you're telling me, and that's bullshit. No secrets between us, remember?" Kenny finished his lukewarm coffee and scooted his rolling chair toward the pot again. "You already check in?"

"Nope. Still in the parking lot. My phone's battery is about dead, too."

"Why not stay with me tonight, Josh. I've got plenty of room and I know you well enough to know when you need to talk to someone."

Josh did need to talk to someone, but things were getting too complicated too quickly. The whole crazy mess was developing a life of its own, beyond his control. He needed to find some badly needed answers before everything he cared about imploded. He tried to console himself that he'd only withheld information—easily explainable in the confusion created by Dianne Lane introducing herself as Pamela Morrow—and had not committed any crime, and had certainly not contributed to Dianne Lane's death. Maybe she was only a wacko. The thought pained him, but also caused him to look inward, to remember. "What ever happened to truth and justice, Kenny?" he asked solemnly.

"What the hell are you talking about? This isn't going to turn into one of your philosophical discussions, is it?"

"What we've talked about a hundred times: good and bad, caring more about people than things." The headache raged, like lightning striking his brain.

"What happened? Simple. You started making money, lots of

money. You always said you didn't want to rely on your rich parents for the rest of your life. That's why we had to starve all those months before Hightower came along; you didn't want to run to mommy and daddy for a loan, even though they could have given it to us out of pocket change. You had to do it your way. Well, my friend, by your own definition, you're a success. You've got everything you ever wanted, everything you've ever talked about. But so do I for that matter, so quit your bitching."

Kenny activated his monitor's screensaver, a personally modified version of "After Dark" that featured not flying toasters or big fish eating little fish, but a *Carcharodon megalodon*—a prehistoric shark that was sixty feet in length and weighed thirty tons—encircling and then devouring software mogul Bill Gates. After each attack and subsequent feast, the monstrous shark would burp noisily, producing a flurry of crimson bubbles in the shape of little Microsoft Windows, and then swim off, only to return a minute later when another Bill Gates plopped into the water, screaming and thrashing about.

Programmer humor.

Though a screensaver was employed, the development system Kenny used was never turned off and was connected to an uninterruptible power supply—an APC Symmetra Masterframe UPS—as were all the development workstations and the Sun Ultraspark server. Lost code was lost revenue. Hightower fought such waste with a vengeance.

For some reason tonight, Kenny was ready to leave the dreary basement and get out into the cool night air. The walls were closing in as they always did after several long days in the lab.

As he was about to speak, Josh broke the uneasy silence. "I've got everything I ever *thought* I wanted, Kenny. It's not the same thing." The cell phone beeped twice, indicating less than a minute of battery life. It was a welcome tone. "Gotta go. Battery's gone."

"You coming over?"

"Not tonight, thanks."

"You still here at eight?"

"Have a cup of that black mud you call coffee ready for me."

"I haven't emptied your cup since last time," Kenny laughed, though he felt like anything but making jokes.

•••

After pulling his travel bag from the back seat and his laptop from the front, Josh locked the Volvo and stuffed the keys in his pants pocket. He threw the clothes bag over his shoulder, filled his left hand with the computer bag, and wandered sluggishly toward the front door.

The La Quinta Inn was quiet at nine P.M., with no guests in the lobby and only one clerk behind the desk, a round-faced woman of forty with a crisp uniform and an easy smile. She welcomed Josh as soon as the front door hissed closed behind him. He didn't recall having seen her; she wasn't the woman normally at the desk.

Behind the clerk, an unseen television softly played an old movie running on one of the local stations.

Josh set his bags on the tile floor in front of the desk and fished in his back pocket for his wallet and credit cards. He laid his wallet on the desk in front of him, his hands cupped patiently over it, as the woman finished entering some data in her computer.

The movie paused for an on-the-hour news update. The first story the reporter covered in brief was the brush fire still raging in the San Juan Mountains, followed by the tragic suicide in Carmel of Dianne Lane, curator of Chinese antiquities for the internationally renowned Richmond Museum and Gallery of San Francisco. Though Josh could not see the screen—the television was in the small office behind the registration desk—he could picture Pamela's cold body being covered by the sheet.

As his mind began to take him back to the beach, a commercial for one of the auto makers came on at twice the volume of the newsbreak, snatching him from his melancholia.

"Sir," the clerk repeated.

"I'm sorry, what did you say?" Josh asked, embarrassed.

"I asked if you have a reservation with us?" Her broad smile was firmly carved in the middle of the round face, like a jack-o'-lantern.

"Uh, yes, Mitchell, J.T." As the woman punched in his name, Josh asked, "Can I buy a newspaper in your gift shop?"

"I'm sorry, Mr. Mitchell, it's closed."

Josh glanced briefly at the glass-encased gift shop across the lobby, its interior dark. His expression conveyed his disappointment.

"You're welcome to this morning's *USA Today*."

Josh thought for a second: the story would not have made a national newspaper yet. "A local paper would be preferable if you have one. Or better still, a paper from San Francisco." He folded his arms on the desk, his best smile spanning his face. It was a forced gesture, but one with which he was well versed: clients were not always pleasant to deal with.

"I think I saw a copy of this afternoon's *Examiner* in the office," she said in a perky tone. "Will that do?"

"That'd be perfect, thanks." His smile gained a bit of authenticity.

The clerk disappeared for a moment but quickly returned with the San Francisco paper. "It's out of order, I'm afraid. I was reading it earlier."

"It's fine, thanks. May I borrow it for a minute?"

"You can have it. I'm through with it." She slid the paper across the counter.

"Do you need to finish with me first?" he asked, holding up his wallet.

"It's no problem, Mr. Mitchell. Take your time. I'll complete your registration whenever you're ready."

Josh nodded pleasantly, tucked the newspaper under his arm, grabbed his bags, and moved toward a couch in the lobby.

He dropped his bags on the floor beside the couch and opened the newspaper on his lap, going quickly to the front page of Section One. No mention of Dianne Lane, just Mid-East problems and Wall Street news.

He turned to A2—still nothing.

A3, however, had been devoted almost entirely to the bizarre and unexpected demise of Dianne Lane. Josh began at the top of the page, beneath the heading "Richmond Museum Curator Dead By Own Hand." The photo that had been printed with the story did justice to his memory of Pamela Morrow, if not the name in the caption. It looked like one of those elegant platinum prints of a Hollywood starlet from the Thirties. He could still feel her incredible presence, even in a two-dimensional black-and-white image.

He read on: Since 1989, Dianne Lane had been curator of the largest private museum and art gallery on the West Coast, the prestigious Richmond Museum—the vocation and passion of Lloyd Richmond, recently deceased husband of billionairess Madeline Kennerly-Richmond. At the time of his death at seventy-four in February, a month earlier, Lloyd had not been active in the Museum's operation for several months, the result of a minor stroke—but had continued to monitor the operation of his life's work through his most trusted protégé, Mrs. Brandon Craig (for business purposes, according to the article, she'd always gone by her maiden name Lane). When Josh read that the woman he'd spent the day with had been married, the lump in his throat dropped into his chest, pressing against his ribs. He loathed the thought of Pamela having lied to him, that she could have any resemblance to Monica.

Changing her name, he was sure that was somehow explainable and certainly forgivable, but *not* lying about how she felt.

Lies had defined his life for too many years, at first as a tool for forcing open the doors of opportunity he felt would have otherwise been closed to a small-town country boy from West Tennessee. Then slowly, but as surely as night follows day, they had begun to erode the walls he had built around his private Camelot.

Now, lies had become the architect of his greatest fear.

As the article continued, Josh read that the autopsy—required by California law in questionable death—had been completed by the Monterey county coroner and Mrs. Lane's body had been released for burial. A private ceremony for family and close friends had been hastily arranged for Skylawn Memorial Park in San Mateo. The service was set for ten A.M. tomorrow.

Josh found himself staring at a point in space somewhere between the coffee table at his feet and the beach in Carmel, his mind a mélange of partially formed thoughts and rapidly developing fears. The grief he was experiencing at the sudden and mysterious loss of someone for whom he felt intense, if inexplicable, feelings, induced very real pain.

He was also having difficulty rationalizing the fact that he felt such depth of feelings after so few hours. It was not like him, at least not like the man he had become. At the same time, the threat the dishonest relationship now posed to his career—perhaps to his very freedom—was quickly corrupting any good there had been.

He knew he needed answers before he could begin to solve the riddle that tormented him: How could he have such feelings about someone he knew only in a lie.

He lowered the paper to his knees. *All right, Mrs. Brandon Craig, if you weren't Pamela Morrow, why did you tell me you were? Why did you pretend to be someone else all the hours we spent together? How could you have lied about something as important as that?*

He knew, however, two far more important questions needed answers: Who was Pamela Morrow, if such a person even existed, and what the hell really happened in the hour after she—or rather, Dianne Lane—left Room 5 at the Sandpiper Inn Tuesday morning?

There was only one logical place to start.

Josh knew he had to begin relying more on his mind instead of his heart. He had to turn off all feelings.

He tore page A3 from the paper and folded it twice, stuffing it in the front zipper pocket of his computer case. He grabbed his bags and walked deliberately toward the lobby door.

"Mr. Mitchell, I have your suite ready, all I need is your signature."

When Josh turned toward the desk, he could see that the round-faced woman's smile had not changed in ten minutes. He put his back against the front door and pressed the locking handle with his hip.

He forced a brief smile, his mind already on the road. "I'm sorry," he said. "Something's come up and I've got to be in San Francisco first thing in the morning."

# 5

Barnett Air's avant-garde façade—six stories of stainless steel and mirrored glass—reflected the morning sun, painting the building in a broad wash of warm amber and crimson that changed shape in harmony with the protean veil of clouds that lay just above the eastern horizon. In a few minutes, the desert heat would burn away the pale gauze, driving off the pastel hues until they were needed again at day's end.

Richard Hightower squinted momentarily as he caught a clear view of the sun through the windshield of his gleaming silver three-seater McLaren F1. Amid a squeal of thirteen-inch-wide Michelin radials, searching for a grip on the smooth asphalt, he whipped the sleek coupe beneath his covered space. His was the only secured spot among the fifteen hundred neatly striped and meticulously kept slots in Barnett's five-acre parking lot. The teal canopy, plus the million-dollar British sports car that spent its days hiding from the sun beneath it, had been two of the many requests he'd made after selling Aero-Tech's Stealth tracking software to the military for a quick fiftyfold return on Barnett's initial investment.

The CEO didn't mind appearing to all a notch above, a notch better. In his mind, he was better, infinitely better, and the image of a consummately successful executive living the good life at the helm of a powerful multinational corporation was not, to his way of thinking, bad for Barnett's image: winners did business with winners. In six short years, his carefully choreographed acquisitions, staffing changes, and extensive fat-trimming had propelled Barnett Air from a mid-sized industry player to an industry leader. To be sure, he deserved the credit, and he had a large PR staff to make certain the praise was never misdirected, especially in the media.

He checked his watch and satisfied himself that he was sufficiently early to visit his office before joining Kanazawa and Mitchell in the development lab. He wanted to check on Kanazawa's progress with Casper as soon as possible, and while his chief of software development always stayed late, he never arrived early.

He still had forty minutes.

Hightower made it a point to have his car under its cover before any other employee, not counting security, arrived for the day. He knew it put even his most senior vice president in a competitive mood right out of the gate: it would take each man or woman's best efforts all day to keep up with their boss. To his credit, it was a sound managerial strategy that had worked brilliantly for some of the top executives in the country; Richard Hightower was not above emulating the best, as long as it was never suspected the idea had not originated with him.

He walked with long, confident steps toward the lobby and the first of three levels of security every employee had to pass when entering the development lab in the basement. Floors one through five required only two security checks: the main guard station in the lobby and a redundant guard desk near the elevators on each floor. The executive suites on the sixth floor, however, could only be reached by the first of the four elevators, and only then when visual verification of the car's occupants, via security camera within the car, had been made at the main guard station. If approved, the car was then sent to the top floor by remote control. The 6 on the car's call panel in elevator-one merely alerted security that you desired access to the top level. The steel doors at the stairwells on each floor (other than ground level for fire escape reasons) could not be opened without security buzzing you through—again supported by surveillance cameras.

Kenny Kanazawa pressed the left mouse button and his screensaver vanished, leaving the last screen he'd been working with in view. He squinted at the tiny lines of code for a long moment and then activated the screensaver again.

It was too damn early to be doing code. He needed coffee.

After adding a packet of French roast ground with chicory to the coffee basket and pouring a fresh carafe of distilled water into the tank, Kenny dropped into his rolling swivel chair, threw his feet on the desk, and clicked his mouse. His mind was still on the problem with the scanner image-interpretation software, and he wanted time to explore the suggestions Josh had made last night before Hightower arrived demanding answers.

He knew he would not get it.

The senior programmer looked at the small digital clock running in the upper right-hand corner of his workstation monitor and smiled when he realized his old buddy was already a few minutes late—he should be popping through the door at any moment. He dropped his feet and with one precise shove, pushed the chair across the floor, ending up directly in front of the coffee pot. It had been done many times.

The smell of coffee beans percolating filled his senses.

Kenny grabbed a pair of clean, though not matching, cups (he had no fewer than fifty to choose from, all gifts of hardware and software manufacturers), skillfully substituted each momentarily for the carafe beneath the drip spout, and produced two early mugs of the hot, dark brown liquid.

Before the twenty-cup pot was empty at day's end, the contents would have turned a tarry black.

He added two sugars to his plus a large shot of creamer, but left Josh's black, as always. Whenever Kenny finished with or misplaced one cup, usually by leaving it half empty on another programmer's desk in the basement lab, he would grab another, as many as six or eight in a day. Once a week, generally Friday afternoons, the other programmers would collect their boss's cups and drop them in the large sink in the utility closet between the restrooms on their way out. Someone in maintenance would then wash them en masse and redeposit them beneath Kenny's table. As far as Kenny knew, he had an endless supply of cups. He didn't concern himself with such trivialities as where they came from. The development staff affectionately tolerated his absentmindedness. They didn't mind looking after him, after all he was a fair and knowledgeable leader who did more than his share of work.

When his office door opened at eight-ten, Kenny's back was to it. "Hi ya, old buddy," he said in a mischievous voice. "Got a cup o' that black mud ready for you." He spun around with Josh's mug extended.

"Never have developed a taste for black mud, Kenny. Must be a programmer thing. Will take a little of that coffee, though."

It was Richard Hightower.

"Sorry, boss," Kenny said. Though he didn't fear Hightower's retribution for such a slight, especially when not overheard by another employee, he had an inbred respect for the chain of command within big business and would never have intentionally addressed the president of the corporation in such a manner. "Thought you were Josh."

Hightower took the mug and wrinkled his nose at its odd aroma, but took a short sip anyway. At least it was hot. "I understood he was to be here at eight," he said, glancing at his watch.

"Me, too. Probably got held up in traffic. Should walk through the door any minute. You know what a stickler he is about punctuality." Kenny looked for another seat for Hightower to use. There wasn't one in his office. "You're welcome to my chair, sir."

"No need. Here's fine." With that, Hightower rested one hip casually on the edge of Kenny's desk, the opposite leg extended. He'd left his suit coat in his sixth-floor office and was in shirtsleeve and tie. As he sipped on his coffee, he looked around the cluttered room and then to the workstation screen, long enough to watch Bill Gates be eaten. It produced a brief smirk.

Kenny started to laugh but knew, despite Hightower's curt smile, the boss would not likely be in a joking mood, not with the latest software still full of bugs.

Before Kenny could think of something clever to say, Hightower spoke. "So, Kanazawa, what's the latest scoop on Casper? We going to be ready for the demo that's scheduled for Saturday with the Navy?"

"Think so, sir. I spoke with—"

"You think so! That doesn't sound like much of a commitment to me. Will you or will you not be ready? Because if you aren't certain we'll be able to give a successful demonstration, I've got a hell of a lot of people to call before they fly in here to watch nothing."

Kenny wanted to respond by saying that he wasn't the one who arranged the Navy's demonstration for March 14, weeks before it should have been set. Had he been asked, it would have been planned for much later, after the software had been proven reliable and not while it was still being written, for Christ's sake. But, of course, development was never asked about such matters; they were simply told what had been sold and then ordered to create it—possible or not.

He took a long draft of coffee and then a deep breath, determined to get a complete thought out before being interrupted again. "When I spoke with Josh last night, he got me thinking in a direction that has not been investigated as thoroughly as it needs to be. The problem could very well lie in the client server IDLs. If you don't mind, I'd like to have him work with me for the next three days to see if his hunch is correct."

Though he hoped the pressure Hightower was feeling from the Navy would get him what he wanted, Kenny knew the boss wouldn't like the idea of losing his top producer for even a day. Josh's sales annually totaled nearly two hundred million dollars, or more than $750,000 each business day for Barnett. And though Hightower had structured it so that Josh was paid strictly on monies collected, which meant only a fraction of the total sales commission paid per month on a long-term lease (most corporate jets were purchased under such leases), there were still enough dollars in question, more than $440,000 last year alone, for Josh to also complain about being pulled from the road for several days. In fact, Josh's dogged determination to make the most of his career opportunity—the break he felt represented a once in a lifetime chance to realize all his childhood ambitions—had kept him from taking a single day of vacation in nearly three years.

And while he was religious about saving money, Josh was equally enthusiastic about spending it: his three-bedroom, three-and-a-half-bath apartment in the Village, with its huge terrace and lavish furnishings, cost more than six thousand dollars a month. With taxes, the exorbitant cost of parking his Porsche and Mercedes in the city, and Monica's proclivity for shopping and eating out, little of the last several years' income was left. Hard work, if he wanted to maintain his lifestyle, was not an option for Josh, but then, he'd never minded hard work.

Hightower set his cup on the desk but kept it in his grip, his mind elsewhere.

Kenny knew not to interrupt.

Finally, after five silent minutes, the CEO stood and took another sip from his cup, then returned it to Kenny. "You're right, Kenny, that is black mud."

Kenny gave a tight smile.

Hightower continued: "Can't let you have him, Kanazawa, certainly not for several days. We've got a hot property out there with the new BA-35, and Mitchell needs—we all need—to capitalize on that as fully as we can. Dassault, Learjet, Cessna, Beech-Raytheon are all scrambling to get out similar designs, and they'll do it too, you can bet your ass on it. All we've got is a little lead time. I'll let you have him for one day, but only if he tells me personally he thinks he can be of help." Hightower looked at his watch again. "Thought you said he would be here by now."

Kenny checked the time on the monitor. It wasn't like Josh to be fifteen minutes late. He shrugged his shoulders. "Should have been. Want me to try his cell phone?"

"I want you to fix Casper so it's demonstrable by Saturday morning, whatever you have to do. If you do, the Navy will give us a sackful of money and everyone's stock will go up, including mine, yours, and Mitchell's. If you don't, however, I'm going to look like a fool. You really want me to look like a fool, Kanazawa?"

"I think I'll try his cell phone."

"Fine, you do that, and when you reach him, tell him I want to hear all about that sale he made in Santa Cruz yesterday. I'll be in my office." Hightower turned toward the door, but stopped as though a thought had just struck him. He turned back to Kenny. "Did Mitchell stay in Carmel Monday night?"

Kenny knew the head of the corporation read four different newspapers at six o'clock every morning while listening to CNN on one television and MSNBC on another, and would know at least as much about the drowning of Dianne Lane in Carmel as anyone not actually connected with the events. He also knew the man never asked a question without good reason— he was in search of something specific, though what, Kenny had no idea. Hightower knew he and Josh were close, so it would be futile to feign ignorance. Kenny smiled. "You know Josh, sir, creature of habit. He loves that old inn there."

Hightower pursed his lips. "He mention anything about the woman who drowned Monday? Dianne Lane? I know you heard about it."

Kenny's muscles tensed. "I think he said there was quite a commotion on the beach as he was leaving. Asked at the hotel, if I remember correctly, and was told someone had drowned in the bay. I believe that's all he had to say about it."

"He didn't mention having flown beside the woman from New York?"

Kenny hesitated, but then said, "Oh, yeah. You know, with all the code problems we're having at the moment, I can barely remember one conversation from the next. I think Josh said that when he learned the dead woman's name, it was the same as the woman who had been seated beside him on the plane Monday. Imagine that."

"He say anything else?" Hightower asked flatly, as if inquiring about the weather.

"Like what, sir?"

"Like, can you imagine your old buddy 'Lucky' Mitchell flying beside a beautiful woman for six hours and not learning all there was to know about her?"

Kenny grinned momentarily, then his eyes locked into Hightower's. He shrugged his shoulders but didn't answer directly, not wanting to dig a hole for his friend.

Finally Hightower turned again and grabbed the door handle. He stopped in the opening, his back to the programmer. "You will send him to my office if you see him before I do, right?"

"The second I see him."

"I hope it's soon," Hightower said as the door closed behind him.

When the CEO had cleared the outer door of the lab, Kenny punched the number on his telephone's speed dialer that would connect him with Josh's cell phone. After three rings, he impatiently mumbled, "All right, 'Lucky,' pick up the damn phone."

He'd barely finished his words when the prerecorded message announced: "The cellular customer you are trying to reach has either turned off his telephone or has moved beyond the cellular area. Please try your call again later."

"Shit!" Kenny said through clenched teeth, anticipating Hightower's predictable ire if Josh didn't show for some reason. "Josh, you son of a bitch, you better let me know what the hell's going on while there's still time for someone to help you."


The Volvo crept silently down the narrow paved access road that meandered lazily through the rolling hills of Skylawn Memorial Park. He looked at his cell phone lying on the passenger's seat, its display blank, and considered turning it on for the first time since the battery had died the night before.

He knew as soon as he did, it would start ringing.

He had no answers for why he wasn't at the office, for why he was going to the funeral of a woman he'd known for less than a day. How could he make others comprehend what he himself did not begin to understand.

The phone remained off.

Skylawn Memorial Park occupied over five hundred eighty acres on San Mateo's Pacific side, at the foot of the Montero Mountains with a stunning view of Half Moon Bay, a rare place in a time when land available for the living, to say nothing of such a huge expanse being reserved for the deceased, was typically priced by the square foot.

Everywhere Josh looked, fresh flowers adorned headstones that stood not upright—which would have broken the tranquil flow of the hills—but placed in natural harmony, level with the verdant plain. It had been intended by its designers, and probably was, Josh considered, a place where visitors could feel peace about the final resting place of their loved ones.

For a moment, he felt uncomfortably mortal. "Calm down, Josh," he mumbled in an effort to recapture his previous mood. "This is normal after someone close to you dies."

*Someone close to you,* he thought, intrigued by his own words.

As the car wandered down a slowly descending hill, more than a half mile from the simple stone entrance to the grounds, Josh spotted a large gathering ahead on the left. Both sides of Skylawn Drive were lined with limousines and expensive cars of all makes, constricting the cramped road even further. Quite a number had turned out for the private service, Josh noted. In a confused rush of feelings, the thought pleased him, as if Pamela had been a member of his own family and he was glad to see she had been so well thought of in life.

He moved the S70 carefully through the line of vehicles and stopped just ahead of the last car parked against the right curb, at the highest point in the park. He was now fully a hundred yards from the green-and-white striped canopy beneath which the mourners were beginning to gather. A man with his back to Josh—obviously the minister by his dress—stood alone on the far side of the polished bronze casket, facing the crowd.

Josh had planned to be at the cemetery by a quarter of ten, but had not anticipated the traffic he'd encountered on the oddly busy Wednesday morning. By five after the hour, he was apparently the last to arrive.

Staying on the pavement, he made his way along the line of cars, toward a ten-foot break in the black ropes that had been set up at the curb to direct the guests to the rear of the canopy. Nearing the gap in the velvet fence, he noticed for the first time a pair of huge . disagreeable-looking men—dressed well but more casually than the others—standing motionless, like stone sentinels at the entrance to a pharaoh's tomb. Josh remembered reading in the *Examiner* last night that the service was to be private, closed to those not invited by Madeline Richmond, widow of the founder of the Richmond Museum, Dianne Lane's employer. He slowed only slightly as he reached the two men, maintaining a deliberately confident air in his step, hoping to appear no different than any other guest, if a bit tardy arriving.

"One moment, sir," the one Josh recognized as former San Francisco 49ers defensive lineman, Derek DiAmo, said in a firm but low voice as he stepped in front of Josh, blocking his entrance. "I don't believe I've seen you before. Would you mind giving me your name, please."

"Joshua Mitchell. From New York. I'm . . . was, rather . . . an old friend of Dianne Lane's," he said softly, a catch in his voice. It was a considerable stretch of the truth, of course, but Josh felt— without any logic—that he had as much right to be here as anyone.

He awaited permission to enter.

A number of the mourners turned their heads to the right to catch a glimpse of the newest arrival. He avoided eye contact with them, his attention on the wall of a man before him.

DiAmo gave the other sentinel a well-understood head gesture, indicating that he should hold Mr. Mitchell at the outer perimeter while he left to check out his story. Josh took a step backward to assure the second man that he understood that he was to wait.

The former football player, whose promising career had been cut short because of four knee surgeries in his first two seasons, now worked full-time as a bodyguard and chauffeur for Madeline Richmond. She had hired him at the request of a friend in the Art League of San Francisco to whose daughter he had been married since college. Madeline treated him with an uncharacteristic level of respect, not simply as the hired help—as she did her other domestic employees—earning his unquestioned loyalty. She also paid him far better; he made her feel safe in a world that had changed too much and too quickly for her liking.

DiAmo approached the elderly woman quietly, bending to whisper in her ear so as not to disrupt the service that had just begun.

When he'd finished delivering Mr. Mitchell's explanation for his appearance, Madeline Richmond lifted her black veil and put her glasses, hanging around her neck from a silver chain, on her nose. She studied the stranger for a moment and then removed the glasses. She shook her head no ever so slightly and then lowered the veil again, her mind on the minister's delivery of the eulogy she'd written by hand yesterday. Despite her late husband's occasional encouragement, she had never cared to learn anything about keyboards or word processors, considering them a tool for the clerical and not worth her time.

DiAmo returned to his post. "I'm sorry, Mr. Mitchell, but I'm afraid I'll have to ask you to leave. This is a private ceremony and you are not on the list of invited guests." Despite the man's polite delivery, Josh was certain that attempting to dissuade him would be futile.

He strolled back toward the Volvo, moving slowly and listening to the minister's glowing words about the many contributions to art, community, and life Dianne Lane had made during her short tenure on earth, and how sorely she would be missed by so many.

He strained to hear the words as long as he could. He would say his last goodbye when everyone had left.


When he arrived at his car, at the top of the hill, Josh could no longer hear the service, though solemnity moved slowly through the air like a mist hanging over a swamp. He looked around, able to see much of the cemetery's five hundred-plus acres from his vantage point. He noted that Dianne Lane's appeared to be the only funeral being held at the moment, though two other plots had been readied. The ground had been dug and the removed earth covered with the same broad drape of fake grass.

*So many people dying . . . so many ways to die*, he thought, reminded again of the fragility of life.

At a point where the crest of the hill upon which Josh now stood disappeared into a small stand of Hollywood junipers, thirty yards to the west, a groundskeeper performed routine maintenance on one of the cemetery's several riding mowers; it had been switched off before the service began. The man used the opportunity to tighten the drive belts on the cutting blades. He regarded the man who had left the service with curiosity for a moment, then returned to his work.

As he stood high above the casket, his mind filled with images of Pamela, Josh felt more alone than he'd felt at any other time in his life. He was sure the other mourners had been aware of his having been turned away from the service, and though he didn't give a damn about any of their feelings, he couldn't help feeling out of place, a voyeur eavesdropping on another's moment of sorrow.

He knew he had a right to be there, and no hulk, no matter how large, was going to keep him from paying his final respects.

From his toolbox beside the lawnmower, the groundskeeper withdrew a powerful, but extremely small, spotter's scope and a 4 x 6 digital color photo of a man with the ocean over his left shoulder. At the bottom of the picture were three words: Joshua Thomas Mitchell. He laid the autofocus telescope across a shop towel on the seat of the mower, and pointed it toward the man standing near the blue Volvo. As he crouched down and pretended to be working on the blade adjustment, a crescent wrench in his left hand, he put his right eye to the eyecup and used his free hand to aim the scope. After a few seconds, he looked back at the photo: it appeared to be the same man, though with his hair neatly combed instead of windblown across his forehead and a suit and tie instead of a polo shirt. Content that the photo and the man were the same, he withdrew a small GPS transmitter from the toolbox and stuffed it in the pocket of his navy overalls. When slipped beneath fender or frame—a quick and simple matter with its magnetic base—its continuous signal would allow his team to position a car on a computerized map to within fifty meters of its actual location anywhere in the hemisphere. He returned the photo and scope to the toolbox. The right opportunity would present itself.

Josh chose a spot of broken shade beneath a tall pine near the front of his car and dropped wearily to the lush grass, his back against the rough bark. Seated, and in deep shade, he was still able to view the service but could not easily be seen by the others. His mind went back to his flight from New York, when he'd first seen Pamela Morrow . . .

. . . "I'm sorry to awaken you from such a pleasant dream," she says in a soft tone.

I turn my head and see her standing in the aisle, patiently awaiting my return from a daydream about making love to Samantha. For reasons I don't understand, I feel a pang of embarrassment, as if she knew exactly what I had been dreaming. I know it's impossible, yet the feeling persists.

I stare in silence for an awkward moment. My God, she's the most stunning woman I've ever seen. I wonder at first why she is just standing there, but finally understand that she is waiting to take her window seat beside me. It is then that I realize I'm staring at her, like a kid looking at his first *Playboy*, and I spring to my feet, bumping my head on the overhead storage compartment. It doesn't hurt, but I shut my eyes involuntarily—I cannot remember a time when I've been more embarrassed.

"Oh, are you all right?" she asks concerned. Her voice is soft and gentle.

When I get the courage to make eye contact with her again, I'm pleased she isn't laughing. The man in the seat opposite isn't so polite, though he is careful not to let such a beautiful woman see his silent, but animated, ridicule of me.

"Yes, thanks," I say, rubbing the spot on my head before I realize I'm doing it. I drop my hand to my side and step into the aisle, making room for her to pass. "I'm so sorry. I had my mind on something and didn't see you standing there."

She smiles as she slips gracefully into her seat, indicating that she understands, though I am sure she knows about my dream.

I am careful not to hit my head again when I sit. "Were you there long?"

"No, not very." She bends down and pushes her bag beneath the seat in front of her, her wool coat remains across her shoulders. "Must be quite a woman if you're dreaming about her in the middle of the day."

*I knew it, she did know about Samantha,* I joke to myself. I tell her, "I was thinking about work, not a woman. Wish it had been." She doesn't believe me, I'm sure, but gives no indication I have been discovered.

The flight attendant delivers the drink I ordered when I first sat down. I raise my tray from the armrest to receive it. She asks the beautiful woman if she'd like something to drink.

She studies my black coffee and small bottle of Bailey's and then says, "I believe I'll have what the gentleman's having, thanks."

"It's decaf," I say.

"Perfect," she smiles, settling comfortably in the thick leather seat. She chooses a copy of *Southern Living* magazine when a selection is offered to her by the second attendant and begins to thumb through the pages, seemingly content to spend the entire trip in solitude.

I moan my disappointment silently; I want to talk to her, get to know her, but am not surprised she has no time for me. It was, after all, an inauspicious beginning.

To my great satisfaction, I notice that she has no ring on her left hand, though why such an idiotic thought has entered my mind escapes me: she couldn't be less interested in me if she were married to Mel Gibson.

I have to remind myself to look straight ahead and not stare at her, but it takes willpower. I feign interest in the magazine I took from the stack in the flight attendant's hands without having looked at the title. To my dismay, I discover that it is the latest issue of *Cosmopolitan* and I have just opened to a two page, full-color Victoria's Secret ad displaying a bevy of gorgeous models in skimpy underwear. I close it as furtively as possible and hope she hasn't noticed.

I stuff the magazine in the pocket in the seatback in front of me and grab American's *In Flight Magazine*. I've read it cover to cover on two previous flights, but pretend the words are fresh. I sip my coffee and pray I won't pour it in my lap.

When the first attendant brings the beautiful woman's coffee and leaves, I seize the opportunity: "Nothing like coffee and Bailey's to knock the winter chill from your bones," I say, then realize I have just done my worst James Earl Jones voice. I can't believe it, I'm acting like a clumsy kid. Beautiful women never have this effect on me.

Maybe I'm just being hard on myself. She is just a woman like any other, nothing special about her. Now who the hell am I kidding? She's a goddess! But much more than just pretty, she has an aura about her, like a force field in a sci-fi movie. It lends a sense of majesty to her, visible in the fluidity of her movements, the grace of her posture, the tone of her voice. I'm staring again and must remind myself to close my mouth.

She looks at me and I would swear she hears my teeth clack together. "It does seem to have a warming effect," she says in that voice. "I'm glad you thought of it."

My brain goes completely blank. No response whatsoever comes to mind, I just smile like a first-grader infatuated with his teacher. She waits for what seems an eternity for me to speak then returns to her magazine.

I feel a cold sweat coming over me and I adjust the tiny blower overhead. It doesn't help much. I realize the heat is coming from within, produced by a need to learn everything I can about this woman in what little time we have, as if survival itself depended upon it. I take a deep, silent breath and sip on my coffee, thinking.

She closes her magazine and cradles her cup with both hands, alternately blowing gently across the surface and then sipping the hot liquid. As I think of how to introduce myself, the hardest thing I've contemplated since asking my first girl out, she speaks. "You have business in San Francisco, or is this a pleasure trip?" Her soft gray eyes draw me into them.

"Business," I say, then add, "but I try to include some relaxation in every business trip. Helps keep me sane." Thank God, a complete sentence without mishap. I can't believe I'm nervous.

"I know exactly what you mean."

Finally a connection! I rejoice.

"What type of business are you in, Mr. . . .?"

"Mitchell, Josh Mitchell," I say, filling in the blank.

"Is Josh short for Joshua?" she asks.

"Yes, it is. Only my mother calls me Joshua, though."

"Why? Joshua is a beautiful name."

My heart pounds. "Most people just tend to shorten names."

There is a long pause before she speaks again. "Well, Joshua," she says with a warm smile, "it's nice to meet you."

She extends her hand and I take it.

It's warm from the cup.

Though we shake, she doesn't offer her name.

I let it pass, fearing it will make her uncomfortable if I ask. "The pleasure is mine," I assure her, my normal voice having returned.

My nervousness has finally passed. This just may turn out to be a glorious flight . . .


A lawnmower's exhaust sputtered momentarily, rudely yanking Josh back to the present. He looked to his right and saw that the groundskeeper was still tinkering with his mower, though it had not been the one that had made the sound. He then looked over his left shoulder and saw a second man cutting a wide expanse of lawn at the base of the hill behind him, between two huge ponderosa pines. It was doubtful his mower was heard by the mourners.

Josh stood beside the tree, his knees stiff, and brushed off the seat of his suit trousers. He had lost track of time.

When his attention returned to the service, he saw that the casket had already been lowered. The majority of the guests was gathered in tight clusters away from the tent, to the south, while a small group of mourners was filing past the grave, each member dropping a flower or handful of rich, brown earth into the pit.

It took less than ten minutes for the group to disperse and the street to clear. The minister was the last to say good bye to Madeline Richmond, and handed her the bible from which he had read. She sat alone on the front row of chairs, where she had been when Josh first saw her, DiAmo and the other sentry having taken up positions behind her on each side. Only two cars now remained on Skylawn Drive.

Josh had intended to visit the gravesite as soon as everyone left, but decided he would come back in half an hour, after the elderly woman and her twin towers were gone.

He walked toward his rental car, hands in his pockets, his right fumbling his keys. He had no idea what he would do for the next thirty minutes, perhaps just drive to a remote part of the park, switch off the engine, and allow his thoughts to find their own course. He had been trying to understand this dilemma for two days; he wanted to let it go now.

He knew he'd have to deal with what had arisen in Carmel soon enough, not to mention the problems that were inevitably brewing at the office, but he didn't want to think about any of that at the moment. For a few minutes, he just wanted to be with the feelings that were crying out for recognition and attention. Feelings he hadn't experienced since . . . he wasn't sure when the last time was, or if he'd even felt these things before.

Pamela had touched him, and his life would never be the same.

As Josh was about to unlock the door of his rental car, DiAmo called out to him by name. When the huge man was sure that he'd gotten Mr. Mitchell's attention, he returned to Madeline Richmond's side, and, joining the other man, continued helping the elderly woman toward her limousine.

Josh walked without hurry toward the long black Bentley, his hands still in his pockets. He imagined the woman intended to offer some measure of apology, or at least an explanation, for having denied him entrance to the service. He would accept either graciously, assuming she had her reasons. Perhaps the recent loss of her husband, and now her husband's "right arm," as the story in the Examiner had put it, had been too much of a strain, and the sudden arrival of a stranger at the gravesite was more than she could deal with.

A capricious gust of wind from the north blew several locks of his thick, black hair into his face and he promptly swept them back in place.

As Josh continued toward Madeline Richmond's limo, the groundskeeper darted north, over the small rise, then quickly east, toward the Volvo, his movements hidden by the crest of the hill. He then approached the vehicle from the passenger's side, using it as a shield. He completed his task of planting the GPS transmitter and was back at the mower by the time Josh reached the bottom of the hill. From the toolbox, he withdrew a small digital camera, removed the cup and eyepiece from the spotter's scope and attached the scope to the camera's lens mount, this time laying the scope across the flat hood of the mower to steady it.

He did not know the woman who had summoned Mitchell, but was under orders to photograph anyone he spoke to, even an old lady.

Madeline Richmond had removed her hat and veil and her glasses were again on her nose by the time Josh arrived. She and the two bodyguards were standing beside the Bentley, near its open left rear door. It was when he was close to the woman, her face now exposed, that Josh realized how frail she was. She appeared to be at least seventy-five, with thinning white hair—though fashionably styled—and could not have weighed more than ninety pounds, and while she had a proud, even defiant, manner about her, she was plagued with an excessive dowager's hump that made her appear much shorter than the five-six Josh imagined she had been in her youth. She stood without benefit of walker or cane, assisted by the man at either arm.

She spoke as Josh reached the front of the car, her voice shaky. "Who exactly are you, Mr. Mitchell, and why are you still here?" No amenities of any kind, no attempt at pleasantry on her part.

Josh was taken aback.

He somehow found his best smile. "Mrs. Richmond, may I extend my sincerest sympathies at the loss—"

"Spare me your patronizing words, young man, and save your sympathies for someone who gives a damn. I asked you two simple questions, and I expect answers." She coughed heavily several times, holding a linen handkerchief to her mouth. It was a deep, painful cough that Josh recognized as the advanced stages of emphysema, the disease that had claimed his mom's only brother. He now understood her barrel chest and wraithlike appearance, but was surprised by her lack of common courtesy.

His smile vanished. "My name is Joshua Mitchell, ma'am. I live in New York City and I was a friend of Dianne Lane's. I'd hoped to see her one last time before she was laid to rest. I'm sorry, I didn't realize the service was private." As he spoke, he studied the two men in a glance. The man unknown to him appeared neutral, but DiAmo had icy hatred in his glare.

The coughing spell ended. The elderly woman processed Josh's words, regarding them warily. "You couldn't have known where to come this morning without having learned of the arrangements from the newspaper or from television, and in either case would have also known, without the slightest possibility of misunderstanding, that the service was closed. Furthermore, I knew all of Dianne's friends, Mr. Mitchell, on both coasts, and you were decidedly not one of them. I must warn you, I'm not predisposed to patience, and you are wearing what little I have left painfully thin."

Josh had dealt with hundreds of businessmen in his sales career, and had met many tough characters, some even ruthless. He was suddenly grateful he'd never attempted to sell anything to the diminutive woman before him.

*Lies had not worked,* he complained in silence, *perhaps the truth will fare better.*

"Actually, Mrs. Richmond, I only met Dianne on the plane from New York Monday. I read yesterday where she'd drowned and wanted to pay my respects before I headed back to the East Coast. She was a very special woman. It didn't take knowing her a lifetime to appreciate that."

Madeline Richmond began coughing again, this time more violently. Josh feared she might die right in front of him. Her glasses fell from her face and she indicated that she wanted to be helped to her seat in the car. When the heavy door had sealed her in, and DiAmo and the other man had taken their places in the passenger and the driver's seats respectively, Madeline Richmond lowered her window. The coughing had subsided, though her face was more drawn than ever, her voice tenuous, her eyes bloodshot.

Josh knew the pain must be relentless, and despite the elderly woman's brash, mannerless nature, felt sympathy for her. He knew it would not be long before she would return to this place.

She began to speak and Josh leaned closer to the open window. Her words were faint but still deliberate. "You seem oddly, may I say unnaturally, concerned about someone you say you just met only two days ago, Mr. Mitchell. Either you are a liar, which we have already determined, or you are a fool, and I do not believe you to be the latter."

She pulled a long, slender cigarette from a gold filigree case. It was immediately lit by DiAmo. Smoking was the last thing on earth this woman needed to be doing, Josh considered sadly, but understood that such lifelong habits often accompanied the addicted to their graves.

The woman coughed as she inhaled but turned her attention back to Josh. "In my many years, I've observed that no man would form such an attachment for a stranger without having first slept with her, and if we are to take you at your word that you only met Mrs. Lane hours before her death, then you would likely have been the last person to have had sex with her . . . though certainly not the first." She stared directly at him, her eyes hard. "I wonder if the police know about you and Dianne?" she said as the black glass raised between them.

An Hispanic man in dark blue coveralls, identical to those worn by the groundskeeper, moved a backhoe skillfully into place between the open pit and the mound of earth his assistant had just uncovered. As he lowered the stabilizing feet at the rear of the bright yellow machine, the assistant busied himself with the mat of faux-grass that had covered the excavated ground, first folding it in the middle, then rolling it into a long tube so it could be more easily removed from the work area. This done, he pulled a wrench from his back pocket and began to dismantle the canopy. In an hour, the bronze and granite marker bearing her name and the dates of her birth and death would be in place and little evidence of the events of the morning would be visible. What soil remained would be scattered by the next cutting and dissolved by the rain.

Very soon, too soon, it would appear to a stranger who visited this spot, that Dianne Lane had always been a resident of Skylawn Memorial Park, a disembodied name which had never occupied a place in the living world, or in the heart of another.

Instead of the peace of closure he'd hoped to find, Josh felt a profound sense of violation at the thought of the woman he'd come to know disappearing forever beneath a piece of cold marble into which a few letters and numbers had been cut.

He stood silently at the west end of the grave—as he had done since the Bentley disappeared over the hill twenty minutes earlier—staring blankly at the dark brown casket, its shiny surface now partially obscured by the earth and flowers that had been heaped upon it. The lid to the sarcophagus would be lowered into place as soon as the backhoe had a stable footing, putting yet another impenetrable layer between him and what might have been.

His mind searched for refuge and he found himself seated beside her on the plane again, when her eyes were still bright and her soft voice could still be heard . . .


. . . "Doesn't life seem so unfair at times, so not worth living?" she says in a sincere, even sad, tone. I can tell she is referring more to unspoken things in her own life than to the story of Monica which she has somehow pulled from me. I am pleased to find I can speak of her without regret.

"At times," I say. "Though it is more often good."

She nods. "I wish that just once in my life, I could meet someone who understands what truth and loyalty mean. Don't you, Joshua?"

I like the way she calls me Joshua, but her words are both a prayer and a damnation to me. Though I had never cheated on Monica, our entire relationship was based upon one lie after another. I answer sincerely, "More than you could possibly know. I'm no longer sure such people even exist. I believe it was just a childhood hope, the kind you inevitably lose when you've lived long enough."

"Oh, they do exist, I assure you," she says. "The trick isn't finding such a person, it's recognizing it when you have." She takes a bite of her scalloped potatoes and then a sip of white wine. I've barely touched my dinner, more interested in listening to her than in eating. "More brief associations are squandered because we're blindly searching when what they've been looking for is right before their eyes."

"I know what you mean . . . but how can one be sure?" I ask. I still haven't learned her name.

"Your heart will tell you," she says simply. "People are afraid to listen to their hearts. They're so conditioned to think their way through life that they miss the most important parts, the things you *feel*. The mind can't feel, only the heart can do that. Our brain tries to tell us how something is supposed to feel, but it's almost always wrong. People confuse such thoughts for feelings." She spears a piece of broccoli and eats it quickly. "Do you know the longest and most difficult journey any of us will ever undertake?" she asks, her eyes aglow, her gestures animated.

"No," I answer honestly. I love the open and simple way she talks. If only I could find the courage to do the same.

I watch as she slowly moves her index finger from the center of her forehead to a spot between her breasts. I can't help but follow, my pulse missing a beat. "The twelve inches that separate head and heart," she says sincerely. "If people would only get out of their heads and into their hearts, what a world we could have. Don't you agree?"

"Absolutely," I answer earnestly. "But, as you say, it's the hardest journey we face in life."

"It *is* life, Joshua" she smiles, her voice soft and sensual.

I nod but can think of nothing that will add to what she has said. I find her captivating, no longer merely beautiful but so much more. In the three hours we've been talking, I've discovered nothing at all about her work or her life, yet I seem to understand her better than anyone I've ever known. I've never met anyone as in touch with their inner self as she. There's something at once new and yet familiar about her, and I find that I'm drawn to her like no other woman . . .


"Hey, watch out, buddy," the man on the backhoe yelled to Josh as the huge slab of white concrete swung in a wide arc to within inches of his head. The machine upon which the man sat made a series of thunderous shuddering noises as the hydraulic arm reined in the eight-hundred-pound lid. "Sorry, I thought you had moved back," he shouted when the noise subsided.

Josh signaled with a wave that he was okay and took several steps backward.

In another minute, the vault lid was in place and the operator had begun filling the hole.

The last mourner at Dianne Lane's gravesite blew her a silent kiss and then ambled back toward his car.

When he arrived, he hung his suit jacket on the hook in the back and dropped heavily into the front seat, loosening his tie. He stared at his reflection in the rearview mirror, his eyes tired, weary of the lies and the unforeseen consequences that always accompanied them.

He knew what had to be done.

Josh switched on his cell phone and dialed local information. When it was answered, he said, "I'd like the main number for the San Francisco Police Department."

# 6

*The cruelest lies are often told in silence.*

—Robert Louis Stevenson (1850-1894)

Although the location on Valencia was the number Josh had been given by the operator as the closest police precinct, he was redirected to the Hall of Justice at 850 Bryant, between Gilbert and Boardman Place. Detective Duane Lefler had been put in charge of the Lane case, he'd been told.

The drive from San Mateo had not been a pleasant trip. He felt like he'd swallowed a live serpent. Force of will alone kept him driving steadily north toward a man and a dilemma he'd rather not encounter.

Josh knew, however, that the trip was inevitable: In addition to his commitment to Pamela's memory, there was an intense desire to come clean and begin living life as he'd been raised, honestly and with pride, even if it meant losing his job. He hoped it wouldn't mean losing his freedom as well.

He also understood Lefler wouldn't need a Ph.D. in criminology to make more than mere coincidence of Dianne Lane and him having been in the same small inn, five hours after they'd flown side by side to the West Coast and two hours after they'd shared a dinner in

Sausalito. His hope was that the San Francisco Police would believe that when he spoke to Fachini in Carmel he didn't realize, until the *Examiner* story and picture were printed on Tuesday, that the woman who'd introduced herself as Pamela Morrow was actually Dianne Lane.

He knew it was an anemic story, and would likely sound as improbable to them as it had to him as he practiced his lines en route to police headquarters, but it was his only chance of staying out of jail for withholding information and lying to the police.

He'd done nothing truly wrong, he kept assuring himself, and therefore had nothing to fear.

It sounded as hollow as it had at the coffee shop in Carmel.

As Josh's rental car vanished over the hill to the south of the gravesite, the groundskeeper took a cell phone from the tool kit and called for his ride. Within thirty seconds, a white panel van with no side or rear glass appeared over the north hill on Skylawn Drive, collected the groundskeeper and his tool kit, and was gone.

"Yeah, it's me," he said when the call he'd placed from within the van was answered. The man from the surveillance van in Carmel was on the other end. "Mitchell was here just like you guessed. Didn't get in, though."

"What do you mean?" the man asked.

"Some rich old biddy at the service with a couple of huge sumbitches at her side turned him away."

"She about seventy-five, black Bentley, coughs a lot?"

"Yeah, that'd be her."

"Madeline Richmond. She runs things now that the old man's dead. Always did really. What'd Mitchell do when he couldn't get in?"

"He stayed, watched the service from the hill a short distance from where I was," the man pretending to be a groundskeeper said. "What's his deal?" He, like the rest, had been told only what he needed to know for the operation.

"It's not your worry. You didn't let him see you, did you?" the man asked, irritated by the thought.

"Yeah, but he don't know shit. I watched him for half an hour and he doesn't have a fucking clue what's going on." The groundskeeper lit a cigarette and put his foot on the dash.

"You willing to guarantee that to Mr. Roland?"

The groundskeeper had no desire to do that; he liked his work too much, and while the man on the other end could be a worrisome pain in the ass at times, Mr. Roland was to be feared. "Hey, listen, it's okay. I planted the locator without being seen and got all the pictures you could want. Everything's cool." He moved the mouthpiece away and yelled into the back of the truck, though the man on the other end could still hear his words: "You getting the mark's signal, Brad?" he asked of the man seated at the GPS tracking screen.

"Two miles ahead on US-101. Moving north at fifty-five," Brad announced proudly.

"Brad's riding the mark like he's got a saddle on him. Now relax, I told you it was covered."

"What about Madeline Richmond? I wonder how she figures into Mitchell's world?" Hetzler hated open-ended situations, preferring to know everything about everyone in any operation, including how they thought. That's how he'd put the mark at Dianne Lane's funeral after his team in Sacramento had failed to spot him last night. He tried to imagine what Madeline Richmond and Josh Mitchell had in common.

The groundskeeper considered the question as well. Finally, "Can't say. They talked for a while after the service, face to face at her car. Something he said didn't make her any too happy. It looked for a second like she was gonna keel over right there. They talked for another minute through her window after her boys put her in the car. Then, the Bentley shot off like it was headed for a fire. We should have had audio on 'em both."

"I agree with you for a change, but the screwup last night left no time for such luxuries. What'd Mitchell do after he pissed off Richmond?"

"Like I said, she and her boys drove off but the mark stayed at the grave until they finished filling it back in. Then he left and I called you straight away."

Hetzler tapped a pencil against his desk, his computer screen displaying the complete file on Madeline and Lloyd Richmond. He knew Mitchell hadn't met Dianne Lane before Monday, and there was no evidence that he knew either of the Richmonds, even casually, so what the hell was the connection? "Alert me the second he lands *anywhere*," he said brusquely, ending the call.


The sun shone as brightly as an arc lamp as it poured through the Volvo's windshield and open sunroof. Though it had initially been a pleasant contrast to the March air gusting through the hills around San Mateo, and the cooling breeze had helped clear Josh's mind, in the stop-and-go noon traffic of San Francisco proper it was just plain hot. To provide some measure of relief, Josh tilted the driver's visor down fully and closed the tinted-glass sunroof panel. The sudden absence of outside noise allowed his thoughts to wander into areas that had been kept at bay by the wind's dulling sound. His guilt returned, demanding an explanation for this insane journey, a trip that would undoubtedly end in disaster.

*What the hell are you doing, Josh?* his inner voice tormented.

Just as in football, where he'd played quarterback for four winning seasons during high school, Josh understood that you couldn't stand idly about while the other team scored against you, and then hope to answer them point for point. No victory had ever come from such a strategy. The best way to win had always been a deliberate offense. In three years of selling, it had worked exceedingly well, and it stood to reason it should work in this situation, he kept repeating.

When Lefler came for him, demanding an explanation for why he'd lied to the Carmel Police about not having known anyone named Dianne Lane, with a hundred witnesses reportedly having seen them together in Sausalito just hours before her death, nothing he could say about her having gone by the fictitious name of Pamela Morrow while she was with him would have the slightest credibility. Besides, who could corroborate such a fantastic story? It wouldn't matter to the cops that he really hadn't heard the name Dianne Lane until Fachini had spoken it in the lobby of the Sandpiper Inn—and then his own shock at having seen her lifeless body lying beneath a sheet on the sand minutes before had disoriented him—he would become suspect number one in her murder. Or at the very least, if it proved to be suicide, dragged through the media like some monster who'd driven a troubled woman, an admired and respected woman, over the edge.

He felt disconnected from reality, as if he now existed in a frightening world from which there could be but one chance of escape.

At an intersection, as he sat waiting impatiently for the light to change, his thoughts maundering, no logic to them, he found himself looking at first with disbelief, and then staring in horror, at a massive billboard across the street. Several of the most damning lines from the note he'd written in Carmel were displayed in block letters three feet high, the words *lies, lies, lies* highlighted in blood-red neon. The billboard's background beneath the words displayed a slender form wrapped tightly in a sheet, like a sailor's body readied for burial at sea.

He snapped his head to the left to see the reaction of the two young women in the convertible beside him, but they had apparently not noticed the billboard yet. They were busy loudly singing the words to Eric Clapton's rendition of "Change the World," though with considerably less ability. When they realized the man in the Volvo was staring at them, his eyes wide and darting, they fell silent, then began laughing at the weirdo beside them.

Josh turned his eyes back to the sign but now saw only an advertisement for Ricoh copiers.

The light changed.

He looked back toward the convertible, but the car had already begun its left turn; all he saw was the rear of the Chrysler Sebring LXI and a pair of raised right arms, swaying to the music.

He didn't blame the women for their reaction: He could only begin to imagine how he must have appeared to them.

"Son of a bitch, Josh," he whispered. "This is no time to lose it."

A man behind him honked impatiently.

The sudden thought of prison made him lightheaded, like a whiff of nitrous oxide at the dentist's office, and he found it difficult to judge speed and distance. It took all his willpower just to stay in his lane until the sensation abated. He remembered that he'd not eaten since early Tuesday evening, after leaving Santa Cruz, and hoped that at least some of the dizziness was due to the food his body craved.

When a Wendy's appeared on the right, he cut across two lanes of congested traffic to make the entrance.

Detective Sergeant Duane Lefler was a stocky, rugged-looking man, completely unlike his counterpart in Carmel, with a threadbare tweed jacket and shoes that needed polishing. He looked like the failed pollination of John Wayne and Columbo. Between thin, hard lips, the fattest cigar Josh had ever seen protruded like a joke store prop. To Josh's astonishment, the detective didn't smoke the monstrosity but instead regularly took a large bite from the end, munching it like a chaw of Beech-Nut.

He eyed Josh, seated in a hard wooden chair opposite his desk, much as Josh's coach in high school had looked at each new player at the beginning of football season: with a disquieting indifference that compelled you to say something on your behalf.

"Our boy just entered the Hall of Justice on Bryant Street about five minutes ago," the pretend groundskeeper said into his cell phone.

The other man checked his activity log on Mitchell's cellular. There had not been a call placed to it from the Hall of Justice, or anyone else for that matter. He couldn't imagine what Mitchell was doing there, but intuition told him it might have something to do with his conversation with Madeline Richmond since he'd gone straight to the station from the cemetery.

He studied the screenful of pixies downloaded and transferred from the groundskeeper's camera and selected one that clearly showed Madeline Richmond's face, apparently displeased by something Mitchell had said.

The man let his mind run free, trying to figure out what the mark might have said that would have angered the old woman so. He drew a blank; he should have had audio on them.

"Want me to find out what he's up to in there?" the groundskeeper asked after a long silence.

The other man thought about it for a moment. "Nope. You just sit tight and keep out of sight. I don't want to spook Mitchell at this juncture. I'll take care of finding out what's going on inside." He hung up. "Which detective is handling the Lane case, Tommy?" he asked the black man who'd been with him in Carmel.

"Lefler, Duane M.," he said, the answer already on one of the computer screens. He'd anticipated the question.

"We have his direct number?" The man was sure they did.

"On the screen now."

For several agonizing minutes, the detective sat and chewed his cigar, his eyes never leaving Josh's face.

As Josh was about to blurt out that he had nothing whatsoever to do with Dianne Lane's death—with all the conviction and sincerity he could muster—Lefler slid his chair back noisily and stood. Josh froze. The other man walked around to the front of his desk and sat on the edge, a small pale blue slip of paper in his hand.

"So, Mr. . . ."—he glanced at the note bearing the basic information the cop at the front desk had jotted down—". . . Mitchell, Hanover tells me you drove all the way here from Sacramento because you have something to add to the Lane case."

Josh had never been in a police station before and believed, based upon the way his head felt detached from his body, that his appearance must convey absolute and abject guilt. He managed a pitiful nod and his lips parted, but his voice wouldn't work. Had he actually managed to blurt anything out a minute earlier, it would have sounded more like he was clearing his throat than speech.

He looked around the small office—anything to break eye contact without appearing nervous.

*Wonderful, dickhead, you're doing great so far! Now, just calm down and get on with your plan. It'll all work out, but not if you lose it again like you did in the car.* He looked at the cop and hoped he hadn't just spoken the words aloud.

Lefler had turned his attention back to the note.

Josh wet his lips and tried again as Lefler read. "I was already in the city, San Francisco I mean . . . well, San Mateo, really. I didn't have to come all the way from Sacramento."

"You went there for the funeral, did you?"

*How the hell did he know?* "Yes," he said evenly.

Lefler's eyebrows raised. "You knew Dianne Lane well, then." He glanced back at the note, but only for a second. "I was under the impression you lived in New York. You two do business?"

Josh wanted it clear that he did not know Dianne Lane, and therefore had no reason on earth to wish her dead.

*But you did know her, you idiot,* his heart reminded, *better than you knew anyone.*

*No one knows that!* his analytical side countered protectively, *nor do they ever have to.*

"No, not well at all," Josh said. "We flew out together from New York on Monday." He fought to keep calm, though he was sure his efforts were ineffective. "I came here today because of the article I read last night in the *Examiner.*"

"So, Mrs. Lane had been in New York with you?"

"No. I met her on the plane for the first time Monday afternoon. Only after I read the article in the paper did I realize that she and the woman I knew as Pamela Morrow were one and the same. I had no idea before that. That's why I didn't tell Fachini." His heart pounded in both ears.

Lefler stood and went back to his chair, dropping heavily into it. He took a bite on his cigar, and then after a full minute said, "Forgive me, Mr. Mitchell, I'm usually pretty quick on the uptake, not dense like today, but I don't have a clue what you're talking about."

*Shit,* Josh cursed, *he doesn't know who Fachini is.*

"Sorry. It's simple really. In Carmel, on Tuesday morning, I talked with a Detective Sergeant Louis Fachini, I think his name was, and he asked me whether I knew the woman who'd committed suicide earlier that morning—"

"Why would he have thought you'd have known her?" The man chewed animatedly.

"He was asking all the guests at the Sandpiper Inn where I was staying." Josh felt the walls moving in.

"Had the decedent been staying there as well?"

Josh started to say yes, but then realized he didn't have any idea. If she had been staying there, Fachini would have known it, but Josh got no impression that had been the case. Still, there was some reason the Carmel detective had been in that hotel Tuesday morning. Josh decided not to say anything he was uncertain of. He answered sincerely, "I don't know."

Lefler watched him as he chewed. "Go ahead, Mr. Mitchell."

Josh gathered his thoughts. "Fachini showed me a picture that I didn't recognize and said the woman who had drowned was named Dianne Lane. I told him honestly that I didn't know anyone by that name . . . until I read the newspaper Tuesday night. It all became clear to me then."

"I'd hope so, Mr. Mitchell, because it's still hazy to me. What became clear?" Lefler put his elbows on the desk.

Josh sat erect in the hard chair. "That the dead woman was Pamela Morrow."

"We've got a second body?" Lefler asked, his lips now tight.

Josh ran back the last few seconds of conversation in his mind trying to understand how the cop had come to such a ridiculous conclusion. "No, of course not. I mean the woman you know as Dianne Lane was Pamela Morrow to me."

"Why would you have thought Dianne Lane was this Pamela Morrow woman?"

"That's who she told me she was. How was I to know any different?" Josh tried not to sound indignant.

"Let me get this straight," Lefler said, bending to his right and spitting his tobacco in the waste basket. "The woman we all know as Dianne Lane, the woman who died at one-thirty Tuesday morning in Carmel Bay, identified herself to you in New York as someone by the name of Pamela Morrow."

"Exactly," Josh said, pleased the man finally understood.

"Why on earth would Dianne Lane have told you she was some-one else, Mr. Mitchell? That seems a bit odd to me. Doesn't that seem a bit odd to you?" The elbows were back on the table.

"Now it does, sure! But I've told you my name is Josh Mitchell and you believe me, right?" Lefler nodded. "Nothing strange about it all. How about if you find out tomorrow that my real name is Cole Younger . . . what then?" Josh felt like he was making progress. Perhaps he only hoped he was, so intensely that it seemed to be true.

"Why would you lie about your name, unless you had something to hide?"

"I guess she did. She was planning on taking her own life, right, who knows what other craziness was in her mind?" Josh felt again like Judas.

*It won't serve her memory for you to go to jail,* he reminded himself, though it did little to relieve the uneasiness.

Lefler stood and slid his chair back from the desk. He walked over to Josh who stood instinctively. "Well, Mr. Mitchell, it might not have been a neat little suicide after all, despite that unbelievably convenient note alluded to in the *Examiner*." His sarcasm aimed at the press had not been wasted on Josh. "I'll share a little secret with you: Whenever anything looks, sounds, and smells like manure to me, I usually consider it manure until I've been proved wrong, and for the moment, this whole Lane thing stinks." He moved toward the only door in his office. "Excuse me while I go speak with a cou-ple of colleagues, will you? Please make yourself comfortable until I return. I shouldn't be long." Without awaiting an acknowledgment, Lefler disappeared into the hall.


Josh Mitchell had the suspicion that things were not about to get bet-ter, but were about to quickly spiral toward the worse. He considered walking out of Lefler's office and taking his chances at some other time, after he'd formulated a logical plan, and was no longer reacting to his need to do something honest and forthright in Pamela Morrow's name. After all, they hadn't charged him with anything; he was free to leave, despite the detective's request that he stay.

He sat again and leaned his head back against the corkboard behind him, studying the office. It was cluttered with paperwork on every horizontal surface, and bulletins, photos, and notes tacked and taped on all the walls. The commercial green paint was visible only from head height to the ceiling. Four or five used coffee cups scattered about the 10 x 10 room were filled with chewed cigar, and the carpet looked like forty gallons of coffee had been deliberately spilled on it. It felt like one of Hell's anterooms.

When he again chastised himself for his cowardly words questioning Pamela Morrow's sanity at the time of her death, he remembered a time when she was still within his reach . . .


. . . We have talked so intensely since leaving Kennedy that we are landing before either of us realizes it. It is only the flight attendant's caution that we fasten our seatbelts that forces an end to our conversation.

The DC-10 pulls into its allotted space at San Francisco International, the jetway is connected, and the exodus begins in a confusion of bags being retrieved and aisles being jammed with passengers eager to leave.

I stand as well, grab my suit bag and laptop from the overhead bin, and set them quickly in the empty seat ahead of me. I ask the beautiful woman if she has anything in the overhead, but she has only a small bag and the wool coat that has been beside her during the trip. She slips effortlessly toward the aisle, bag in hand, her coat on her arm. I still haven't learned her name.

In less than a minute, she will be absorbed into the population of San Francisco, and I will have no idea how to reach her again. I haven't the slightest notion what she does, where she works, or even in what part of the Bay Area she lives. While we talked, such things as names and occupations seemed unimportant.

We exit together, ahead of most of the other passengers, the involving conversation of the last quarter day replaced now by an awkward silence. It is the first time we've stood side by side and I find her much taller than I had imagined, at least five-nine, and strikingly proportioned. Her deep, wine-colored suit jacket and knee-length skirt are well-tailored; her tan legs are bare, the calf muscles sharply defined; her two-inch heels of nude suede. I can't move my eyes from her.

The end of the narrow jetway yields to the expanse of the main terminal and a sea of bodies, half moving hurriedly toward gates, bound for distant places, the other half returning home or to business. It's seven-oh-one according to the large round clock near our gate and the airport is packed. I lose the beautiful woman in the crowd when I allow eight or ten children with helium-filled balloons and brightly painted cards to pass between us. For a moment, it is as if the throng is a bog of quicksand and has swallowed her up.

Then I spot her ahead.

She pauses when she realizes we have become separated and turns back, her eyes searching. When the children pass, I hurry to her and we both smile but don't speak. She leads slightly as we advance with the flow of bodies moving toward baggage claim and ground transportation. I know time is running out.

"Have dinner with me," I say over the noise of the terminal.

"I'm sorry, what did you say, Joshua?" she says, looking toward me. We are moving at a rapid pace, driven forward by the human river. My suit bag crashes against the leg of a man running in the opposite direction. The beautiful woman has advanced a step ahead when someone crashes into me from the rear, without an apology, and literally knocks me alongside her.

At her left shoulder again, I repeat my invitation. "I said I'd like to have dinner with you tonight." She looks at me, having heard this time, but merely smiles.

It is time for desperate measures: We are at Gate 4 by now. I see an opportunity ahead.

I sling my clothes bag strap over my left shoulder and transfer my computer to my now-free left hand. I put my right arm around her waist and guide her gently, but swiftly, toward the only empty gate we've passed. The torrent flows past us, spreading out quickly in the main lobby like a river meeting a delta.

She knows why I have maneuvered her here, evident in her sympathetic expression, and answers my question before I can ask it again. "I can't, Joshua," she says politely.

"Give me one good reason why you can't," I say, not to be beaten by a simple no. "It would mean a lot to me."

She touches my arm with her right hand. "I really can't, honestly. You're sweet for asking, though."

I set my two bags on the carpet and take her shoulders in my hands, my face as close to hers as I dare. She is so beautiful, such a rare person. Her perfume fills my senses. I am speaking before I realize I've formed complete thoughts: "I'm not sweet. This isn't about being polite or kind or . . . I don't even know your name."

The beautiful woman looks beyond me for a long moment, silent. When she focuses on me again, she says, "My name is Pamela Morrow, Joshua, but I still cannot have dinner with you tonight."

Pamela Morrow. I repeat it silently because it feels so good to know after all the hours of wondering what it might be. I think it fits her perfectly. "Listen, Pamela, you'll have to forgive me for being forward—I don't have time for tap dancing." She smiles. "I have known lots of women in my lifetime, if that's what you're thinking, but this is different. I'm not trying to win some ego contest. I've never known anyone like you. I know that sounds like a come-on, but it's true. Your words have touched something that has lain dormant since I was a kid. I believe what you said on the plane about trusting your feelings, and about not appreciating what's right before your eyes until it's gone. I don't just *want* to have dinner with you, Pamela, I *need* to. We can't just let this chance pass us by."

I surprise myself by my candor and worry I've gone too far. I realize she has not encouraged me to say these things, and can only hope, even if she tells me to drop dead, that she believes the sincerity of my words. I wait for her to run like she's just been scalded, but her face softens, her bright gray eyes glisten.

She puts her free hand on my left arm which is still holding her shoulder. "Joshua, when we first talked on the plane, you said you had a very busy client schedule this week. You haven't the time to bother with me right now."

"No client I have is more important than this."

"I find that hard to believe."

"It's true, Pamela."

She hesitates. "What do you have in mind?" she says.

I tell her, "I know the perfect place, Scomas in Sausalito. Best seafood on the coast. It's one of my favorite restaurants. We can be there in forty minutes."

"Sausalito is in the exact opposite direction you said you were heading. You'll need your rest if you're going to be driving up and down the coast all week."

"I'll drive all night if that's what it takes to have dinner with you, Pamela. This isn't some lark, I meant what I said about you touching a special place inside me. There are so many things I want to know about you. Please say you'll join me." I know not to speak again until she does. I've done my best, there's nothing I can add; the rest is up to her.

I wait, but not without wanting to say more.

"Just dinner," she states, capping any other ideas I might have had.

I cross my heart quickly.

She looks toward that secret place again, her eyes a little sad. Finally, she returns. "It's so far out of your way, Joshua. Are you sure you wouldn't rather eat somewhere closer? San Francisco has many wonderful restaurants."

"Have you ever eaten at Scomas?" I ask, relieved that she has accepted.

"No. I hear it's good, though." She is looking directly at me now.

"It's wonderful. You'll love it. Can we go now or do you have things you have to do first?" I grab my bags again, one in each hand, hoping she can leave straight away.

"I'll have to meet you there," she says, throwing a wrench in the works. The fear of being stood up grips me.

My heart drops a jagged stone into my stomach. I start to speak but she stops me: "I know what you're thinking and you're wrong. I know where Scomas is and I'll be there. I give you my word, Joshua." She looks at the clock near us. "It's seven-ten now. How about nine o'clock sharp, inside the restaurant? First one there gets a table."

I have little choice but to concede. I realize that if she doesn't meet me, I'll probably never see her again. I feel like the first time I skydived, not entirely sure the chute would open.

"Nine's perfect," I tell her. "But since I've got nothing to do in the meantime, I'll get there early and reserve a table for two by the water."

"Sounds romantic," she says with a wistful smile.

I stop breathing. "Nine o'clock, then."

"I'll be there, Joshua."

I watch until she has disappeared from view . . .


"What'd you and Mrs. Lane talk about on the plane, Mr. Mitchell?" Lefler asked as he shut his door with a loud slap. Josh had not heard him enter.

"Talk about?" Josh said. He watched as the cop, carrying a manila folder he'd not left with, took his seat.

"Yeah, you know, talk, chit chat. The woman died six hours after the two of you landed. I'd kinda like to know what she and the last guy on earth she spent time with discussed as they flew coast to coast. You did talk, didn't you?" The cigar was stuffed back in his mouth, another inch of it bitten off. His eyes conveyed nothing about what he might be thinking.

Josh tightened his muscles. "Sure, we talked about lots of things. I'm not certain I can repeat the conversation verbatim." He thought about what he *could* tell him without lying.

"I'm not looking for a tape recording of the trip, just a clear idea of what she had to say to a stranger before she died . . . or was murdered. Might be helpful in understanding what was going on."

Josh said carefully, "We spent a lot of time talking about the disappointments we'd both had with love. About how some people fail to recognize the person that's right for them until it's too late."

"Heavy conversation between two people who'd just met, would-
n't you say?"

"Not really. We talked about other things, too." *What things, you
idiot?*

"Would you characterize her mood as despondent?"

Josh didn't have to think about the question. "No, not at all. I
never imagined that she could be planning on taking her own life."
Josh realized what he'd just said.

"Yeah, considering her file, her schedule for the next several
months, made me feel the same way, Mr. Mitchell." He spit into the
waste basket. "Kinda leads me to believe there might have been
another party interested in her 'suicide,' someone who might have
served as a facilitator, if you know what I mean."

Josh wanted to come clean, to tell the detective all there was to
tell, but not to become embroiled in a murder investigation. Still, he
couldn't find fault with Lefler's logic that it sounded more like murder than suicide.

He nodded that he understood.

"Can you think of anyone who might want to see Dianne Lane
dead, Mr. Mitchell? Perhaps someone who believed she presented a
threat of some kind." The cop set his elbows on the desk, his eyes
narrowed.

Josh saw the end of a small cream-colored envelope sticking out
of the manila folder, but couldn't tell if it was the one he'd mailed on
Monday. He decided to tell Lefler about dinner at Scomas, about the
way they had connected, even more than they had on the plane, and
about the feelings he knew they shared. If he phrased it just so, surely
the detective would know he couldn't have caused her any harm.

He wet his lips. "Detective Lefler, I never could have—"

The phone in Lefler's office sliced his words.

"Yeah," he answered tersely, standing to fish the receiver from
beneath a stack of papers. For the next two minutes, the detective
sat on his side of his desk, his back to Josh. He never spoke, only listened.

Josh felt trapped, now realizing that the hardened cop wouldn't
give a shit about his supposed feelings for a stranger. He'd heard such

things a million times and knew love, however intense, didn't make someone immune from violence—even murder. History was littered with such cases, from common men to celebrated heroes.

He decided to keep quiet and seek the advice of counsel. It would piss Lefler off, but so be it.

Better that than incriminate himself further.

Lefler hung up but faced away from Josh for another minute.

When he turned back, his expression had changed. There was a malignancy in his eyes. He opened the manila folder and read from it before speaking. Finally, looking up, "Mr. Mitchell, is there anything at all you would care to tell me about how or why Dianne Lane died?" He never blinked.

"No," Josh said. The deliberate way in which Lefler had worded the question unsettled him. He would request the presence of an attorney before speaking further. He wanted to stand, hoping to appear less vulnerable, but didn't know how it would be perceived by the cop. He remained seated.

Lefler tossed the folder into the chaos of the desk and moved quickly toward the door, holding it open. "Well, Mr. Mitchell, I can think of nothing else to ask you at the moment. You're free to go, and thank you for coming in. You've been most helpful."

Josh was dumbfounded. He remained seated, certain that what he'd just heard was born of hope or anxiety, and not what had actually been said.

"Mr. Mitchell?" Lefler said, making the opening wider.

Josh stood, sure he would be called back as he walked down the hall. He passed the detective in slow motion, his movements tentative.

"Good day, Mr. Mitchell," Lefler said, closing the door behind him.


Josh was at his rental car before he allowed himself a wide grin. *Survived!* he shouted internally. Hell, he'd come through with flying colors.

It appeared that life as he knew it was going to continue after all.

"Yes!" he shouted when he dropped into the front seat and closed the door, the broad smile still spanning his face. "Yes, yes, hell yes!" He'd never been more relieved, as if he'd just been informed his brain cancer had been misdiagnosed and was only a common cold. He bounced his head against the headrest, his eyes closed, the actuality of it all sinking in slowly.

He didn't notice the van in the alley, and could not have seen the high-powered binoculars that were trained on him from within it.

Lefler answered the phone in his office on the first ring. He already knew who it'd be. He didn't speak.

"Mitchell looks like he just won the lottery, detective. You did real good," the man said. "We'll take it from here."

Lefler boiled. He hated the FBI and especially the odd little man on the other end. "Understand something, Hetzler, I don't believe for a second that Mitchell didn't see the Lane woman at his hotel after having spent half a fucking day on a plane with her playing 'let's swap life stories at thirty-nine-thousand feet.'"

Hetzler had met cowboys before. "I don't really give a damn what you believe. When we've gotten what we want from him, you can have the bastard for the murder of Dianne Lane, or anything else you want for all I care. Until then, and I say otherwise, Detective Lefler, if you go anywhere near Mitchell, by the end of that same day the only police work you'll be doing is guarding rubber dog shit in a fun house."

Lefler grumbled some muted obscenities and hung up. He took a big bite of his cigar and spoke with a grin to the phone: "If I find one solid link tying Mitchell to Dianne Lane's death, Hetzler, you overdressed little pissant, I'll hang him by his heels and gut him in the town square whether you're through with him or not. And you can take your threats and stuff them straight up your tight Bureau ass."

The Volvo moved easily into early afternoon traffic, heading northeast on Brannan Street toward the China Basin area, though Josh hadn't chosen the direction intentionally. He was simply driving, his mind processing the disquieting events of the last half hour.

As Josh thought more about it, Lefler now appeared too eager to accept his story. *What the hell kind of detective is he to simply accept at face value everything I told him?* his mind taunted. He remembered the call that had changed Lefler from an animal of prey to a man unnaturally eager to dismiss Josh and whatever remaining information he might have.

"What the hell was that all about?" he wondered aloud.

Traffic moved slowly in downtown San Francisco, a cloudless sun now creating true early-summer temperatures. Convertibles were everywhere, from a rag-top Volkswagen Beetle to a Ferrari 348.

He opened the sunroof. The euphoria of a moment earlier fell prey to his natural sense of self-preservation.

He knew that he would be hearing from Lefler again—soon.

Despite the momentary reprieve, and his desire to hold on to the euphoria, Josh sensed the presence of an outside influence that had driven the detective from a hunting posture to one of inexplicable indifference.

"Why the hell can't this just all be over and my life back like it was!?" he shouted through the hole in the roof, his face held high, hoping that by doing so, his angry words might land squarely in God's lap, and not get lost in the cosmos.

*My life back like it was* . . . He replayed his words silently.

"It's not really what you want, is it?" he said. It occurred to him that all this had come about because he'd desperately wanted his life to be different, and not as it had been for the last ten years. "How's this for a change, dickhead?" he laughed out loud, amazed at the irony of it all.

He knew he needed to discover whether Dianne Lane had committed suicide or, as Lefler had intimated, been murdered. He forced to think such things dispassionately because his very freedom depended upon what he learned. He would either be in the clear, at least legally; or his career, perhaps his future, would be in ruin if he was implicated in her death.

He found the S70 driving itself toward its home at San Francisco

International, like a horse heading for the barn at the end of a ride.

In his heart, Josh didn't believe the Pamela Morrow he had known would have taken her own life. It wasn't in her nature, of that he was certain.

In his mind, he couldn't deny the possibility that she'd been killed.

But why? The answer wasn't remotely within reach.

If Josh could discover the reason, that knowledge might enable him to identify someone with a motive, or at the very least, direct suspicion away from himself.

He held no illusion that Hightower would forgive anyone who brought disgrace of this magnitude to the corporation. The job he'd temporarily saved moments before was now up for grabs again.

"Screw it," he said. "It's only a job."

*Sure, and it's only half a mill a year doing what you love.*

Josh played back the dinner in Sausalito and remembered Pamela Morrow mentioning she'd graduated from Ole Miss in Oxford, her best childhood memories had been of carefree days at Braden High in the sleepy, picturesque Mississippi River town of Natchez.

"Maybe I'll find the answers there," he said, turning onto the interstate.

He had a plane to catch.

# 7

Whitney Lawrence answered the phone in the office of field sales for Barnett Air, located on the fifth floor of corporate headquarters in Sacramento, with her customary easy professionalism, her friendly enthusiasm evident to each caller. She loved her job, and thought her boss not only the nicest man she'd ever worked for, but the sexiest as well. They were two sentiments that would never be shared with him. Those were not the things professionals did in the late Nineties, she understood. She had often told her buddies, however—when asked over a beer on Friday evenings what kind of ogre she worked for—that she had been blessed with a boss whom they would kill to have.

"Barnett Air, corporate aircraft sales," she said cheerfully. "Mr. Mitchell's office."

"Hey, Whitney."

Josh's voice was unmistakable. "Oh, hi, boss. Sounds like you're at some airport. SFO or SMF?" She was referring to the FAA designations for San Francisco International Airport and Sacramento Airport—she knew well the lingo of her field.

The multitude of background noises surrounding Gate 65 at San Francisco International competed for attention with Josh Mitchell's words as he spoke from a pay phone near his gate. After his bizarre morning with Madeline Richmond and Detective Lefler, it occurred to him that the cops might begin keeping a log of the calls made from his cell phone, and he wanted to be able to act freely for the next few days. He knew it was probably only paranoia, but it brought him some badly needed peace of mind.

"Thought you were going to be here this morning," Whitney continued before he answered. "Something come up?" She chose Save from the File menu in Microsoft Word to protect the mail-merge sales document she'd begun creating.

Josh was used to his petite brunette secretary keeping him on track, and thought nothing of her asking him why he was late getting to the office. He hated the fact that he was going to have to lie to her, but there was no alternative with what he was planning.

What the hell am I planning? he wondered.

He reminded himself again that his actions made sense only if you looked at them with a desperate eye, and not from a standpoint of logic. Logic told him to leave the detective work to the police. They would see that justice was served and that he was vindicated.

His instinct knew otherwise.

"Something's come up, Whitney, and I've got to head back East right away." He didn't want to disclose his destination even to her, though he knew where her loyalties lay.

"You okay, boss?" she asked, sensing something out of the ordinary.

"Sure, fine, just some rich farmer who discovered a little oil on his land has a yen for a new bizjet. I'm going to try to snatch the sale from Cessna before they can get in the guy's pocket. From what my contact tells me, I've got just enough time if I hurry."

"Need me to set up your flight?" she asked efficiently.

"Already did it."

"A room tonight? Rental car?"

This woman was the best, he thought, but he didn't need her help right now. "I'll just pick up a car when I land . . . and I'm not sure where I'll be staying tonight. I'll wing it."

Whitney recalled the conversation she'd had with the CEO earlier in the morning. "You speak with Hightower yet, Josh?" she asked. Josh not only permitted the familiarity of first names, he liked it. He welcomed her opinion and valued her integrity and humor. If Whitney felt blessed in her employment, so did her immediate boss.

"No. Is he looking for me?" Josh asked. The way Whitney had put the question prickled the hairs on his neck.

"I'll say. He's got some . . ."—she made sure that Vickie, the woman at the desk across from hers and secretary for the manager of composite materials technology sales, wasn't able to hear her—". . . bug up his butt this morning. Asked me, ordered would be more like it, to let him know the moment I heard from you." She lowered her voice. "You make the big guy mad or something, boss?" she jokingly asked, though she knew Josh was Hightower's favorite, and that little he could have done would have earned the CEO's anger.

"Hope not," Josh said, though he didn't understand why Hightower would be so insistent on knowing when he called in. Numbers were all he'd ever cared about, not putting leashes on his salesmen.

Numbers and image, Josh corrected. His muscles tightened.

He hoped the odd request had stemmed from Kenny having directed some of the deadline heat he'd been feeling back at the CEO and cited Josh as the only one who could turn down the flames in the time that remained before Saturday's demo.

Screw the Navy. They'd wait. He didn't have time for Kenny's problems right now, knowing his friend could solve them without his assistance. Kenny, on the other hand, could not help solve Josh's problem. No one could, except the killer, assuming Lefler was right. *You're getting in way over your head, old buddy*, his inner voice cautioned. "Whitney, I need you to cover for me for a while."

The request got her full attention. "What's going on, Josh?" she asked with genuine concern. "You sound funny."

Josh squeezed his eyes shut and tried to sound more normal. "I smell money and don't have time to be playing Hightower's games right now, that's all. Jeez, Whitney, you know how he is, he thinks I should live on both coasts simultaneously while at the same time sitting in daily meetings accommodating his big-dog 'fill me in personally on every promising lead' routine. If I don't see this 'Jed Clampett' first thing in the morning, he'll be sitting in the back seat of a Citation by tomorrow afternoon and I'll be eating peanut butter and listening to a sermon from the president of the company about my lack of sales initiative."

Whitney laughed. "I doubt if one missed sale will put you on a peanut butter diet, boss. Besides, you're not going to let this one get away. You never miss 'em when you smell money." The use of a familiar expression had eased her mind. "I'll tell Hightower you left me a voice mail while I was at lunch; we're both covered that way." She swiveled away from Vickie. "What can he say to that? That I should eat at my desk? Ha! I'd like to see him try to get that one by me. Besides, he'll get over it when you drop a check for eight mill on his desk."

*What if I don't come back with one?* he considered. More deception and the baggage that always comes with it.

He swore, his hand over the phone. He couldn't change his plans now. He knew that while the cops might be concerned with justice, successful prosecutions interested them far more.

Josh leaned back against the divider between the pay phones and bumped the man on the phone to his left. "Sorry," he said when the man glared at him.

The white-legged man from the beach smiled and nodded, then put his back to Josh again, pretending to be engaged in his own conversation. He wasn't, but the ruse had allowed him to place a tiny, sensitive, directional microphone, in the form of a pen, and its digital microrecorder, hidden in a small, leather-bound Day-Timer, on the top of his phone's body without drawing attention. Even three feet away, amid the noise of the concourse, it had clearly taped every word Josh had spoken on the line since initiating the call to his office, and while it couldn't hear Whitney's responses, the man would learn what he needed from the one-sided conversation.

Josh heard the announcement for last boarding. "Gotta go, Whitney. Thanks for the white lie."

"He'll be steaming by tomorrow morning, you know that, don't you?" she cautioned.

"Yeah, I know. I'll try to have good news by then."

"Call if you need anything. I'll be here until six. You've got my new home number, right?"

"You gave it to me last week."

"Just checking."

"You're the best, Whitney."

"I know. Just remember that when evaluation time rolls around."

As they both chuckled, he set the receiver in its cradle and grabbed his two bags.

The man at the pay phone retrieved the Day-Timer and shoved it back in his inside jacket pocket. He watched as his man boarded the American Airlines MD-Super80 bound for Jackson, Mississippi. When Josh entered the jetway, Hetzler stepped to the counter at Gate 65.

He produced his credentials. "Is Flight 754 nonstop to Jackson?" he asked of the startled attendant.

"No," the woman answered quickly. "It makes a stopover in Dallas. They have to change planes." She took a good look at her first FBI special agent. Though she kept the thought well hidden, to her the man seemed oddly out of place to have been with the Bureau, small, frail-looking, not at all the James Bond she had once imagined all federal agents resembling.

"I want the schedule on this flight, not one like it, this flight." He put his arms on the counter.

The woman obediently called up the data on her terminal. "They left exactly on time, one forty-five, so they should reach Dallas by their scheduled arrival time of seven-fifty-four P.M. Those going on to Jackson have to change planes, transferring to American Eagle Flight 5073, scheduled to leave Dallas at eight-thirty-seven P.M. The weather is clear so they should arrive in Jackson, at Gate 2, on time at ten-thirty-two P.M." She smiled at the little man.

"What seat did you assign to Joshua Mitchell?" The gate, which had been bustling minutes before, now enjoyed the company of only these two people.

Again to the terminal.

"Seat 2D in First-Class," she said efficiently. The well-rehearsed smile returned.

The man nodded. "Thank you," he said as he disappeared into the river of bodies flowing through the concourse.

At the newsstand near Gate 65, another man had watched Josh Mitchell, as well as Special Agent Hetzler while he watched Mitchell. The man at the newsstand hadn't missed the Day-Timer recorder that had been set on the top of the pay phone. He also hadn't failed to note Hetzler's interest at the counter. He knew he'd been noticed by neither Mitchell nor the agent. He wondered just what the hell they taught at the Academy, though he knew— he'd been through it.

He realized, from Mitchell's lack of awareness of what was going on around him, that he was going to be pathetically easy to take out, and it could be done right under the noses of the feds. He appreciated the irony.

When Hetzler, blending into the crowd like a ripe lemon in a stack of red apples, had again passed his position, the man at the newsstand took his cell phone and scanned its memory for a number he wanted in Biloxi, Mississippi, his closest operative to the state's capital. He'd thought about going after Mitchell in person—the money was certainly good enough to warrant it—but decided to share the wealth with an old Army buddy. Biloxi was only three and a half hours from Jackson; there'd be plenty of time to make it to the airport and intercept Mitchell when he landed at Gate 2.

When his associate answered the phone on the fifth ring, the man still leaning against the wall near the newsstand said, "Hey, Ron, it's Jack. Catch you at a bad time?"

"Farris, you old fucker, it's good to hear from you after all these months. You in town, I hope?" The man dropped into an overly padded cushion in a rattan chair on the front porch.

The temperature in mid-March in Biloxi, while not cold, was still thirty-five degrees from the scorching heat that would sit over this seaside town like Satan's skillet in late July and August. Today, a seventy-five degree breeze wafted across the beach, the highway, and the man's front yard, drifting pleasantly through the open windows and screen doors of his modest home. The view six years before, when he'd bought the ocean-view cottage, had been nothing but white sand and endless miles of the Gulf of Mexico. Now, a massive floating casino designed to appear like a stern-wheeler from Mark Twain's era, blocked most of the view. It pissed him off, but he liked the convenience of Vegas-style gambling at his doorstep too much to do more than grumble over the lost panorama.

Jack Farris could picture his friend perfectly. "You're sitting on the front porch in one of those old cane chairs you got when we were in Nicaragua, aren't you?"

"You bet. On my fat ass square in the middle of one," Kisber said. Jenny, his woman of six months, brought him another Miller and set the snack tray she'd been preparing on the table between their chairs. He squeezed Jenny's knee when she sat. She was the only woman he'd ever been with longer than a month. "If this gal of mine keeps feeding me étouffée and crab dip, I'm gonna get permanently stuck in one of them." He dug a chip into the center of the tray, filling his mouth with the spicy dip.

"You too fat to make a buck?" Farris asked.

"Never be that fat," Kisber said, his mouth full.

"Well, stop eating for a moment for Christ's sake and listen closely. You've got to act on this right away." A number of departing passengers filled the newsstand, browsing its wares. Farris moved toward the now-empty Gate 65, speaking as he walked. "There's twenty grand in it for you, old buddy." He knew he'd have Kisber's full attention now.

Ronald Kisber moved the phone from his mouth and spoke to his woman. "Give me a minute, sugar. This is business." He winked at her.

Jenny stood. "Sure. I've got to check on dinner anyway." She vanished into the house.

"Go ahead, Jack," Kisber said. He stood, moving to the end of the porch farthest from the front door.

"You gotta be in Jackson no later than a quarter of ten tonight. At the airport, Gate 2. You'll be meeting American Eagle Flight 5073 from Dallas."

"Who's the target?" Kisber already knew that for the kind of money he'd just been offered, someone was going to die. The thought didn't bother him—everyone dies eventually, he figured—but he didn't want his woman involved in his second business. As far as she was concerned, he was a charter fishing boat skipper and nothing more. It wasn't a lie, he did have a twenty-eight-foot Bayliner that made him a fair living—more if he'd worked at it—but his easy money came from the jobs he took on two or three times a year. Not too frequently, he'd calculated, just often enough to supplement the budget nicely.

"Name's Mitchell. Twenty-eight to thirty, six-foot, black hair, wearing an expensive gray wool suit. He's carrying a laptop in a black leather case and a black leather suit bag. He's sitting in First-Class, so he'll be one of the first off." Farris wanted a cigarette so bad he started to light up and sneak a couple of drags before anyone saw him. He decided it would be better to wait. He crammed two pieces of gum into his mouth.

"What's the setup?" Kisber asked. He checked his watch, noting that he had two hours at the most before he had to be on the road. Plenty of time to eat a good dinner and still pick up his fishing partner.

"He'll rent a car. Hertz if he follows his pattern. I don't know where he's going after he lands, but my employer wants this information in hand before anything happens to him."

"Got it. And then?"

"He has an accident before he leaves Mississippi."

"A serious one?" Kisber asked.

"I fear it's going to be fatal."

"Too bad. I could be friends with any guy who drops twenty grand in my lap." Kisber swallowed the rest of his beer. "And the eleventh hour?" he asked, referring to the latest time the target could be taken out.

"Doesn't matter as long as he never leaves your fair state, my friend." Farris chewed the gum noisily.

"Hey, it's a great state. He's gonna love spending the rest of his days here."

"Yeah, especially since he's only got one left."

Both men began to laugh.


San Francisco disappeared over Josh Mitchell's right shoulder as the MD-Super80 climbed toward its cruising altitude of thirty-six thousand feet. He had four hours before landing in Dallas, and would have normally already been at his keyboard, hammering out database corrections or drafting potential-client letters. Unlike previous flights, however, his mind was far from business.

He wished he were traveling to Natchez to see Dianne again, and not for the purpose of rummaging through the secrets of Pamela Morrow's past, if such a woman even existed. He regretted that he'd not made love to Dianne, instead talking away his only opportunity while she lay there wanting him. It had, at the time, made sense; he was thinking of the future.

*What future?* he thought. *There'll be no future now.*

"Care for something to drink?" the flight attendant asked. The main cabin was only half full, and he was one of only four passengers in First-Class. The woman was a slender, attractive blonde with long hair and full lips. Her nametag identified her as Kristi. Ordinarily, Josh would have made conversation with her, but not today.

"Bailey's and coffee," he said out of habit. He remembered the last time he'd had the combination and a pain darted through him. "No, just make it a glass of orange juice, please."

As he sipped the tart liquid, the mountains began to rise up to meet the plane, their snow capped peaks clearly visible out the starboard window. The cobalt blue of the sky gradually yielded to the gray then yellow hues of the atmosphere as it neared the ground seven miles below.

Josh was no longer sure if he was running toward the truth, or from the lies; if it was about uncovering the reality of Dianne Lane's past—or his own. Sometimes, the two concepts appeared to be the same, yet he knew only too well how great the difference was. He closed his eyes and tried to sleep, something he'd gotten precious little of in the past few days. He touched the empty seat beside him, "Pamela's seat," and his thoughts drifted back to Scomas . . .


. . . I arrive at the restaurant an hour or so after we land in San Francisco, grateful that it isn't a Friday or Saturday evening. A table by the water, as I have requested, will be ready in fifteen minutes, the maitre d' assures me.

I sit at the bar and have a vodka tonic. I'm as nervous as a teenager. I find the feeling not unlike many I've experienced today, driven by the bright gray eyes and warm, sensual smile of Pamela Morrow. I like the way her name sounds when I say it aloud.

In little more than ten minutes, the maitre d' tells me my table has been readied and I follow him toward the rear of the building, through a pair of French doors, and into a room that is isolated from the main dining area.

"Will this do, Mr. Mitchell?" he asks with genuine interest. Apparently the fifty bucks I slipped him when I first came in worked.

I note that the Bay Bridge is clearly visible from this table, the full moon adding an amber glow to the ruddy tones of the steel expanse. Though not beautiful by Golden Gate standards, it is nonetheless perfect, I consider pensively. "It's wonderful," I say, content to slip him another hundred if he so indicates. He doesn't and seems pleased to have been of service. I sit, choosing the seat that has its back to the bridge, but with a clear view of the main dining room through which Pamela must cross.

"Will the other party be joining you before long, sir?" he asks as he hands me a wine list. The waiter is standing behind him with a pair of menus.

"I certainly hope so," I say, though I know it sounds like I'm waiting for my first date to arrive. Who cares what they think? I'm excited at the thought of seeing a woman again from whom I have been apart less than ninety minutes.

As the man is about to speak again, my change in expression silences him.

He follows my eyes.

Fifty feet away, just entering the main dining room, is a woman as stunning as anyone this place has ever seen. In a snug-fitting black silk and wool suit, her every curve clearly defined yet tauntingly concealed, Pamela Morrow glides across the floor toward me. The three of us in the anteroom can only watch in silence as she approaches.

When she nears the table, I rise, brought to my feet by the mere sight of her.

"I hope I'm not late," she says in that voice.

The maitre d' takes her chair, allowing her to sit opposite me. The waiter dutifully hands her a spotless napkin, which she places across her lap, then offers her a menu.

"Thank you," she smiles. Both men are in love.

"Would the lady care for something to drink?" the waiter asks. The maitre d' goes about his duties with a silent sigh.

"What are you having?" she asks.

"I had a vodka tonic when I first arrived. I was considering a glass of red wine with dinner. I'm not a big fan of white."

"You have a good Merlot?" she asks the waiter.

"The Truchard '94 is excellent," he says with pride.

She sees the approval in my eyes. "I think we'll share a bottle of that." She looks to me again. "You hungry?"

I am, starving, though I shake my head no.

"Would it be okay if we ordered a little later?" she asks me. Who could refuse her?

I nod that it is.

"Very good, madam," the waiter says. "Your wine will be right out. I'll be nearby whenever you're ready to order." Then he disappears and we are alone for the first time.

Pamela notices the bridge over my shoulder. "My God, I didn't think the Bay Bridge could be so beautiful. Have you seen it, Joshua?"

I nod and she knows I have chosen my seat so she could enjoy the view.

"Thank you," she says, her voice low, then her eyes narrow teasingly. "I suppose now you're going to tell me you ordered that unbelievable moon especially for me."

"It took some persuading, but when the 'Big Guy' finally understood how much this evening meant to me, He relented. You like it?"

She places her hand on top of mine. "I love it." She moves her hand and sits up straight as our wine arrives. She quickly takes a sip. "You're right, it's an excellent vintage," she says to the maitre d' who appears pleased he has suggested well.

"Will there be anything else for the moment?" he asks when he has filled our glasses.

"I think we're fine for now," she says.

I like the way she has taken a gentle hold on the reins. When the man leaves, she leans toward me a bit, touching my hand again.

"So, Joshua, what did you say to convince the 'Big Guy' to let you borrow such a moon tonight?"

I take a long, slow breath, the nervousness I felt at the bar is now far worse. "I told Him that I had been on a quest to find the perfect woman, and that, after a dozen years of failed attempts, and coming to the conclusion that no such person exists, she winds up almost literally in my lap. I've always heard you get what you want most when you look least hard for it."

I do not anticipate the reaction my words will cause.

She sits erect again, pulling her hand back, her eyes fixing on the bridge in the distance. For an agonizing moment, she doesn't speak. Then she directs those wide gray eyes toward me, though they are not warm as before. She sips her wine, her face drawn, her voice sad. "All my adult life, Joshua—and I have lived a few more years than you—since I first began to fill out, someone has wanted to own me, to possess me like a piece of jewelry. I'm their answered prayer, even before they have learned the slightest real thing about me. I find it hard to believe a person will experience true love and lasting feelings in so little time. It's possible, I suppose, but I've never felt it.

"In the end, after a week, a month, or in the rarest instances, a year, my instincts always proved correct. The 'love' was gone . . . and yet the possessiveness always lingered.

"True love, as I see it, Joshua, stems from a feeling that is the opposite of possession. Something truly loved is free to exist on its own terms, to enrich the life of its partner while never giving up its own identity. I've never met anyone yet who understands that." As I am about to speak she adds, "Oh, sure, all men swear they do in the beginning, but their actions always prove they haven't a clue about real love." She sips her wine again. "You appear to be a very dear man, Joshua, but I'm hardly the answer to your prayers."

After an awkward silence between us, the waiter approaches and we order a dinner of lobster tails and steamed vegetables. He leaves.

I'm glad I've had a moment to think. I understand what she is saying, know only too well how she feels about love, or at least the *promise* of love, gone bad, but her comments have left me no defense without repeating some lame promise that I'm not like the others. I rest my arms on the table, my eyes never moving from hers. "Pamela, I won't try to convince you that I'm different from the men you've known. I don't know any of them, I only know me, so I'll ask you to listen while I tell you what prompted my words earlier.

"Even when I was a kid, I knew I was looking for something that was different from what my friends wanted. They either wanted to score quickly and move on, no strings attached, or they wanted to control a girl—possess her, as you put it. There never seemed to be any middle ground." A slight nod told me she'd been there. "I knew there had to be more and I tried to find it. Back then, most of the girls I knew were so eager to get out of that small town that they would marry the first guy available. I had to run from one myself, harder than I ever ran on the football field."

She smiles at my little joke. I'm glad to see some light return to those dazzling eyes.

I empty my wineglass as our salads arrive. The glass is quickly refilled by the waiter. In a minute, we are alone again.

"My life today is perfect in the eyes of my friends: I've got a great job that I work with a passion; until recently I was dating a model they all wanted themselves; I get to travel and stay in the finest hotels; eat at all the best restaurants; I have a terrific home, a couple of great cars, and a few bucks in the bank; my boss thinks I'm doing a great job; and I can still wear the jeans I wore in high school—in short, as far as they can see, I've got it made."

A wide smile now graces her face. God, she's incredible.

I continue while my mind is still unaffected by the wine and the ever-present waiter is at bay. "As good as it must have appeared on the outside, Pamela, there was one important thing missing . . . I'd come to believe that love was just a naïve boyhood dream, that what I had was all there was, all there ever would be. No one I met seemed to comprehend that, though I was always led to believe that your sex instinctively understood such things.

"To be fair, most grasped the basic concept, but it's the subtleties that make life worth living, and it was the finer points that escaped them. Love is a lot like flying, I suppose. A heavy hand on the stick, as well as a lack of control, will cause a crash. Only by being one with the plane, in tune to its needs, as well as those of the ever-changing environment, will ensure a smooth flight and a safe landing."

"Do you fly your own plane?" she asks.

"Every chance I get," I smile. I don't want to get off onto another subject so I don't elaborate.

She eats her salad with a healthy appetite. I start on mine as well, ravenous from half a day without food.

"Just listening to you on the plane convinced me you understood that most people spend their whole lives in their heads, and never make the journey to their hearts, though it's only, as you put it, a short twelve inches away. You're the only woman I've met who knows that there's a difference between what we feel and what we think we feel. To most, it's the same thing."

Pamela touches my hand again. "It's not, of course."

"A successful life together for two people is a lot like flying over the Rockies, if you'll forgive the metaphor. Too long away from flying can be fatal, while too much attention to the controls will rob you of the spectacular views. Some couples are so concerned with making their marriage work that they never get to enjoy it."

"It helps if both are qualified pilots," she says, "so they can take turns at the helm whenever their partner needs a break."

"It sure does make it a hell of a lot easier to keep the plane off the rocks," I say. The lobster arrives.

"This looks heavenly," she says as the waiter removes the eight-ounce tails from their shells. She cuts a tender bite and dips it in the drawn butter. The sound of pure enjoyment emanates from behind closed lips.

A tingle in my toes rises slowly through the large muscles of my legs and courses its way toward my chest. I don't speak, but cut into my lobster as well. It has been steamed to perfection.

After a few bites without conversation, Pamela says, "So tell me, Joshua, whatever became of this model?"

I nearly choke on the bite I have just taken when I realize her eyes have a hint of mischief in them.

I feel her foot nudge my leg . . .

"Would you care for dinner?" the flight attendant asked. Josh removed his dark sunglasses and looked to his left. Kristi held a tray with warmed hand towels before him. "You have your choice of roast beef with mushroom gravy and garlic mashed potatoes or a cold seafood salad with crabmeat and scallops."

Josh's mind was still fuzzy from the half-sleep he'd been in for . . . he checked his watch . . . an hour and forty minutes. "I think I'll have the roast beef," he said, suppressing a yawn. His drink had been removed, though there had been little left but melting ice in the glass. "Could I get another—"

"Orange juice," Kristi answered.

"Yes, please." Josh took the hot towel and pressed it to his face. Its heat radiated through his closed lids, soothing his tired eyes. He turned to his right, wishing that Dianne was still sitting beside him, safe and sound.

The seat was as empty, though, as he knew it would be. He mumbled an obscenity and wadded the towel into a tight ball dropping it onto Kristi's tray as she passed his row on her way back toward the cockpit and galley.

*She's gone, Josh,* his heart reminded him. *You know what has to be done if you're going to have any peace about her.*

He turned his eyes to the oval window to his right, and the possibilities—and obstacles—that lay beyond it.

●●●

With the change of planes having occurred precisely on time in Dallas, and a brisk tailwind from the west, Flight 5073 touched down in Jackson, Mississippi twenty minutes ahead of schedule, at ten-oh-six. By now, Josh had been up for eighteen hours, and that on only two hours of sleep the night before. He felt and looked exhausted, needed a shower and a shave, and was weary to the bone from carrying his bags everywhere he went like a refugee.

As he sluggishly exited the jetway, two pairs of eyes picked him up with ease. Jack Farris had done an admirable job of describing their prey, though at this time of night, only one other man on the small turbo-prop could have possibly been mistaken for Joshua Thomas Mitchell, and he'd been in a seat in the very rear of the plane, not First-Class. Josh was the third passenger off the plane.

Ronald Kisber turned to his fishing buddy, Brian Mills, and winked. They were leaning against opposite concrete support columns at the mouth of Gate 2, where Josh had to pass directly between them. To Kisber, it was like a lamb grazing blindly within inches of a pack of hungry wolves. He enjoyed being close to a man he was going to kill before he snuffed out his life, often sitting at a table beside him at lunch, pulling beside him in traffic, or asking him for a light.

When Josh neared the columns, his mind on the hundred-mile drive ahead, Kisber spoke. "How was the flight?" he asked as naturally as any other waiting party.

Josh hadn't expected to be engaged in conversation before reaching the rental car counter and had to look around for a second before identifying the origin of the question. He tried to smile. "You know, up, down, lots of nothing in between. Just another flight."

"Road warrior, huh?" Kisber grinned.

Josh nodded, rounded the column, and strolled toward Ground Transportation. The man's face hadn't even registered in his wearied mind.

Kisber and Mills fell in behind their lamb, staying well in back of the small exiting crowd.

"You reckon he'll meet whoever he's come to see tonight?" Mills asked.

"Don't expect so," Kisber said. "He seems pretty beat to me. I imagine he'll grab a room nearby and do his business in the morning."

"That suits me fine. The drive up here always wears my ass out."

Mills had been called by his friend of six years only twenty minutes before Kisber had picked him up. They had arrived an hour ahead of the plane from Dallas, and still had work to do before the real business could begin.

"Don't go to sleep on me yet, Brian. We've still gotta stash my Vette and grab us some wheels before morning. I'm thinking maybe a nice big Chevy pickup. Black with a chrome roll bar and driving lights all across the top. What d'ya think?"

They continued to follow Josh toward the rental cars.

"You think you're gonna find a truck like that?" Mills asked. Though technically new to the "business," he possessed the three most desirable traits Kisber required in an assistant: guts, loyalty, and a total absence of conscience, not unlike the Special Forces from which Kisber and Farris had been spawned.

One sweltering summer evening in the Gulf, six years prior, when the fish weren't biting well, and it was just Kisber and him on the Bayliner, ten miles out from shore, Mills had taken the deer rifle Kisber always kept handy and trained the 14x scope on the only boat besides Kisber's they'd seen in an hour, a hundred yards to the southwest in a dead calm sea. The trawler was manned by just one person, a seventy-three-year-old fisherman and grandfather of nine who'd made a living from the waters south of Biloxi since his return home from Europe at the end of WWII.

When Kisber jokingly asked the man he'd met only a week before what the hell he thought he was doing, Mills fired once, striking the old man in the back and sending him over the transom into the Gulf. Knowing that the bullet would pass through the man's slender body and be lost forever in the murky sea—negating the possibility of a ballistics match even if the old man's body was ever found—Mills had answered simply, "Eliminating the competition, my friend." He and Kisber had been close ever since, joined by a bond of secrets that could never be revealed.

Kisber now patted his friend on the back. "Hell, Brian, this is Mississippi. If I can't find me a truck like that in ten minutes here, there ain't one in the country." The two laughed as they stopped a hundred feet from the Hertz counter, and watched as their lamb follow his predicted pattern precisely.

The man arrived at Gate 2 out of breath. "When did the plane from Dallas get in?" he snapped, obviously agitated. He scanned the area as he spoke, looking for the man who'd been described to him over the phone.

The woman standing behind the counter regarded the fellow in the polo shirt and khaki slacks with caution, wary of the anxious expression which distorted his otherwise pleasant face. She glanced at the clock on the wall. "Ten minutes ago," she said flatly.

"Dammit!" the man grumbled.

The woman seemed surprised by his reaction. "Is there something wrong, sir?"

The man glared at her. "Why the hell are you people always late unless being early fucks up someone's day?!"

She chose not to respond, digging deeply within her for the "corporate smile." It was slow coming, but when it arrived, nothing she could have said would have been more effective.

She said pleasantly, "I'm sure I don't know, sir. Would you care to fill out a complaint form?"

The man cocked his jaw and stormed away, heading straight for the nearest pay phone. He dialed Hetzler's cell phone number from a slip of paper in his pants pocket. He knew it wasn't his fault—he'd only gotten the call to meet the plane twenty minutes ago, and he was fifteen miles from the airport at the time—but he also knew the man who'd called him wasn't going to be happy.

"Yes," Hetzler answered, still in his office in San Francisco.

The man in Jackson took a frustrated breath. "I missed Mitchell," he confessed.

"That's just fucking great! How the hell did that happen?!" The man stood before his window on the thirteenth floor, watching the last of the sun's orange rays being consumed by the nearly black Pacific. He saw no beauty in it.

"Plane arrived twenty minutes early. I missed it by less than ten minutes."

"I thought you assured me you could make it."

The man's breathing was almost normal again. He'd sprinted from the curb in front of arriving flights, slowing only for the security check. "I would have made it easy if the damned plane had been on time—or late, like most of them. It's not my fault, sir."

"Yeah, well maybe not, but now we've got our mark running around the state of Mississippi, headed for God knows where." Hetzler squeezed his eyes shut and rubbed the bridge of his nose. The headache that had been with him all day was much worse. "Find out what he did for transportation and see if you can locate the car. It's a long shot, but give it a try. I doubt it'll be spotted before midday tomorrow at the earliest."

"Headed there now," the man said.

"I want to know something soon," Hetzler seethed.

"I'll call the moment I know anything."

Hetzler dropped into his chair and laid his weary arms across his desk. "Maybe it's time to turn the heat on from the other direction, Mr. Mitchell," he said. "Let's see how you like this."

He punched up Josh's file on his computer and scanned the list of phone numbers.


"I sure wish I knew where that son of a bitch was heading at this time of night," Mills bitched after they'd followed Josh south from the airport for forty miles down I-55 and then southwest on an isolated two-lane blacktop road. They were on State Highway 28, traveling at sixty-five miles an hour but staying well in back of Josh's rented Pontiac Grand Prix.

There was no danger of losing him on this road.

As they moved steadily toward the Mississippi River, a sign

indicating Natchez 70 miles, shot by the passenger's window of Kisber's black 1994 Corvette. "If that bastard is trying for Natchez tonight I'm gonna kill him with my bare hands," Mills said through clenched teeth.

Kisber laughed. Patience was not one of his friend's better traits. "Don't know who's so God-awful important in that old town he's aiming to see, but I don't figure he'll be stopping anywhere else along the way."

"Son of a bitch!" Mills barked. He lit another cigarette off the remnants of the previous one, then flicked the butt out the side window he lowered only briefly. It was nearly midnight and the air had turned cold. "Where're we gonna find a truck like you want in a town that's still living in the Civil War?"

Kisber gave him an amused look.

Mills said, "I know, it's Mississippi, right? Yadda, yadda, yadda. Still, the sumbitch ain't making this as easy as we'd hoped."

"You that anxious to see the inside of your first prison, Brian?" his friend asked, like the ever-patient teacher to the overly eager, yet ill-prepared, student.

"Me? Hell, no! Why the hell should the cops give a shit about me?"

"Because those without patience always attract unwanted attention, my friend. Patience is not just a virtue, like you were told in school—you did go to school for a couple of years, didn't you?—it's also your greatest asset. It's more helpful in bagging a prey than all the weapons you could carry. Mitchell will be plenty easy to take out when the time comes. Meanwhile, sit back and enjoy the view."

"Enjoy what? You can't see shit out here in these pitch-black boonies except dickhead's taillights a mile ahead. We haven't passed so much as a house trailer in miles."

"Precisely," the teacher grinned sadistically.

"Now I'm lost for damn sure."

"Can you imagine a better place for our little buddy's accident than in this desolation of cotton stubble and backwater?"

Brian Mills looked beyond the windshield into the nothingness that lay on either side of the two-lane road.

It produced a grin.

• • •

At one-fifty-five Thursday morning, Josh pulled the rented Pontiac into a space in the parking lot of the Day's Inn on Highway 61. He rested both hands on the wheel, too tired to open the door. Once along the deserted two-lane road, and then again on Highway 61 near Stanton, he'd fallen asleep momentarily, and had only reawakened when the sound of the Grand Prix's right wheels growling in the loose gravel of the shoulder came screaming in through the blackness that had pulled his lids shut.

Even his inner voice was too tired to chastise him for nearly killing himself twice.

When the pall of sleep began to drag him into its abyss again, Josh found the door handle and gave it a pull. He lifted himself out of the car, dragging his twin bags like a pair of anvils.

Within ten minutes, he was in Room 224, asleep in his clothes across the bed nearest the door.


Kisber and Mills rolled quietly in behind the rental car and stopped momentarily. "He's down for the night," Kisber said wearily.

"Well, I'm sure as hell glad. I wish your buddy in San Francisco had known the son of a bitch was heading for this shit hole so we could have just met him here and saved four hours of fuckin' driving." Mills finished his tenth cigarette since leaving Jackson Airport, flicking it on the trunk lid of the Pontiac.

"You'll ruin his paint job doing that," Kisber quipped.

"When I get done with this bastard, that'll be the best spot on his car. Can we for Christ's sake get some sleep now, Ron?"

The Vette rolled away, out of the parking lot. "Got to find me that black truck first."

"You gotta be shitting me!"

"Patience, my friend."

"Screw patience. You take care of the patience half of this arrangement and I'll take care of Mitchell. Deal?"

Kisber shook his head, amused. "Deal," he said.

# 8

When the wakeup call he'd ordered for nine A.M. announced itself impatiently, Josh managed to open only the eye that was not buried against the bedspread. The ringing continued, as annoying as a tomcat crying outside a bedroom window on a still summer night. He extended his left arm and raised the receiver an inch, dropping it noisily against its cradle, silencing the incessant peal. The need to use the bathroom won out over the desire to continue sleeping, forcing him to his feet.

As soon as he flicked on the bathroom light, his eyelids slammed shut defensively, causing him to bash his right shin against a toilet bowl that was much closer to the door opening than he'd anticipated. "That hurts," he said, groping for the lid. "Wonderful way to start the day, butthead."

Josh removed his razor from its black carry pouch and laid the soft case on the vanity beside his shaving kit. A brisk wipe of the mirror with a hand towel cleared the shower fog again, revealing an image that startled him: he looked like he'd been on a three-day drunk.

He rummaged in the kit for his Visine.

The Norelco razor complained in a low rhythmic murmur as it consumed the last of more than a full day's stubble. Unable to sleep Tuesday night, he'd shaved several hours before leaving for the cemetery in San Mateo, and not since. With his thick black hair and coarse beard, Josh normally shaved before work in the morning and again prior to dinner. If not, by bedtime he would look more like he was reliving his carefree fraternity days at MIT than assuming the image of a national salesman with a Fortune 500 firm.

When he'd returned the razor to its pouch and had brushed his teeth and hair, he rested his palms on the vanity and stared at his nude reflection. He recognized the body and face of the man who stood before him, but did not know him. "Okay, Josh Mitchell, you've made it to Natchez, Mississippi. What the hell are you gonna do now that you're here? You don't even know why you're here, do you, except you think you remember Dianne Lane mentioning that she was from Natchez? So, you think you'll find answers in this place?" He shook his head. "More than likely, only more questions." He raised his eyes toward the fluorescent light and allowed the thoughts to form themselves. "How about this for starters: Why would Dianne Lane have told you the truth about her childhood home when she flat out lied about things as basic as her own name? There is no Pamela Morrow, remember? The person you thought you knew . . ."—he paused as the rest of the unspoken sentence formed in his head, ready to be spoken; his heart forced a modification—". . . the woman you fell in love with doesn't exist, fool. Her name was Dianne Lane, she was married, and now . . . she's dead." His mind played continuous name games, swapping Pamela Morrow and Dianne Lane beneath the same image, his heart wondering why it mattered what she'd called herself. He lowered his head, chin against his chest, eyes on the cold marble countertop. "So, why are you here then, Josh Mitchell? What can you hope to learn?"

They were the same two questions he'd asked all the way from San

Francisco, and still he was no closer to arriving at an answer than he'd been when he'd decided to come.

He chose a pair of comfortable jeans, loafers, and an old MIT sweatshirt instead of a suit and tie today. Surprisingly, he found that it lifted his spirits, reminding him that he'd once had a life away from work.

Again, soon, he swore.

Though he'd been certain there would be no Braden High listed, believing it to be as fictitious as the rest of Dianne Lane's story, its address and phone number stared back at him from the white pages of the phone book in his room. "I'll be damned," he mumbled in disbelief. He circled it, tore the page from the book, and folded it twice so the address was centered in the quarter page that remained on top. He stuffed it in his back jeans pocket and finished packing his suitcase.

When he zipped the suit bag closed, his stomach growled loud enough to have been heard in the hall. "Okay, okay, relax. I'm gonna feed you." The growling continued.

With his travel bag and laptop stowed in the trunk of the Grand Prix, Josh hurried back to the lobby for the breakfast buffet.

In the far corner of the motel parking lot, a black Ford pickup with a chrome roll bar sporting four Hella fog lights across its top waited patiently. Kisber would have rather had a Chevy or a GMC, but Mills had complained so vehemently when the Ford had initially been spotted then passed, that he'd relented. To ensure that the truck wouldn't be reported stolen before they'd finished their work, the two men had slipped into the isolated trailer of the man from whom they intended to "borrow" it and had put a bullet in his ear while he soundly slept off the empty bottle of vodka lying on the filthy carpet beside his bed. They had then put a simple hand-printed sign, scribbled on the back of an unpaid bill (they'd had their choice of many) between the storm- and inner door that read: *Gone Fishin'*. Since it had been apparent the man lived alone, they doubted anyone would miss him for at least a full day, probably two. By then, they'd be back in Biloxi, relaxing on the front porch in Kisber's rattan chairs, sipping beer and eating Jenny's crawfish étouffée, twenty thousand dollars to the good, and the state of Mississippi would have yet another unsolved murder on its hands.

With his back to the passenger's door panel, arms folded across his chest, legs spanning the center hump, his feet resting on the driver's mat beneath Kisber's legs, Mills finally snored loud enough to wake himself up. He'd been asleep for only three hours and his mood had improved little from the previous night. Killing the man in the trailer had eased the tension of waiting for the action to begin, but it was a short-lived fix.

"Jesus, Brian, you sound like a pig rooting in the mud with that damned snoring of yours." It was chilly in the truck, the engine having been off since five-fifteen, when the two men had first staked out a spot as far from Josh's Pontiac as possible, while still ensuring they'd not lose it in traffic when he headed out. The Corvette had been left at a used-car lot whose sign indicated that it was closed on Thursdays. The tag had been removed and hidden under the seat. Kisber knew that, there, the car would not be noticed or thought of as abandoned by the local police. "Hide in plain sight," he always said. The simplicity had amazed his friend.

"So, what's with the damn heat? You worried about using all the dude's gas?" Mills complained.

"Piece-of-shit Ford's got a leaky muffler. I smelled exhaust fumes in the cab after we'd sat here a while and I didn't feel like dying in my sleep. I told you we should've picked a GM product. Next time you'll listen to me, Brian." As he spoke, Kisber surveyed the lobby entrance like an eagle watching a ground squirrel. "I'll turn it back on as soon as we get moving."

Mills looked at his watch: nine-fifty-five. "Great, and when the hell's that gonna be, might I ask? First the son of a bitch wants to drive all night, and now he's gonna sleep all damned day. Christ! Just let me go in there and do him right now, will ya?"

"No need," Kisber grinned, squinting his eyes and pointing his hand like a pistol at the front door of the motel. "I told you patience would deliver our prey to us in due time."

Mills quickly spotted Josh. "Yeah, well, just remember what I said about patience . . . that's your deal, not mine." Mills sat up straight and watched as Josh climbed into the front seat of the Grand Prix, a Styrofoam coffee cup in one hand and a stuffed paper napkin in the other. After a few seconds, the car left the parking lot.

The Ford sprang to life as soon as the key was turned, as eager for the day to begin as its two occupants. Its massive V-8 lumbered and complained until they had turned north onto Highway 61 and Kisber was able to apply some throttle. It then smoothed out, sending three hundred horsepower out through twin mufflers that were barely legal.

"Hot damn, let's do it!" Mills shouted as they fell in behind the Grand Prix, five cars back.


Josh repeated in his head the simple directions the desk clerk had given him, and drove with confidence toward an address in the center of town. "Heck, nothin's far from anything else in Natchez, Mr. Mitchell," Bridget had said with a proud smile. "Be sure and take the historic home tour while you're visitin' with us, ya hear? The ladies that put it on would love to have you join 'em."

The misplaced and troubled Tennessean, who now made his home in Greenwich Village, deep in the most populous city in America—a world and a lifetime away from his roots—remembered with fondness just how much he missed the easy manners of Southern folk. With most of his jet sales coming from either coast, or from the money-rich central cities of Dallas, Chicago, or Houston, he'd gotten little opportunity to visit the true South since leaving for college in 1987.

"It's truth time, Josh," he whispered as he drove the three lights north on Highway 61, past several fast food places, a mall, and the Natchez Regional Medical Center, to John R. Junkin Drive. "You could have gone home anytime you pleased . . . it just didn't matter enough to you, did it?" His own words tasted like acid.

He knew the reason he'd avoided home was not because his hectic schedule had prevented his return, but because his "hick" friends and uncultured parents would have been an embarrassment to him amid the sophisticated world he'd too quickly adopted. Most of his friends in Cambridge, Massachusetts, where MIT was located, had never met a farmer, and believed things like corn and beans came from Del Monte or Green Giant, with no thought to the months of backbreaking work—by farmers—prior to canning.

It had been easy to fall into his new world, where his good looks and sharp mind had gained him rapid acceptance, and it had suited his purposes to deny his true past, especially when he quickly learned that the Northeastern liberals, who set the style and tone in Cambridge and Boston, thought of all Southerners as ignorant racists. They were often referred to as "rednecks" and "crackers" by those who would have rather bitten off their tongues than have said something equally disparaging about Hispanics or blacks.

Inventing cultured parents who lived in a villa in the south of France, and who had been too busy sailing around the ports of Europe to attend his graduation, had been a necessary elaboration of the original lies, the lies of survival, as he'd seen it then.

In truth, the couple from Selmer, Tennessee—happily married thirty-one years in July—had looked forward for four years to attending the commencement exercises of their only son, and would have, had he given them an actual date. Instead, to continue the lie that had begun to fit less comfortably with each passing month, Josh had made up some tale about needing one additional credit for his aeronautical engineering degree, and that graduation for him—unlike most of the class—would occur sometime the following fall. He'd crossed the stage in May of 1991 with no one celebrating his academic achievement but a handful of rowdy fraternity brothers.

It had been a hollow victory.


Braden High was a large redbrick building, three stories high, constructed in the late Fifties, with a large expanse of well-kept rolling front lawn and towering oak trees on either side of a wide concrete walkway. A dozen steps led from the street to the front entrance.

Josh stopped in the middle of the first landing, a great gray plateau fifty feet from his car parked at the curb, a hundred feet from the building.

He wondered again what the hell he was doing there.

He mumbled to himself, running the conversation through his head as he imagined it might go when he stood in the school's office. "Hi, my name is Joshua Mitchell, and I'm here to learn all I can about a woman I believe was possibly one of your former students, a Ms. Dianne Lane."

Josh pretended to take the school secretary's inevitable position. "And why should we tell you anything about a former student, Mr. Mitchell? Are you family?"

"Why should you tell me what I want to know, you ask? Good question. No, I'm not family, I'm a complete stranger. Actually, I was hoping to use the information to clear myself of an impending first-degree murder charge in the drowning death of Dianne Lane." He couldn't even begin to imagine what the school secretary would do after hearing that admission, but he was pretty certain she wasn't going to hand over the school's records on Dianne Lane—even if she had attended Braden High.

His shoulders slumped in despair.

The black Ford pickup rolled past the front of the school at just below the speed limit, unseen by him.

As Josh turned toward his car again to rethink his strategy, his eyes caught sight of a pleasant-looking building that lay directly across from the school. Standing defiantly alone in an age when malls and strip shops had become the norm was a Rexall Drugstore that looked like it had stood in this same location for thirty years, changing little with the passing decades.

The sight of it produced a smile.


The air inside the old pharmacy smelled clean and antiseptic, like the place had been mopped with Lysol the night before. Josh was pleased to find the business looked exactly like the Rexall that used to be in his hometown when he was a kid, and that with the slightest suspension of reality in his mind, he'd be standing there now, like he'd done a thousand times over the years.

It was this feeling of certain familiarity that had caused him to jog down the steps, past his car, and across the street, toward a place he was sure Natchez high school students—like his friends and he had done so many times after class let out in Selmer—had congregated for decades. He craned his neck above an aisle of Johnson & Johnson products for what he'd most hoped to find: a fountain. It was there, but now, in addition to the Cokes and milkshakes he remembered from his youth, diet drinks and four flavors of yogurt had been added to the menu. A man in a white lab coat stood at the prescription counter, adjacent to it, talking on the phone.

"Can I help you, young man?" a woman's voice asked.

Josh turned toward its origin. A wide smile spanning a face which had celebrated at least sixty birthdays met his gaze.

"Oh, hi. I'm sorry, I didn't think anyone was up front," Josh said.

The woman had been kneeling down, an aisle over, putting up stock from McKesson. "Didn't mean to scare you," she said, realizing she'd startled the stranger. She walked around the end of the aisle toward him. "Don't see many faces in here I haven't seen a hundred times before. I'm Betty Jean Price, I take care of the front." She leaned toward Josh and wrinkled her nose. "I get to yack with all the customers that way, and my husband Robert . . . well, that's his world back there in the pharmacy. He doesn't talk a whole lot, but then, I guess I do enough talking for the two of us. Folks say if we both talked as much as me, there'd be no air left in the store for the customers." Josh grinned at the woman's innocent candor. "Guess there's some truth to that . . . opposites do attract. We've been married forty-one years next July third," she stated with obvious pride. Betty Jean extended her hand. "Welcome."

Josh smiled and shook Betty Jean's hand. Her shake was firm and animated. "Nice to meet you, Betty Jean. I'm Josh Mitchell. How long have you and Robert operated this drugstore?" He hoped it had been at least twenty years, remembering that the *Examiner* article had given Dianne Lane's age as thirty-six at the time of her death Tuesday.

"We had the first Rexall in Natchez. Opened right here in 1964. Been here ever since." A woman came in the front door with an infant in her arms. "Mornin', Glenda, how's the new baby getting on?"

The woman stopped between Josh and Betty Jean, rotating the infant so both could see his face clearly. "Little Ryan's put on two pounds since we finally got rid of that nasty old colic. Isn't he just the most beautiful thing you ever saw?" Josh guessed the young mother to be no more than twenty, with a slender face, wide smile, and a pair of the bluest eyes he'd ever seen.

Betty Jean pulled the blanket back from his arms so she could play with his tiny hands. "He sure is. You and Gary must be very proud."

Josh agreed that the baby was indeed beautiful and Glenda smiled at his approval.

She said, "I'm picking up a prescription Dr. Norsworthy was supposed to have called in. Do you know if it's ready by chance?"

Betty Jean turned her head to the rear. "Hey, Robert," she shouted, gaining his attention. He'd ended his phone call and had begun filling out his weekly stocking order. "You got little Ryan's scrip ready?"

Robert waved a small brown bottle with a gleaming white cap in the air with a smile.

"You're all set," Betty Jean said, giving the baby's hand a squeeze.

Glenda smiled and headed toward the back.

When the mother and child had gone, Josh started to speak. Betty Jean beat him to it. "Oh, I am sorry, Mr. Mitchell, I got to yacking so much, I never did find out what we can do for you."

Josh decided folks were right about Betty Jean's love of gab, but found her charming and not the least bit offensive. He was pleasantly reminded for the second time in an hour how different people were in the deep South. "I met a woman earlier this week, in San Francisco, who said she was originally from Natchez and attended Braden High School in the Seventies. I was wondering if you might remember her coming in here back then." Josh knew it was a long shot, but it was the only shot he had.

"Are you with the police, Mr. Mitchell?" she asked, her expression now serious.

"No, I'm not, Betty Jean. I'm just someone trying to find out a few things about this woman's past, that's all. I read that she committed suicide on Monday and it really bothered me. I was hoping to learn what might have been troubling her." His expression betrayed him.

Betty Jean studied his eyes. They were sad. "You liked her a lot, didn't you?" she said.

"Yes," Josh said. "I did, and I don't understand what happened." His voice almost broke.

"But, how could anything that occurred twenty years ago tell you what was in her mind three days ago?"

"I don't think it will . . . or can, but I've got nowhere else to turn. She spoke so warmly of her life here, as a young girl, that I thought there might be some answer among the memories. I guess it sounds crazy. You're right, it's been too long."

Betty Jean touched his arm. "What was her name, Josh?"

Josh pulled the newspaper photo from his back pocket and showed it to the woman. The name Dianne Lane was beneath it.

As she walked toward the counter to ring up Glenda's prescription, Betty Jean studied the photo. She thanked the young mother, patted the baby on the cheek, and told them to hurry back. When they were alone again, she looked up from the picture. "Nobody by this name ever attended Braden High School, at least not in the Seventies. I'm sure of that."

"But it's been twenty years, Betty Jean. How can you be so sure?" Josh's heart sank.

"Back then, the girls would all come in after school and browse through the makeup and hair color, always hoping to look more like the big-city girls they saw on television. They all came in at one time or another, some a couple of times a week. Anyone as pretty as Dianne Lane here would have been a regular customer, and I'd have remembered her. Besides, for ten years, from 1969-1979, I was also the school nurse. Every girl from freshman to senior came to see me at least once, for some Midol or when she'd run out of . . . you know . . . girl things. I never remember the name Dianne Lane crossing my desk."

Josh took the photo and returned it to his back pocket. "Thanks,

Betty Jean. You've been most kind. I really appreciate the time you've given me." He turned to leave.

"Oh, no trouble at all, Josh. Sorry I couldn't give you the answers you're looking for." Her regret was genuine.

"Thanks again." When he had the doorknob in hand, Josh turned back to the checkout counter. "You don't by any chance remember a student named Pamela Morrow from that same time, do you?"

Betty Jean's eyes lit up. "I should say I do, Josh. If ever there was a young lady who merited remembering, Pamela Anne Morrow would be her."

Josh walked back toward the woman with mixed feelings. Instead of the truthful direction his quest was supposed to take, he found himself again chasing lies. *Why had Dianne Lane called herself someone else?* he repeated for the thousandth time.

Maybe now, he'd learn.


"This is the craziest son of a bitch I've ever seen," Mills bitched as he sat in the cab of the pickup, sucking on his last Marlboro. "I'm gonna need some smokes if we're gonna keep on with this patience shit."

"I suppose if it were up to you, you'd go in the drugstore right now and kill the son of a bitch in broad daylight." Kisber shook his head in amusement and reached inside his windbreaker pocket. He tossed a pack of Winstons in his buddy's lap. "Those should hold you for a while."

"It'd sure beat the hell out of all this waiting around."

"And what about it needing to look like an accident? You forget about that or what?" The black Ford was sitting in the corner of the high school's parking lot, diagonal to the Rexall, a hundred yards southwest.

"Hell, no, I didn't forget. It just seems to me that dead is dead, *how* don't much matter." Mills opened the Winstons.

"Well, it seems to matter to my friend Jack, and so it matters to me. Clear?"

"Sure. I just want to get on with it, that's all." He pulled a cigarette from the pack and lit it with the butt of his last Marlboro. "What the hell you figure he's doing in the damned drugstore anyway?"

Kisber again shook his head, this time puzzled. "What was he gonna do at the high school before he changed his mind? That's what gets me," he said, rubbing his bottom lip with his thumb.

"Reckon he went there?"

"Maybe. Jack would know. I guess it's not important, but it still bugs me." The air outside couldn't have been more still if they'd been sitting in a closed room, the leafless branches of the trees without movement. Overhead, the sun shone almost white in a sky as clear and hard as stainless steel, warming the March air and coaxing the temperature to nearly seventy degrees. Kisber rolled his window down, feeling claustrophobic in the truck's cab. He unzipped the Gore-Tex bag between them and withdrew a pair of .40 caliber Glock 27s. "Check your piece," he said to Mills. Both men withdrew their slides in unison, chambering a round from the clip in each barrel. Kisber then ejected his clip, reached into an open box in the bag, and added a bullet for the one that had just been chambered, bringing the available total to eleven.

Mills followed suit. "What about that accident shit you just bitched at me about?" he said.

"Mitchell looks to be in pretty good shape to me. He just might not want to die accidentally," Kisber said, his eyes narrow and mean.

"Hot shit!" Mills yipped.

"Only if he don't go along with the program," Kisber warned.

"Oh, of course, Ron. Absolutely. You know me."

"Yeah, I know you," Kisber said, shoving both weapons back in the bag and zipping it shut. "That's what worries me."


Josh Mitchell sipped on a glass of ice water as he sat alongside Betty Jean Price at the four-stool counter in the rear of the Rexall. She had fixed herself a Diet Coke. Robert had come over and said hello, but had quickly disappeared back into the pharmacy when the phone began to ring.

"How do you know Pamela Morrow?" Betty Jean asked, making herself comfortable on the end stool.

Josh thought for a minute. He didn't know how to answer the question without sounding like a nut. He decided to try the cold truth and hope the woman didn't think him crazy. "I thought the woman I met on Monday was named Pamela Morrow. I only found out after she'd died that her real name was Dianne Lane."

"Why would you have thought that?" she asked, her Diet Coke untouched.

"Dianne Lane didn't tell me her name during the entire six-hour flight we shared, and when I finally pressed her about it after we'd landed, that was the name she gave me. I had no reason to doubt it."

"I guess not. Does seem queer, though, using someone else's name, don't you think?"

Josh nodded.

"Any idea why this Dianne Lane person would have done such an odd thing? You think she was trying to hide something from you?"

It was an idea Josh had toyed with, without an answer. "I thought of that. Dianne Lane had been married, I found out the next day, though she and her husband were either divorced or she was a widow. I couldn't find out anything about the man other than his name. I don't think she would have been worried about people seeing us together. All we did was fly beside each other on a crowded plane and talk."

"You seem pretty concerned about this stranger to have only talked with her. Am I wrong, Josh?" Betty Jean raised an eyebrow knowingly.

Josh knew his feelings for Dianne Lane were far more apparent than he would have liked, but saw no point in involving Betty Jean in the rest of the story. "She was a remarkable woman. I could tell that right away. It's not right that she's dead."

"No, it's not. How can I help you?"

"Tell me what you remember about Pamela Morrow," he said, impatient for anything of substance.

Betty Jean put her straw to her lips, drawing in a bit of the sweet brown liquid. "Pamela Morrow was that one of a kind girl no one ever forgot once they'd met her. She was tall, slim, beautiful, smart, and truly kind—all the things every woman wants to be. I think she was the most attractive and capable girl to have ever attended Braden High School. She was Homecoming Queen twice, in her junior and senior years. No one before or since has been selected more than once. She was also voted most likely to succeed in her senior yearbook. The kids also joked that she was 'most likely to move away from Natchez.'"

Josh grinned, but thought about Dianne Lane, the woman he'd known for only eighteen hours, trying to picture her as a teenager in high school. Every characteristic of Pamela Morrow that Betty Jean had just described could have just as easily applied to her. Then reality coldly invaded his dream: The person he'd met was Dianne Lane, not the stranger Betty Jean had just described. He'd never laid eyes on Pamela Morrow, though he knew that he had no choice now but to meet her, to learn what he could about the strange connection that existed between these two remarkable women.

As he was about to ask Betty Jean if she possibly knew where he could find her today, she spoke. "There was just one odd thing about Pamela, Josh, one thing none of us could quite figure out."

He was stopped in his tracks. "And what was that, Betty Jean?"

"She was always such good friends with that Marie Edwards, ever since they were little girls. I never did understand it myself, but then, to each his own, I always say." She took another drink of her Diet Coke. The small drugstore remained quiet except for Robert's abbreviated responses on the phone and his constant rattling of pill bottles twenty feet away.

"Why was her friendship with the Edwards girl so odd? Was Marie . . . I don't know how to put it . . . a bad girl?"

"Oh, I guess Marie was nice enough all right, even back then. Never seemed to be in trouble and always did real well in school. Went to college at Millsaps in Jackson. I understand she even worked for the Governor's Office for a bit while she was up there. It's just that . . ."

"Yes," he pressed, baffled.

"Well, she was half-black. You know, part Negro." Betty Jean glanced over her shoulder to ensure the store was still empty. She hadn't heard the bell over the door chime anyone's arrival. She turned back to Josh. "None of the 'regular' blacks would have anything to do with her and neither would the white kids, but it didn't seem to bother Pamela one little bit. No, sir. They hung around together all the time like Marie was an ordinary person."

*An ordinary person,* he repeated silently. Josh had almost forgotten how deeply seated bigotry still was in much of the South, especially among those who had been raised in previous generations, where tolerance was discouraged. He imagined Betty Jean's "world" had never been much larger than the county, perhaps the state of Mississippi at most, and as such, she would have had little opportunity to shed prejudices that had now been with her more than six decades. He decided not to try to bring the woman into the late Nineties, though his respect for Pamela Morrow had been raised appreciably by Betty Jean's last remark. "I see," was all he chose to say.

"But then, Pamela always did seem to have her own agenda in life," Betty Jean added with a sad smile as she finished her Diet Coke.

Josh had never met the real Pamela Morrow, but understood exactly what Betty Jean meant. He found himself hoping fervently that she still lived in the Natchez area, though he was more than willing to go wherever necessary to meet her. The belief that some mysterious link still existed between the two women teased his mind. It couldn't be coincidence that Dianne Lane had chosen Pamela's name hours before her death. An odd thought struck him. "Did Pamela Morrow have a sister? A half-sister, perhaps?"

"No. She was an only child. It was just her mama and her. She told me her daddy had been killed in the Army. I remember meeting her mama once, at a football game—real nice lady she was—and we talked about kids all the way to halftime. Robert and I have four grown boys and nine grandchildren ourselves, and I distinctly remember Mrs. Morrow telling me that Pamela was an only child. I thought, how sad for her. No brothers or sisters and no daddy either. Her mama passed away after Pamela left for college, 1979, I think."

Josh suddenly felt doubly disloyal to his own family, and a knot moved slowly down his throat. His own actions had effectively made him an orphan, while simultaneously robbing his parents of their only child. He vowed to call them tomorrow.

He knew there was nothing left to do; he had to meet Pamela Morrow as soon as possible. His pulse raced nervously. "Betty Jean, is there any chance you can tell me how I can get in touch with Pamela Morrow?"

"Oh, you can't get in touch with Pamela, Josh. She's been gone, what, nine years now."

Josh did the math quickly in his head. "Was 1989 the year Pamela finally left Natchez, as everyone had predicted?" Though he was pleased Pamela had lived up to the expectations that had been put to her in high school, and had probably become a huge success in whatever career she'd finally chosen, he knew finding her meant more travel and more time.

Time was something he had precious little of.

Still, he was determined to find her, to hire a private detective if necessary.

He waited for the woman across the counter to tell him where Pamela now lived, assuming she knew. He crossed his fingers.

A sad look painted Betty Jean Price's face as she reached across the counter and touched his arm. "No, Josh, I'm so sorry—1989 was the year Pamela Morrow was killed."

# 9

Needing to hear a familiar voice more than at any other time in memory, Josh phoned his apartment. Though his mind had convinced him it was only to retrieve his messages, his fear of being alone wanted Monica to pick up, to tell him that she loved him with every cell in her body and that she would be waiting for him when he returned. He knew it was neither what he needed nor truly wanted, yet the confusion and the sense of being adrift in an emotional sea overwhelmed him.

When the same snide greeting she'd left on the answer phone Monday afternoon played hatefully in his ear, whatever false hope he'd harbored for relief coming from Monica vanished.

Nothing made sense anymore.

He extended his arms against the steering wheel and forced his body into the bucket seat of the Grand Prix, hoping to rein in his confused emotions, to let his analytical side dictate his actions for a change. It was useless. His perfectly ordered world, everything he'd built over the last ten years, was on the verge of collapse, with no foreseeable hope of preventing it.

And while the thought of losing it all mattered less today than it had when he'd first faced the prospect on Monday morning, it still mattered and it still hurt.

Lefler's face haunted his mind, adding to the misery.

Josh grabbed the phone and dialed his parents' home in Selmer, the blood in his ears pounding. Before it rang the first time, he pressed End. How could he call them for the first time in months with nothing to offer but trouble?

Of the dozens of people he knew, many quite well, he realized that not one genuine friend existed in the lot. Not one of them would stand beside him if he was charged with murder. They would party at his apartment, drink his booze, dance to his stereo, let him pick up the check at dinner, but there wasn't a real friend among them.

Yes, there is one, he reminded himself.

Perhaps it was time to bring Kenny Kanazawa fully into this crazy puzzle, to get a rational perspective from a concerned outsider, someone he trusted fully, someone who cared—a true friend. Kenny would never lead him astray. His would be the voice of reason, even if that voice was occasionally tinged with cynicism and locker-room comments—that was simply Kenny's style. Josh knew he meant well.

From his cell phone's speed dial he called the direct number to Kenny's office in the software lab.

"Development, Kanazawa," his friend said in a somber tone. He sounded more exhausted than usual.

"Hey old buddy," Josh said.

"Josh?"

"Yeah."

"It's about time, you worthless son of a bitch! So, where the hell are you?!" Kenny barked.

"On the road. Didn't Whitney tell you?"

"Shit, no. She doesn't know where in the hell you are. Said you left a vague voice mail telling her you were going to be somewhere in the Southeast chasing a sale. And what's with your damned cell phone? You forget how to turn it on?"

"I let the battery run down. Sorry."

"It's a lithium-ion, Josh. It'll recharge fully from any outlet or cigarette lighter in the world in forty minutes. Don't give me that dead battery shit. You forget I'm not one of your customers who doesn't have a clue about technology."

"Listen, Kenny, I really am sorry. I know you were counting on me to help with Casper and I let you down—"

"Screw Casper," Kenny interrupted. "It's your dumb ass I'm worried about, old buddy."

"My ass?"

"Damn straight! Hightower's on one of his tirades. Ran around in a pissy mood all day yesterday, and then this morning—BAM!—he's Attila the Hun."

"What's he on a rampage about?" Josh asked innocently, though he was sure he was most of the reason.

"Because he hasn't been able to find his favorite boy for two days, and you know how crazy it makes him whenever one of his chickens is out of the coop too long." Kenny scooted his chair backward toward the coffee pot, cup in hand. It would make his tenth cup since arriving at work at eight.

"I've been out of touch longer than this before," Josh said, adjusting the car's visor to keep the rock-hard sun out of his eyes.

"Not while the FBI was looking for your butt, you haven't."

Josh's stomach became a stone. He switched the phone to the ear away from traffic, putting his palm flat against the open ear. "The FBI?" he repeated. The signal had become scratchy.

"Yeah, you remember, the Federal Bureau of Investigation. J. Edgar Hoover. Big sandstone building in Washington, DC. I know you've seen them on TV. I think Efrem Zimbalist used to play—"

"Enough! for Christ's sake, Kenny. I know who the damned FBI is! I was just wondering what the hell they wanted with me."

"Well, that makes three of us: you, me, and the old man."

"What did Hightower say exactly?"

"He said the FBI phoned him at his home late last night wanting to locate you. When he pressed them for a reason, they told him it was none of his business. Jesus, you just don't say things like that to a man with a McLaren F1," Kenny said in a tense laugh.

Josh closed his eyes, unable to respond.

"It really pissed him off. He stormed into your office first thing this morning and practically fired Whitney because she didn't know exactly where you were at that very second. Poor girl, he really gave her some serious shit, but she kept her cool. Kept assuring him that you would call in any moment. He's had no choice but to wait, and you know he doesn't wait worth a damn."

Josh stared at the headliner. "Shit," he mumbled, his chest tight. Things were getting way out of hand. "Is she okay?" he asked.

Kenny said, "Whitney? Oh, sure. I wish I had a secretary like her. Hell, Hightower wishes he had her, but he knows she wouldn't work for him for five seconds. You need to call her, Josh. She's worried about you."

"I will. Soon."

"Soon, my ass! What the hell's going on, Josh? I don't think those FBI guys want to talk to you because they're shy a striker on their beach volleyball team." Kenny took a large swig of his coffee, then put his feet on his desk by his computer. "This has something to do with Dianne Lane's murder, doesn't it?"

"Since when has her suicide become a murder?" Josh asked hurriedly. He'd decided it was not a good time to confide in Kenny. He needed to be back at the office, face to face with his friend. It looked like he was going to have to return sooner than he'd planned.

"Since the Ten O'Clock News last night, when some San Francisco cop named Lefty or something announced to the press that he was not at all convinced the neatly packaged death of Dianne Lane was a suicide."

"Lefler," Josh corrected.

"Yeah, that's right. You see the same story?"

"No," Josh said without thinking, then bit his lip.

"How come you know his name?"

"It's not important right now. Listen, Kenny, you've got to cover for me for a little while. I need a few more hours to pull some things together. Don't tell Hightower that I called in yet, okay? Do that for me, will you?"

Kenny was on his feet by his computer. "Bullshit, Lucky, you tell me what the hell's going on right now!"

"You know I hate that name."
"Fuck you! Talk to me, dammit!"
"Thanks, old buddy. I knew I could count on you."
"Josh!"
"Later, man."
"Dammit, Josh!" Kenny shouted.
A dial tone greeted his anger.

Josh knew he had to meet with the FBI shortly, before the whole insane situation escalated further, before they called Hightower back no longer simply wanting to find him, but to inform the president of Barnett Air that they had a warrant for the arrest of one of his salesmen.

He was sure he could still convince the authorities that he had nothing to do with Dianne Lane's death—suicide or murder—though the fragile belief was becoming harder to hold on to.

He had to act quickly. If they were looking for him in California, he wondered if they had followed him to Mississippi—to where he now sat.

He spun in his seat, trying to spot any vehicle in which a pair of men in suits sat patiently, looking out of place in the river town. The thought brought a nervous smile to his tight lips. He realized how stereotypically ridiculous his image of the FBI was. He had only television's view of such things, with no practical experience in matters of running from the law. He knew that, while he might have been more than qualified for survival in a sales world, he would be quickly consumed on the "street." His heart thudded like a platoon of soldiers marching across a wooden bridge.

Though he hadn't the slightest idea what he was looking for, Josh continued to scan the area, determined to find the agents that might be surveilling him. He spotted a black truck in the corner of the school parking lot, its two male occupants apparently waiting for someone.

*You're really a dumb shit, you know it, Josh?* his analytical mind taunted when it had taken a moment to process Kenny's words. *If they're still looking for you in California, then they don't have any idea you're in Natchez, now do they?*

The logical realization eased his tension. Of course the FBI wasn't following him. Why would they be? He was no criminal. For the moment, the San Francisco or Carmel police might think he was involved in some way in Dianne Lane's death, but not the FBI.

*What if Fachini or Lefler called in the feds?* he considered. *This is getting crazy.*

Though he could only speculate about what the FBI wanted with him, he understood that he wasn't going to reach a definitive answer just sitting there letting his paranoia run wild.

While he had been talking with Betty Jean in the pharmacy, Josh had decided to locate Marie Edwards, to speak with her and hopefully get some feel for the close friend who was killed in 1989. Maybe, by doing so, he would discover why Dianne Lane had used Pamela's name hours before her own death. Perhaps, if he could learn something of substance about Pamela Morrow, it would shed some light on the reason for Dianne Lane's suicide, or, at best, point the finger of suspicion at someone with a motive for her murder.

Josh was groping for anything that would remove him from the possible suspect list and show Dianne Lane as the victim of someone else's wrath, jealousy, or greed.

Or perhaps, as someone who was genuinely troubled, a woman capable of taking her own life.


"You think he's spotted us?" Mills asked when Josh turned to look toward the black truck. The thought made the hired assassin nervous.

"Nah. He's just looking around, like everybody does when they first get in their car in a strange place. We're cool." Kisber chewed on the filter of his cigarette, his eyes never moving from the Grand Prix.

"Hell, man, it's nearly eleven o'clock. Are we gonna just follow this son of a bitch around all day like a couple of dogs in heat, or are we gonna actually do him sometime soon?" The younger man's legs had begun to go to sleep and his bladder was screaming for relief. "I gotta piss."

"Well, hang it out the door, or wait until we stop again. We got no time to pull through McDonald's."

"We're stopped now. I'm getting the hell out." Mills reached for the door handle.

"I'll leave you if you do," Kisber said, his attention never diverting from their prey. "He's fixing to move again."

"Dammit to hell!" Mills said, slamming the door closed. "I'll just piss in his dead face after I've blown his brains out."

The truck eased into the street, careful not to close too rapidly on the Pontiac.

From a third-story window in the school, two young men—seniors switching classes—watched as a distinctive black truck exited the parking lot.

"Hey, Scott, isn't that your uncle's rig?" the boy nearest the window asked.

Scott moved closer, watching the familiar vehicle with concerned interest. "Sure is, man, but that's sure as hell not Eddie behind the wheel."

"Or in the passenger seat either," the other boy added.

Scott watched as the truck vanished among the stately oaks sheltering the street. "Hey, Chuck, reckon Amy's got her cell phone with her?"

"Always," Chuck said with confidence.

"Get it from her, would ya? And meet me at my car."

"Now?"

"Move your ass!" Scott said, darting for the stairs.

At the curb in front of one of the more impressive examples of antebellum architecture to grace a city abundant with similar testaments to a grand lifestyle long vanished, Josh switched off the Grand Prix's engine. He checked the address on the ornate mailbox with the number he'd written down fifteen minutes earlier: they matched.

In the yard, a man Josh guessed to be in his mid- to late sixties, slowly and lovingly carved the end of a piece of crown molding with a coping saw, shaping it so that it would fit precisely into the peaks and valleys of the ceiling trim to which it would be married. The man worked with the unhurried patience of an old-world artisan, obviously content in the belief that any contribution he made to the restoration of this 1839 mansion on the Mississippi River must be as fine as he could craft, irrespective of time, regardless of cost.

He'd seen Josh drive up and park, though he showed no interest in his arrival.

Josh approached with an easy posture, aware of the temperament of many craftsmen when disturbed. He stood directly in front of the elderly man, five or six feet back from his work table, waiting for the carpenter to acknowledge him.

"Can I help you?" the man asked after a full minute, his eyes on his saw blade.

"Yes, please. I'm looking for Marie Edwards. Can you tell me where I might find her?"

The man looked up from his work. "I believe Ms. Edwards is in the parlor. Is she expecting you?" He studied Josh from head to toe, giving no indication of approval or disdain.

"Not really, but I phoned her office and her secretary told me that Ms. Edwards would likely be here. Would it be all right if I went in?" Josh wasn't sure why he was asking permission of the elderly man. It just seemed as if he should.

"She's pretty busy today, but I suppose it'll be okay." He returned to his sawing as quickly as he'd left it. "Be sure to wipe your feet on the mat before you go inside," he mumbled.

Josh smiled, amused at the man's protective manner, as if the house were his own.

*Artists*, he chuckled.

He crossed the expansive wooden front porch and, as instructed, wiped the soles of both shoes on the hemp mat lying in front of the massive oak door. While he didn't turn to check, he was sure his actions had been dutifully noted by the carpenter.

The fretted handle turned with ease, though a slight squeak came from within its heavy brass workings. Similarly, a quartet of brass hinges announced the arrival of the home's most recent guest.

As he stood in the foyer with the door to his back, Josh heard footsteps approaching from the room off the right of the wide entrance hall. He guessed it to be the parlor.

"Finished with that piece of crown already, Henry?" a pleasant voice asked as the footsteps neared. In another second, a woman carrying a full set of architectural blueprints appeared, her surprise revealing that she had not been expecting visitors. "Oh, I'm sorry," she said, juggling the thick book of plans to her left arm. "I didn't think anyone else was here." She extended the right hand that was now free. "I'm Marie Edwards."

"I thought you might be," Josh said with a warm smile. "I hope you don't mind my stopping by unannounced."

"Are you the electrician?" she asked, rolling the plans back into their original tubular shape. She sounded hopeful.

"No. Sorry. My name is Joshua Mitchell. I was given your name by Betty Jean Price at the pharmacy across from—"

"Braden High," she completed, recognizing the name at once.

"Yes. I see you know Mrs. Price then."

"Everyone in Natchez knows Betty Jean Price. In fact, everyone in Natchez knows everyone else in Natchez, Mr. Mitchell."

"Please call me Josh."

"Well . . . Josh . . . since you're obviously not from here, I must warn you that it's like that in a small town, I'm afraid."

"How well I know, Ms. Edwards. This is a metropolis compared to the town I grew up in."

The woman returned his smile. "Please call me Marie." She let her eyes wander beyond the huge window on the east wall of the parlor. "It's funny, the inability to put on a pot of beans without someone immediately calling from across town suggesting that you should add a little more salt was the main reason I originally left Natchez."

Josh nodded his understanding. "But you returned."

"I guess your first home will always be home." She turned her eyes back to the attractive stranger. "So, Josh Mitchell, what can I do for you today?"

In a glance Josh studied the woman as he thought of the best way to phrase his request. She was much shorter than he, no taller than five-four but solidly built, with skin the color of mocha, and long, wavy hair as black as a raven's wings. Her corduroy blazer, starched white blouse, and pleated khaki slacks presented an air of casual professionalism. And while not beautiful in the classical sense of the word, Marie Edwards possessed soft, dark eyes and pleasant, even features that seemed to fit her personality perfectly. Within the few words she'd spoken, Josh sensed a confident, capable woman with intelligence and charm in equal measures. He could easily understand why Pamela Morrow would have befriended this woman despite others turning away.

"I wonder if you could spare me a few minutes of your time, Ms. Edwards?" he asked. His expression conveyed more distress than his words.

Though initially hesitant to say yes to his request, Marie quickly realized that she felt no sense of danger from the handsome young man, despite his troubled eyes.

"We can talk in the ballroom if you'd like," she said.

"That'd be fine," he said, following her into a room opposite the parlor—on the south side of the mansion—that appeared to have been completely restored. The most prominent piece of furniture in the majestic room was a brightly colored camelback sofa sitting before a whitewashed brick fireplace. She invited Josh to join her as she sat.

"From your expression, Josh, I gather you have a matter of some urgency you'd like to discuss with me. I certainly hope I can be of help."

Josh felt foolish for having alerted her unnecessarily. "I apologize, Ms. Edwards for—"

"What happened to Marie?" she asked in an attempt to lighten the mood.

"Marie . . . I apologize if I've caused you any concern. It is a matter of some urgency to me." He could tell by her look that he wasn't stating his case very well. "I'm trying to clear up a mystery, and I believe you may be the only one who can help me with that." He tried not to fidget, though he felt undeniably nervous. He was, at this moment, as close as he was ever likely to get to Pamela Morrow—the woman indirectly responsible for his deepest fears, and paradoxically, the woman who might be able to put an end to them.

Marie had to tell him everything she knew about Pamela Morrow.

Laying the cumbersome blueprints on the oriental rug at her feet, Marie settled back in the curve of the delicate sofa and folded her hands in her lap. "I've never been the solution to a mystery before. Sounds terribly interesting. Just what kind of mystery are we talking about, Josh? Murder, I hope," she added with a broad smile.

Josh knew that, despite her humor, the woman was not prepared for the response he was going to give. He thought of couching it for less effect but opted for the cold truth. "It appears you get the prize on the first guess," he said.

Marie sat up straight. The smile had disappeared.

"I hope you're kidding with me," she said.

He pulled the photo of Dianne Lane from his back pocket, handing it to her. "Do you recognize this woman?"

"Should I?" she asked with the photo in hand, but before she'd glanced at it.

"Don't know. Perhaps. Either way, after you've taken a look at it, I'll try to explain."

Reluctantly, Marie Edwards turned her gaze to the wrinkled *Examiner* photo, showing Dianne Lane in an evening gown in front of a simple, dramatically lit background. It had been taken during one of Richmond Gallery's annual fund-raisers.

She studied it for a long while, then said, "I gather the woman was obviously Dianne Lane, but I'm afraid I recognize neither the face nor the name. Sorry." She handed the photo back to Josh.

*Dammit to hell!* his mind shouted. His disappointment showed.

"You promised to explain," she said.

Josh stood, moving to the fireplace. He turned back to the couch, resting his hips gently against the brick. "You have a few minutes?"

Marie nodded hesitantly.

• • •

The Ford pickup sat on a side street in the shade of a row of tall ever-greens, the front of the mansion and the rented Pontiac clearly vis-ible. As the two men waited within, the patience of one exhausted, the other's waning, Kisber's cell phone began to ring.

"Yeah," he answered in an annoyed tone. He'd known it would be Jack Farris even before the man spoke, and he knew the reason for the call.

"So?" Farris said in a terse tone.

Kisber knew what his employer wanted. He'd phoned Farris last night with a full update when they'd arrived in Natchez, but had not called since. "Dude's still running around town like he's on a damned scavenger hunt or something. Doesn't seem to be any logic to his moves."

Mills tossed another spent Winston out the window. He had four left.

Farris asked, "What's he done this morning?"

"Left the hotel around ten and drove to some school across town."

"What kind of school?"

"You know, a high school."

"Why'd he go there?" Farris asked.

"Beats me. He didn't go in or nothing. Just parked in front, started up the stairs, and then beat a trail for some drugstore across the street."

"What the hell?"

"Exactly what I thought. Spent half an hour in the place talking with some old broad. After twenty minutes, I sent Brian up to the glass to take a look and he said they were just sitting in the back of the store gabbing."

"You get her name?"

Kisber lit a cigarette. "Nah, but it'll be a piece of cake. Brian says he thinks her old man and her own the place. He's apparently the druggist."

Farris made the appropriate notes. "What then?"

"Made a couple of calls from his car as he drove, then ended up where he is now, inside one of those big old Civil War houses along the river. You know, the ones they're always fixing up and running bus tours through."

"The address?"

Kisber gave it.

"Any idea what he's doing in there?"

"Not a clue. Some old guy's out front cutting trim, but we're not able to see inside the place from where we're sitting without making a big deal out of it. You want me to send Brian up to the house to have a better look anyway?"

Mills nodded that he was ready to get the hell out of the truck and would be more than happy to go.

"Better not. My employer is still very insistent that Mitchell's death have every earmark of an accident. If we spook him, it'll sure as hell fuck that plan up."

"And what if the dude don't want to die accidentally?"

Mills grinned, patting on the bag.

Kisber shook his head, amused by his buddy's one-track mind.

"Unless you hear otherwise, he had better die just like I said. If not, no green. Got it?"

"Sure, Jack. But as long as I gotta follow him around like a lame dog, until I get *official* permission to take him out from the idiot you're working for, I'm warning you, if he makes me, I'm doing him where he stands, permission or not." Kisber bit heavily on the filter of his cigarette.

"You afraid he might make you?"

"We're being careful enough," Kisber said firmly.

"Are you worried about Mitchell getting the better of you, Ron?" Farris asked sarcastically.

"Fuck, no!"

"Then we've got no problem, do we? Listen, I gotta report in with what you've told me so far. Who knows, I might call you back with news that the brakes are off."

"Make it soon, Jack. I've got a feeling this boy's gonna split this town before too long, and there's only one sweet place between here and Jackson to do him like you want."

Farris said, "I'll call you back within the hour."

● ● ●

Josh spoke, his voice low, his tone reverent. "On Monday of this week, on a flight from New York to San Francisco, I met the most fascinating woman I've ever known. For nearly seven hours, I listened as she described her view of love and life, a view that, to my delight, paralleled my own. When we landed in San Francisco, and as she was about to walk away, I asked her name."

"You hadn't learned her name before then?" Marie asked, still sitting upright on the sofa.

"It hadn't seemed important before. I can't explain it, but it just hadn't mattered when we were talking."

"Go on."

"Before she left the airport, and after more than a little persuasion, she finally told me her name was Pamela Morrow, and that she was originally from Natchez, Mississippi." Josh watched for the response.

Marie stood as soon as the name was spoken.

Without a word, she went to the window at the rear of the home, and stared out at the legendary river flowing swiftly southward at the foot of the property. In a few weeks, the azaleas, dogwoods, and Bradford pears which lined and dotted the mansion's manicured lawn would be in bloom. Spring was her favorite time to be working among the stately homes on the bluff.

The front door opened with a series of familiar squeaks, causing both Josh and her to turn instinctively toward the sound, though neither could see the door from their position. Marie knew Henry had completed his work on the ceiling trim and was coming to install it in the parlor.

She called to him. "When you're through with that piece, Henry, why not grab some lunch?" She was sure he'd heard her despite his lack of a response. That was just Henry's way.

She turned her eyes to Josh, their rims glistening. "I don't know what game you're playing, Mr. Mitchell, but I don't find it the least bit amusing. If you'd please leave now, I'd appreciate it."

Josh knew he had to say something quickly, something that would convince her of the absolute sincerity of his words. "I fell more deeply in love with Dianne Lane in eighteen hours than I believed possible, Ms. Edwards, and now she's dead." Marie's hand went to her mouth. "My only clue to her death is the name Pamela Morrow, the woman she claimed to be, and the woman you knew better than anyone else. Please, don't send me away before you help me understand this insanity."

Marie wiped a tear away with a tissue she pulled from her blazer. "What happened to her?" she asked.

"She either killed herself or was murdered. There was a suicide note, but I'm not sure how valid it is." He heard the wind pressing against the ancient panes of glass, eager to gain entrance, like the demons of repressed images that tried to invade while he slept.

"Where did this happen?"

"In Carmel, California," he said.

"How did she die?" she asked.

"She drowned." The vision of Dianne Lane lying beneath the sheet tore at Josh. He fought to keep it at bay.

Marie sat on the sofa again, and dabbed at both eyes with the tissue. "You say this woman Dianne Lane called herself Pamela Morrow, and never once used her real name around you."

"That's correct." Josh took a seat at the other end of the sofa.

"Why? Why would she do that?" she asked.

"I have no answer for you."

"You say you knew this woman well enough to have fallen in love with her, and yet you didn't even know her name."

"I believed the name she'd given me. If you had met her, you would have too," Josh stated as if there could be no argument.

"I don't know about any of that. What I do know, if this woman killed herself, she was nothing like Pamela Morrow, the real Pamela Morrow. Pamela would have never taken her own life, and certainly not in *that* way."

"How did Pamela Morrow die?" Josh asked respectfully.

Marie's eyes grew harder. "What do *you* know about Pamela, or her death?"

"Nothing. Absolutely nothing. I want to know, though. Will you tell me about her, Marie . . . please?" He touched her hand.

She looked at his hand on hers but allowed it to remain. "Where are you from?"

"A little town in Tennessee called Selmer."

"Any blacks there?" she asked.

Josh nodded.

"Anyone like me?" Her tone had taken on a bitter flavor.

Josh felt uncomfortable. He shook his shoulders and said, "Not while I lived there, no."

Marie smiled, though not a smile of pleasure. "You have any idea what it was like growing up in a small town in Mississippi in the Sixties and Seventies when you're half-white and half-black and accepted by neither?"

Josh's eyes said he could not possibly know. He remembered Betty Jean Price's words and understood that it couldn't have been easy.

"The only friend I had in the world back then, besides my mother, was Pamela Morrow." Her eyes illuminated. "We were like sisters from the time we first met. I made it through my first twelve years of school because of her, not just with her academic help, which she was always willing to give, but because Pamela made it possible for me to exist day to day without the torment and ridicule I would have otherwise suffered."

"How did she do something like that . . . back then?" Josh asked. The hammering in the distant room had stopped.

"You say you were impressed with the woman you thought was Pamela Morrow, right?"

Josh nodded.

"Well, Josh, all I can say is that you should have known the real Pamela. She had a quality about her that took everyone's breath away. When she made it clear to everyone we met that they couldn't have her friendship without at least giving me an even break, they backed off. I won't begin to tell you I had the ideal childhood, but it would have been pure hell without Pamela. She probably saved my life."

"She was beautiful?"

"Oh, absolutely, but much more than physically beautiful. You know how one person in a thousand can enter a room and suddenly no one else exists? I don't mean in the vain sense of the word, like some kind of show-off, but in that special way we all secretly admire and yearn to have ourselves."

"That's the way I felt about Dianne Lane. The two women appear to have shared so much."

"Including death now," she said coldly.

Her words felt like a blade passing through him. How could the world lose two such rare and precious people while seeming to be overrun with low-life trash? The thought angered him.

"You said Pamela would never have committed suicide, especially by drowning. Why?"

"Like I said before, I was Pamela Morrow's best friend ever since we were little girls, before either of us knew there was such a thing as race or inequality. I knew her better than anyone else in the world and she would have never chosen that way, even if she were the type to commit suicide—which she wasn't. Pamela was a fighter, a survivor, always. Besides, she was deathly afraid of the ocean since being caught in a riptide on summer vacation down in Mobile when she was a small child. Her mother barely reached her before she was pulled out to sea. She never went within a hundred feet of the ocean again, even when the senior class all went to Panama City Beach on spring break."

"Tell me about her death, Marie."

It was obviously not a subject she was eager to address. She took a long time responding. Finally she said, "One rainy Saturday night, October 18, 1989, Pamela stepped out of her car in front of her home in Jackson, just like she'd done a thousand times, only this time a driver, probably drunk, sideswiped her little red Toyota, killing her instantly. They never caught the guy, but there were several witnesses who saw the accident. One guy who lived next door to Pamela even jumped into his truck and tried to track the guy down, but he was never able to spot the car again." Marie looked off into the distance, her eyes rimmed with tears again. "We buried her the following Tuesday morning here in Natchez."

*So, she never really left town, at least not for good as everyone had predicted*, Josh thought sadly.

"She had family here?" was all he could bring himself to say.

Marie didn't respond.

Josh imagined her eyes were fixed on a simple marker in a cemetery not far away. He knew exactly how the horrid image felt as it wormed its way through the soul. He vividly recalled Dianne Lane's marker from the cemetery in San Mateo.

"Marie?" he gently prodded.

"Yes," she said softly.

"Did Pamela leave any family . . . other than a loving 'sister'?" He squeezed her hand.

Her eyes thanked him for his insight.

"No. Her mama died of cancer while Pamela was away at college at Ole Miss in 1979. Pamela had no one else."

"Her dad?"

"She never knew her father. Her mother spoke of him only once, when Pamela pressed the issue at thirteen, I believe it was. Her mama said simply that they had been together only once, and had never seen each other after that day. I can tell you this, Josh, it troubled Pamela deeply to be fatherless in a school where almost all the kids at that time came from 'proper' families. Perhaps," Marie smiled for the first time in minutes, "that's the reason she and I got along so well: we were both misfits, bastards in our own ways."


As they stood together on the front porch of the mansion, Josh found it difficult to think of anything to say. He'd gotten the answers he'd secretly wanted, but none of the answers his mind needed, nothing that would keep Lefler off his back or satisfy the FBI if they, too, wanted solid information about Dianne Lane's death. Still, he was grateful for Marie's confidence and openness. Best friends, especially those like Pamela Morrow, come along so infrequently that when one is lost, it leaves a void that never completely fills.

He took both of her hands in his and looked into her eyes. They looked much different now that he knew her better, or perhaps he simply saw deeper into them. "Thank you, Marie."

"You did love Dianne Lane, didn't you?"

Josh's eyes said he did.

"I didn't help much, did I?" Her concern sounded sincere.

"You did all you could. I don't know if anyone can help at this point. It's okay, really."

"You're in some kind of trouble, aren't you, Josh?"

He felt her hands grip his. "It's nothing for you to be worried about."

"Is it about her death? Are the police trying to blame you in some way?" she asked, her face turned up to his, the cold that had tried to steal its way inside her earlier now finding an opening. "Why not just tell them how you felt about her?"

"It wouldn't help. I'm afraid it might even make things worse. Most people can't understand feelings like that. They'd just label it some kind of weird obsession."

"Do you think Dianne Lane shared your feelings?"

Josh took a slow breath, considering the question; he'd wondered the same thing. "I know she felt *something* for me. I think I frightened her away before we had a chance. Now, I'll never know."

"Why not just let it go then?"

"I can't."

"Because of the authorities?"

"At first it was that. I admit it. It sounds cowardly, but I was afraid of losing my job and going to jail."

"Not cowardly, just normal," she said.

"Thanks," he nodded.

"And now?" she said.

"I'm not sure why I can't just let it go. Maybe I can't bear the thought of someone having taken her life and gotten away with it."

"What if she did kill herself?"

"Dianne seemed so much like the Pamela you described. I know she was a fighter. I just can't see Dianne taking her own life."

"I wish I could help you more."

"It's okay, I promise. You've done all you can. You've been more than generous. I've got to be going now." He raised a hand and touched her cheek, then turned to leave.

"Josh," she called to him.

He turned back at the edge of the porch and she came over to him. "Take this. It has all of my numbers on it, including my cell phone and my pager." She handed him a business card. "If there is ever anything I can do to help, call me. I mean it."

"Thanks, I know you do."

As he descended the steps, Marie couldn't help wondering just how much Josh really knew.


When Josh had pulled from the curb and was halfway down Canal Street, the black pickup fell in behind.

"Get the bitch's license number, Brian," Kisber ordered when they passed Marie Edwards's silver BMW, the only vehicle remaining in the mansion's circular brick drive with Henry's truck having pulled away fifteen minutes earlier.

"You think Jack will want us to do her as well?" Mills asked, relishing the thought.

"I'd like to do her," Kisber said with a twisted smile as he studied the lovely woman standing between a pair of massive white columns.

"Reckon that's who Mitchell came here to see?"

Kisber nodded. "I'd bet on it."

He gave the powerful truck a bit more gas when the Grand Prix made a turn at the end of the street and disappeared from view.

He didn't want to lose it now.

## 10

One stop remained before Josh could begin the long drive to the state capital and his plane ride back to San Francisco. He pulled into the space nearest the entrance of the main branch of the Natchez Public Library and walked toward the front door. By noon, much of the early-morning chill had been chased away by a fat, yellow sun hanging like a teasing promise of summer above a clear southern sky. He'd practically lived in libraries in college and knew exactly where to go once inside.

The librarian on duty greeted him with a pleasant "Yes, sir," in a soft voice. The counter placard identified her as Cindy Crane.

"Hi, Cindy," he said. The woman had chestnut-brown hair and glasses that seemed perfect for her face, though her light complexion spoke volumes of too many days behind a desk in a dark library, and not enough outdoors enjoying a world beyond her books.

"Hello," she smiled.

"I need to use the microfilm reader for a few minutes, if I could." He placed his palms on the wooden counter and returned the smile.

"Follow me, please," she said. The woman walked around the long counter and headed for a small room on the west end of the building. When she and Josh stood before a pair of film readers and a tall file cabinet against one wall, she said, "You have a specific publication in mind?"

"What was the name of your local paper in 1989?"

"Same as now, the *Natchez Democrat.*"

"Great. I'd like to see the reel covering November 18th of that year."

The librarian opened the third drawer of the cabinet and studied the collection of identical white cardboard boxes inside, each measuring four inches on a side by one inch thick. She chose one. "This reel covers July 1st through December 31st of 1989. Are you familiar with this type of reader?"

Josh made a quick inspection of the nearly matching cream-colored cabinets with their blackened glass screens. They hadn't changed a bit since school, probably not since he'd been born, he guessed. "Just like I used in college," he assured her.

She handed him the box containing the microfilm. "Will you be needing to print anything?"

"Perhaps. I'm not sure yet." Josh took the box and opened it. He withdrew the single reel of film and set the empty box on top of the file cabinet.

"Use the machine on the left in that case," Cindy said, pulling its chair back. "It's also a printer. Just center whatever you want between the lines on the screen—you'll see them when the lamp is on—and press the Print button here." She indicated a big red button beneath the view screen. "Your prints will come out of the slot here in a few seconds. Copies are twenty-five cents apiece."

"I'll show you everything I print," he said, crossing his heart.

The woman gave a broad grin and returned to her desk.

Josh took his seat and loaded the film on the left reel, threading it carefully over the lamp and onto the take-up reel on the right. When the advance knob was given a turn, the reel whirred busily, flashing across the screen a series of unintelligible newspaper images from a decade ago. He slowed the reel four times to check his progress and then stopped within a few days of the date he wanted on the fifth try. It took only another minute to locate the cover story of Pamela Morrow's death by a hit-and-run driver that had not been found as of the article's publication. He remembered Marie Edwards telling him that the man had never been found.

A primal resentment stirred within him, though he knew it had no legitimate outlet. Such criminals had to be left to the universe for their just punishment. It was wrong, but he also knew it was fact.

He aligned the first article for printing, though the entire story wouldn't fit on a single sheet of paper.

"Damn," he chuckled, "that means another quarter."

When he'd read and printed the entire cover story in the *Democrat*, which had been continued on page A3, he turned to the Monday edition, hoping to find anything else that might be of help. The original story, which had been written in the early morning hours of Sunday, November 19, 1989, had been filled with glowing prose eulogizing one of Natchez's brightest youth, extinguished well before her time, but had offered little of substance about the accident investigation or Pamela's career and life since she'd moved to Jackson. The only two photographs in the article were Pamela with one of her Homecoming courts from high school and her 1977 graduation.

A familiar name jumped from the first column of Monday's article.

Josh had to read the words again and then a third time to make certain his subconscious hadn't invented them. Like Dianne Lane, Pamela Morrow had been an art historian, and just like her successor, she'd been employed by Lloyd Richmond at the time of her death.

"Hot damn!" Josh yelped, clenching his right fist. He realized his voice had carried past the room. He was relieved to find that Cindy Crane had not come to check on him at once.

A solid link at last! he thought, his pulse increasing.

He printed the full article, stacking the three sheets of paper on top of the four that held Sunday's story.

The second article contained two photos of Pamela Morrow, one taken only weeks before her death, at the University of Mississippi, when she'd been honored for her work with the Art Department there, and the other with her employer and a second man. It was Josh's first look at the woman who had become such a prominent influence in his life. She was stunning, as beautiful as Marie Edwards and Betty Jean Price had led him to believe she'd been. He pulled the *Examiner* photo of Dianne Lane from his pocket and laid it alongside the print from the microfilm reader. Clearly two of the most attractive women he'd ever seen, ever imagined, and yet very different.

As he found himself drawn first to one, then to the other, he couldn't help noticing the similarity in the women's eyes—warm and inviting—though in the black-and-white photos he had no way of knowing whether Dianne's and Pamela's were the same color. It didn't matter, he decided, and went to put the *Examiner* photo back in his pocket. Something kept it before him.

His emotions tried to make a connection but his mind refused to acknowledge it. He yielded to logic; he'd been a victim of his run-away emotions and imagination for days and was drained from it.

Still, if he hadn't trusted Marie completely, he'd have sworn that the two women . . .

"You're going nuts, Josh," he whispered with a twisted grin, then shook his head as if to clear it of the improbable thought.

When his eyes continued to dance between the photos, he finally settled on Dianne Lane's badly wrinkled photo, closed his eyes, and his mind readily returned to his room at the Sandpiper Inn in Carmel . . .


. . . It's late Monday, past midnight, and I'm lying in my bed, try-ing to sleep but unable to get the woman I left two hours before off my mind. Despite my best efforts at dinner, she declined my invi-tation to join me in Carmel, but happily, I didn't leave the restau-rant empty-handed. I have her address in my wallet, and she has agreed to see me again next week.

Though I am as excited as I can remember, I am also exhausted from the flight and the long drive. I must try to get some sleep; clients hate it when I yawn while trying to coax six million bucks from their company treasury. I turn onto my right side, facing the large windows that look out onto the Pacific Ocean, and stuff both pillows beneath my head. The windows are cracked several inches and a breeze floats through the room, carrying the hypnotic melody of the surf in its gentle embrace. In a few minutes, my eyes are too heavy to keep open any longer and I feel myself slipping into that familiar world of peaceful stillness.

I know I will dream about Pamela.

Then I hear her calling my name. "Joshua . . . Joshua," she says in that voice I can never forget.

I roll onto my back, toward the door and the origin of the sound, and see the silhouette of a figure standing above my bed. My heart pounds loud enough to be heard by the shadowy visitor, I am sure.

"Joshua," she repeats, and I know it is her.

"Pamela?" I say hesitantly, certain I am imagining it all and afraid that my own voice will banish this vision to that confine where dreams perish.

I reach for the switch that will turn on the bed lamp but she stops me by placing her hand gently on mine, keeping the room illuminated only by the faint glow rising from the lights below my windows.

"You want to make love to me, don't you?" she asks.

My eyes have begun to adjust and I can see her more clearly now, still wearing the black suit she wore at dinner. In the ghostly half-light that slips through the thin veil of curtains, she is unbelievably gorgeous, a dream stolen from the emptiness of night.

"I do" is all that I can say.

"I want you too, Joshua. Spending the day with you, getting to know you as I have, only made it that much more difficult for me to say no to you in Sausalito."

"But you're here now. . . ."

She says in a whisper, "Yes. Now is all we have, but it's all that matters, isn't it."

"Yes," I say, afraid I will awaken at any moment.

I can see her smiling down at me as she slowly begins to undress

•••

"Having any difficulty finding everything you wanted?" the librarian asked efficiently. Cindy had finally gotten up the nerve to check on the man who had filled the library with exuberant profanity a few minutes before.

Josh looked at the woman with his eyes, but his mind stubbornly refused to leave his room in Carmel. He knew the unfinished dream would vanish again as soon as he came back to the present, but he was unable to keep it alive by willpower alone.

Then, it was gone.

"I apologize for my outburst earlier," he said but offered no explanation for it.

"Apology accepted. I assumed you found something important in your research," she said supportively.

Josh was more embarrassed now that she'd confirmed that his faux pas had been heard at the front of the building. "Thanks for your help, Cindy. I found what I needed." He counted the copies he'd made. "It appears I owe you a dollar seventy-five." He handed her two ones pulled from his front jeans pocket.

"I'll get your change," she said.

"No, that's okay. My mom always charged me a quarter whenever she heard me cussin' so I figure I got no change coming."

"Fair enough," Cindy said. She gave him a broad smile and left the room.

Josh took a last look at Pamela Morrow's image on the microfilm screen, standing between the two men, Lloyd Richmond and the man the article described as his closest associate, Morris Goldman.

He turned the knob fully to the left and rewound the reel.

In a minute, he was in his car, driving north on the road that would lead him to State Highway 28.

## 11

Thirty-five minutes after he'd left the library, Josh turned his rented Pontiac onto the narrow two-lane road that led east to Interstate 55. He was only an hour from Jackson. No longer comfortable with the silence that filled the car's interior, and his head, he poked at the buttons on the radio until he'd located the Scan control. He stopped the automatic searching when he found a station that was free of static, not really caring what kind of music it played, so long as it was loud, upbeat, and wasn't heavy-metal.

It had been five minutes since he'd passed another vehicle, and, with his mind on the radio for much of that time, was startled to find the Pontiac's rear window virtually filled with the gleaming chrome grill and huge electric winch of a black Ford pickup.

The truck gave no indication it wanted to pass, though there was certainly adequate room at the moment, yet it remained dangerously close to the Grand Prix's bumper. Josh checked his speedometer: at an even sixty, he was already five over the speed limit. He wasn't exactly poking along holding up traffic, but decided to give the accelerator a boost for good measure. The needle passed seventy. The vehicles remained as close as cars of a train.

"What the hell's his problem?" Josh mumbled, adding another five miles per hour.

The first bump occurred even as Josh was trying to add distance between the two vehicles.

"You crazy bastard!" Josh shouted, unable to decide whether to bury the gas or the brakes. He opted for power.

The second collision was far more violent, with the truck having had fifty feet more distance in which to gain momentum after the last impact. The Pontiac's rear end fishtailed when struck this time, but was brought under control by Josh before the tires had found the loose shoulder. "You bastard!" he shouted angrily again. He looked for a side street or a Y in the road, but none presented itself. There wasn't even a driveway down which he could make a quick evasive turn.

The third bump was the most damaging, noticeably deforming the trunk lid of the Pontiac as the winch punched its way into the car like a hammer striking a pie pan. He heard the sound of shattering plastic being swept beneath the howling tires of the truck. "Get the hell off me, you son of a bitch!" Josh screamed as the chase reached 100 mph, but then an idea came to him. In a move that would have made a Nascar driver proud, Josh yanked the rental car into the oncoming lane of traffic and buried the antilock brakes, propelling the black truck instantly past him as its driver tried to wrestle the behemoth to a stop without the benefit of the Pontiac's computer technology. Massive plumes of black smoke billowed from its four tires as the iner-tia of the truck was slowly, clumsily, brought under control.

A hundred yards now separated the two vehicles, and the truck was still shuddering to a stop.

Josh whipped the wheel one hundred eighty degrees and nailed the gas, using both lanes and part of the shoulder to effect his turn. He bolted west as fast as the car would take him, adding needed dis-tance between himself and the truck.

"Those crazy bastards!" he shouted, repeatedly hammering the side of his fist into the passenger's seat back. In his mirror, Josh could now see that the truck had also made the turn and was in pursuit. "What the hell do you want from me?!" he screamed at its reflection, the adrenaline flowing through him like an icy river, tensing his muscles to the point of pain.

He frantically looked for options, anything that might give him more of a chance than a duel on this narrow strip of asphalt. He knew he couldn't win in a clash of vehicles, for the truck was at least a thousand pounds heavier than his rental and had been built for off-road punishment. He checked the mirror: The truck had gained back half the distance it had lost. "What the hell's that thing got in it?" he yelled, pressing the accelerator harder, though it had no room left to move.

When he passed a hundred again, he found himself on the stretch of road littered with the fragments of the rear bumper, taillights, and rear trim panels of the Grand Prix. Without coming to a near-dead stop, there was no way to avoid them; hopefully none of the debris would shred a tire. At his speed, the shards of plastic slammed against the car's undercarriage like a series of hammer blows, but to his amazement, and immense satisfaction, all four tires remained intact.

"Yes!" he celebrated, then returned his attention to the rear.

The truck was closing at a phenomenal speed, its two occupants now clearly visible. Josh's fear mounted immeasurably when he saw the passenger brandishing a handgun like a veteran proudly waving a flag on the Fourth. He couldn't imagine what he'd done to warrant such insane behavior, and tried to remember encountering the truck after he'd left the library. Perhaps, he thought, he'd accidentally cut the two men off in traffic somewhere along the way or had unknowingly forced them onto the shoulder while he was screwing with the damned radio. Maybe they were drunk or drug-crazed, but they drove too well for such simplistic explanations.

"What the hell do you want with me?!!" he repeated at the top of his lungs.

He braced himself for the inevitable impact, knowing that he had to take the collision squarely. Another attempt at an evasive maneuver would spell death as the driver—prepared for such a possibility now—slammed into the Pontiac, crushing it like a child's toy.

He had to keep his speed, all the car would give.

Josh looked for another car, for *anyone* to appear and intercede on his behalf. He couldn't believe the road was so deserted, but then, as a form materialized within half-seen images, maybe that's what the men had had in mind all morning. "The school parking lot," he mumbled, putting words to the image that had begun to surface. He could clearly see the truck in his memory now, and the two men who had appeared to be waiting for someone. "Me?" he questioned aloud. "What the hell could they want with me? The bastards have been following me all day. Why?"

*They can't be with the police*, he reasoned. *The police don't act this way. Then who the hell are they?* he wondered, more frightened for the lack of a logical answer.

He'd grown up in an area where true rednecks still existed, though thankfully in ever-diminishing numbers, and he knew that members of their narrow-minded, easily angered sect knew few limitations when it came to expressing violence.

Whatever he'd done to anger them, it didn't matter at this point. Only staying alive mattered.

The fourth impact was so violent that Josh saw the left rear quarter panel buckle in his side mirror and the back left door spring ajar. When the rear deck spoiler was slammed through the rear window, the glass shattered into a million razor-edged crystals, many of them propelled like miniature missiles toward the dash and front windshield. Several struck Josh painfully, one slicing the back of his right ear and two others leaving a pair of tiny gashes in his scalp. Before he had time to curse or wince from the hot sparks of pain, he discovered to his horror that the car's right rear wheel had gotten fully onto the shoulder. When he instinctively tapped the brakes to begin the necessary correction—the car's front end pointing toward the center line—his eyes met a sight that locked his breathing. The truck, which was now alongside the Grand Prix, slammed into its left front corner, ripping off the front bumper and disabling the airbag sensor mounted there. The car spiraled into the cotton field north of the highway in a dizzying flat spin.

The noise was deafening; the spinning, bouncing, jarring, jolting images that flooded his vision made less sense than those which filled the tube of a kaleidoscope.

The left tires suddenly bit into a deep plow rut and the Pontiac rolled onto its left side, then its roof, right side, wheels again, the left, roof, and right sides a second time before ending upright. Within the maelstrom, Josh's head was bounced against the headliner and door pillar, finally striking the side glass and shattering it, dimming the lights that burned behind dazed and frightened eyes. The narrow, evenly spaced ruts of last year's cotton crop jarred what was left of the car that danced across them at forty miles an hour buffeting its contents as if it were in a giant paint shaker. He fought to retain consciousness as a warm river flowed into his left eye and across his lips.

Then violently, but mercifully, everything came to a stop: the flipping, the spinning, the shaking, even the hodgepodge of unfamiliar noises. As dust from the arid field choked the interior of the car, like a morning fog drifting in through the doors that had been twisted and the windows that had been blown out, Josh began slipping toward the beckoning darkness.

He turned his head in the direction he felt the highway lay, the frightening awareness that they would be coming to finish the job.

His left eye, filling with blood, was unable to distinguish anything but meaningless shapes; the last blurry image his right eye beheld was the sight of two men sprinting toward the stricken Pontiac from the black truck stopped at the edge of the cotton field, its doors open and outspread like the wings of a vulture.

Mills arrived at the car first, but had to wait several seconds for the dust to settle enough for him to see clearly inside. His prey certainly looked dead, his face painted in blood, his head slumped against his chest. Only the shoulder harness prevented Mitchell's lifeless body from falling into the center console.

Kisber arrived. "He dead?" he asked out of breath.

"Gotta be," Mills said, rapping the side of Josh's head with the butt of his pistol. There was no response.

"Check his pulse," Kisber ordered, looking back toward the road. He noticed that a car was approaching, though still several hundred yards away. "Shit!" he snapped. "We've got company!"

"Cops?!" Mills asked excitedly, his attention as well now on the sedan that was traveling at high speed from the west.

"No, civilian," Kisber said with certainty, relieved, though he would have readily shot it out with the authorities before being taken prisoner. "His pulse!" he repeated.

Mills put his fingers against Josh's neck and waited for an indication that the man's heart no longer beat within the battered body. "Shit!" he yelled to Kisber, "he's still alive!"

"Put a bullet in his brain—now!" the senior man ordered.

"What about them?" Mills said, pointing a finger at the bright red sedan which had slowed because of the activity in the dry field north of the highway. Neither man could tell anything about the car's occupants.

"Fuck 'em," Kisber barked. "I'll deal with those bastards while you finish Mitchell." He raised his weapon threateningly toward the sedan which had now stopped a dozen yards west of the truck, though realizing he couldn't hit anything at that distance. He hoped it would, however, rid them of the unexpected and unwanted "do-gooders" that had stopped to volunteer roadside assistance.

At the same time, Mills put the barrel of his gun against Josh's temple.

The two shots that rang out echoed off the trees in the distance.

Mills was immediately thrown to the ground, the side of his head missing.

Kisber couldn't understand the intense burning in his chest and looked toward the origin of the pain. Though he put his hand against the spot where blood had quickly begun to soak the material, the hot, crimson liquid continued to gush from the unseen hole in his left lung, oozing between his fingers.

In a pathetic attempt at self-defense, he again raised his pistol in the direction of the sedan. A third and fourth shot from the pair of deer rifles exploded in unison, shattering the early-afternoon air and leaving his corpse sprawled across the hood of the Pontiac.

"Joshua," the woman's voice repeated softly.

"Pamela?" Josh said.

"Who?" the woman asked.

Josh opened his eyes. He was surprised to find both of them work-ing properly, then even more surprised to discover that he was appar-ently still among the living. He was lying on his back on a firm, but pliable, surface of some type, an anvil-hard sun overhead. The nearly white, cloudless sky caused him to squint his eyes shut as soon as he'd opened them. Then a silhouette blocked out the source of the light, bringing welcome relief.

It was the woman who'd called his name. "You're going to be okay, Joshua," she said.

He tried to focus on her but she was a featureless silhouette. He tried to roll his head to the side but found it restrained by a neck col-lar. All around him was a flurry of activity: men in suits talking with men in coveralls; men in uniforms talking with men in jeans; every-one talking with everyone else at the same time—it made him dizzy, adding to the nausea already unsettling his stomach. "Where am I?" he asked of the woman who hung above him. When he tried to move his head, it would not respond.

"We've just removed you from your car, Joshua. You were in a ter-rible accident. You're okay, we're—"

"Is my neck broken?" he interrupted, his heart accelerating when he realized a cervical collar enclosed his neck, pressing against his jaw. The feeling was claustrophobic, frightening.

"You're doing fine," she answered reassuringly, touching his arm. "You were moving your arms and legs quite a bit while we were extracting you, so I'd say the likelihood is slim that you've sustained any permanent injury. The doctors in Jackson will be able to tell you a great deal more after they've completed their examination, but I'd say you were just beat up pretty badly. You're also one of the luckiest people I've ever seen."

"Mr. Mitchell?" a man said.

Josh turned his eyes toward the new voice. He didn't speak as the man knelt beside the gurney.

"Mr. Mitchell, do you have any idea why those two men would have been trying to kill you?" The voice belonged to a man in some type of uniform, though Josh couldn't make out his features well either.

"No," he said honestly.

*Why?* he questioned, though he knew it must have something to do with Dianne Lane or Pamela Morrow—or both.

"Where are they?" Josh asked.

"Both are dead," the man in uniform said coldly.

It seemed impossible. "The last thing I remember, they were alongside me at a hundred miles an hour. Did they wreck as well?"

The man grinned. "No, Mr. Mitchell. They didn't know it was open season on worthless sons of bitches." A number of the men who had been standing around began laughing robustly.

Unable to see even a portion of the activity around him, Josh felt claustrophobic again. "Can I please sit up?" he asked, turning his eyes back to the woman.

"I wouldn't recommend trying it, Joshua, not yet. We're not sure if anything is broken, and we won't know until we get you to a hospital and take some X rays."

Josh did a quick analysis of his body, wiggling his toes and moving his fingers. He seemed intact. Screw it: he still felt intensely claustrophobic and wanted up—now!

He touched her arm. "I promise I won't hold you liable," he smiled, then tightened his stomach muscles and rose quickly to a seated position, startling her.

"Mr. Mitchell, I really must insist—"

His head tried to explode; the left side felt like someone had taken a ball peen hammer to it. As his socks touched the soil of the cotton field, he put his left hand to a spot where his brains felt like they were pouring out. He found a large soft bandage covering the area.

"Please lie down, Joshua," she insisted.

His expression said she was wasting her breath.

"Fine. You don't have any idea how sore you're going to be tomorrow. Much worse on Sunday." She touched the hand that was still pressed against the square bandage. "You'll need stitches there, I'm afraid. Nice little gash, probably from the side window. I've stopped the bleeding for the moment, but it's only a temporary fix until we get you to the hospital in Jackson. Your right ear is going to be sore for a few days, but I don't believe that cut or the three or four in your scalp will need suturing."

Josh appreciated her concern and he was grateful she'd been the one to administer to him. "Thanks for taking such good care of me," he said.

"You're still going to the hospital," the woman assured him.

"No argument," he said. Then he spotted the sheet that had been draped over a bloody shape on the hood of the Grand Prix and a second one, covering the corpse on the ground by the left rear door—awaiting crime-scene photographs. The sight loaned a sense of hard reality to the situation that had not been present before then, despite all that had occurred. He couldn't help thinking about the last person he'd seen lying beneath a similar sheet.

He grew lightheaded and felt he might vomit when he noticed the fragments of bone and hair splattered across the side of the car.

"Mr. Mitchell?" the man in uniform said, snatching him from the realm of death and horror.

Josh turned to him. The man was with the Mississippi Highway Patrol, his sunburned face and distinctive uniform clearly visible now that Josh no longer had the sun in his eyes. The patrolman stood. He was squarely built, in his mid-twenties. He repeated his question. "I find it hard to believe that you have no idea why these two men wanted you dead?"

The dozen or so other men at the scene stopped talking and turned their attention to the stranger on the gurney. Josh was amazed at how many people now cluttered this field since his last memory of it. Closest to the front of the Grand Prix he saw two men with long deer rifles with telescopic sights. With their camouflage overalls, they looked like hunters who had stumbled out of the woods and into this surreal scene. Other than the patrolman, they were the only two with any visible weapon.

A jumble of questions skittered across his mind. He tried the most basic one first. "Who killed them?"

"That'd be us," one of the men with the rifles answered proudly, receiving pats on the back from several other men for his response.

"How? Wait, now I remember something. The last thing I saw, the two men who'd been chasing me were running through the field toward me."

"The little one had his gun stuck in your ear when I dropped him like a sack of corn," the other hunter said. "I was really afraid Charlie wouldn't get his T-Bird stopped in time for Bud and me to get off clear shots."

"Mind you, friend," Bud said defensively, addressing his remarks to Josh, "Derek had a sweet shot already lined up from the back while I had to climb out of the front seat and throw my Browning across the roof. That's why he took the one with his gun on you."

"Yeah, and I got a kill on my first shot," Derek said. "If *your* sumbitch had been a deer, we'd be eating hot dogs tonight instead of venison." The friendly ridicule brought choice comments from several men as Bud tried to explain his precarious shooting position.

Josh looked at the cop and found him to be smiling at the story along with the rest of those gathered. He was no longer sure he hadn't died and mistakenly gone to some kind of hunter's afterlife. He was, however, grateful to the men who'd saved his life.

The coincidence bothered him, his paranoia mounting.

"How did you two happen to come along at this exact time?" Josh asked the men.

The patrolman answered for them. "Didn't just happen along, Mr. Mitchell. Charlie's brother owns the black truck there. His son, Scott, spotted it sitting in the high school parking lot just before it took off after you. Scott called his dad from his car as soon as he and a friend set out after it. They lost it for a while, but picked it up again sitting near the library. Boy's got a good head on his shoulder, even if he is family."

Josh processed what he'd just heard as his head pounded. Though he felt strangely ashamed that he was glad the two assassins were dead— as was everyone at the scene apparently—hunting down car thieves with large-bore hunting rifles seemed a bit extreme to him. He was astounded to find the police condoning such behavior, and the "family" remark had only added to the confusion. "Don't get me wrong, officer, but do you go after all car thieves with such . . . enthusiasm?"

"Do when they kill to get someone's property," a man at Josh's back muttered quietly.

Josh turned toward the man he knew to be Charlie, the driver of the red T-Bird, and could see that the intense anger he was feeling was poorly hidden. He understood that Charlie's brother had somehow died at the hands of the men beneath the sheets, and now they'd paid in full for their sins. How close he'd come to joining Charlie's brother made him shudder.

The EMT noticed his body shivering and wrapped the blanket lying at the foot of the gurney across his shoulders.

"Time to go to the hospital, Joshua," she said. "I need you to lie back."

As the events of the last hour began to take hold in his consciousness, Josh felt too shaky to argue with her. With her supporting his head and neck, he resumed his prone position. "Will you get my bags out of the trunk?" he asked her. "Also, I had a number of pieces of paper lying on the passenger seat. Would you see if you could find those as well?"

"You mean these?" the patrolman asked, taking the material Josh had printed off the microfilm reader from one of the men in a suit and holding it in front of Josh's face.

Josh realized there would be a lot of questions in Jackson, though he still didn't know how to answer most of them. He nodded.

The officer knelt beside him again. "Mr. Mitchell, I don't know why these two worthless pieces of shit wanted you dead, but you came within a gnat's ass of obliging them. They're not going to bother you again, but I'm not so sure about whoever sent them. I think the least you owe us is the truth, don't you, sir?"

*The truth! What the hell is the truth?* he mocked. After a decade of lies, he didn't know if he could still recognize it.

"I'll tell you anything I can," he said.

The EMT and her male counterpart, joined by two of the men from the crowd, lifted the gurney and walked slowly toward the waiting ambulance at the edge of the field.

Josh lifted his head and made eye contact with the two hunters, who were standing on either side of their friend Charlie. "Thank you," he mouthed.

Derek nodded and Bud winked before spitting tobacco juice at the feet of the corpse on the ground, but the man who'd lost a brother for a reason none of them understood only stared silently back, his eyes glistening with a sadness no retribution could quell.


Dr. Wilkerson carefully studied the last of the series of X-rays his technician had taken of the lucky young man from New York City and found his newest patient to be in surprisingly good shape—considering. He attributed much of the good fortune to Josh's remarkable physical condition, the rest to his shoulder harness and seat belt.

Except for the persistent headache from the minor concussion he'd gotten from the door pillar, a tender spot from the six stitches required to close the laceration to his scalp at the hairline, and more bruises than he'd sustained in a full season of football, Josh felt surprisingly good. The Darvocet the nurse had given him when he'd first arrived had begun to work, numbing the cluster of aches and pains.

Tomorrow will be another story, he was assured for the second time. He stuffed the remaining five pills in the amber vial in his pocket.

Two uniformed patrolmen were waiting in the outer office when Wilkerson pronounced his patient fit for questioning, and the men escorted Josh in silence to the Criminal Justice complex on Pascagoula Street.


For the next two hours, until well past six P.M., Josh tried to provide an explanation for the bizarre happenings on Highway 28. He examined photos that had been taken of the men, neither of whom had been identified yet, but was unable to remember seeing either of them before spotting them in the stolen truck in the high school parking lot. In every instance, he leveled with Detective Carl Brownell, the man assigned to the case, as best he dared, telling him everything he knew for certain up to the moment his rental car had been bumped by the men the last time.

Just as with Lefler, he left out the part where he'd seen Dianne Lane after their flight had landed in San Francisco. Nothing had changed—such an admission still couldn't improve his position.

In the midst of questioning, another detective came into Brownell's office with a series of faxes he'd just received, from New York and the FBI. From their hushed conversation, Josh knew the information must be about him.

Brownell took the several sheets of paper. "I'll be with you in a minute, Mr. Mitchell." The detective then dropped into his chair and began to read the material. When he'd finished he put the report in a manila envelope which bore Josh's name.

The sight of his name on a second folder in a second police station in two days was unnerving.

His inner voice would not be silenced: *Wonderful, Josh, since you've been poking your fool head into this mess, your life has gone from great to shitty. You've never been in trouble in your life and now you have police files in Mississippi and California, and you haven't even started talking with the FBI!*

His headache tormented him.

To get his mind off the file folder, Josh tried to remember when the last flight to San Francisco left Jackson Airport. He wasn't eager to see the FBI, but knew the sooner he got it over with, the sooner he could begin to regain some stability in his crumbling life, perhaps even learn from them who the men were that had tried to kill him.

The flight schedule he had checked yesterday eluded him.

Brownell leaned across the desk. "From what I read here, it appears you've never been in trouble of any kind before. I can't even find a parking ticket unpaid. That means you're either real honest or real smart." He glared at the man seated across from his desk with obvious displeasure. "So which is it?"

"I've done nothing wrong."

"I've never known a criminal yet who had."

Josh locked his jaw to prevent a retort he would regret. He didn't care at all for the man's insinuations. His gut had been right: innocent meant nothing.

"I also see you've got a Top Secret clearance."

"Had," Josh corrected, taking a deep breath and exhaling slowly through his nostrils to restore calm.

"Okay, had. What's that all about, Mitchell?"

"I used to develop computer programs for the government," Josh said.

"You mean the military, don't you?"

"I really can't say for whom, detective. You understand I hope."

"What I understand, Mitchell, is that I've got three men dead within twenty-four hours of your happy ass arriving in my town—one of them the first cousin of a state trooper—and it all seems to center around you . . . and a woman who's been dead more than eight years. I've listened to you propose a lot of far-fetched theories this afternoon, but I've heard damned little fact." He stood, moving to the side of his desk. "I want to know why two hit men from Biloxi, neither of whom you'd met before in your life—supposedly—wanted you dead?"

"For the tenth time, detective, I don't have the slightest idea." Josh hated police stations, and vowed to never enter another one once this horror was over.

*Will it ever be over?* he wondered. *It's no longer just the loss of your job or even prison—now someone wants you dead. But who?* his mind tormented.

"Well, you'd better come up with something more substantial than that, or we're gonna be here all night. You got me?"

Josh had heard enough. "I'm not the criminal here, detective! You continue to lose sight of that one important fact. I'm the poor bastard these two cretins tried to kill, not the other way around. I'm the victim, remember, or doesn't that matter to cops anymore?"

Brownell took a step toward Josh when his door opened.

"Got a minute, Carl?" the detective who'd delivered the faxes earlier asked as he stuck his head in the office. Brownell gave Josh a hard look and followed the other man into the outer room, closing the door as he went.

When he returned five minutes later, Brownell was accompanied by two men Josh had not remembered seeing as he was escorted to the detective's office. The three of them crossed the small room and stood immediately before Josh, who felt compelled to stand despite the soreness which had begun to wrack his body just as the EMT and Dr. Wilkerson had warned. He made eye contact with each, awaiting the inevitable explanation for their presence.

It was Brownell who spoke first. "These two gentlemen are with the FBI, Mr. Mitchell. They've come to take you to San Francisco." He leaned toward Josh, jabbing a finger painfully into his chest as he spoke. "When they're through with you, you and I are gonna finish our little conversation. You can bet on it."

The agents allowed the detective to say his piece before the one on Josh's right spoke. "Good evening, Mr. Mitchell. I'm Agent Larson and this is Agent Sims. We're with the Bureau's office here in Jackson. How are you feeling after the events of this afternoon?"

"Sore, but I think I'll live," Josh said, suspicious of the man's concern.

"Good, I'm glad to hear it. Special Agent Hetzler of the San Francisco office has instructed us to deliver you to his location for questioning on the next available commercial flight. Are you feeling well enough to leave now, sir?" As opposed to Brownell's gruff demeanor, Josh found the agent's manner unnaturally pleasant, disconcerting.

With little choice but to oblige, Josh nodded and held out his hands to accept the handcuffs.

"Will that be necessary, Mr. Mitchell?" Sims asked.

"No," Josh mumbled. "I just assumed . . ."

He didn't finish his thought, but let his arms drop back to his sides. Within the hour, the three men were on board a jet bound for the West Coast.

Once in the air, Josh turned his eyes, and his mind, to the south, toward a blood-soaked cotton field a few miles east of the Mississippi River.

He wondered who in hell had sent the pair of assassins to take his life.

And, more importantly—why?

# 12

*In the consciousness of the truth he has perceived,*
*man now sees everywhere only the awfulness*
*or the absurdity of existence . . .*
*and loathing seizes him.*

—Friedrich Nietzsche (1844-1900)

At eleven-fifteen Thursday night, Josh and his escorts arrived at Karl Hetzler's office on the thirteenth floor of FBI Headquarters on Golden Gate Boulevard in San Francisco. For most of the second leg of the flight, after their departure from Dallas at eight-twenty Central Time, Josh had slept soundly, the result of having taken a second Darvocet to silence the shards of pain that had begun pricking every muscle and joint in his body. Though not fully rested, the three hours of sleep he'd stolen had helped, despite awakening once in silent agony, over Santa Fe, New Mexico, when his head slumped to the side and he'd banged the recently sutured scalp wound squarely against the plane's port bulkhead. The familiar sight from the air reminded him how close to his final destination he was.

To their credit, when he'd banged his head, Larson and Sims had appeared sympathetic. Sims—in the aisle seat—even offered to get Josh a pillow, which he had gratefully accepted.

The elevator door opened with an efficient mechanical hiss, revealing a large cherry reception desk in the midst of an expansive foyer that probably measured twenty-five by sixty, with the long dimension paralleling the front edge of the desk. A wide floor-to-ceiling window—at each end of, and perpendicular to, the wall which housed the twin elevators—afforded a majestic view of the Bay Area skyline. Four cherry-stained solid-wood doors, two directly behind the receptionist and one to each side of the desk, remained tightly closed and were secured by reinforced locks with case-hardened card access slots. Small digital cameras in decorative, but also reinforced, housings announced the presence of anyone who wished to enter one of the portals.

To Josh's surprise, the desk was manned at a time when most private corporations would have been closed for five hours, his included. The receptionist, an attractive black woman in a crisply pressed charcoal suit with an open collar, announced their arrival in her soft, intentionally neutral voice that still betrayed a hint of New England upbringing to a discerning ear. A small clear tube originated from behind her right ear and terminated in a brushed-steel tip at the corner of her mouth. Josh recognized it as being similar to the telephone headsets used by the receptionists who manned the floors at Barnett Air.

Agents Larson and Sims presented their credentials to the receptionist who studied them carefully, having seen enough authentic badges to spot a fake, no matter how adroitly counterfeited, more quickly than a machine. She swiped each I.D. badge through a card reader, then asked the men to stand on the mark on the floor at the left end of the desk while she captured a head shot with a camera dedicated to that purpose. The digital image was instantly entered into the server's main database, where a comparison (similar to fingerprint analysis but much quicker, as the logical match to the image was already known) was made and the proper level of access granted.

It seemed overkill to Josh, a bit too much like a James Bond movie, but he readily admitted to himself that he didn't begin to appreciate the frightening variety of resourceful foes, both organized and solo, facing the Bureau in the late Nineties. No one wanted another Oklahoma City, and steps aimed at preventing a repeat tragedy, even those which appeared overly elaborate, had been instituted by security agencies at their facilities throughout the country.

Both men had been approved within forty seconds.

"He's expecting you, gentlemen," the woman stated as she pointed a finger toward the door on the west side of the lobby.

Josh was hand-delivered, as ordered, to the office at the end of the hall bearing the words *Special Agent in Charge: Karl W. Hetzler* on its door. Larson knocked twice gently, waited a few seconds, and then opened the door.

"You're a difficult man to keep up with, Mr. Mitchell," Hetzler announced in a serious tone when the door had shut behind the three weary travelers. He studied Josh for a moment before speaking again. "Please wait outside, gentlemen," he instructed. When Larson's eyes narrowed with concern, Hetzler added with confidence, "I'll be all right."

The agents vanished, leaving Josh alone with a short, pale, balding man who looked less like an FBI agent than any of the numerous cops he'd encountered in the last eight hours.

"Have a seat, Mr. Mitchell," Hetzler said dryly, indicating an expensive blue-leather couch on the east wall. A brass table lamp at one end of the couch provided the only illumination, leaving the spacious office conspicuously dark. "We're going to be here quite a while, I imagine." When Josh had sat down, the agent took one of the matching leather wing-back chairs, the one to Josh's right, and scooted it several feet closer to the couch. In the amber glow of the single lamp, Josh's expression seemed reserved and cautious, but also filled with questions. "I suppose you're wondering why I had you brought here."

"The question had crossed my mind," Josh said, his voice less assured than he'd have liked. "I assumed it has something to do with Dianne Lane's death." He found the couch comfortable enough, but not the surroundings; they gave him the creeps. Given his choice, he would have been at Richard Hightower's home in Loomis, saving what was left of his job. Hopefully, he and this strange little man would finish their business in time for him to still make it to the office when it opened at eight.

*Hopefully,* he revised, reevaluating his circumstances, *I'll actually be allowed to leave when he's through with me!*

After placing a Sony microcassette recorder on the coffee table in front of the couch, its tape already rolling, the little man settled comfortably in his chair. He smiled broadly at Josh. "Such a good start. I like a man who doesn't beat around the bush. It'd be such a waste of your breath and my time and intelligence for you to sit there and pretend you had no idea why you were here. I think we're going to get along nicely."

Josh didn't agree with Hetzler's assessment. He didn't like the man and felt an instinctive distrust he'd rarely experienced. Because of the uneasy feeling, and the innate sense that he was not in safe hands, Josh was uncertain about how much information to offer once the interrogation began in earnest, and decided it would be better if he simply answered the questions put to him, adding nothing. He was reminded of an old rule in business which warned that a man who says too much often gives back a sale that he's already made.

Hetzler seemed put off by the fact that Josh did not respond to his attempt at pleasantry. "Perhaps not," he amended. "Let's begin, shall we?"

Josh took an involuntary breath, and felt himself pressing backward against the cushions. He knew neither motion had been missed by the agent. *Calm down, dickhead, before you have a damned heart attack. If the man knew anything, he'd be telling you—not asking you. Breathe slowly and think before you speak.* "Shouldn't I have an attorney present?" Josh asked.

"Why? You have something to hide, Mr. Mitchell?"

*Hell yes! If I told you that Dianne Lane was in my room, naked in my bed, an hour before she was murdered, you'd throw my ass in jail so fast it'd make me dizzy!*

"Of course not," Josh assured him.

For the first time—the paranoia he'd felt for four days now validated by the bizarre and frightening events that had taken place in Natchez—Josh knew that Dianne Lane had, indeed, been murdered, and that her "suicide letter" had been planted to mislead the cops.

Fachini had been right: it had all been too neat.

"Well, then you've got nothing to fear, do you?" Hetzler said with a smirk twisting his narrow lips.

"It wasn't a question of fear."

"What then?"

"My rights, I suppose."

"And the FBI has no intention of violating those rights, Mr. Mitchell. You're simply here to volunteer what you know about a woman you were likely the last person to see alive."

"Not the last," Josh said defensively.

"No? Who then?" Hetzler seemed intrigued.

"Whoever killed her." Josh's eyes reflected the defiance he felt.

The pale man put an index finger to his lips. "The newspaper called it a suicide, Mr. Mitchell, but apparently you don't agree. What do you know that they don't know?"

*Hetzler, you son of a bitch!* he thought.

"Nothing at all, except I doubt you and the San Francisco Police get this involved in every suicide."

Hetzler lowered his chin, his finger still against his pursed lips. "When did you first meet Dianne Lane?"

*Thank God we're moving on.* "Monday afternoon. Three-forty, give or take a few minutes."

"How can you be so certain of the exact hour?"

"That's when our plane left Kennedy. She took her seat beside mine just before departure."

"*Your* plane?" he asked, raising an eyebrow. "You were traveling together?"

"It's a figure of speech, for God's sake. It was simply the plane on which we, and about three hundred other folks, had been booked." He'd been right, he was not going to like this man.

"And you contend that you'd never seen or spoken with Dianne Lane before that moment on the plane at Kennedy?"

"Why do you guys always rephrase what people say that way? Contend? I don't contend a damned thing. I'm telling you flat out that I'd never laid eyes on her before that moment, and she was not the kind of woman you'd easily forget. If I'd met her before, I'd have remembered it, and I'd have said so." Josh's pulse hammered in his ear.

"Okay, Mr. Mitchell, relax. I'll accept that for the moment. Did you two talk on the flight?"

"Of course. Can you imagine sitting beside someone for six and a half hours without speaking?"

"Yes."

Josh's eyes narrowed.

"But not if that someone was as beautiful as Dianne Lane, I must admit," Hetzler taunted. "You did find her quite beautiful, didn't you?"

"Did you ever have the chance to see her in person?"

"On the news once or twice, if I recall."

"Did you find her beautiful, Agent Hetzler?"

"Not my type, really. But I gather she was yours."

*Where did the Bureau find this guy?* "We spoke during the flight. Yes, I found her attractive. She was a dynamic woman anyone with half a mind would have found stunning. What's your point?" He thought about the Darvocet in his jeans pocket.

He would tough it out.

Hetzler grinned. It was obvious he was enjoying this. "I have no point, Mr. Mitchell. I'm simply trying to get at the truth. That's my job. You have a problem with my wanting the truth?"

Josh's eyes told him to go to hell. "Of course not."

"Tell me what you and Mrs. Lane talked about for six and a half hours."

"Everything. Nothing. We just talked."

"About?"

"About things . . . life, for example."

"And death?"

"You're a bastard, you know it?"

"So I've been told, but I didn't kill her, Mr. Mitchell."

"Neither did I!"

"No one said you did. Do you feel like you're being blamed for her death?"

"I get the feeling you don't believe a single word I'm saying."

"You haven't yet said anything as far as I'm concerned. Would you like to begin saying something? Perhaps then I'll know what to believe and what not to believe. Whatever you think of me, Mr. Mitchell, I'm not one to form opinions without reason."

Hetzler was made of stone, unfeeling, uncaring, virtually unmoving. If not for the bony index finger tapping gently against his thin lips, he would have seemed frozen in his chair.

Josh didn't know what had caused his ill-considered confrontational mood. Perhaps it was the anger he felt toward whoever had directed Dianne Lane's death and had almost choreographed his own. Whatever it was, he realized for his own good, it had better come to an abrupt end. "I'm sure by now you've heard about the two men who tried to kill me in Mississippi."

Hetzler nodded and produced a slip of paper from his jacket pocket. "Ronald Allen Kisber and Brian Edward Mills, both of Biloxi. Kisber, formerly with Army Special Forces, ran a small charter fishing business in the Gulf since 1991. Little is known about Mills at this time. He seems to have been a nobody who never distinguished himself in any way. We'll know more about him in a day or so. We do know that neither man had a criminal record." The agent chose not to read the line at the bottom of his notes about Kisber having been tossed out of the FBI Academy in 1990 for being overly aggressive during mock arrests. He looked up from his paper. "Guess they thought killing would pay better than fishing."

That the lunatics who'd chased him halfway down Highway 28 had no felony records seemed unthinkable to Josh. But perhaps, besides a complete lack of conscience, that was one of the requisites of their employment, or more likely, their past had been deleted, or at least modified. As a programmer, he knew such things were not only possible, but all too easy to accomplish. But of the many clever individuals, corrupt corporations, or covert fingers of the military who had such resources, which one wanted him dead? And why? "Whoever sent those bastards after me may well have been responsible for Dianne Lane's death, too. You can see the logical connection, can't you?"

"I'll concede it's one of many possible explanations."

"I'm sure you have a better one, though," Josh said sarcastically.

"Consider for a moment that Kisber and Mills, or whoever hired them, wanted you dead because you have considerable knowledge of Lane's death instead of none at all. Such a scenario seems far more plausible to me, Mr. Mitchell."

"It doesn't sound plausible . . . it sounds ridiculous. I'm nothing in this equation, I don't know shit!"

"Apparently someone thinks you do, Mr. Mitchell, and it's my bet they'll try to kill you again."

"What about protection?" He knew no one could be truly protected from a determined assassin. What had happened along the highway outside Natchez was a fluke, a piece of celestial good fortune that had certainly used up whatever reserve of luck he'd been holding.

"The only way I can possibly protect you, Mr. Mitchell, is to gain a full understanding of from whom, or what, I'd be protecting you. Are you ready to tell me everything I want to know about the six and a half hours you and Dianne Lane spent together before landing in San Francisco on Monday evening?"

Josh knew that nothing he and Dianne Lane had shared during the flight would be of any help in clearing up this mess. He'd gone over every word of it in his head a dozen times and not the slightest clue to the mystery had presented itself. *Maybe*, he thought, *this guy can do better. It's worth a try at least.*

"Can I get a drink of water?" he asked, his mouth as dry as talcum powder.

For the next three hours, Josh recalled every nuance of the soulful and at times intimate conversation he'd shared with the woman who'd entered his life so abruptly and had altered it so dramatically. He'd surprised even himself with the level of detail he'd been able to recall. Neither the odd little man nor his tape recorder, now into its fourth cassette, had missed a word. Josh knew that the letter he'd written in Carmel had surely been discovered by now, and while there had been nothing said to indicate Dianne Lane had been in his room before her death, he remembered a sentence or two that had alluded to their dinner at Scomas. Reluctantly, but with absolute candor, he'd painted a vivid image of their hour together beside the Bay, with the silver moon suspended just above it.

Not even the part about Dianne Lane having called herself Pamela Morrow all day changed Hetzler's expression. Throughout it all, his poker face remained inviolate.

By two-thirty Friday morning, there was only one thing left to tell—about the time she'd spent in his room—and Josh determined that it was not going to be revealed at this time. He'd made a serious decision, he knew that, the most serious of his life, but the consequences of such an admission would be far more dire, he was sure. Apparently, to his amazement, no proof existed that Dianne Lane had come to his room at the Sandpiper. So be it. The proof that she had come to be with him, to make love to him, was in his heart, and he'd be damned if they were going to have access to that as well.

When Josh reached the point where he'd walked Dianne Lane to her car, parked along the waters of the Bay, and had watched her drive away from the restaurant, he swallowed the last sip of water Larson had brought him. "That's all there is to tell," he said, his voice scratchy.

"And that was the last time you saw her?"

Josh nodded, praying that his eyes didn't betray him.

Hetzler stood for the first time in an hour. He walked to the window in his office, opened the blinds, and looked toward the Pacific. "Interesting story, Mr. Mitchell." With his back still to Josh, he said, "You told Detective Fachini that you didn't see Dianne Lane in Carmel."

"That's right," Josh said as evenly as possible. His heart froze.

"She didn't even so much as phone your room?"

Josh shook his head. "Not once."

"So, why do you think she followed you all the way to within sight of your hotel, a drive of more than two hours, if she hadn't planned to see you again, Mr. Mitchell?" He turned to face Josh.

"I think she did," Josh said, hoping his willing admission to the obvious would alter the agent's direction of thought.

"I beg your pardon?"

"Sure, I'm human enough to hope she was there because she wanted to be with me again, and I'd like to think that she would have, too, if she hadn't been killed first." Every time he spoke of Dianne's death, the denial that she'd been with him, holding him, wanting him, only an hour before she died, felt like long, steely fingernails scraping a blackboard in the back of his mind. "I'll never know now, will I?"

Hetzler returned to the coffee table and picked up the recorder, removed the tape, and scratched the number four on its label with his pen. He set the tape on the table alongside the other three. "I think that'll be all for now, Mr. Mitchell. You're free to go. I'll have one of the agents you came here with take you to a hotel of your choice nearby."

"So, I'm on my own now? Two guys try to kill me a few hours ago, and you're offering me a ride to a hotel."

"If Kisber and Mills were working for someone, we'll find out soon enough. If you know nothing more than you've already told me, you have little if anything to worry about."

"I know exactly as much as I knew at noon, Mr. Hetzler, nothing more and nothing less, and an hour later those two bastards in the truck tried to make a hood ornament out of me. I'd say I have plenty to worry about."

"I see your point," the pale man said, showing no emotion.

"Is dropping me at a hotel your idea of protection?"

"We'll be following all leads thoroughly, I assure you. If there's a conspiracy, we'll uncover it."

"Before or after I'm dead?" Josh said. The question was rhetorical.

Hetzler opened the door. "You have a hotel of preference, or would you like me to recommend one?"

Josh stood with obvious difficulty, his muscles stiff, his body hurting in every cell. He wanted desperately to take another pain pill, two of them, and sleep for a week, but knew he had to be in Sacramento in five hours. Hightower was waiting, and so, too, he hoped, was his job.

He was too tired and too sore to care really, but his ever-analytical brain reminded him that he'd still need the job long after he was rested and the soreness had passed. "Could he drop me at a rental car agency?"


Josh and his escort hadn't reached the elevator before Brad Munford entered Hetzler's office from a door in the least lighted corner of the room. He'd watched and listened and videotaped everything Mitchell had said about Dianne Lane, as instructed, and was eager to get his boss's first-hand impression. "I say he liked the woman . . . a lot. It's obvious," he said upon entering.

"You think?" Hetzler said sarcastically.

Munford was used to Hetzler's often irritating ways. "You still figure he killed her, sir?"

Hetzler collected the four microcassettes and dropped them in an envelope, hastily scribbling Josh Mitchell's name across it. They would be transcribed in triplicate and be back on his desk before noon. He looked up from his pen. "When I first saw him in Carmel, I would have bet my pension he was the killer. Now . . . I'm not so sure anymore. The part about Lane calling herself Pamela Morrow intrigues me, though."

"You think there actually could be a Pamela Morrow?" The agent had never heard the name.

Hetzler nodded pensively. "There was a Pamela Morrow, but it was before your time. Who she was is not as important as how Dianne Lane knew about her. And, how much she knew about her."

The younger agent shrugged his shoulders. "So what do you make of it all? I know you've at least got a theory, sir."

"Don't know yet, Brad, except that Mitchell couldn't possibly have known Morrow's name without Lane feeding it to him. It just may be that he really doesn't know anything about all of this, like he said, and simply fell for the wrong person at the wrong time."

"Think the banker knows that by now?" He was referring to whoever hired Kisber and Mills.

"Not a chance."

"Then the boy's still in jeopardy. Think there'll be another attempt to take him out?" The agent remained standing at the edge of the desk.

"Probably before the weekend's out."

"We gonna provide him protection?" It had not been asked out of concern, but simply for information.

Hetzler stood and grabbed his suit jacket, moving toward the door; he was beat. Munford followed. When he'd flicked the switch that killed the one lamp that had been burning, the little man pulled the door behind him. "I'd do my dead-level best to keep him alive if I thought he had any further value to the Bureau, anything of substance to offer that might help clear up the stinking little mess Dianne Lane started long before you'd even entered the Academy. But you know what, Brad? My gut tells me Mitchell's just one unlucky bastard, and we're not in the business of protecting unlucky bastards from the pitfalls of life." The two agents walked toward the elevator.

"So he's completely on his own, as he said."

"Aren't we all?" Hetzler said philosophically.

"He seems like a nice guy, too bad for him."

"I don't know, Brad. You heard Mitchell say that he'd hoped Dianne Lane was going to join him again so they could spend time together. I figure he'll be just as satisfied joining her. Don't you?"

Munford nodded half heartedly, pressing the Down arrow. "Now that you put it that way, sir . . ."

When Larson and Sims left the underground parking lot adjacent to FBI Headquarters, with Josh already half asleep in the back seat, fighting to keep his eyes open, a black Dodge Intrepid fell in loosely behind them, affording the agents and their charge as much lead as they wanted in the light early-morning traffic. There was little chance of the Intrepid losing the white Ford Crown Victoria—besides standing out like the bride at a wedding, the Intrepid's driver had installed a tracking device under the Ford's rear bumper while its occupants were waiting patiently and obediently on the thirteenth floor.

The Dodge followed with confidence, the laptop computer on the passenger seat keeping the Ford centered at all times in its on-screen digital map. The driver placed the call he was supposed to make as soon as Mitchell was on the move again.

# 13

Josh stood in the shadow of the headquarters of Barnett Air, his head pounding, his left shoulder filled with a dull burning, the left knee feeling as though someone was trying to drive a sheetrock screw into the joint. Though he'd showered in his suite at the La Quinta Inn on Jibboom Street—without the benefit of even five minutes rest—and had managed to salvage a fairly crisp suit and dress shirt from his banged-up travel bag, he still looked as bad as he felt.

Probably worse, he thought, though he doubted that were possible.

His watch indicated that ten minutes remained before the company's doors officially opened, but he didn't need to look at its face to tell that; he could have set its time by the massive influx of employees from the parking lot. Ten minutes early, never late, was Hightower's mandate.

Few disobeyed.

"Hi, Josh," came the friendly greetings from junior vice presidents and sales reps as they hurriedly passed, eager to be seen at their respective posts before the CEO made his regular morning rounds.

"Good morning, Mr. Mitchell," from the less lofty as they scurried by like army ants, pulled to cubicles, keyboards, and telephones by a silent voice that called to them from empty checking accounts and burgeoning bill drawers.

"At least no one asked me what the hell I was doing here," Josh muttered with an uneasy smile, pleased at the thought that his name had not yet been given to security as one of the previously employed. He knew the office grapevine carried information such as a major termination—and his firing would be considered major—faster than e-mail. At two minutes before the hour, he pulled on the stainless handle of one of the sextet of wide front doors and was greeted by the familiar rush of cool air.

"Good morning, Mr. Mitchell," the receptionist said as he approached her desk in the center of the mammoth lobby. "It's good to see you again." She noticed the sizeable bruise on his left cheek and the small, flesh-colored bandage at his hairline he'd substituted for the large white gauze pad after he'd showered. "If you don't mind me asking, what on earth happened to you?"

"Cut myself shaving," he smiled.

She knew at once he didn't want to talk about it. "You should be more careful. I believe the president is—"

"Looking for me," he completed. "I heard." He leaned across the desk and wrinkled his nose. "I think he's looking for someone to wax his McLaren," he whispered.

She smiled as she always did when Josh spent a moment with her. "He should be in his office. Check with Dot when you go up."

"Thanks," he said, already moving toward the elevator.


Dorothy Guinn had been Richard Hightower's private secretary since he assumed Barnett's presidency five years ago. At forty-five she was quite attractive and carried no extra weight, was incredibly organized, typed ninety words a minute, understood Microsoft Office better than the people at Microsoft, and most importantly, was tough enough to put up with Hightower's considerable ego, lengthy list of peculiarities, and occasional vile temper. When Josh stepped off the elevator, she found one of her rare smiles. "Hi, Josh." She, too, noticed his various contusions and bruises. "Jesus, you look like you've been mugged. Are you all right? Stitches?" she asked, pointing toward the scalp wound.

"A couple." He sat on the edge of her desk, as always. He was the only salesman permitted such familiarity.

She stood behind her desk, but leaned toward him for a better look, the need to mother coming out in her. She had no children of her own and her only marriage had ended twenty years prior. Barnett was her family. "What the heck happened?"

"Cut myself shaving," he repeated.

She looked squarely into his bloodshot eyes. "Make the incision lower next time, maybe those eyes of yours will clear up."

Josh chuckled; he knew she was genuinely concerned. "Actually, Dot, I wrecked my rental car yesterday."

"Anyone else hurt?"

Josh saw no point in relating the full story to her, despite the fact that the two had shared more than one beer after work over the years. "Nope, just me."

"Where'd this happen?"

"Mississippi, south of Jackson."

"You poor thing. You on any pain medication?"

He shrugged his shoulders. "Got a couple of Darvocet left, but they make me sleepy as hell."

"Want a couple of Tylenol?" She kept a bottle in her desk, mostly for the headaches Hightower gave her.

"Took some Advil at seven. Thanks." He looked toward the door behind her. "Is he in?"

"I hate to put it this way, Josh, but to say he's been waiting to see you for two days would be the understatement of the month."

"So I heard."

"You up to it?" she asked sympathetically.

"Why, you gonna cover for me, Dot?" He knew she would.

"If need be, you bet." Still standing, she threw back her shoulders as if preparing for battle.

Josh smiled and squeezed her arm. "Might as well get it over with."

He took a long breath. "I hate starting off days like this, don't you?" "Do it every day," she said with a grin. "You'll be fine. Don't let him rattle you. You know how he can be sometimes, Joshua, especially when an important deadline is at hand. Whatever he's upset about will eventually pass."

*God, I hope so,* Josh thought, turning the doorknob.

Richard Hightower's office had been opulently crafted and meticulously appointed, becoming his private domain. Century-old hand-knotted oriental rugs covered pickled hardwood flooring while kidskin leather covered couches and chairs; solid cherry library paneling on all but the west wall, which was made entirely of tinted glass; seven-piece crown molding adorned ten-foot ceilings; custom cherry cabinetry, complete entertainment center, and bar with Italian marble countertops provided amenities while a hidden master bath with Jacuzzi, stair climber, and dry sauna provided the luxuries. On one wall—behind a moveable bookcase—computer, video, and satellite screens linked him to every outlying branch in Barnett's international dominion. A pair of original Frederick Remington bronze sculptures in lighted display cases, an extremely rare Michelangelo wood carving in a temperature- and humidity-controlled glass case, plus no fewer than a dozen other art treasures from the Americas, Europe, and the Far East had been placed for maximum visual impact throughout the fifteen-hundred-square-foot top-floor office.

He'd seen to the room personally. It was his private palace where congressmen, generals, and even competitors met to discuss secret—and extremely lucrative—business dealings with the most powerful man in the Barnett empire.

Though Josh appreciated the room architecturally, and even thought it possessed a certain sense of artistic harmony, the setting always reminded him of the gauche world of junk-bond salesmen and S&L presidents of the early Eighties.

Hightower stood as soon as Josh entered, ending his phone call abruptly. For an interminable moment after he'd cradled the phone, he didn't speak, and only stared toward the door with a blank expression on his face.

"Good morning, sir," was all Josh chose to say, allowing the CEO to set the tone of the meeting.

Hightower waved Josh to one of the seats across from the desk—there were five plush leather chairs to choose from.

Josh settled uncomfortably in the center one, his bruised knee barking at him like an angry dog as he sat.

Finally, Hightower took his seat, leaning back in his huge kidskin swivel chair, elbows on the armrests, fingers interlaced with the two index fingers making a steeple and touching his lips. He wanted to be furious, to explode at Mitchell for any number of reasons, least of which was having been told to mind his own business by the damned FBI, but he chose to listen to his favorite salesman's story first. It should be interesting. "You've been a hard man to find the last couple of days."

"Sorry, sir."

"It's not like you, Josh."

"No, sir, it's not."

"I thought you were going to be here Wednesday morning at eight, helping Kanazawa with Casper. This is not Wednesday morning."

"I had a good reason for not being here, sir."

"I thought you might, I'd love to hear it. I assume looking like you've been thrown from a train is part of the story?"

"Yes, sir. It might take quite a while to bring you fully up to date."

"I've got nothing but time, Josh. Just start at the beginning."

Josh knew it was only a figure of speech, and that while he and the CEO were in the plush office chatting, Dot was outside shuffling and reshuffling her boss's schedule every time a quarter hour passed and the door remained closed. But he also knew they would not be interrupted. He relaxed a bit, knowing that whatever happened from this point forward, his fate was going to rest on the truth. He was going to tell his boss everything that had happened since Monday afternoon in New York—*including* Dianne Lane having been in his room before her death—and trust to fate.

• • •

For more than an hour, Josh retold the story in detail, and for the second time in ten hours he relived the hours spent with the incredible woman on the plane, at dinner, and in his room in Carmel. He chose to avoid intimate details, though Hightower had asked how they'd spent their time there. It had seemed more out of curiosity than anything else, but Josh had still been uncomfortable with things that were just between him and Dianne.

Each time the memories were summoned, the images became clearer, with more and more emotional energy. He found himself speaking of a dead woman as he'd never spoken about, or to, any woman before. As he sat in the chair across from Hightower's huge desk, his mind was less on saving his job than trying to understand the situation himself.

And while he faithfully retold the story of the woman who'd changed his life, he realized that he had loved Dianne Lane from the first moment. Not like he'd loved Samantha, or Monica, or anyone in between, but in a way that surprised him.

At nine-thirty, he finished his protracted tale, ending with the conversation between himself and Special Agent Hetzler last night. The CEO had remained seated the entire time, scarcely adjusting his position in the chair, speaking infrequently. He seemed riveted to Josh's every word, encouraging ever-greater detail as the relationship between Dianne Lane and Josh progressed through the waning hours of Monday evening.

Though having expected to be mentally exhausted from repeating essentially the same words he'd spoken only a few hours earlier, Josh instead felt himself invigorated by them. Something stirred deep within, as if finally being true to Dianne Lane's spirit and memory had freed a long-imprisoned portion of himself. He no longer cared what Hightower might say or do about the decisions he'd made or the actions he'd taken, he knew he'd chosen correctly by following his heart and searching for the answers to the questions that had haunted him since Tuesday morning on the beach in Carmel.

The awareness alone had proved a powerful stimulant.

When Josh had finished, Richard Hightower stood and walked to him, pulling one of the remaining four chairs around so he could be closer to him. "My God, Josh, it's a miracle you weren't killed. We're damned lucky you're still with us." He shook his head. "I always knew such things happened, of course, but I really find it difficult to believe there are actually men out there willing to kill someone for money—an absolute stranger, for Christ's sake. Shocking, and one of my own people, a friend. Absolutely shocking." He continued to shake his head, patting Josh repeatedly on his left knee. Josh didn't let on that it felt like the man was striking it with a mallet.

"I'm just sorry I didn't tell you what was going on earlier, sir," he said, genuinely apologetic.

"If you had, perhaps I could have helped in some way, and a lot of this might have been avoided, not that I mind, but it's obviously taken its toll on you. Understandably, I might add." He put a hand on Josh's shoulder. "Josh, remember, you work for a powerful organization, and as its president, I have no shortage of influential contacts all across the country." Hightower suddenly stood, moving behind his desk again. "But, hell, that's all water under the bridge now, no sense in dwelling on what's done. What's important is that you're okay and still with us. It's time to let the federal boys sort out the nasty mess of Dianne Lane's tragic death, and time for you to put the whole unfortunate incident behind you. There's nothing to be gained by living in the past, is there?" Their eyes met.

"No, sir. Nothing at all," Josh said, his heart not agreeing with his voice. "Thanks for listening, sir, and understanding."

Something began to bother Josh, something either in Hightower's tone or manner—or both. He wasn't sure what it was or why it had arisen, but he knew he had to keep his emotions from running away with him again. After all, this man was his friend, practically a father to him.

Hightower's words evaporated the troubling thought in Josh's mind before it could take firm hold. "Of course I understand. Hell, I'm human, despite what most of my board believes. I've been dumb-struck by a beautiful woman before, more than once. They'll do that to you. But nothing lasting has ever been built in a day. You'll get over this thing in short order. What you need is a big sale or two under your belt to get your life and mind back on the right track." He grabbed a thick folder with a bright red corner, holding it toward Josh. "By the way, Legal sent up the paperwork from the Thurgood Hydro-Dynamics sale. Sweet. Good margin, and good work." He dropped the file back on his desk. "Tell you what, it's Friday, take the rest of the day off and kick back for the weekend. Go fishing or just sit on your butt and watch a ball game. On Monday morning, be back here ready to saddle up again."

"Thanks, I could use a little down time. Been at it pretty hard the last couple of months . . . and then all of this craziness with the FBI and the San Francisco Police thinking I might have had something to do with Dianne's . . ." Josh didn't finish his thought as he stood, his knee reminding him that he'd been in a near-fatal crash twenty hours before. Something felt unsettling, beyond the injuries, but he attributed it to his lack of sleep.

Richard Hightower noticed the flash of pain in Josh's eyes and knew it reflected more than just physical discomfort. He came to Josh's side, putting an arm around his shoulder. "I may be your boss, Josh, but I'm also your friend. At times, I feel almost like a father to you and Kenny; we three have a history together. Trust me on this: screw the cops, don't let the thought of them bother you one more minute, and get this nutcase out of your mind. Barnett is behind you corporately, and more importantly, I'm behind you personally. Let the FBI do their thing, you do what you do best, and everything will turn out fine. It'll all blow over in a few days, a week at the most, and you won't hear another peep out of any of them. It's obvious you're not a criminal, right?" The CEO put both hands on Josh's shoulders. "If you were, you wouldn't be working for me, right?"

Josh nodded, but his boss's cruel description of Dianne Lane echoed in his mind.

Josh forced a smile, though he still felt the uncertain rumbling deep within his gut.

As Hightower walked Josh to the door, arm again across his shoulder, Josh began to feel better, as good as he'd felt in five days, and even his injuries seemed to have quieted somewhat. He faced his boss at the door, extending his hand. "I'll be ready Monday morning, sir."

Hightower nodded, his eyes narrow but smiling. "Before you leave, mind dropping in on Kanazawa to see if he needs anything? I understand he solved a long-standing problem yesterday, thanks to your suggestion, and things are now progressing nicely, but I'd like a second opinion. We've still got that demo with Admiral Whittier scheduled for tomorrow afternoon. I'd really appreciate it, Josh."

"I'll go straight there, sir," he said resolutely, quite willing to do virtually anything his boss wanted at this moment.

When the door had closed behind him, and the smile he was known for once again spanned his face, Dorothy Guinn gave Josh a wide grin. "Told you things were going to be all right," she said. "He knows he can't run this place without you or me."

"You were right, Dot. As usual. Say, why not take the rest of the day off with me and we'll get knee-walking drunk? It'll do you good to get away from that phone for a while." Just then, a pair of lines began to flash rapidly, accompanied by a short verbal communication from the main switchboard that the president had two calls waiting.

"Because you'd still have a job on Monday, and I'd be standing in the unemployment line." She punched the first of the blinking lights as she waved him away with a grin.

Josh stood before the gleaming elevator doors, across from Dot's desk, rocking rhythmically on his heels, a half-remembered song teasing his memory, his mind otherwise blissfully blank. The moment was short-lived as his thoughts soon returned to Hightower's cruel verbal indictment of Dianne Lane. Calling someone the man had never had the pleasure of knowing a "nutcase" tasted like bile in Josh's mouth as he repeated the words. Though he had known her for less than a day himself, Josh knew instinctively that this woman had been no wacko, despite claiming to be someone dead nearly eight years.

Still, if she had committed suicide and had not been murdered, his problems would become insignificant. Hightower now knew all there was to know and had still pledged his full corporate and personal support. His worst fear about his career had not been realized, and, in that respect, it felt like a great weight had been lifted from him.

On the other hand, if she had been murdered, he considered—unable to dismiss the idea that the hunches of seasoned cops like Lefler and Fachini were right—Josh knew it would take all of Richard Hightower's powerful connections just to keep him out of jail while he awaited trial.

How soon would that occur—six months after his arrest?

Twelve?

How backed up was the docket? he wondered.

It was not a subject on which he imagined he'd ever have invested a second's thought, and yet now, the image of even a day in jail with murderers, rapists, child molesters, and drug addicts made his heart race.

*You're imagining things, Josh,* he told himself. *It went great with Hightower. Everything's going to be fine.*

The image persisted and he had to force himself to push it away.

After Josh pressed the Down button a second time, as if the impatient act would miraculously speed the car's arrival, he looked to his right, toward the door to the southwest stairwell, and decided not to take the elevator to the basement after all. His years of playing football with one injury after another told him it would probably do his sore knee good to be exercised a bit before he propped it up on his bed at the La Quinta Inn and began two and a half days of well-deserved R&R.

The thought of sleep was luxurious, euphoric, and he vowed not to think of the events of the week again before he'd enjoyed twelve uninterrupted hours of it.

The heavy fire door closed with a vaultlike echo behind him.

On each floor of the Barnett building, at the southeast and southwest corners, a reinforced steel door provided access to a staircase that ran the full height of the structure, from the sixth floor to the basement level. Entry to these stairs was possible from the interior side without intervention, for fire safety reasons, but armored electronic locks at each door required anyone desiring admission to a floor from the stairwell side (other than ground level) to be buzzed in by the main guard desk. In keeping with the architectural harmony of the building, the stairwells had been enclosed in mirrored glass with supports of alternating brushed and polished stainless steel.

The left knee complained at first, but then grew more subtle as Josh descended the levels slowly and deliberately, taking each step carefully and noting how things felt. After a full flight, he decided he agreed with Dr. Wilkerson's assessment, he'd done no serious damage, only a minor sprain to the joint with surface bruising. It would be healthy in a week or two, he concluded as he reached the fourth floor.

The silo-shaped stairwell was noticeably warmer than the air-conditioned floor he'd left a few minutes ago, and in the stale, still air a bead of sweat trickled down his back. He looked out toward the parking lot, fumbling the keys to his rented Lincoln in his pants pocket, wondering if he could see where he'd parked from where he now stood, anxious to be on his way to his warm, waiting bed.

As he scanned the crowded lot, looking for the distinctive gold-tone paint of the Town Car, Josh saw a man he didn't recognize standing beside his rental, the man's attention on the interior of the vehicle. Josh moved closer to the wall of glass until his face was practically touching its surface.

That was where he'd parked, he was sure, and that was his rental, but what the hell was the man doing looking inside his car?

He considered pounding on the glass and shouting out, an instinct triggered by a sudden flash of anger, but knew nothing he could do would be heard. His analytical side quickly told him that it was best he'd not made his presence known.

Josh watched in troubled silence as the man peered through the glass of the four doors in turn, making a complete circle of the car around its front, cupping his hands around his eyes to block the light as he put his forehead to each window.

Finally, the man looked all around him—obviously to ensure that he was not being watched—stuck his hand inside his windbreaker and removed a small object, then knelt behind the car. At more than eighty yards, Josh could not tell what the man had withdrawn from his jacket, but was certain that whatever it was, it had just been placed under the Lincoln's rear bumper.

Was it a bomb? A homing device of some kind? In either case, it was not something he wanted on his car.

He watched as the man stood again, strolled casually to a space not far from the Town Car, and took his seat behind the wheel of a black Dodge Intrepid.

In thirty seconds, the man had left the property, but Josh soon noticed that he pulled his car into the parking lot of a medical supply firm across the street from Barnett and a block down. He could no longer see the man behind the wheel, but he knew he was waiting. And would continue to wait as long as it took.

"Hetzler, you lyin' dog," Josh said as he pulled his cell phone from his pocket. He took a business card from his shirt pocket and punched in the number that had been scribbled on the back in pencil.

"Hello," Hetzler answered indifferently. His mind was on the file before him. He got few calls on his direct line.

"I thought you said you believed me, Hetzler!"

"Mitchell?"

"Damn right!"

"Believe you about . . .?"

"About Dianne Lane, of course!"

"Well, in fact I do. What's seems to be—"

"Then why are you having me followed!?" Josh barked. "I told you everything I knew!"

The agent rocked back in his chair. He had no time for this shit, but was intrigued by the angry call. "What makes you think you're being followed, Mr. Mitchell?"

"I don't think, I know. What does the FBI want from me that it hasn't already gotten? I don't know a damned thing more than I've told you, I swear."

"And, as I said, we believe you, Mr. Mitchell. No one with the Bureau is following you, for any reason. You have my word on that."

"Right, and the check's in the mail, too."

Hetzler grinned. "I appreciate your skepticism, sir, even understand it, but my agency doesn't deal in stealth. If we want something from a suspect, we've found that good old-fashioned intimidation and harassment serve our purposes far better. If you are indeed being followed, as you fear, you need to look elsewhere, Mr. Mitchell."

Josh was puzzled. He'd been sure it was Hetzler and company. "What about Lefler?" he said, moving unsteadily to his second choice.

"You still in the city?"

"What?"

"San Francisco. You still in town?"

"No. I'm at my office in Sacramento."

"It wouldn't be Lefler then." The agent was ready to get on with his life, a life that, at this moment, didn't include Joshua Thomas Mitchell.

"How can you be so sure, Hetzler?"

"No jurisdiction. Besides, it's much easier for him to simply arrest your ass. Costs less, too."

"But—"

"Mr. Mitchell, if there's nothing else, I've got better things to do than assuage your paranoia. Have you considered it may not be cops at all?"

The stunned silence on Josh's end granted the agent permission to hang up, which he promptly did.

"Shit!" Josh shouted, his angry voice echoing throughout the stairwell. He now understood whoever hired the thugs in Mississippi was ready and eager to correct his mistake.

But why?

No longer would he be safe simply not knowing.

He had to see Kenny, but not for the reason Hightower had requested.


"Development, Kanazawa," the senior programmer answered when his office phone rang. He pressed Control-S to save his work.

"He's on his way down to have a look at Casper," Hightower

said, his voice low even though his office was virtually soundproof.

"Where's he been the last two days?" Kanazawa asked, though he knew the boss wasn't about to engage in small talk with him. He was right.

"I've just finished an in-depth conversation with him about that very subject, and his relationship to Dianne Lane—"

"What's she got to do with anything?" he interrupted.

"More than you could imagine. You don't think her dozen trips a year to mainland China were merely for collecting objets d'art, do you?"

Kenny's mind raced.

"Anyway, Mitchell swears I heard all there was to hear, but I'm not at all convinced he told me everything he knows, or even most of it. He seems to really have been affected by Lane's death, not something you'd expect after a one-day acquaintance. I want to know everything he knows, Kanazawa, everything the two of them talked about on Monday—and before, if he knew her prior to then. My bet is that he did, and the two of them were working some kind of elaborate plan to steal Casper and make their own deal with our overseas friends."

"How could he? He doesn't have one line of Casper's code."

"You sure about that, are you?"

"Positive," Kanazawa said, though he was even at that moment considering ways his clever former partner could have infiltrated the development server and offloaded Casper without detection. If anyone could do it, he knew Josh could. *Dammit!* he said silently, determined to find out how it had been done, now believing Hightower's distrust merited further investigation. "There's only one way Josh could have done it," he said.

"Great, only *one*, Kanazawa!? And I was afraid you'd left half a dozen flies open so 'bright boy' could yank our dicks any time he chose."

The programmer didn't appreciate the sarcastic jab, the implication that he was incompetent. "It's still only a possibility, sir, not a probability. Do you think he suspects us?"

"I'll tell you what I think, I think it was dumb luck that some rapist or junkie popped his bitch of a partner before they could steal our sale, and because of it, and for no other reason, we're still in business. But we can't count on luck saving us again. I need Casper debugged and operational in twenty-four hours. And I need to know what's in your buddy's head that he didn't see fit to share with me. You think you can deal with two problems at the same time, you know, multitask, as you nerds call it?" His voice had risen.

"I may be a nerd, sir, but don't forget, without me we'd have nothing to sell."

Hightower seethed. "And without me, you and the Boy Scout would be living out of a refrigerator box, dreaming of making it someday instead of living the good life. I can ruin you both."

"And neither of us could do anything to prevent this, nothing to bring you into the mix as well?"

"How much cash can you put your hands on, Kanazawa? A couple of hundred grand, tops?"

Kanazawa knew it was that amount at most—he'd lived a very good life the last three years. He chose not to answer the question, knowing Hightower would make his point regardless.

"I've got over a hundred and fifty million in banks throughout the world," the CEO continued. "I could flush the two of you and live forever in style in any one of a dozen countries that don't honor American extradition treaties. What could you do, either of you?"

"It wasn't a threat, sir." It had been, but one without teeth.

"Just rhetorical chit chat, then?"

Kanazawa took a frustrated breath. He reminded himself that Hightower wouldn't think twice of destroying Josh, or him, if either ever posed a genuine threat to his plans. "I'm on your side, I think I've proven that. We've worked perfectly together on the last two projects and I haven't let you down yet, have I?"

Hightower grew benevolent in his tone, though his voice had again lowered. "That's why your big payday is right around the corner, Kenny, because I know that no matter how loyal you may be to Mitchell, your true allegiance is to your own welfare. And mine."

"Is that why you've withheld my share of the last two sales, to keep me on a string?" Kenny wanted the ten million he'd already earned but had yet to receive, as well as the ten he'd soon earn from the sale of Casper. If Josh got in his way . . .

"Insurance, Kenny. That's all. To keep you on the straight and narrow. But with this being the last deal we'll do together, you'll soon have every cent that's owed you, with interest. I've got nothing but gratitude for the excellent work you've done to date. We've got one remaining hurdle, however."

"I'll find out what Josh knows about the woman and her plans, and if there's a door into Casper that isn't secure, I'll clamp it so tight *he'll* have to be a ghost to get in."

"Don't spook him. He needs to talk. If there's someone else out there trying to steal this sale, I—we—need to know who it is."

"I'm not a fool."

"Ninety-six hours, Kanazawa, then you and I will be splitting fifty mill from our little rice-eating buddies."

Kanazawa hated that damned expression, but the thought of sitting on a tropical beach and drinking piña coladas for the rest of his life, without ever having to look at another computer, softened his sensitivities.

Josh pushed open the door to the software lab and headed for the glass office in the center of the room. He could readily tell that his friend wasn't at his normal post. He scanned the many familiar faces that looked up from busy keyboards searching for Kenny's. He spotted him near the development server, at the rear of the room, talking with his chief hardware engineer. Kenny spotted Josh at the same time.

"Hey, old buddy," he shouted above the din of the bustling room. He made a final comment to the engineer and then hurried toward his friend. Josh waved back and together they entered Kenny's cluttered office.

As Josh pushed past his friend, Kenny noticed the bruise on his left cheek and the stitches protruding from the laceration in his scalp like a handful of whiskers growing awry.

"What the hell happened to you?"

Josh was tired of the question. He felt like he had "Ask me what the hell happened" tattooed on his forehead.

He chose not to respond. "Where are your car keys?"

"Where are my keys? That's not an answer." Kenny folded his arms across his chest.

"You don't really want to know."

"Then I wouldn't have asked."

Josh huffed. "Someone tried to make a hood ornament out of me. Satisfied?"

Kenny processed the information, such as it was; it told him nothing. "No," he said.

"A wreck, that's all. I'm okay, really, thanks for the concern. Your keys?" He held out his hand.

"They're in my pocket and they're going to stay there until I get some answers."

Josh's expression removed any doubt about him being serious.

"What's wrong with the car you drove here, or is that the wrecked one we're talking about?"

"No, that was in Mississippi yester—"

"Mississippi?" Kenny said incredulously.

"Just let me have them, please," Josh said, his face drawn.

Kenny had loaned Josh his car numerous times over the years, as Josh had done for him, and handed over the keys without further resistance.

"Thanks," Josh said, turning. "I'll have it back tonight."

"Hey, hold on a minute," Kenny said, surprised by his friend's sudden departure. "What the hell's going on?"

Josh stopped with his hand on the doorknob. "I haven't time to explain now, maybe later tonight. I gotta run."

"Bullshit!" Kenny snapped. "You were supposed to be here on Wednesday, you don't show, and when I see you for the first time in two days, you look like you've been dropped from a third-story window and all you can say is give you my car, maybe you'll explain later. Fuck you. Give me back my keys." He held out an open hand.

"I can't. I really need to borrow your car for a while."

"And the reason is . . ."

"I don't feel like walking a hundred miles."

Kenny shook his head, bewildered. "Sit down and tell me what's going on, Josh. Now. Do it, or hand over the keys."

Josh looked at his watch; it was past ten. "Can't you trust me on this? Please. If I wreck it, you can have mine. It's in better shape anyway."

"I don't give a shit about the car, Josh, but I do care about the lunatic behavior you've been exhibiting the last few days. Let's you and me take an early lunch, grab a beer or four, and talk it all through. If you can convince me you're not losing your mind, and I haven't gotten you too drunk by then, you can borrow my car." He refolded his arms resolutely.

"Like old times, huh?"

Kenny nodded, but there was no smile to be seen.

"I can't, not now. I gotta go, really."

Kenny placed himself between Josh and the door. "Over my dead body. Talk to me, dammit."

Josh sat on the corner of the table that held the ever-gurgling coffee pot, Kenny barring the only exit. "You remember the name Dianne Lane?"

"Sure, the woman who died in Carmel while you were there." He let him continue.

"I think I loved her, Kenny. I didn't realize it at the time, but I loved her. Can you believe it?" His eyes were sad, his face tired, his shoulders drooped.

They had been through a lot together in seven years—long hours and short relationships, tears of frustration and tears of celebration, near bankruptcy then financial security, and more—but this was the first time Kenny could recall his friend using the word "love" in conjunction with a woman's name. It surprised him. "Then you did know her before Monday?"

Josh shook his head. "Never saw her before in my life. That's the damnedest thing about it, Kenny. I always thought love took months, years, to develop." He looked into his friend's eyes. "I know now that it can happen in a single heartbeat."

Kenny felt sorry for his friend; he'd obviously suffered a loss, however inexplicable, just as Hightower had surmised. But it still did not explain his errant behavior since Tuesday morning.

"So, why my car?" he asked.

"I think someone's watching my rental." '

"Who?"

"Don't know, but I don't think it's the cops."

"This is freaky shit, you know that, don't you?"

Josh nodded.

"Why would someone be following you?" Kenny lowered his arms to his side.

Josh shrugged his shoulders. Kenny knew he either didn't know, or wasn't going to tell.

"Where are you going when you leave here?" he asked.

"I need to talk with a man who used to work with Pamela—"

"Who?" Kenny interrupted.

"I mean Dianne Lane. Maybe he'll be able to tell me why she had to die."

"How would he know that?" Kenny asked, still puzzled by the mention of a name he hadn't heard before.

"It's a very complex story, and one I'll share with you when this is all over. We'll get drunk as a couple of skunks."

"I've got time now."

"I don't, unfortunately," Josh said. He knew Kenny would never understand what he hoped to learn from Morris Goldman. Hell, he wasn't really sure himself.

"How about calling the guy?"

"Tried. If he has a phone, it's not listed."

Kenny stood mutely, his eyes focused on a thought rather than an object, trying to decide what to do. There was so much at stake; Hightower would be livid.

Josh stood, putting his hands on his friend's shoulders. "I gotta know, Kenny. This may be the only man who can help me."

"Who is this man?"

"It's not important." He gently moved Kenny aside.

"You really loved this woman, didn't you?"

Josh nodded, his eyes deep, lost.

"You're my friend, right?" Kenny asked.

The question seemed oddly phrased. "Of course. Your best friend. Always."

Kenny nodded with a tight smile. As far as he could tell, there was nothing substantive about Josh's relationship with Dianne Lane that was being withheld from him, and nothing that posed a threat to the sale of Casper. Whatever the Lane woman had been planning, if anything, Josh had merely been an innocent bystander, in the wrong place at the wrong time.

This Kanazawa would bet his life on; he hoped it wouldn't come to that. "Take it," he said, moving fully out of Josh's way. "You know where I keep it."

"In back, as always. Thanks, my friend," Josh said.

"If you wreck it, you *will* sign over the title to yours." It had been said with a twisted smile that Josh hadn't missed.

He jangled the keys in the air, crossed the distance to the lab door in wide strides, then disappeared into the hall.

Kanazawa grabbed the cleanest cup he could find, rolling it between sweaty palms. The pot chugged and hissed and the French roast within it smelled burned. He filled it halfway, turning toward the door that had just closed behind his best friend. He raised the cup to his lips. "God, I hope you know what you're doing, old buddy," he whispered into the black liquid. "This is no game we're playing."

## 14

The map he'd grabbed at the Exxon station leaving Sacramento indicated that Idlewild, California—supposed home of Morris Goldman, Lloyd Richmond's and Pamela Morrow's former business associate—sat on the west shore of Lake Tahoe, twenty miles south of Interstate 80, halfway between Tahoe City and Meeks Bay; he knew the area. It was a long shot, he understood, but Josh was determined to find Goldman if it took all weekend, or longer. He didn't allow himself to even consider the possibility that the man had died in the decade since he'd posed for the picture he'd uncovered at the Natchez Library.

Josh had pushed the Porsche Turbo much harder than he knew was prudent—the California Highway Patrol loved busting weekend speeders rocketing toward Tahoe and Reno—but he'd left an hour before lunch, while the rest of the world was busy wrapping up the week, and a full four hours before even the earliest gamblers typically headed toward the glitter palaces in Nevada. He'd crossed his fingers and hoped that he would not attract unwanted attention at this time of day.

Whether or not it would prove a sound strategy on any other Friday, the poppy-red Porsche left the Interstate at the Highway 89 junction, heading south toward the tiny town of Idlewild, without having encountered the first radar gun in the hundred-plus miles from Sacramento.

He looked at the clock in the dash: 12:15 P.M. It brought a smile. Though he owned a twin to the car he now drove, Kenny's showed sixty-three thousand miles on the odometer, while Josh's hadn't left four digits yet. He vowed to make more time for long drives in the country, then felt a sharp pain as he thought about never having the opportunity to share a winding Rocky Mountain road with Pamela at his side, her hair tossed by a cool Colorado breeze.

*I'm sorry to awaken you from such a pleasant dream.* Pamela's first words replayed hauntingly in his mind, and he knew at that moment there would always be a portion of him that would never awaken from his dream of her.

Overhead, the sky threatened gray and black, pregnant clouds moving and churning like the North Sea, the air thick with the humidity that often accompanied a storm in the mountains. It seemed much later than noon, ominous, threatening, the electric smell of ozone and pine needles adding to the sense of urgency.

He pressed on, the need to know the truth about Pamela Morrow and Dianne Lane drawing him like a voice that had to be answered.


Morris Goldman's cabin sat along Blackwood Creek, shrouded in a blanket of evergreens, its shake roof and redwood walls stained nearly black by decades of tree sap dripping from a thick canopy of pine and cedar boughs. The dense pack of fallen needles crunched beneath Josh's shoes as he made his way toward the front door. He wished he'd changed out of his dress clothes before leaving Sacramento and had grabbed a coat heavier than his suit jacket. In the mountains, mid-March was still winter, the air cold.

A shiver that he attributed as much to a deep sense of uncertainty as the outside temperature washed his skin in goose bumps. He took the three wooden steps leading to the covered porch hesitantly, having no idea how his strange quest would be received by the cabin's owner. He rehearsed his opening line for the tenth time as his feet touched the landing.

> Gone fishing; if I want to talk to you,
> you'll know where to find me.
> If you don't know where to find me,
> I probably don't want to talk to you.

Josh read the typed note that had been thumbtacked to the door; from its yellowed color and tattered edges, it appeared to have been in this same spot for a while, its author apparently not eager to encourage visitors.

*The man comes right to the point,* he grinned. *Maybe he's home anyway,* he hoped, knocking softly.

No response.

His second round of knocking could have been heard next door, had there been a neighbor.

Nothing. His eyes scanned the note again.

"Dammit," he grumbled. He, of course, had *no* idea where the man was now. Perhaps the woman across the highway who'd been kind enough to point out Goldman's home also knew where the old man liked to fish.

"It's me again," Josh said with his best smile, arriving at Sarah Young's house for the second time in ten minutes. He'd walked the two hundred yards from Goldman's cabin. She was still seated comfortably in her well-worn rocker, halfway through an elaborately embroidered Christmas stocking for her newest grandchild—little Ethan, who lived with her youngest son and daughter-in-law in Boise (she had yet to see the baby, though the proud parents had dutifully sent a video of the birth)—and started to get up when Josh neared the porch.

"No, please," he said, gesturing for her to remain seated. "I'm so sorry to bother you again, Mrs. Young."

It had been dumb luck that he'd located someone in Idlewild, on the first try, who not only verified that Morris Goldman was still alive—and quite well—but who also knew where he lived. Josh got the impression that Mrs. Young knew everyone in Idlewild. Her rocking never stopped as she waved him into a chair next to hers.

"Thanks," he said, sitting.

"Not home?" she said.

Josh shook his head.

"Should've thought of that before I sent you over. Sorry, young man. Morris goes fishing every day after lunch . . . unless it's storming out, of course."

"Of course," Josh said. "Does he have a place he prefers to fish?"

"Would you care for anything to drink?" she asked.

"No, thank you."

"You sure? It's no trouble. I've got some tea made. And a little lemonade too, I believe."

"I'm fine, thanks." In truth, he hadn't thought much about food or drink for days. "Do you think you might know where Mr. Goldman might be at the moment?"

"Today's Friday, right?" It had been more stated than asked.

"Yes, ma'am," he confirmed.

She appeared to be thinking, her attention on the dark water that lay across the highway from them, and which framed Morris Goldman's back yard. Josh turned toward the lake as well, clearly visible from the front porch of her modest home at the base of sixty-five-hundred-foot Eagle Rock. He hadn't paid it much attention earlier, his mind on other things, but now found it breathtaking as his eyes swept across the lake. Its normally deep blue waters mirrored the afternoon's wintry mood, echoing the sky's ashen hues, the reflected clouds appearing as massive ice floes teased by a chill wind drifting out of the north.

"Tahoe Pines."

"I'm sorry?" he said.

"I'll bet he's down toward Tahoe Pines." She picked up her appliqué and began attaching a small red bow. "Goes there Fridays, I believe. That's where I'd start looking." She made eye contact, her lined face kind and generous. "Of course, you could take a seat on his porch and wait for him to get back, or visit here a spell with me."

A feeling of intense nostalgia swept through Josh, as he was immediately reminded of home. Not his apartment in Greenwich Village, but his boyhood home in Tennessee. Without knowing anything about the woman beyond what he'd gathered in twenty minutes' conversation, he knew she lived alone, was deeply devoted to her children and grandchildren, and probably made the best peach cobbler, or carrot cake, or chocolate pie in Idlewild.

He longed to see his mother.

"You're too kind. How far is Tahoe Pines?" Josh asked.

"Oh, it's not far. Quarter mile maybe. Just over there." She pointed toward the lake just south of Goldman's cabin.

Josh retrieved the microfilm copy of the newspaper photo of Lloyd Richmond, Pamela Morrow, and Morris Goldman. Their names were printed at the bottom of the picture. He handed it to Sarah Young.

"Does Goldman still look like that?" he asked.

She studied the picture briefly. "You bet. A bit older perhaps, but aren't we all?"

Josh smiled.

"You won't have any trouble recognizing Morris from this," she assured him. "Sure I can't get you something to drink?"


"Hand me my net, will ya," the old man shouted from the edge of the lake, the small wind-blown waves lapping to mid-thigh; his tall, green rubber boots were still several inches out of the water. He afforded himself a longer look at the man he'd called to, his well-cut suit oddly out of place in the gray mist that had begun to fill the air, then turned his attention back to the five-pound mack he'd been fighting for ten minutes, its tender flesh now only five feet from his net and twenty minutes from his frying pan. "Today, if you don't mind," he barked. He couldn't imagine what the hell a city lawyer wanted with him, but it would have to wait.

Josh grabbed the aluminum handle and turned it around,

extending its red rubber grip toward the man he recognized from the photo in his suit pocket. The lake lapped across his four-hundred-dollar Italian shoes, filling them both. "Mr. Goldman?" he said, stepping back onto dry rocks and hiding his discomfort. His toes squished within icy socks.

"Not now, sonny," the man snapped, holding the pole high, at arm's length, the net buried in the gray-blue water. A few moments later, the fight was over and the five-pound spotted silver fish had been safely placed in a small Igloo cooler. "Lake minnows," the old man yipped as he snapped the lid shut. "Got this pretty fella the first time I pitched one in. Ninety feet—can't miss 'em at that depth this time of year." He grabbed one of the handles of the cooler and motioned for the stranger to take the other.

Josh took it at once. "Mr. Goldman?" he repeated, though he was certain the man before him was the same man as in the photo.

"You a lawyer?" Goldman asked sourly.

Josh tried to keep from falling on the slippery rocks as he helped carry the cooler up the bank toward the highway. The trek would have been far less difficult in hiking boots or sneakers than in slick-soled dress shoes. "No, sir," he said. "I'm no lawyer."

"Good, 'cause I hate the bastards. Lawyers are like hyenas, they don't care whether they feed off the living or the dead, so long as they feed." They reached a narrow foot trail Josh had noticed in his descent to the lake. "Set her down," the man ordered.

Josh obeyed, standing erect after he did. He was still an inch shorter than the other man, though five decades his junior. Josh was surprised at the man's apparent physical condition at nearly eighty, and hoped he'd look as good at fifty.

"Are you Morris Goldman?" he asked.

"Why do you want to know?"

"I need some information. If you are Morris Goldman, I think you might be able to provide it."

"Information, huh? That's refreshing. Since you're not a lawyer, I was afraid you were an encyclopedia salesman." He began to disassemble his rod, storing the individual pieces in a canvas tote on his hip. "You have a name, sonny?"

"Joshua Mitchell. I'm from—"

"I didn't ask you where you were from, did I?" he said, looking directly into Josh's eyes.

"No, sir, you didn't," Josh said, doing his best to remain pleasant, though the man looking hard at him wasn't making it easy. Josh knew he couldn't afford the luxury of alienating him.

The man then said in a curt tone, "That's because I don't care where you're from, and furthermore, I've got a news flash for you, Joshua Mitchell. If for some strange reason you think I possess information of any kind that could be of value to you, unless of course you're interested in the fishing around here, then you're sadly mistaken. You either have me confused with someone else, or you've been lied to. In either case, I have no time to waste with you."

He slipped the net through a loop in his canvas belt and pulled a pair of dry gloves from his jacket side pocket, depositing his wet ones in the opposite pocket.

Almost soaked through from the misty air, his feet like ice, Josh was freezing.

The man seemed completely indifferent to his misery, and with both hands now free, grabbed his cooler. "Good day," he said and started down the trail toward his cabin.

Josh watched as the distance between them grew quickly. He'd anticipated Goldman being reticent to talk, but he had not expected him to be downright rude. He raised his jacket collar and pulled the coat tightly across his chest. "I need to know about Pamela Morrow," he shouted down the trail.

Morris Goldman stopped at once and turned slowly around, the cooler drooping against his thigh-high boots. He didn't speak as Josh walked quickly toward him. When Josh had reached his position, Goldman said, "What do you know about Pamela Morrow?"

"Very little. Practically nothing, really," Josh said.

The man studied the stranger's face carefully.

"That's what I figured," he finally said, and turned to go.

Josh started to grab his arm, but reconsidered. "I had dinner with her on Monday night, though," he said instead, his words hurried.

Goldman stopped, turned again, and focused a cold stare directly into Josh's eyes. "Bullshit. Pamela Morrow died in 1989. If you knew anything about her at all, you'd have known that."

"I do know that," Josh said.

"Well then, you're not just misdirected, you also appear to be crazy."

"Perhaps. More than once since Tuesday morning, I'd have agreed with you readily, but I don't think I'm crazy, Mr. Goldman. I am, though, way over my head in something I don't begin to understand, and if you can't help me, by this time Sunday I'll probably be dead."

Goldman cocked his head. "I'm not sure I care either way, but I'll give you thirty seconds to convince me you're not a lunatic."

Josh took a deep breath and spit out his thoughts. "On Monday afternoon, I caught a flight from New York City to San Francisco. During the flight, I met and got to know an incredibly beautiful and fascinating woman who told me her name was Pamela Morrow. We had dinner together after the flight, she came to my hotel room later, and by one o'clock Tuesday morning, she was dead." The breath was spent.

Goldman's eyes narrowed on the word "dead."

"You kill her?" he asked as evenly as asking the hour.

"God, no!" Josh said. "I loved her." Several drops of water made their way past his collar and down his back.

"In one day?" Goldman said.

Josh knew *that* part, if nothing else, did sound crazy. "She was a remarkable woman, Mr. Goldman, even if she wasn't really Pamela Morrow. But, from what I've been able to learn, the woman she pretended to be was also quite remarkable."

Morris Goldman continued to look into Josh's eyes, studying them as if they held a truth his words hadn't spoken. "That she was," he said, and Josh could sense a pain that had not fully vanished in more than eight years since her death.

"I could really use a few minutes of your time, sir," Josh said, knowing not to speak again until the man responded.

After what felt like several minutes, the old man turned one end of the cooler toward Josh. "Grab a handle, sonny."

• • •

The cabin was warm and rich with the aroma of a roaring fire. Pine needles sizzled and the damp logs the old man had pulled from the porch hissed as the flames licked at them. While Josh tried to warm himself before the wide fieldstone hearth, Goldman made a pot of coffee in the kitchen. Outside, it was raining heavily now, the far shore of the lake dissolved by a gray curtain that began just beyond the rear deck; it seemed to Josh like a metaphor for his life.

"Mind if I take off my shoes?" Josh asked. "They seem to have gotten a little wet."

"Make yourself at home," the man said pleasantly, a grin twisting his lips. He'd noticed Josh's soaked shoes earlier.

Josh slipped off his shoes and socks, putting them on the hearth as close to the flames as he dared. It wasn't the first time he'd dried wet shoes by an open fire, and knew that it wouldn't take long to chase the lake water from them.

"Black okay?" Goldman asked, entering the room with a pair of heavy ceramic mugs. He was sipping from one.

"Yeah, black's fine," Josh said, his front warm but still noticeably damp. He took the mug handed to him and the two men sat opposite each other by the fire, Goldman selecting a rocker that was obviously his favorite chair.

For a long while, Goldman just sat, sipped, and rocked in a slow, steady rhythm, staring at the yellow flames. Josh watched his face— it appeared older and more drawn than it had by the lake. He wanted to talk, to break the interminable silence that filled the small room, but forced himself to be patient.

Finally, the old man lowered the cup to his lap.

"By the lake, you said you loved her," he said, never turning his eyes from the fire.

"I don't think I knew it at the time, or maybe I was afraid to think I could actually fall in love with someone in so few hours, but I know now that I did love her, like no one I've ever known." He watched the orange, yellow, and amber fangs greedily consume the three fat logs that were now red with heat. The room had warmed and his clothing had begun to dry.

"What was this remarkable woman's real name, or have you never learned it?"

"Dianne Lane. Perhaps you read about her earlier this week or saw something about her death on the news."

Goldman rocked his head softly. "Don't have much use for the news anymore. It's never done a thing to improve my life one little bit."

It had been said without cynicism. "You're probably right," Josh grinned, longing for such simplicity in his own life. He liked the old man.

"What happened?" Goldman said.

"I don't know, except that she apparently drowned sometime after midnight Monday—"

"Drowned?"

"Yeah. In Carmel Bay."

"I thought you said the two of you flew into San Francisco."

"That's right," Josh said.

The old man's faint smile told Josh he understood how the two had ended up in the picturesque village by the sea, a town made for lovers.

"Do the police know what happened?" Goldman asked.

"There was a suicide note, but neither they nor I believe it."

"Why not?" he asked, turning to Josh. He studied the eyes again.

"The first detective I talked to said her death was too neat."

"Too neat?"

"Yes. He said death was seldom neat unless brought about by someone calculating, deliberate." Josh still felt the primal anger at such a thought. He wanted one minute alone with the man responsible for Dianne Lane's death, and wondered for a moment if it was the same person who had tried to have him killed. It made as much sense as anything else so far.

"And you?" the old man said.

Josh looked toward the lake for a while then back to the man on his right. "Dianne Lane wasn't the kind of woman who would have run from something in her life. She wouldn't have killed herself."

"You made that determination in less than a day?"

"Yes. You would have too," Josh said as if no other conclusion could have been reached.

Goldman nodded.

Josh continued: "Anyway, now—"

"Now, you're suddenly suspect number one, right?" Goldman finished.

It was Josh's turn to nod.

They both took a minute to consider the situation, Josh sipping on his hot coffee, Goldman rocking like the steady sway of the pendulum in a grandfather clock. One of the chair's rockers squeaked with each backward arc, but neither man seemed to notice.

"I notice you're still free. They obviously couldn't think you had much to do with her death."

"They will, soon," Josh said, and proceeded to tell him about the letter he'd written and mailed in Carmel.

Goldman put the mug to his lips, then back to his lap. "Earlier, you said you might well be dead before the weekend was out. Even in the worst case, it's unlikely they'd treat you like you were an armed serial killer. Perhaps you're just a bit—"

"It's not the cops I was referring to," Josh interrupted. "Someone out there apparently doesn't want me to make a connection between Dianne Lane and Pamela Morrow. They've already tried to kill me once."

"Really? How?"

Josh vividly related the chase and crash outside Natchez.

When he'd finished, Goldman stood and set his mug on the mantel. He strolled toward the kitchen and returned with the coffee pot and a bottle of French brandy. He added half a cup of coffee to his mug and poured in a double shot of the Delsay. When he extended the bottle toward his guest, Josh took a generous slug of the brandy as well.

Goldman rotated his chair toward Josh, then sat again. "And you think I can somehow prevent this from happening again?"

"No, sir, I don't, but you may be able to help me understand *why* it's happening. That way, I might be able to point a finger at who-ever's responsible." The brandy warmed all the way to his stomach.

"What do you think I can tell you?" Goldman asked.

Josh pulled the photo from his pocket. It was miraculously still dry.

For the first time in almost a decade, Goldman looked into the faces of an old man and a young woman who had once been two of his closest friends. He studied it silently, reverently.

Josh said, "I know first-hand that Pamela Morrow was well-loved in her hometown of Natchez, and read that she graduated from Ole Miss with honors, served as an art historian and librarian for Lloyd Richmond, and was killed by a hit-and-run driver outside her home in Jackson, Mississippi in October 1989. I know virtually nothing at all about her life between college and her untimely death."

"What would you like to know?"

"I gather you worked with her."

The man nodded.

"How long?" Josh asked.

"Six years. Maybe a little less. I was with Lloyd for twenty-eight years."

"What exactly did Pamela do for Lloyd Richmond?"

"Just as you said."

"There's got to be more to it than that."

"What are you implying?" Goldman's face grew stern.

"The newspaper said they had traveled to China numerous times together. Was that only to gather paintings and porcelain?"

"Why else?" Goldman said.

"You tell me. No one living knew them better."

"I'm not sure I like what you're driving at, sonny."

"I didn't establish the rules of this game, Mr. Goldman, but I'm forced to play by them. Listen, no one would be trying to kill me sim-ply because I was about to discover that Pamela Morrow was the world's greatest secretary."


At a gas station in Truckee, California, along I-80, and less than twenty miles from Morris Goldman's cabin, Jack Farris waited impatiently as the phone went unanswered on the other end, the rain still tapping steadily on his rented Taurus. He'd been driving for hours and was tired and hungry. The last thing he wanted right now was to make this call, but it was time—and inevitable. His watch told him he was three minutes early.

It was finally answered.

"Yes," came the deliberate response.

"I'm sorry, we missed in Mississippi," he said quickly, wishing to get the bad news out of the way, like a dose of paregoric.

"I've known that for hours, Mr. Farris. Since it's apparently not ability, or the timely delivery of information, tell me just what purpose you do serve in the scheme of things. You'll forgive me if it escapes me at the moment."

Farris had been well-paid in advance for the "accident" that was supposed to have ended Josh Mitchell's life, and was not about to return the money, but with the mishap outside Natchez, could feel the bonus for a successful mission slipping away. It represented a great deal of money, and despite having saved Kisber's portion—by default—didn't want the balance to get away.

He'd already spent it in his mind.

"I was on the road. You said not to call until eight." Farris knew it was a weak defense.

"I'd assumed you'd have good news for me."

"I'm sorry. Some unforeseen things have happened."

"You came highly recommended. Was I misinformed?"

"Not at all. I know where our boy is at the moment and I'm going there now to finish things personally. It'll all be over shortly. You'll wake up tomorrow morning to a world blissfully free of Mr. Mitchell." He switched the cell phone to the opposite ear.

"That won't be necessary." It was put in command form.

"I'm sorry?"

"I've other plans for you. I hope they won't prove too difficult."

"I'm listening."

"I've decided a simple passing is too good for our little friend. I want him to rot in jail, on death row, with a decade behind bars to think about his poor choice in women. I would like the police to suddenly become acutely interested in Joshua Thomas Mitchell and his involvement in Dianne Lane's death. Do you think you can arrange that, Mr. Farris?"

Farris silently cursed at the phone for the unnecessary hundred and seventy-five mile drive he'd just made in the pouring rain. "It will be difficult to link Mitchell to Lane's death, beyond circumstantial evidence, I mean. It's unlikely he'll get the death penalty, even if convicted." He didn't know why he was giving this idiot a lecture on the legal process.

"Then we need to give the police something more solid to sink their teeth into, perhaps another atrocity that can be clearly attributed to our friend. Atrocities: that is what you deal in, isn't it?"

"It is." A woman and child came out of the gas station's convenience store and Farris instinctively lowered his voice, though his words could not have been heard within his car. "You have someone specific in mind?"

"I'll leave the choice entirely up to you. Be creative, but there is to be no trail to me whatever, understood."

"Of course."

"If you succeed in this, there will be a generous second bonus in it for you."

"Fine," Farris said, his mind already on the work to be done. "Consider it past tense."

"Like Mississippi?"

He started to respond, but the line was already dead.

"Rich prick," he said.

He was pleased he hadn't wasted the trip after all and pointed the Taurus toward the tiny hamlet of Idlewild.

Goldman stood again, his back to the fire, his eyes squarely on Josh's. "Lloyd Richmond was a great man," he said with emotion.

"I don't doubt that, sir."

"And there's never been a more loyal and capable woman than Pamela Morrow. The Richmond Museum would have been a meaningless collection of pretty trinkets, with no soul or logic to it, without Pamela Morrow's hand in it. Madeline Richmond may have provided the money, Lloyd the drive, but Pamela gave the Richmond Museum soul, and the art world knew it." Goldman took a long drink of his brandied coffee. "There was never any impropriety between them."

"Fine. I'm glad to hear that. But there was something going on that someone doesn't want me to know about. I'm certain of it, and I think that whatever it was will provide the link between Dianne Lane and Pamela Morrow."

"You keep saying that. What kind of link?"

"God, I wish I knew. All I've learned so far is that they both worked for Lloyd Richmond, in what would appear to have been the identical capacity, and now they're both dead."

"But Dianne Lane's death is being considered a murder, if your suspicions are correct, while Pamela's was clearly accidental. Hardly a similarity there."

"I wonder," Josh said to himself, though it was heard by the old man.

"You think Pamela may have been murdered as well?" His tone didn't carry the level of surprise Josh would have expected.

"There's a thin line between a hit-and-run accident and a 'hit.' Who would have wanted Pamela dead?"

"No one. Everyone loved her."

Josh's look forced the old man to recant.

"No one is universally loved, we both know that, but Pamela Morrow came as close as anyone I've ever known. Besides, she was an art historian, for Christ's sake, not a drug runner or a diamond thief." The rain had slowed outside.

Josh knew Pamela Morrow hadn't been married, but knew nothing of her private life. "Did she have a boyfriend?"

Goldman emptied his mug and set it on the mantel. "She dated some, but there was no one steady if I remember correctly, no one she brought around work. I can't even recall the name of anyone she ever dated."

"Doesn't that strike you as odd for someone so beautiful?" Josh stood, taking a spot opposite Goldman at the fireplace.

"Perhaps. Oh, sure, many men tried to get her to go out with them, some got downright pushy, but she knew how to handle them. Pamela always kept her mind on her work; she was completely devoted to the gallery and Lloyd Richmond."

Though it hadn't been intentional, Josh's expression changed.

"Get your mind out of the gutter," the old man said quickly, noticing the change in Josh's expression. "He was like a father to her— nothing more."

Josh remembered Madeline Richmond's center seat at Dianne Lane's gravesite in San Mateo. He wondered if she'd been as close to Dianne's predecessor. "What'd Mrs. Richmond think of Pamela?"

Goldman took Josh's mug, his own, and wandered toward the kitchen. He didn't answer.

Josh followed him. The sun tried to peek through the heavy clouds in the north, sending shafts of amber light onto the rippled waters of the lake. In the kitchen, the old man ran water in the mugs.

"Mr. Goldman?" Josh said.

Still no answer.

Josh moved to his side. As he did, the man took a small towel and dried his hands. He leaned against the countertop where it made a right angle at a corner. "She hated her," he said, dropping the towel on the counter. He strolled toward the rear deck.

Josh was stunned. Goldman had just said everyone loved Pamela.

He slipped on his hot, but wet, loafers, stuffed his damp socks into his pants pockets, and followed the man onto the deck. The air was cool and damp, the wooden shingles soaked and dripping rhythmically onto the barren flowerbeds bordering the deck.

"Why?" he asked, leaning on the rail beside the old man.

"It doesn't take a genius to figure that out. You jumped to the same conclusion in the first five minutes."

"But you said there was nothing between them."

"Nothing improper," Goldman repeated, his gaze fixed on the clearing lake. He loved the life he lived now and wanted the past behind him.

He turned to his guest, whose welcome had worn thin. "I think it's time for you to leave. You know all there is to know."

Josh faced him squarely, defiantly. "I can't believe that, sir."

"I'm sorry you feel that way. Go away, Mr. Mitchell. There's no peace here, only misery."

The response was not what Josh had expected. "What do you mean?" he pressed, his guts knotting like a snake writhing in his belly.

"Go away, son. I've said all I'm going to say." He stepped heavily down the deck steps and walked toward the water.

Josh followed. "You have to tell me what you know . . . don't send me away, please. I've nowhere else to turn." He grabbed the man's arm, stopping him.

"I'm truly sorry," the old man repeated, pushing Josh's hand away.

# 15

Josh locked Kenny's car and walked toward the lobby door. He'd secured a reservation at the Tahoe Seasons Resort in South Lake Tahoe by cell phone after leaving Goldman's cabin—the closest room within fifty miles—and knew a warm, dry room and a hot shower awaited him. It was all he'd ask for the moment. Later, when his suit and shirt had been hung to dry, and he'd languished beneath a scalding shower, he'd add a few more items to his short list of life's essentials. For now, his mind was too fuzzy, his body too tired and too sore, and his headache too recent to consider much else.

He checked in with no trouble—other than the look he got from the desk clerk, who must have thought it odd that the man in the wrinkled suit, no socks, and shoes that squished when he walked, had no apparent change of clothes—got his key, and strolled sluggishly toward the elevator that would take him to Room 826.

Josh stripped off his still-damp clothes, hung them on the wooden hangers in the closet, widely spaced, and stepped naked into the bathroom. The image that greeted his tired eyes was worse than he'd expected, though his groaning muscles had reminded him repeatedly that he was not at all healed from Thursday's fracas. His left side, from mid-thigh to shoulder, including his upper arm and much of his ribcage, was an unearthly shade of purple with brownish-yellow edging adding as much as an inch to each side of the darker areas. The seatbelt bruise was now the worst, dark, wide, tender.

He twisted the Hot knob counterclockwise, ran a hand under the tub faucet, then added a touch of cold and stepped in. Chill bumps instantly painted his entire body but were soon dissolved as the water poured across him. He put both palms against the wall with the showerhead, leaned forward lowering his chin to his chest, and let the full force of the spray strike his neck and shoulders.

He would remain there for the better part of a half hour.

After Josh shaved, combed his hair, and wrapped a towel around his waist, he fell into the bed, his back against the headboard. Whitney would be gone by this hour, but she would have left his important messages in his voice mail. He was sure something of note had occurred since he'd left the development lab. He wished he'd taken time to see her before leaving, and hoped she'd understand.

He called the office and waited for the automated answering system to pick up. When the prerecorded woman's voice began to announce pleasantly that Barnett Air was closed at this time, he punched in his pass code to bypass the annoying levels of routing that allowed an outside caller to leave a message for nearly any of Barnett's fifteen hundred employees. Normally, entering his four-digit code took him directly to his personal electronic mailbox; he grabbed the hotel's cheap plastic pen and pad by the bed to jot down any messages that required immediate attention, the phone cradled between his head and right shoulder. He was not prepared for the words he heard:

"I'm sorry, your personal identification number has been removed from the system. If you feel this has occurred in error, please consult your supervisor or department head during regular business hours.

"Further attempts to reach this mailbox from an outside line will result in an immediate disconnect."

Josh sat erect and swung his feet to the floor, dropping the pen and pad on the bedside table. "I'm screwed," he grumbled loudly.

He tried the number again, thinking he might have punched in the wrong pass code, perhaps the code of a former employee—he was tired and knew anything was possible.

On his second attempt, despite dialing more deliberately, he was cut off as soon he entered the last digit of his number.

His ear was filled with an annoying busy signal.

"What the hell's this all about?" he growled, though he knew instinctively that he'd been terminated. At this moment, he wanted to hear it from someone other than Barbie (the company nickname for the voice on the answering system), to vent some of the frustration that gripped him. He punched in Kenny's home number, hoping it wasn't one of the normal nights when he'd glued himself to his computer. "Be there," he whispered hopefully, the feeling of desperation surprisingly strong, despite thinking he'd been prepared for this moment. His chest felt like someone was standing on it.

"Hello." Kenny finally answered, sounding exhausted.

"What the fuck's going on, Kenny?" Josh said without the usual pleasantries, surprising himself with his curt tone. He knew his dismissal wouldn't have occurred without Kenny at least knowing the basics of what had happened.

"Josh? Where the hell are you? Are you okay?"

"At least you didn't ask about your car first."

"Screw the car. Talk to me, dude." Kenny set his glass of vodka on the kitchen counter.

"You talk to me, old buddy. I'm the one on the outside looking in." Josh stood, wrestling with the towel that was trying to unwrap. He didn't feel like bothering with it and pitched it across the bed, pulling the phone cord to the end of its length. He touched his underwear hanging in the closet: still damp from the rain. "Dammit," he muttered, dropping to the bed again, shoulders slumped.

"Where are you?" Kenny said, his voice tinged with concern.

"A hotel . . . near Tahoe. What the hell did Hightower fire me for, Kenny? Everything seemed fine when I left his office." Josh felt truly bewildered, betrayed. Chilled, he pulled the covers around him.

"Yeah, seemed that way to me, too. He came down after you left— I didn't tell him you took my car, of course. . . ."

"Thanks."

"He seemed okay with everything; asked if you'd checked on Casper and I told him you had, but that I didn't need any help so you went to get some rest. Then, with no warning, about four o'clock, all hell broke loose." Kenny strolled across the den.

"What do you mean?"

"He came storming into the lab shouting something about how he'd trusted you, treated you like a son, and you'd outright lied to his face."

"Bullshit!" Josh said. He'd been completely honest with Hightower. "I told him everything."

"Hey, I'm not in the middle of this, Josh, I'm just telling you what the old man said."

"He say what I lied about?"

"Said you didn't tell the Carmel or San Francisco Police about Dianne Lane being in your room before she died."

Josh knew his letter had tripped him up, as he'd feared, and that it must have found its way into Lefler's hands sometime prior to four o'clock. It didn't take a physicist to put two and two together, even if the actual sum wasn't four. He'd hoped to have an answer to the puzzle by now, something that would explain the letter's contents credibly. On their own, the words might seem to provide a motive for killing the woman to whom they'd been addressed. He suddenly missed Dianne Lane more than ever, and not just because her being alive would put an end to all of this. He missed her deeply, like a friend he'd known all his life.

He pressed a palm to the wound on his head; a headache thundered just below the stitches.

"I didn't kill her, Kenny," he said, his words low.

"You don't have to tell me that, my friend, I never suspected you did." Kenny reached his Caller-I.D. unit. The name on the LCD panel was from the Tahoe Seasons Resort in South Lake Tahoe, its area code and number displayed beneath. It brought a smile. "You okay, Josh?" he asked with concern in his voice.

"Shit, no! I'm out of work, the only woman I've ever really cared about is dead, I'm the principal suspect in her murder, and some asshole is out there trying to kill me for a reason I can't even guess. Yeah, Kenny, my life is just peachy! Thanks for asking."

"Hey, Josh, don't go south on me, hear? I'm on your side, remember?"

Josh fell back against the mattress, rubbing his eyes. "Sorry. It's been a shit week and getting worse. I don't mean to bark at you."

"It's all right. I doubt I'd be half as calm."

"Finish telling me about Hightower."

"Like I said, about four, he came into the lab shouting and cursing, bitching about how you'd let him down. He asked me where the hell you were, since you hadn't gone back to the La Quinta like he thought. I told him I didn't have the slightest idea, and I think he half believed me. I was really glad I hadn't told him earlier I gave you my car.

"As the lab door slammed behind him on his way out, he was shouting about how you were history. Sorry, man. Is there anything I can do? I really think he'll calm down over the weekend." Kenny didn't sound like he believed the words he'd spoken.

"Not a chance," Josh said, his arm across his forehead, eyes shut. "Did you hear anything about the cops looking for me as well?"

"No, not a word. Hey, maybe the old man's just overreacting. Maybe it's not as bad as he thinks. I mean, if you didn't kill her, they can't prove you did, right?"

"Even if I manage to get a complete exoneration, after the lawyers are through with me I'll be broke, ruined in the business, slandered in the media, dragged through the legal circus like a freak, and the news of my acquittal will be printed on the last page of the paper below an ad for driveway repair. It's a lot to look forward to."

"Shit, man, what are you gonna do?"

"I'm thinking." Josh sat up, his headache worse.

"Leave the country," Kenny said suddenly.

"What? You mean run?"

"Fuckin-A! I'll sell all your stuff and send the money to a Swiss account you set up. You could live for years."

"And then?"

"Hell, I don't know, but I'd think the prospect of continued freedom would sound pretty good right now."

It did, actually, but Josh had never fancied himself a quitter. He knew a life on the run was no life at all. He remembered Dianne Lane's beautiful face, warm eyes, generous smile. He couldn't let the world go on thinking he'd killed her, even if staying to deny it meant his financial ruin—or worse. To run would be to betray what she'd meant to him. He'd been running from the truth all his adult life. No more.

"Can't do it, Kenny. Whatever happens, I've got to see this through."

Kenny clenched a fist in frustration; he'd tried everything he knew to try. He wanted his friend to leave the damned country, to run like hell while he still could. He knew if Josh remained, if he stayed and fought for the truth of Dianne Lane's past, he'd be dead before he could see it coming. He remembered Josh's words about someone trying to kill him in Mississippi and knew in his gut who was behind it.

"Think about that for a moment, Josh. You've got nothing to gain by staying and proving your innocence, everything to gain by leaving this crazy place before the shit hits the fan for good. Do it, tonight. I'll get top dollar for all your stuff and send it right away, I swear. You've already got enough money in the bank to live on for a couple of years. Send me a power of attorney and I'll get that to you in a few days. Go, man—please."

Josh stood and moved to the window, the phone cord stretched fully. In the lights of the parking lot, people were coming and going with no knowledge of any of this, moving about freely with their minds only on vacation or the money they'd won or lost at the tables. It had been such a trying week. He longed for sleep.

"I'll think about what you've said, I promise, but for the moment I'm really tired. I'll call you tomorrow. You be at home?"

"I got that demo with the Navy in the afternoon. After that, I'll be here waiting for your call."

"You're a good man, Kenny," Josh said, allowing the curtain to fall into place again.

"Run, Josh. Don't think about it, just run. Please, for me. It may be my only chance."

"Your only chance?"

"What?"

"You said, 'your only chance.' Don't you mean my only chance?" Josh asked, teasing his friend for his choice of words.

"Yeah, sure, of course that's what I meant," Kenny said, though his voice had changed.

Josh gave it no further thought. "Goodnight, my friend," he said, his mind already elsewhere.

Morris Goldman rocked in a slow, steady rhythm before the stone hearth, the scrapbook opened on his lap, the fire he and Josh had shared now a mound of glowing embers, his eyes tracing the images from another life. Pamela Morrow and Lloyd Richmond stared back from silent photos, neither approving of nor condemning his treatment of the stranger who had come seeking help.

"Maybe I should have told the boy, Lloyd," he whispered to an image of Richmond captured beside one of his beloved terra-cotta soldiers, buried at Xian in 200 B.C. and unearthed, with the help of Richmond funding, in 1974. "What could it have hurt?"

A faint noise came from a room behind him and the old man stood to investigate. After Josh had left, he'd opened several of the cabin's windows a bit to allow the clearing breeze to waft through the house, as he often did after a storm, and anticipated the wind having knocked something over in the kitchen. Several of the tiny pine cones he collected were lying in the sink, having fallen from their perch on the windowsill.

He closed the window and carefully restored the pine cones to their original order among the others.

As he set the last one in place, a second noise came from the opposite end of the house, from the area of his bedroom. He tried to imagine what it might be, and while the wooden cabin was hardly free of creaks and groans, this sound was different, sharp and mechanical, not organic like most of the colorful sounds that gave the old home its character. He put the scrapbook under his arm and retraced his steps to the den, depositing the cherished photo album in his rocker.

When he stood again and turned toward his bedroom, he got a sense of something moving in the shadows of the darkened room. Cautiously, he felt for the light switch on the wall to the right of the door and flicked it when his fingers had found it.

The object in the shadow darted toward him.

"Damn, Lucifer, you scared the stew out of me," he said as the solid black cat crossed the hardwood floor and wrapped itself around his left pant leg, begging for attention. The old man stooped and filled his arms with the mischievous feline, the scamp of the neighborhood, without permanent home or apparent desire to find one. "Looking for a dry bed for the night, eh? Lucky for you I left a window open."

When Lucifer had been fed a small portion of grilled mack and a saucer of warmed milk, he found his occasional spot beside the dying fire and curled up on Morris Goldman's jacket, which had been turned inside out just for him. The self-grooming in earnest began as his benefactor returned to his memories.

Pamela Morrow's wide, dark eyes haunted him as he reached his favorite photo of them, the one taken arm and arm with her at a charity barbecue after they'd won the three-legged race.

"Tell me what to do, Pamela. Knowing can't help the boy, can it?"

He stared at the photo as he thought about the frightened young man he'd turned away earlier.

"How about you, Lucifer, you have an answer for me? I could sure use one about now."

The cat looked up momentarily at the mention of the name most used to address him around Idlewild but found nothing of greater interest than cleansing and straightening his coat.

Morris Goldman leaned back in the rocker and closed his eyes in deep thought, the album pulled against his chest.


Jack Farris peered through the narrow slit between the bedroom's open window frame and the damp sill, his eyes slowly adjusting to the dark and finally coming to rest on the solitary figure that snoozed peacefully in the old cane rocker. The lights had been turned off, another log put on the fire, and Morris Goldman now slept quietly beneath an afghan his wife had made more than two decades earlier, six years before her death from cancer. He often slept that way, even after all these years, the empty bed too often a painful reminder that his beloved Becky had been taken long before her time.

The damp ground squished quietly beneath his soles and had allowed him to move about the cabin's exterior undetected. He cursed himself for having not seen the man's stupid collection of pine cones on the kitchen sill, but no real harm had been done.

He put both feet on his makeshift step, and with gloved hands, pushed up on the bedroom window. It moved quietly, but with the resistance of a window that had been painted numerous times over the years.

As it raised an inch, then two, Lucifer suddenly filled the opening, his eerie green eyes glowing in the near darkness.

*Goddammit!* Farris thought, losing his footing on the soggy log he'd propped against the stone foundation. He fell the six feet to the ground, landing squarely on his back in the rocky soil. His breath was momentarily knocked from him, though he soon recovered and bolted for the cover of a thick ponderosa pine.

"You little black bastard," he muttered, wishing he could put a bullet in the worthless cat and get on with his business.

The interruption gave him a moment to rethink his hastily laid plan; perhaps too much time had lapsed since Mitchell's departure; perhaps the old man had spoken with someone in person or on the phone since Mitchell had checked into the Tahoe Seasons Resort. In either case, perhaps now wasn't as good as later, or perhaps someone else would present themselves as a more credible opportunity. He'd follow Mitchell for a while and make a more logical move in a day or so. Moneybags wanted results, but hadn't dictated that it be done by morning.

There was time, though not much.

Guessing the owner of the home hadn't been roused by the commotion, Farris started back toward the car he'd secreted in the woods a half-mile away.

• • •

Josh wrestled beneath the covers, alternately kicking them from his body and then pulling them back across himself as he grew cold beneath the wall vent that lay directly over his bed. His mind was filled with horrid images of wrinkled, pallid flesh, and cars tumbling through the air. Despite his efforts to ban the image, the face of the stranger lying in the field beside his battered Pontiac—or what had been left of the man's face—flashed across his retinas.

Sleep came hard, though it eventually came.

When his mind finally let loose its need to control the lunacy of the week, the dream of the woman soon followed : . .

. . . She slips the third button through the eye of her suit, then the fourth, and I can now see the gentle curves of her breasts. I have waited for this moment impatiently and now it is here. I fear she'll be disappointed in me, but quickly dismiss such thoughts. I know her, as I know myself, and everything will be all right.

Our eyes meet; hers knowing, warm as a summer breeze; mine anxious, hopeful. In the light from the windows, I watch as she slips the suit jacket from her shoulders and then the skirt past her hips, finally letting each fall to the floor. In another second, she is nude and moving toward the bed where I am sure I am still dreaming.

"May I join you?" she asks. I could never tire of her voice.

I pull back the covers and allow her to slip in beside me, her skin warming mine as our bodies touch. I didn't realize how chilled I'd become until she pressed against me.

Feeling no need to speak further, she kisses me without reservation, her mouth on mine, hard and sensual, her hands pulling my head to hers, her fingers in my hair. I experience a sensation of lightheadedness, like the first time I kissed a girl as a young boy. I want her.

Pamela pulls me onto her, my chest against her breasts, her nipples hard against my skin. We kiss as if it's not possible to get enough of each other. Her breath floats past my ear, her breathing deep, intense. Our hips meet and begin to move in harmony. We are still apart, the need to join overwhelming.

"Oh, Joshua," she whispers in my ear. "I'm glad you wanted me too."

"I do want you," I tell her, but already know it has to wait. For a little while. She is too important to me to make the same old mistakes.

She has to know the truth before we can have anything honest, anything lasting. That is the only thing that matters more at this moment than making love to her.

I know that if I don't force myself to do this, now while the thought can still be distinguished from the passion that torments me, I will never do it. It has been too hard getting to the point in my life where the discomfort of truth matters more than the false comfort of lies.

I raise my body from hers, elbows locked, my hands alongside her shoulders. Even in the darkness, I can still see her haunting eyes.

"Pamela," I say, scarcely able to believe I am doing this. My body is screaming to make love to her, to hold whatever has suddenly materialized in my lunatic brain for some other occasion, yet my heart knows there will never be another first time to make love to this woman, and it must be perfect. Lies will kill us, and whatever chance we might have.

She looks up at me, her hands touching my face, her thumbs caressing my lips. "Yes."

"I have to tell you something first," I say. My heart pounds.

"And it can't wait?" she says with a soft smile.

I shake my head, though my eyes have already said it can't.

I roll onto my side, my back to the windows. She turns onto hers, facing me, her head cradled in her right palm.

"All right," she says, tracing the lines of my face with the fingertips of her free hand. Without intending to, she isn't making this easier.

"Since I first thought I understood what love could be," I begin, "I wanted someone who felt the same way about love and life as I do. We talked about this at dinner—"

"Won't this keep?" she asks, leaning over to me and kissing my lips softly.

I silently beg my body to be patient so my mind can get out what it needs to say. Desire wants no part of reason.

"No, please bear with me. You said you weren't the answer to my prayer. You were wrong. You're not just a beautiful woman, a special woman, meeting you has put me back in touch with the Joshua I'd lost . . . or had misplaced . . . the Joshua I'd always meant to become. That was my prayer, even more than you."

She sits up, against the headboard. The light from the windows spills across the line of her jaw, the curve of her slender shoulders and firm breasts, across the plane of her stomach. She knows I cannot think and look at her at the same time and pulls the covers across her.

I'm not sure I'm grateful, but I find the presence of mind to continue: "When I left Selmer—"

"Is that where you're from?" she asks.

"Yes. Selmer, Tennessee. A little town near the Tennessee River."

She nods and puts her hand on my arm. Though she says nothing, I know she remembers me telling her on the plane that I was from Boston.

I gather my thoughts. "When I left home for college in Boston, I had no idea what to expect. Here I was, this bumpkin from nowheresville as far as they were concerned, with nothing more going for me than a scholarship and a pretty sharp mind."

"That's a lot more than most enter college with," she says.

"I know that now, but I didn't then. I was afraid that just being myself would never be enough for the pedigree crowd at MIT."

"So you reinvented yourself."

"Yes. To the point of inventing parents who'd retired to the south of France after selling off their agricultural interests in Tennessee. That way, none of my friends would expect me to take them home for the holidays or during the summer. Whenever the question arose, I skirted it.

"By the time I graduated, the lies were an integral part of the life I was living, inseparable and sometimes even indistinguishable. They carried into the business world and even into my relationships with women."

"Didn't your model know the truth?" she teased. Her eyes glinted in the moonlight passing through the blinds.

"No one knew—no one *knows*, I should say. Even my boss. My

employment records are as fake as the rest of my last ten years."

"Why are you telling me this, Joshua, now, if you've never told anyone else?"

"I had to. What we can have, if there is to be anything, has to be based on the truth. I couldn't make love to you with you thinking I was anyone other than who I really am. Do you understand, Pamela, why it matters so much to me?"

I see a sadness wash over her, draining the happiness from her face. My heart sinks.

She pushes the covers back and slips from the bed, grabbing her clothes as she moves for the bathroom, never looking back toward the bed.

A disappointment like I've never known envelopes me. I know she's leaving, and nothing I can say will convince her to stay.

In a minute, she steps from the bathroom, dressed, and returns to the bed. When she sits beside me, she runs her hand through my hair. I haven't moved, my shaky muscles unable to support my weight, I am certain.

"You're a dear and gentle man, Joshua. I wish I could have gotten to know you under different circumstances—"

"What circumstances?" I interrupt. *Please tell me. . . . I'll make them happen, whatever I have to do.*

"Just . . . different . . . that's all. I have to go now. Please don't think badly of me."

"I could never. Please stay, Pamela. Let's talk about this. There's so much at stake."

"You're more right than you know, but it's out of our hands," she says, and I have no idea what she is talking about.

She places the key she has used to enter my room on the table beside the one given me at check-in and stands, backing toward the door, her eyes fixed on mine.

I sit up in the bed and resist crying out for her to stay. I remember her words from dinner, about freedom, and mine about letting things have their own honest identity. They now cut like a knife, sealing my fate.

"Goodbye, Joshua Mitchell," she whispers standing in the open door.

"Wait," I call out. "Can't I see you tomorrow?"

She gently shakes her head no.

"Please. Just breakfast, Pamela. What can that hurt? On the garden patio. Seven A.M." I fill in all the blanks so she can't refuse. *Please don't say no*, I beg silently.

She rests her forehead against the edge of the door, her eyes tightly shut.

After a lifetime, she nods with a faint smile. "Until seven," she says softly, and then, as the door closes behind her, I hear: "Goodbye, Joshua. . . ."

"Freeze, asshole!" came the chorus of excited voices in the darkness of Josh's hotel room. Harsh white beams of light painted the walls and furniture in crazy, searching streaks, blinding Josh through sleep-dilated pupils.

After being ripped from the warm dream of Pamela, cold, rough hands flipped him onto his stomach, his head held immobile by a thick iron bar across his neck. A knee slammed into his left kidney painfully pinned him against the mattress while other pairs of gruff hands held his legs and bent his arms and fingers like saplings in a gale, clamping his wrists into tight steel bracelets. His left shoulder felt like an acetylene torch was being held against it.

Abrupt, angry, cursing male voices filled the tiny room; he had no idea how many there were, but the place was thick with them, like flies on a carcass.

When the room lights were flicked on, Josh realized the men had been operating by flashlight only: long, black, aircraft-aluminum Mag-Lights containing a half-dozen D-cells each—what couldn't be blinded by their intense beam could be hammered flat with little fear of damage to the armored light.

Josh's disorientation was heightened by the confused shouting and fractured sentences flying all around him, though he couldn't tell where one command began and another ended.

He *could* tell that he was at the center of their anger.

With as little regard for the pain it had caused when they'd flipped him onto his stomach, he was now as abruptly rolled onto his back, the bedcovers thrown to the floor. He lay centered lengthwise on the mattress, embarrassingly nude, trying to sort out the different faces that moved about him like worker bees. No one appeared to be in charge as they tore through drawers and looked under and behind every stick of furniture in Room 826.

He'd never seen so many handguns in one small place in his life.

Though they were hardly inconspicuous, Josh noticed for the first time the huge yellow letters spelling out "U.S. Marshall" on the backs of most of the black jackets.

Finally, a man in a dark blue business suit rounded the corner from the short hall that led to the only door, and stood at the foot of the bed. The noise from the other men came to a quick end and most moved out of the room, their work done, disappearing into the hallway.

The man in the suit bent and grabbed the spread that had been on the bed prior to the assault. He pitched it across the lower half of Josh's body.

"Thanks," Josh said, though it seemed little enough to be grateful for.

One of the officers, without the yellow lettering on his black uniform—Josh assumed him to be a member of the SWAT team assisting the marshals—handed the man in the suit Josh's driver's license. He studied the photo for a second before handing it back to the SWAT man who then vanished. Besides Josh, there were now only three men left in the room, the man in the suit plus two marshals.

Josh heard the outer door close.

"Joshua Thomas Mitchell?" the man in the suit asked, though he'd already made the determination he had the right man.

Josh nodded. He no longer believed this to be the worst nightmare of his life, but the worst reality.

"I'm U.S. Marshal William Codrall. I'm placing you under arrest for the murder of one Dianne Marie Lane in Carmel, California, on or about the ninth of March of this year, as well as interstate flight to avoid prosecution. The order was signed by a federal judge four hours ago."

Josh instinctively looked toward the alarm clock on the bedside table, but it had been knocked around so that its dial was not visible to him.

"You have the right to remain silent," Codrall continued. "If you give up that right, anything you say can and will be used against you in a court of law. You have the right to counsel; if you cannot afford one, the court will appoint an attorney for you."

Josh listened to every word as the marshal recited it, though his mind was lost in the surreal moment; it was worse than he'd ever imagined. He should have gone a lifetime without having the Miranda read to him.

When the marshal-in-charge finished his legal speech, he asked if Josh understood his rights. Josh nodded. The man then asked Josh if he had anything to say at this time. Josh shook his head, knowing that to say *anything* to this man, without benefit of sound legal advice, would be foolish if not downright dangerous.

"Do you intend to oppose extradition to California, Mr. Mitchell?"

The question was not one Josh had expected. If he said yes, would he be thrown in a jail in Nevada? Would it be better than one in California? Probably not, he imagined, feeling screwed either way.

"I'll have a document for you to sign to that effect when we get to the car then."

Josh indicated that he understood.

Codrall then signaled for the other men to put the suspect on his feet.

Josh grimaced when the two huge officers lifted him by his upper arms; his left shoulder socket felt like it was breaking.

His controlled, but not entirely silent, expression of pain went unremarked.

When Josh was standing at the foot of the bed, one of the men grabbed his clothes from the closet. Both men then proceeded to dress him from the waist down, including socks and shoes, as Codrall stood back, his 9mm Beretta at the ready.

Josh's shirt was then placed across his shoulders, followed by his jacket, his hands still cuffed behind his back. Neither was buttoned, leaving his chest bare.

In the hall, Josh could hear other guests asking in frightening tones what in the world was going on, why had their sleep been disrupted?

Codrall shouldered his weapon. "Ready, Mr. Mitchell?" he asked politely, as if saying *no* would actually allow Josh to remain in his room.

"Does it matter at all to you that I didn't have anything to do with Dianne Lane's death?" He knew that it didn't even before he asked the ridiculous question.

"Nope. It's not my job to determine guilt or innocence. I just bring 'em in," Codrall said without looking at his catch.

"Where are you taking me?" Josh asked, his mouth dry.

"Carmel. Ever been a guest of their fine jail?" he asked.

"Never been in any jail before," Josh said across parched lips, his words weak, without core. He'd half expected to be heading back to San Francisco.

Codrall studied the man with the wrinkled suit coat across his shoulders. He noted Josh's apparently good physical condition, but also the fear lining his face. For a moment he was silent, appearing sympathetic, then a wicked smirk twisted his lips. "Well, like the old joke goes, Mitchell, you're gonna *hate* Wednesdays."

Josh's knees felt as if they'd buckle. He knew what the man meant.

Both marshals, firmly gripping his arms, chuckled at Codrall's tasteless humor as they led the suspect from his hotel room through a sea of bewildered guests.

Even if Josh's mind hadn't been flooded with the pure animal-like thoughts of the ordeal that lay ahead, he'd scarcely have given Jack Farris, standing in the hall a few doors down from Room 826, a second look.

# 16

Detective Louis Fachini paced beside the table in the interrogation room, his patience thin, the odor from years of cigarettes smoked in nervous desperation permeating the tiny chamber. It was nearly noon, five hours after Josh Mitchell had been delivered back into his hands, and he was tired of the lies and denials. It didn't matter that Josh had told him nothing but the absolute truth since the formal questioning began at nine, suspects always lied, and this one would be no different. Besides, he'd caught Mitchell in two significant deceptions already—he had known Dianne Lane and she had been in his room prior to her death—so it followed that other lies must be waiting to be uncovered.

And he'd uncover them—many who'd occupied the chair upon which Josh now sat could attest to that—but for now the detective was interested in only one: Why had Mitchell killed Dianne Lane? Although it seemed, to Fachini's satisfaction, that Mitchell's letter, written in his own hand and now lying on the table before him, provided more than ample motive.

Josh thought about the most recent question, his mind fuzzy and slow, like he'd been on a drunk for the last week. His hurriedly arranged attorney, John Steven McNeese, a twenty-seven-year-old conscientious and hard-working nonpartner—one of ninety-six such clones from a prestigious old Carmel law firm hastily chosen because of their full-page ad in the Yellow Pages—repeated his demand that Josh not answer anything. Though pleasant enough, and all-too-eager, McNeese was not the man Josh wanted on his right when trial time came. Still, for the five-thousand-dollar retainer this was costing him, Josh at least listened to McNeese's warning again.

And again, he refused to heed it.

Instead, he reread the paragraph in his letter that Fachini had alluded to and chose his rebuttal carefully. "I was talking about how I'd lived my life, that's all. The lies I referred to were about my life during college and the years following. Simple things, personal things, not some earth-shattering secret like knowing who killed Kennedy."

"Would you consider Richard Hightower an image-conscious man, Mr. Mitchell?"

Josh knew he was, to a fault, but didn't want to answer the question directly. He knew where Fachini was heading.

"No more so than most CEOs, I guess," he said unconvincingly.

Fachini gave him a raised eyebrow for his trouble. "Oh, come now, Mr. Mitchell, he's well known as an 'axe man' when it comes to blights, or even *potential* blights, on Barnett's public image. He feels like he built the company to its present status with his bare hands. Fair characterization?"

Josh shrugged, yet did not bother denying what the detective obviously felt he knew to be gospel. McNeese sighed gratefully.

"And yet you shared these . . . personal secrets, as you put it . . . with Mrs. Lane, knowing that if she were to reveal them to your employer, you'd be out on your ear. Am I right, Mr. Mitchell?" Fachini rested his weight on both palms, arms locked, standing across the table from Josh, his black eyes fixed on his prime suspect.

"Why on earth would some relative stranger go to my boss and tell him that I told my college fraternity buddies, nearly a decade ago, that my parents lived in Europe? You're reaching, detective."

"Why? Blackmail. Maybe she was shaking you down for money."

"That's ridiculous. What I shared with Dianne Lane were hardly the kinds of things Hightower would care about. Now you are reaching."

"Am I? It shows a pattern, Mr. Mitchell. A pattern of lies. I think he would care a great deal about one of his trusted employees being an inveterate liar."

Josh didn't like being called a liar and started to rise from his seat. His attorney, sensing the unwise movement, grabbed his arm and again pressed him not to say another word, though he knew by now it was a futile gesture. He prayed Josh wouldn't incriminate himself—he'd never make partner that way.

Fachini saw the reaction he'd gotten and pressed on. "It doesn't matter why, anyway. All that matters is that you believed that if she did go to Hightower, you'd lose that cushy job you had with Barnett Air, and the lifestyle that went with it. Say it ain't so."

Josh hated this bastard. He was not merely doing his job, he was relishing the part where he got to persecute and torture. Josh could no longer think objectively, or clearly. He desperately tried one last argument. "I'm not exactly what you'd call unemployable, Fachini. I'm one of only a handful of salesmen in the world who deal exclusively in corporate jets, and I'm the best there is. Even if what you hypothesize were true, I'd have another job before my dinner got cold. And, for more money. Why in hell would I kill someone to protect something that doesn't need protecting?"

Fachini stood, pulled a chair behind him, and sat, his eyes never leaving Josh's. "You fuck her?"

Josh didn't want the conversation to go in that direction, but knew it wasn't one of his sales calls; that he wasn't in control.

McNeese held Josh's arm, whispering in his ear: "If he knew, he wouldn't be asking you. Don't say another word, Josh, please." His words were level, but his tone reflected the claustrophobia he felt in the cramped closet of a room.

Josh couldn't keep the anger from erupting. "Hell, no! We'd only met a few hours before, for Christ's sake!" He knew the defense sounded like it came from a Sixties TV show, not the sexually free Nineties.

Fachini made an incredulous face, then turned it hard again. "But you wanted to," he whispered, "didn't you?"

"No . . . I mean, of course . . . sure, who wouldn't have?" Josh stammered.

"But she wouldn't let you, would she? She came up to your room, screwed with your head awhile, and then wouldn't screw you? Bet a good-looking guy like you isn't used to that kind of rejection. And after an expensive dinner at Scomas, wine, lobster, the whole deal. What a bitch. No wonder you threw the dick-teasing whore into the ocean." He stood, turning his back on Josh as he straightened his hand-made tie in the one-way mirror.

Josh wrenched his arm from McNeese's death grip.

"Fachini, you're not a good cop who wants to know the truth. You're a foul-mouthed, dirty-minded son of a bitch. Dianne Lane was not a whore, she was the finest lady I've ever known. She came to my room, we talked, she left, and I don't have the slightest idea how she died, except that she left a suicide note you seem to be forgetting. Now, if you think you can prove I killed her, be my guest."

He had risen to his feet without consciously realizing it, and now stood eye level with the detective who'd turned casually back during the outburst.

Josh's angry words brought nothing more than a smirk from Fachini, though the junior lawyer had dropped his head to his arms, folded on the table, and was rocking it slowly back and forth while murmuring, "Sit down, sit down, sit down."

"Oh, I will, Mr. Mitchell. And I'll put your lying ass on death row." He took a step and leaned across the small table, planting his face an inch from Josh's. "I've got you, I've got opportunity, and I've got motive." He grabbed the letter from the Sandpiper and jammed it into Josh's chest. "You got nothing, Mitchell, not even a bad alibi." He stood erect as a pole. "But to show you what a fair guy I am at heart, if you want to cop a plea of second-degree murder, in which case you could be eligible for parole in seven or eight years, you have one opportunity, and one only, to come clean with me. If you leave this room and I don't have what I want, I'm going to the DA and press him for murder in the first, and I won't have any trouble getting him to go along with me. He absolutely loathes New Yorkers."

Josh sat slowly, the desperation of his situation crushing him. He needed to decide what to do next, what he hadn't yet tried. It seemed hopeless. He was trapped in the system, and if he didn't play by Fachini's rules, the cop would flush him and move on, no sleep lost.

He studied the smudges of black ink on his fingers that remained from being printed, and the depth of the abyss into which he was about to be flung became undeniable.

"I'd like to talk with my attorney," he said.

"Sure, take all the time you like. I'll be close by when you're ready to make a statement."

"No mikes," McNeese said, referring to the recording equipment used to tape conversations in the room.

"Of course not, counselor. What do you think we are, unscrupulous?" Fachini let himself out of the room, closing the door exaggeratedly behind him, as if to remind Josh that he had the power to close it for decades—if not forever.

Josh turned to McNeese. "You've got to get me out of here. I can't spend the next six months in the Monterey County Jail awaiting trial."

"Actually, I think they're about ten months backlogged," the lawyer said, trying to be informative before he realized it was not the kind of news his client wanted to hear.

Josh squeezed his eyes shut before training them on the attorney again.

"I'm not sure you'll be eligible for bail, Josh," McNeese said, pulling a reference book from his briefcase. "This is a capital crime and the evidence is pretty strong. Furthermore, the death of Mrs. Lane has been called especially heinous by the press all week, with public sympathy for the murdered woman growing each day. She was beautiful, well-loved, well-respected. Quite frankly, Josh, they want your butt, and whatever judge you get will be all too aware of this. I wouldn't get my hopes up about getting out of here anytime soon. Sorry."

Josh shook his head, scarcely believing what he was hearing. "You think I killed her?"

"It's the responsibility of my law firm to provide you with the best defense possible, Josh, not to determine your guilt or innocence." He stopped turning pages in the thick law book.

"It'd help if someone believed I was innocent," Josh said, "like my attorney."

"All right. If it matters that much." McNeese went back to his text, searching for something that had come to mind.

*Monday*, Josh thought, knowing he couldn't possibly be out of Fachini's private hell before then at the earliest.

He could well be dead by Monday.


When Detective Fachini stepped into the blackened office adjacent to the interrogation room, Karl Hetzler's even voice floated across the darkness. "I need to talk to your suspect a minute, Louis. Alone, if you don't mind."

"Hetzler?" Fachini said before his eyes had readjusted, surprised by the agent's presence. He'd apparently arrived sometime during the questioning.

"I'll need this room cleared as well," Hetzler added.

"Hell, why not just make yourself at home? Want some coffee? A Coke? My office?" Fachini disliked the Bureau, and Karl Hetzler in particular. They'd met on several occasions, and each time, the FBI had interfered in one of Fachini's cases.

He could see the man's face clearly now.

The agent said, "I should have let you know I was coming, but I only learned of Mitchell's arrest two hours ago. Been on the road since the call."

"What's the Bureau's interest in Mitchell?"

"You know I'm not free to discuss that, Louis." Hetzler's tone was especially patronizing. He had no more use for the cop than Fachini had for him, but attempts at pleasantry usually made things go smoother than outright hostility.

"Well, maybe I'm not free to let you use my building for your cat-and-mouse games. What do you think of that?"

"Please, Louis. I'm asking nicely."

Fachini knew this was Hetzler's way of saying that with the help of a federal judge—who was assuredly only a call away—he could have Mitchell moved to another location anytime he chose.

"Come on, boys," Fachini ordered, summoning the other two detectives from the observation room. "What do you want me to do with the lawyer?" he asked.

"I'll deal with him. Thanks for your gracious cooperation, Louis. I'll remember it." The agent moved to the door to the interrogation room.

"I just bet you will," Fachini muttered under his breath, heading toward his office.

Hetzler opened the door.

"Is there something we can do for you?" McNeese asked officially. He thought he and his client had the room to themselves for a while.

"Hello, Josh," Hetzler said with as warm a smile as he could produce.

Josh nodded.

McNeese looked at his client. "Who is this man, Josh?"

"Can we talk for a moment, Josh, just the two of us?" the agent asked.

McNeese and Josh made eye contact, the lawyer wondering what the hell was going on.

Josh patted McNeese on the shoulder. "Give us a minute, will you John?"

"Are you with the police?" the lawyer asked, eyeing Hetzler.

"It's all right, John, really. Just wait outside, please."

Though he didn't like it at all, McNeese acquiesced and Hetzler closed the metal door behind him. Josh flinched at the sound.

The agent sat opposite Josh. "You're becoming quite a popular fellow, Josh."

Josh leaned back in his chair. "Never did care much for the spotlight."

"Really? You were a star quarterback in high school; I find that hard to believe."

"Doesn't surprise me; lately everybody's finding what I say hard to believe."

Hetzler gave a chuckle.

"What can you do to make my life more miserable than it already is, Agent Hetzler?" Josh asked.

Now the agent leaned back, mirroring Josh's posture, if not mood. "I read the letter you wrote Dianne Lane, Josh. Interesting stuff. Want to talk about it?"

"Jesus, you guys are great. I get the feeling none of you has ever told a fib in your life."

"I'm no memory expert, Josh, but as nearly as I recall, your words were, 'My life is what it is today because of the lies I told, the lies I lived. Now it's time to begin anew, a life I was meant to be living all along. I have you to thank, Pamela.' Sounds like more than mere fibs to me. How about you?"

Josh rolled his head against the block wall, eyes squeezed tightly shut. Finally, "Like I told Fachini, I was referring to personal things in my life, not national secrets. I had a Top Secret clearance, for Christ's sake, issued by your agency. You know you don't get one of those if they think you're a liar. Do you?"

"Not usually. It has happened, though." Hetzler's eyes had lost any trace of humor.

"Are you all fucking crazy or something? How far can you blow this thing up?" He leaned forward across the table. "Don't you get it? I didn't want my rich classmates in college to know I was a poor farmer's kid, okay. None of them had even seen a farmer, except maybe from the interstate at seventy miles an hour. They drove BMWs and had bedrooms bigger than my whole house. I was so far out of my element I felt like the country dog headed for the city; I knew if I ran, I'd get bitten in the ass; if I stood still, I'd get screwed. I just wanted to fit in, so I invented a life they'd comprehend."

Hetzler did understand, far better than Josh could have imagined. Mitchell fit the standard profile almost to the letter: an over-achiever who didn't feel he fit in; an attractive guy who could charm anyone out of anything. He'd gotten what he'd come for—more. It was now time to let Mitchell go, despite the vehement objections and threats he knew the overzealous Fachini would direct at him.

If he was right, and he knew he was, the frightened Mr. Mitchell would quickly lead them to the conspirators they'd been trying to identify for four years. Hetzler hated no one more than those who, for the sake of money, turned over national secrets to the enemies of the country he loved. He'd have Mitchell—and he'd have the rest of his group as well, now.

The agent stood, and, patting Josh once on the shoulder, left the cramped room. For the third time, the door slammed shut. Josh knew he'd never get used to the metallic sound. It had an icy permanence to it like no other sound he'd ever heard. He'd never thought of himself as claustrophobic, but knew he could acquire the disorder with little difficulty in a place such as this.

If his memory served him, and the evening news was accurate, prison cells were even smaller.


It took an order from a federal judge to effect Josh Mitchell's release, and, if there had been a thread of goodwill remaining between Fachini and Hetzler, it was now severed.

"Thanks," Josh said meekly as the sergeant slid his possessions through a half-moon opening in a thick glass window. It earned him a disinterested grunt. The officer turned a legal pad toward the two men standing beyond his window.

While lawyer McNeese watched in confused relief, Josh signed for his things and emptied the manila envelope bearing his name and booking number. The sergeant took the pad, reclaimed the envelope, and disappeared.

"Who was that guy?" the lawyer asked for the second time.

"His name is Karl Hetzler."

"And he is . . .?"

"Someone with the government," Josh said, avoiding a more direct answer. He didn't begin to understand what had just occurred, why he was being released when it was so blatantly obvious that the detective in charge of the investigation vehemently opposed it, but he was grateful for the intervention the odd little FBI agent had apparently provided.

*I guess he believed me after all*, Josh thought as he began to put his wallet and keys in their respective pockets, though he would have figured Hetzler for the last person to buy his story.

"Which branch?" McNeese pressed, feeling he'd missed something along the way. He knew he'd have to make a full report, and "the government" simply wouldn't do for the partners.

"The FBI."

"What do they want with you?" he asked as they walked.

"Listen, John, I'm really grateful for all your help, but I simply can't answer your question. If you want to know that, you'll have to ask them. Sorry."

"There's more to this than a simple murder, isn't there?" the attorney said, though a part of him really didn't want to know.

"I honestly don't know, John. I suppose so . . . maybe not . . . I don't care, really. I just want to go somewhere and sleep for a week." Josh reached the front door, McNeese behind.

Josh hadn't seen Hetzler or Fachini since he'd left the interrogation room an hour earlier—another detective had seen to his release—though he had heard part of the heated conversation between the two cops. He didn't care about their jurisdictional differences, so long as he was leaving this place.

He silenced his inner voice as it asked for how long.

He'd deal with that later.

At the front door of the Carmel Police Department, which faced Fourth Street, Josh thanked John McNeese again, assured him that the check he'd given him was good, and told him he'd be in touch in the next few days.

They shook hands and, as the lawyer started toward his car a couple of blocks away, Josh suddenly realized that he had no ride. His car was in Monterey, at some garage the Carmel Police used for storage, ten minutes north. He called out to McNeese, and then jogged to his side.

"Sorry, John, but can you give me a ride to Monterey? They've got my car up there."

"Sure. Hop in. I was going up there to see my sister sometime today anyway, might as well be now. You got the address?"

Josh handed his lawyer the slip of paper bearing the garage's address.

"I know the place," McNeese said, starting his car.

Josh hoped someone had called ahead to have Kenny's car released; the last thing he needed at this point was to be charged with attempted auto theft.

Josh hurriedly checked the Porsche for damage, at the garage manager's direction—it was filthy from being driven to and from Tahoe in the rain—and promptly announced that it was perfect. Whatever damage there might be, though he saw nothing obvious, he'd gladly fix; he just wanted it out of the lockup as quickly as it could be arranged.

He signed his name to an official-looking police document for the fourth time in ten minutes and sank in the familiar leather seat. The engine fired at once and within another minute, the Monterey Garage had vanished in the rearview mirror.

Only then did Josh allow himself a deep breath of relief, his mind focusing on retrieving his few possessions from the La Quinta Inn in Sacramento and on finally getting the sleep his body had been craving.

The air was cool, the sky no longer threatening, and at two in the afternoon, Josh estimated he would reach the hotel by five-thirty. He opened the sunroof to allow the March air to refresh his exhausted brain.

When he did, the loose paperwork the garage manager had handed him rustled on the front seat, stirred by the breeze entering the roof. It needed to be in the glove box.

With his eyes on the road, he folded it in thirds—like a letter to be mailed—and opened the small compartment. A letter that had been previously occupying the space dropped to the passenger's floorboard.

"Great," Josh said sarcastically, as he leaned across the center console and quickly fished around for it. His effort was in vain, but nearly allowed the Porsche to eat one of the roadside markers as the right tires eased onto the shoulder.

He put his mind fully on driving and decided to try again the first time he had to stop.

As he sat at a light several miles northeast of the impound garage, he again fished beneath the passenger's seat hoping to find whatever had escaped the glove box. When his fingers touched the loose sheet of paper, he pulled it impatiently forward, hearing it tear noisily on the seat track.

Josh cut his eyes to the traffic signal and realized that the adjacent lanes had just gotten a long-awaited turn light: he had a few seconds yet. Before he stuffed the loose sheet of paper back in the glove box, he gave it a glance to see if he had inadvertently ruined something of importance to his friend, and was surprised at the odd words that stared back at him.

The brief but curt letter was from an attorney demanding that Kenny's mortgage be brought up to date by the first of the month or foreclosure proceedings would begin immediately thereafter.

"What the hell?" Josh said, closing the glove box. Kenny's home and land had been paid for in cash; Josh had proudly stood beside him as his friend wrote the check in the closing attorney's office not long after they had received payment for *Canterbury*. Had Kenny taken a second mortgage on it? And if so, why? He had a good income from Barnett, even if it didn't compare with Josh's; more than enough to meet his expenses and provide for generous savings.

Josh realized that too much distance had grown between the best friends, and vowed to correct the situation as soon as his neck was out of the noose that presently surrounded it.


Brad Munford followed the Porsche carefully. He knew Mitchell hadn't seen him, and was not likely to in his current state of mind. Later, after the boy had reacquired some emotional stability, he would watch his mirrors more carefully, and the agent would have to be more stealthy, but for now, a hundred yards and five or six cars back of the distinctive German sports car was adequate.

"Think he'll lead us to the rest?" he said after he'd driven in relative silence for ten minutes. They were on State Route 1 heading north, just passing the Monterey Fairgrounds.

"He's way out of his element. Scared shitless. He'll lead us,"

Hetzler said with calm assurance. "He doesn't want to be the fall guy. He's going to tell that to whoever's in charge to his face. It may get him nowhere, but it's my guess he'll tell him."

"Think he'll run?"

"Most do."

"We going after him if he does?" The agent eased around a slower car and shortened the distance between their car and the Porsche.

Hetzler lit a cigarette and blew the smoke through a narrow crack in the passenger window. "With a vengeance," he said as he exhaled. "I got him out for a reason, but when I put him back in, he won't see the sky again until he's too old to move without a walker."

As expected, having driven in a dull stupor, his eyes on the road but his mind as blank as he could make it, Josh pulled into the parking lot of the La Quinta at five-fifteen. He was sure Kenny would be worried about him by now—they hadn't spoken in fourteen hours—but decided not to deal with that until he'd had a shower, some food, and at least a few hours rest.

As soon as Josh shoved his plastic key into the room's electronic lock and turned the handle down, the man was on him, forcing him through the door and down onto the carpet. Josh had rarely been tackled as hard on the football field and his breath was squeezed from his lungs as the man's weight hammered him to the floor.

Josh's first impulse was to fight back, but his mind somehow knew that he wasn't being assaulted. He understood the two-hundred-plus pounds pinning him to the carpet was probably another U.S. marshal, no doubt sent to usher him back to a waiting cell. Fachini had apparently prevailed.

The psychological yo-yo of murder suspect and free man was taking its toll on Josh.

The man felt Josh's muscles slowly yield and his impulse to resist abate. Even in the poorly illuminated room, he could see in Josh's weary silhouette that there would be no further struggle.

Josh could smell the man's breath, and the odor of cigarettes smoked one after another was repugnant.

The man stood. "Put your forehead against the carpet and then don't move until I tell you to," he ordered, his voice low, almost a whisper, but his tone unmistakable.

Josh obliged, waiting for the handcuffs to follow. His sore shoulder and knee had both been awakened in the fall, and were now complaining loudly and sending shards of pain shooting through his joints. He felt his nose bleeding from where his face had struck the floor. The blood pooled in his nostrils, forcing him to breathe through his mouth.

He listened for the sound of others milling about, but heard nothing, unlike before when the room was alive with angry men. It seemed this man was alone.

No, he considered, there would be others in the hall, many, as before, and would respond with guns drawn if called upon. He'd give this man no reason to summon them.

"How 'bout it, Mitchell," the man spoke, his voice a notch louder but still much lower than normal conversation, "life been a real bitch lately, has it?"

Josh didn't need to respond.

"That's too bad, but all the shit that's been heaped on you is your own fault, you know that, don't you?"

Josh clenched his fists but remained silent.

The man saw Josh's fingers knot. "It's about time you stopped playing Magnum P.I. and became just an ordinary citizen again."

Josh now realized that this man, whoever he was, wasn't with any branch of law enforcement, at least not any he'd done business with in the last week, and he felt like he'd met them all. He was someone else, representing other interests, though who or what was as elusive as everything else served up during this mad week.

*Oh, Jesus,* Josh thought, *is this bastard the one who sent the two men after me in Mississippi?* He considered his options for escape or self-defense, but felt as helpless as an animal in a slaughter pen. Then he realized that if this man wanted him dead, he'd already be dead.

"What do you mean?" he asked.

The man put a heavy leather work boot across Josh's neck, adding weight until he elicited a deep groan. "There is no connection between Dianne Lane and Pamela Morrow, understand? Trying to create one will fuck you up beyond belief. Trust me, Mitchell, you don't want to piss us off. Just drop it. Let it lie, and eventually you'll get your life back, or most of it anyway. We can't help it if you got a prick for a boss, but those are the breaks."

"What are you going to do with me?" Josh asked.

"Do?"

"You're not going to arrest me . . . or kill me?"

"You're so melodramatic, Mitchell, and apparently watch too much television. I'm afraid neither of those options would serve our purposes very well. Now, on the other hand, if you don't do as you're told, you'll be dropped back into the gristmill of American Justice, to spout your stupid little pleas of innocence while Fachini and Lefler vie for the right to gas your dumb ass." He moved his foot and knelt on one knee beside Josh's head, bringing his mouth close to Josh's right ear. "I already think Fachini's got a hard-on for you, Mitchell. How much planted evidence do you think it would take to get him all wet for you again? Think about it, my friend. This is not a football game you're playing. Losing is forever."

The man stood and walked easily to the door, showing none of the anxiety or anger Josh felt. When he'd left and the door had latched itself behind him, Josh picked himself up from the floor and stumbled to the bathroom, turning on the light above the vanity and running cold water in the sink.

He stuck his head under the stream, dousing his bloody nose and mouth. The bleeding stopped quickly—he'd been hurt worse in a hundred scrimmages—but he couldn't throw off the shaking that had started shortly after the man's last words. It wasn't fear as he'd always thought of it, but a hopeless desperation that clutched at him. He sank to the toilet lid and stared at his reflection in the mirror.

The hard, narrow eyes that stared defiantly back troubled him. Being told what he couldn't do had meant trouble for Josh since he was a boy in Tennessee, for it always dictated what he would do.

# 17

It was dusk when the gravel forming Morris Goldman's driveway crunched again beneath the Porsche's wide tires. The cabin appeared dark but for the gilded glow of a dim bug-light escaping around the north end of the structure from the rear deck. Josh didn't see the old man until he was practically upon him, standing in the shadows of the front-porch overhang.

"Figured you'd be back," Goldman said, his words sounding as weary as he looked.

Startled, Josh said, "Sorry, didn't see you, sir." He stopped before the first step, awaiting permission to begin something he'd decided two hours earlier to pursue even if it meant his life.

"Guess I know why you're here. Might as well come on in and get it over with." The man disappeared through the front door, leaving it ajar.

Josh was both pleased and puzzled at the ease with which he'd been granted a second audience with the only man alive who might be able to shed some light on Pamela Morrow's years with Lloyd Richmond.

He hesitantly crossed the threshold, knowing that the old man's words of warning yesterday had been spoken in earnest, and should have been heeded. His eyes found the man sitting in his rocker, illuminated only by the orange glow of a dying fire.

"Sit," Goldman said in a voice as faint as air, and Josh wasn't certain he'd actually heard it.

Determined to have his answers, he took the seat he'd used on Friday, barely able to distinguish the man's features in the half-light, though only a few feet to his left.

Goldman sipped on brandy. No coffee this time.

As if reading Josh's mind, he said, "Bottle's at your feet; glass, too. You'll want a drink about now, I suspect."

"Thank you," Josh said, finding with his left hand the bottle of Delsay between the two rockers. A snifter sat upside down over the cork and the glass surfaces tinkled together as he retrieved them. He poured a tall glass, emptying the bottle. The brandy ran like a river of liquid fire down his throat, quieting the tension in his stomach.

It was nice to be expected, but he wondered how the man had known he would be returning tonight. That question, like most from the week, would probably remain unanswered. He was certain, however, that there was no link between this quiet gentleman from another age and the thug who'd tackled him in his motel room. Why he knew this, he wasn't sure, he just did.

"You said yesterday that there would be no peace in my questions, only misery. What did you mean by that, sir?"

"How has your life been since Mrs. Lane's death?" The old man spoke to the fire, concentrating on the black-and-crimson embers that no longer held the bright light of flame.

"You know how my life has been; I told you about it yesterday."

"And since then?" he interrupted, as if he knew the reappearance of his new acquaintance had been driven by external forces.

Josh took another stout slug of brandy. "Hell, pure hell. In the last eighteen hours I've lost my job and now I've been arrested and booked for her murder."

*Eighteen hours.* There was that number again, just like in Carmel, he thought. Strange.

"What's maddening," he continued, not wishing to lose his train of thought, "is that in this whole bizarre situation, I didn't do anything wrong, not a damned thing."

Goldman chuckled mockingly. "Of course you did something wrong, my wide-eyed young friend—you were in the wrong place at the wrong time. That's all it takes now'days. This isn't the Fifties, it's the dawn of a new century, and frankly, I'm glad I won't be around to experience much of it. I rather liked this one, you know." He turned toward the silhouette that was his guest. "You seem surprised that the system finally betrayed you."

Josh didn't speak.

"Well, don't be," Goldman sneered. "We'll all have a turn in the barrel before we're done."

"What's made you so cynical?"

"Cynical? Is that what you believe? I like to think of myself as a realist. I mean, just look at the mess you're in."

"But it's not right. It's not fair," Josh said.

"Fair!? My God, boy, what are you looking for, old-fashioned justice? Forget it, it's gone forever. The best you'll get for your belly-aching these days is a speedy trial and cramped cell with an inmate animal whose civil rights are protected better than the average citizen. If you want your life back, Mitchell, you're going to have to *take* it back." He finished his drink. "There's another bottle in the kitchen cabinet right of the sink. Get it, will you?"

Josh stood and returned with a second bottle of the French brandy. He poured into the old man's outstretched glass.

"How? Everything I've tried has only gotten me in deeper."

"Before I attempt to answer that, tell me one thing. Not counting the two men down in Mississippi, have you encountered anyone else since Tuesday morning you've been suspicious of?"

Josh didn't have to think. He told him about the man in the room at the La Quinta, and his warning.

Goldman nodded his head knowingly. "Figured as much," he said putting the snifter to his lips. "Why don't you just heed his words and go about your life?"

"I can't. It's gone beyond that now. For most of the week, I thought this was about clearing my name, about staying out of prison, even about keeping my job. But I know it's more than that."

The old man gave him a curious look.

"Someone killed the only woman I might have loved, and now they want me to 'go about my life' and forget it or they'll charge me with her murder. Well, fuck 'em. I'd rather be dead than in prison for something I didn't do, especially if I had to sit there for thirty years wondering who took her life. If there's a way, any way, I'm going to find the answers, even if I have no idea what to do with them once I have. I have to know."

Morris Goldman knew Josh was pitifully outclassed by his many adversaries, and would likely end up dead before long. Still, he admired his spirit and felt he had to at least offer him some chance to survive.

"Who was that guy who came to my room?" Josh asked, touching an angry finger to his sore nose.

"Don't be too concerned about him or his affiliation; all the spooks are pretty much the same."

"Spooks? You think this guy was with the government?" The thought seemed preposterous to Josh.

"Most assuredly."

"Bullshit. This guy was a criminal; he acted like no government—"

"Being a criminal and working for the government is mutually exclusive in your mind?"

"Of course not, but—"

"You said you were booked on murder charges."

"Yes, this morning in Carmel. What does—"

"How can you be here then?" Goldman asked simply.

"What do you mean?" Josh failed to connect the dots.

"In California, there is no bail for capital crimes, so I repeat my previous question." Goldman sipped his brandy slowly, pensively, working the puzzle out himself.

Josh replayed the conversation he'd had with Agent Hetzler that had brought about his unexpected release, and tried to find the sinister passages among the words they'd exchanged. The dots remained unconnected. "I convinced the FBI I wasn't responsible for Dianne Lane's death. Simple as that."

"Simple as that? You know, it's a miracle you're still alive. I can't remember having met anyone more naïve in my life."

"But, I didn't kill her. I convinced them of that."

"They don't care, my young friend," Goldman barked. "And even if they did, and this was just a normal murder case, you'd have sat for at least a week in the county jail waiting to be freed. The FBI does nothing quickly, unless it serves their purposes."

"What purpose?" Josh asked, not caring for the direction this was heading.

"You'll know soon enough."

Josh detested guessing games, especially at this moment. "I want to know now! Hell, maybe you're dreaming all this up to satisfy some personal agenda." He stood, setting his glass abruptly on the mantel.

His eyes had adjusted to the cavelike darkness of the den.

"Go to the window and tell me what you see. Don't move the blinds, just look through the spaces between the slats."

Josh hesitated, but his curiosity drove him to the window left of the front door. The partially wooded yard was in full darkness now, the remnants of yesterday's storm clouds blocking the moon and stars. The only illumination came from a generous gaslight at the foot of Sarah Young's driveway. He could make out the outline of the Porsche, the crown of the highway, the silhouette of numerous pines, but little else. Then his eyes detected another form, a trucklike vehicle of some description sitting on the road, parked in front of the house across the street. "There's a car or a truck with its lights out just sitting along the road."

His gut told him it wasn't there to pay a call on the widow Young.

"That'd be your FBI buddies, I suspect," Goldman said in such a manner that there was little way Josh could question his words. "So much for your theory of belief in innocence."

"Why are they following me? If they'd wanted to know where I was going, they could have just asked. I'd have told them."

"Don't you get it?" Goldman said, rising from his chair. "Lloyd Richmond was not just an art dealer and Pamela Morrow not simply an art historian. Your suspicions, however unsupported by evidence, were not that far off the mark."

Josh walked toward the dark figure of Morris Goldman. "What are you saying exactly, that Lloyd Richmond was some kind of government agent? A spy?"

"Lloyd Richmond was a man who believed in many causes, few more ardently than world peace—"

"What's any of this got to do with world peace!?" Josh interrupted.

"On the one hand, everything; on the other, nothing at all."

"Is it possible for you to be any less clear?" Josh snapped, not really angry with the man, but with the mounting frustration he felt.

Goldman ignored his impatience, though he understood it. "Have a seat, Josh."

"I don't want to sit."

"Suit yourself. I'd like some more brandy." The man took his glass and the fresh bottle, and sat in his rocker again. With his back now to the room, Josh was forced to retake his seat.

When he'd sat, Goldman offered him the bottle, but Josh only set it on the floor at his feet again. "Please answer my question, sir."

"How familiar are you with the Second World War?"

It seemed a most unlikely question. "I studied about it in school, of course. I've seen a number of specials on the History channel. I don't know much really; it was a bit before my time."

"It wasn't before Lloyd Richmond's time, or mine." He rolled up his sleeve, pulling a worn Zippo lighter from the breast pocket of his plaid flannel shirt. A yellow flame flickered, painting the immediate area in a buttery glow. He held his forearm beneath the light. "Know what this is?" he asked.

Josh saw the remnants of a series of black numerals tattooed there, partially faded by time but still visible. He knew little about a war that had taken place in his father's generation, but he knew what the numbers meant. "You were in one of the Nazi concentration camps during the war?"

"Dachau. 1937. My family was one of the first interred. My parents were both teachers." The pain had not disappeared in six decades.

Josh couldn't imagine what this man had endured, and it forced him to consider his own situation in a different perspective. He was ashamed for thinking of Morris Goldman as cynical, but was unable to express his regret, his last breath locked in his throat.

"They came one night in April, while we slept, and we were naïvely pleased when we ended up only a few miles from our home in Munich. When they first arrived and took us, we were afraid we'd been deported, thrown from our own country, though we had no idea why such a thing would have happened. My father told us to be strong and to believe that we would be home soon, when they'd figured out that we were loyal Germans. Within a year, he, my mother, and both of my sisters were dead. I managed to escape with the help of a boy named Gerhard Bruenner, the son of a local politician who was forced to watch while his father was shot by an SS firing squad.

"We ran for a week, always east, barely stopping and avoiding anyone and everyone. To our good fortune, I suppose, the SS wasn't as prevalent then as in the later years, and I'm not sure we were even missed for days. We lived in sewers and ate whatever the rats ate, sometimes the rats themselves. Finally, we were discovered stealing food from a garbage can by a prosperous Christian family who smuggled us into Poland as two of their own children; they knew Europe was about to explode."

Goldman took a sip, his eyes focused on some distant object.

"I suffered more guilt than you can imagine in the years that followed, both for having not died along with the rest of my family, and for having denied my Jewish heritage to keep from being found out, but one does what one must, I suppose." He looked at Josh. "Isn't it strange, feeling guilty because you simply lied in order to keep from being killed?"

The words rang deafeningly in Josh's ears.

The old man forced himself to go on: "After a few months, we were able to make it to Moscow and secure passage on the Trans-Siberian Railroad. We had to travel without the benefit of a sleeper car, and we slept sitting up most of the time, mind you, for almost 6,000 miles from Moscow to Ekaterinburg, Novosibirsk, Irkutsk, and Kharbarovsk, ending our journey in Vladivostok in the westernmost corner of Russia. After another couple of weeks on foot, traveling south from the port city, we finally made our way to Singapore. Jews had it far better in China during the war years than in Europe, we had been told, and it proved true, thankfully. I don't think we could have gone another mile. We both soon found a place to live that kept us out of the weather, and work that kept us from starving. It was never home for us, but the next few years managed to pass quickly. Gerhard and I eventually went our separate ways."

Goldman's voice had become dronelike recounting the portion of his past Josh was sure he never forgot but rarely visited. His heart went out to him.

"That was when I first met Lloyd Richmond. His life mirrored my own in many ways and we became friends at once. We were born in the same year, 1923, he in Peking and I in Munich. His parents were American missionaries. They were killed by the Japanese in 1937. Though we were only boys, in terms of years, things were not as they are today. We were hard and tough, with few illusions—you quickly become like that when you're on your own.

"We both went to work for the Chinese Underground, doing what we could, until the end of the war in forty-five. With our families gone, and little reason to stay in China, we followed the returning GIs."

His voice took on a renewed vigor, absent during the last long moments.

He continued: "We met Madeline the following year in San Francisco when her parents hosted one of their famous Nob Hill parties to benefit refugees of the war. Lloyd and I were guest refugees, selected God-only-knows-how. She and Lloyd began to see each other and soon fell in love, mostly because he was the handsome, worldly rebel her parents feared and she had a burning desire not to conform to their wishes then.

A decade later, she had become them, and the romance was over.

"After the museum and gallery were on stable footing, and perhaps to put his mind off the growing tension in his marriage, Lloyd traveled extensively, putting together the collection you see now. Later, as the need to seek refuge from Madeline grew, he would return to his childhood home in search of more and more extraordinary pieces."

"Why'd they stay married all these years?" Josh couldn't fathom a life with someone he didn't love, or who didn't love him. He thought about his own parents, happily married over thirty years.

The old man looked at Josh. "You'd have to have known the Kennerlys of San Francisco's elite in those days; three generations of American 'nobility.' Nothing was worse or more dreaded than a family scandal, such as a very public divorce. Lloyd found relief where he could, but always kept his indiscretions quiet. He knew Madeline no longer loved him, but I think a part of him loved her to the end."

Josh found Goldman's last words—about Richmond finding "relief" where he could—especially biting. He understood now that Pamela had provided such relief.

Had Dianne also? He pushed the thought away.

Still, he was no fool, and spoken or not, they'd both been Lloyd Richmond's mistresses. The thought of them together for all those years, when he'd not been granted even a full day with Dianne, angered him. A horrid thought crossed his mind: Had Pamela been killed to make room for his latest attempt at "relief"?

"Oh, God no!" he said silently.

Then a harder reality slapped him in the face. Had Dianne actually helped get rid of Pamela Morrow, to make room for her to be the new love in Lloyd Richmond's life? Had she been behind the wheel of the car that took Pamela's life?

He didn't want the answers, any of them, for to continue to deny them would keep them untrue.

"What are you thinking?" Goldman asked, puzzled by the odd silence.

The man's voice snapped Josh out of the pointless pursuit of painful images. "Nothing," he said, his voice faint. He forced himself back to his own problems as a way of taking his mind off things he could no more undo than yesterday's lies. "Tell me how art has anything to do with world peace."

"It gave Lloyd the ability to travel between the U.S. and China with little notice. He had extensive and powerful contacts in both countries. There were many who envied that fluidity of movement, as well as his ability to speak several Chinese dialects, and saw the possibility of putting such power to use. It was only a question of time before his political views earned him the attention of the right party."

"What views? Which party?" Josh asked hurriedly.

Goldman's eyes said to be patient, and Josh sighed with exaggeration.

"Both Lloyd and I had suffered the tyranny of nations bent on dominating the planet, and because of the imbalance in world power, came within a breath of accomplishing it. More than any other country, the U.S. prevented this, but in doing so, became the de facto world power herself. Many believed it was only a question of time before the U.S. would enforce her might and do for herself what the Axis had failed to do."

"That's crazy," Josh said defensively.

"Perhaps, but amid the paranoia that ran rampant after World War II, the possibility couldn't be ignored, especially by the USSR and China. The world had learned one lesson from both Germany and Japan—*strike first*. Believing—hoping—a military giant wouldn't come knocking had cost sixty million lives."

Josh's mind reeled. What the hell had he gotten himself into?

And more importantly, was there any exit now?

"You're saying that Lloyd Richmond somehow wished to correct the imbalance in world power after the war? How? No man could do that!"

"Really? Consider: China developed the atomic bomb within a few years of the end of their civil war, thereby neutralizing the U.S.'s global 'trump card' and effectively shielding herself from possible external domination. Mere coincidence? Think again. China had demonstrated no prior technical proficiency in such matters."

"You're telling me that Lloyd Richmond sold U.S. military secrets to Red China? The atomic bomb, for God's sake!?"

"I'm not telling you anything. I'm giving you food for thought, that's all. During the horrid, bloody years of the Thirties and Forties, Lloyd met many young men, often displaced like himself, who would later become powerful leaders in the new Communist China; they developed deep friendships in some cases. Bonds forged in the hell-fire of war are tempered like few others, Joshua." Goldman added

Josh's empty glass to his and, without turning on any lights, stood and deposited them in the kitchen sink. He returned and stood at the same blinds where Josh had looked out earlier. He stared toward Sarah Young's house but saw nothing.

"Richmond was a Communist?"

Goldman took a thoughtful pause. "He believed in mankind, not in governments. Neither his ideals nor mine changed over the course of five decades, the world merely changed around us, and the need to do things as we had always done them changed with it. What he wanted—what we all wanted—never faltered, though, nor the desire to achieve it."

Josh stood beside him at the blinds. "But Lloyd Richmond was a spy. A simple yes or no."

"Nothing is simple," he said.

"Yes or no, dammit!" Josh insisted.

The man turned his eyes to meet Josh's but didn't speak.

"And Pamela Morrow, was she a traitor, too? And Dianne Lane? The whole lot?" Josh asked.

"You need to seek those answers where they can be found."

"Bullshit! You started this, now give me a straight answer, dammit!"

"What does your heart tell you?" he answered instead.

Josh was dumbstruck; his heart had nothing to do with this. "Was Lloyd Richmond a traitor? Did he sell us out?"

Goldman took a deep breath and let it out slowly before he answered. "Lloyd Richmond was a great man, a man who followed his conscience regardless of cost or consequence."

"That's not an answer."

"Then answers that will satisfy you will be found where they spent their last days." He put his hands on Josh's shoulders. "Now go, please, before your watchers feel the need to further disrupt the peace I've tried for so long to create here."

Josh looked out through the blinds and saw that the mysterious vehicle had vanished. Had it moved on, or had the men inside sought a more secretive location, and now lay in wait for him in the darkness?

More questions with no answers.

He didn't like the thought of moving through the blackness toward Kenny's car, but was tired of being pushed around.

He looked again at the still figure beside him, shrouded in darkness, a faint umber light tracing his left side, and knew that Morris Goldman had given all he would.

If there was more, and he knew there was, it would remain with the man.

Jack Farris pushed the bedroom window upward, using slow, steady pressure until the opening had increased to twelve or fourteen inches. Through the wider gap, he could more clearly hear the old man in the den chatting with his guest—it was apparent the lengthy conversation was finally wrapping up—and wondered again how the hell Mitchell had wormed his way out of Fachini's grip.

He knew, in order to collect his bonus, even more weight would have to be heaped on the boy's unexpectedly broad shoulders.

An amount no one could bear.

Having the FBI testify that they'd seen Josh Mitchell enter Goldman's home at dusk, at his invitation, and then spend more than two hours in a darkened cabin with the lone occupant before driving away, was a bonus he'd not counted on, but one he was anxious to exploit.

An hour ago, he'd seen the blue-suited pair from San Francisco move their vehicle from its vantage point across from the cabin to the fire road that bordered the white frame home at the base of Eagle Rock. Too visible, he'd guessed, noting the neighbor's oversized gaslight, and had been pleased the agents had been too lazy or too disinterested to do a walk-up surveillance of the cabin. Had they, he would have been forced to alter his plans for a third time, a prospect he hadn't cherished.

The concern was academic now.

Being careful not to knock over the log step he'd employed unsuccessfully the night before, he slipped through the opening as easily and quietly as a snake entering its lair.

Morris Goldman locked the front door as he heard the Porsche disappear south on Highway 89, and walked to the kitchen for a drink of water. Having satisfied his thirst, he set the small glass upside down in the sink and moved sluggishly and a bit unsteadily toward his bedroom. He was tired, a little drunk, and ready for sleep. Perhaps tomorrow he'd use his small powerboat and give the deep water macks a go. The thought pleased him.

As he entered his bedroom and reached for the light switch, the length of rope was wrapped violently around his neck before he could put conscious understanding to the action. His hands moved instinctively to the source of the pain, fighting and clawing at the snare, but before any measure of relief could be found, the knot that had been tied in the half-inch nylon cord—centered over his larynx—crushed the fragile tube of tissue and cartilage. Goldman's body drooped, suspended by the ropes in Jack Farris's hands like some kind of macabre marionette.

When the old man had been placed in his rocker and the ends of the cord—still tightly around his neck—had been tied to the points of the chair back so the body wouldn't slump to the floor, and so that constant pressure would be exerted on the garrote to ensure a kill, Farris closed and latched the bedroom window. With a rag from his pants pocket, and using the penlight he carried, he cleaned his muddy footprints from the floor.

There was one final thing to do, something which would guarantee that slippery Mr. Mitchell would not go free of Goldman's murder: Farris pulled out the stem on the old man's watch and ran the hands back forty minutes—to a time during which Mitchell was undeniably still inside the house—then reset the stem. He took the man's limp arm and, using it like a hammer, smashed the watch's crystal against the oak arm of the rocker, shattering the glass and freezing the hands where they sat.

Satisfied, his hands still gloved, he unlocked the front door and left as quietly as he'd come.

He smiled as he retraced his steps to his car. "Let's see you get your ass out of this one, Mitchell."

# 18

Sunday morning crept through an unnoticed crack in the tightly pulled curtains of the hotel room, and despite Josh's failed attempt to hold back the day, let it be known that the world cared little for his misery and regarded his fear with indifference. Life was going on, with or without his participation, and the eternal sun beyond ridiculed him for even trying to pretend it wasn't so.

He rolled onto his back and pulled a pillow across his face, his arms locked across it.

It didn't help. Though he'd blocked out the shaft of light, he could still hear its silent voice.

Calling out for him to complete what he'd begun.

Challenging him to a duel.

He'd gotten in bed late, had slept hard, it had been the first night in six that had held no images of Dianne Lane's face, no memories of their short time together.

He allowed the pillow to fall to the carpet, and lay there staring at the pebbled ceiling. When he intentionally brought forth an image of her, from their dinner in Sausalito, he knew in an instant that her memory had not been purged, never would be, and he knew also that, while Morris Goldman may have been correct about his long-time friend, he'd been wrong about Dianne.

An anger rose, forcing him upright in bed and to his feet. He refused to willingly accept that everything he felt about this woman had been based upon a lie—and worse—but then his own life loomed, condemning him. Had he not entered into every relation-ship since high school as a creation of his own fears and vanities rather than a man a woman could depend on for the honesty he so desperately sought himself?

He wasn't alone in such deceits, he knew that, but just because he wanted to believe in Dianne's innocence, it wouldn't alter the truth.

*The truth?* he thought. How little he knew of the truth.

He dressed quickly. Whichever way it turned out, Josh knew he had a rendezvous with destiny.


Richmond Gallery and Museum occupied a half-block on Taylor Street at California, opposite a small park, a monstrosity of lime-stone and marble with tall, fat columns constructed in an opulent era before income taxes had eroded the wealth of America's castle builders. At the dawn of the twentieth century, the Kennerlys of San Francisco, regarding themselves no less capable of architec-tural resplendence than the Vanderbilts or Astors, had commis-sioned the elaborate structure in 1922 to serve as the nucleus of the Kennerlys' North American empire.

It had served the family well until after World War II, when global opportunities forced rapid diversification of the Kennerly interests.

Madeline's father, Randolph III, patriarch of the clan at that time, gave the building—which had outlived its usefulness to the corpo-ration—to his favorite daughter and new son-in-law as a fifth wed-ding anniversary present. He knew of Lloyd's desire to secure a suit-able building in which to house his growing collection of Chinese art treasures—accumulated with Kennerly money—and, after con-siderable renovation, Lloyd began moving his beloved artifacts, sculptures, and paintings into *his* new building in the spring of 1954. The Richmond Museum opened to the public the following fall, the gallery—which sold expensive objets d'art, though not those of historic significance—two years later. In the four decades since their subsidized beginnings, both had grown to be regarded as the finest establishments of their kinds in the Western Hemisphere, and had long since made Lloyd comfortably wealthy and internationally recognized.

More importantly, Josh had discovered, it had given him the ability to move between Mainland China and the U.S. with impunity.

After briskly walking the two blocks to the museum—Kenny's Porsche resting quietly in the hotel garage—Josh stood on the sidewalk and stared up at the row of Gothic pillars that stood like unspoken warnings that not just art but power lay within.

The change of clothes, a good night's sleep, and a sheepherder's breakfast in the Fairmont's restaurant had done more to rekindle Josh's desire to survive than he'd have thought possible leaving Morris Goldman's cabin. The trip to San Francisco last night, his eyes more on his rearview mirror than the road ahead, had proven uneventful, and by the time he'd reached his favorite hotel, Josh had barely been able to drag his walking corpse to his tower suite.

The exorbitant room had been unnecessary for comfort—all rooms in the Nob Hill landmark were excellent—but had done its part in reminding him that life had once been safe and grand, and that, perhaps, it could be again.

Josh ascended the granite steps leading to the museum entrance and arrived just ahead of a pair of Catholic nuns supervising a small party of neatly dressed schoolgirls ranging in ages from ten to fourteen. Josh recognized the nuns' order as the one responsible for orphan care across much of the state, and his heart ached for his own family.

He held the door for the entire group, who, after the nuns had nodded politely and passed, took turns thanking him amid hushed giggles and covered mouths. He smiled generously back at the innocent, giddy faces who, unlike him, had taken no part in removing their parents from their lives.

After the group had vanished into the cavernous interior, Josh still stood in the threshold. He closed his eyes and took several slow, deep breaths, hoping the anxiety would subside, which it finally did.

"Stay focused," he reminded himself. "Find the answers you need." The arrival of another group forced him inward.


From their ninth-floor window in the Mark Hopkins, directly across California Street from the Fairmont Hotel, Agents Munford and Higgins watched with binoculars and video camera as Josh Mitchell finally moved south toward the destination Karl Hetzler had assured them he would head sometime Sunday morning. Two additional agents were already increasing their knowledge of Far Eastern art amid the splendor of the museum, and another pair of Hetzler's best were on board the cable car coming up California Street.

"Jon and Kurt have picked him up," Munford said, training his binoculars on the two men who'd just jumped from the wooden trolley and had discreetly fallen in behind Josh shortly after he'd crossed Mason Street.

"Got 'em," Higgins said, the chip-enhanced 100X digital zoom lens of the palm-sized DV minicamcorder missing nothing of the action. Hetzler had ordered that every aspect of Mitchell's involvement be fully documented, and looked forward to playing a tape of the incriminating footage for Josh personally—in retribution for being made a fool.

"Ready to go?" Munford asked, packing his gear now that Mitchell was under direct surveillance.

"Give me thirty seconds," the agent who'd transmitted the initial images of Josh Mitchell from inside the van at Carmel said. Tommy Higgins remembered Hetzler's words on Tuesday about the Mitchell kid being deeply involved in the conspiracy that had come to a head on the beach in Carmel, and was proud he worked for someone with such field savvy. Making the final bust Mitchell was unwittingly choreographing for the Bureau could only be good for the careers of all involved, considering the nature of the case. "Ready," he said crisply when he'd secured the camera and night vision accessories in the briefcase. Both of the other teams would photograph Mitchell before and after he entered the museum, and with whomever he met or talked, with each frame bearing the date and a sequential number that would be indispensable in federal court.

It was only a question of time now before the last act would finally begin and the curtain dropped on a long list of players. The young man who'd just entered the stately building on Taylor Street was merely the most recent addition to the cast, but perhaps the pivotal actor they'd long sought.

The agents all sensed it, could feel it after two long and often frustrating years, though none more than Karl Hetzler, and it aroused him in a way that was almost sexual.


Josh spotted the woman sitting on a folding canvas seat beneath one of the museum's most valued pieces—a terra-cotta soldier from Shaanxi province kneeling with his hands poised as if still holding the wooden spear which had decayed while entombed for two millennia—a charcoal sketchpad visible on her lap.

"Ms. Chang?" he asked, his voice low as if in a library. One of the older schoolgirls from the orphanage, a slender brunette of thirteen or fourteen and a straggler at the moment, peered at him from over a sealed glass display case housing the wedding dress of a fourteenth century Ming Dynasty princess. When Josh smiled back at her, the girl pretended not to notice and scurried off to rejoin her friends.

Carol Chang looked up from her work. "Yes," she said, offering the handsome young man a warm smile. "May I help you?"

The woman, who stood no more than five-one in her bare feet, had served as Dianne Lane's assistant for the past three years, during her senior year at the University of California at Berkeley and in the two years of postgraduate work that followed. The curator had told her that she'd seen a rare drive and quest for perfection in her that she, too, possessed as a student.

"The woman at the desk told me that today was your day off, and I apologize for disturbing you, but she also said that you might be able to help me. My name is Joshua Mitchell. I had the pleasure of meeting Dianne Lane just before her death." The word had not become easier to say. He stood for a moment admiring the drawing she'd been working on, then knelt beside her. "There are some things about her work . . . your work . . . that I must know."

Carol Chang sensed an urgency in the man's voice that would have troubled, even frightened, her had it been anyone else making such a request, but she feared nothing from this man. Perhaps it was the obvious reverence with which he'd spoken her friend and mentor's name. She looked warmly at him. "You knew Dianne?"

"Yes, but not as well as I would have liked, I'm afraid."

"I understand," she said. "Dianne had that effect on people."

"I hope you'll forgive my intruding this way. I know how hard this last week must have been for you."

"Thank you" was all she said, but her eyes revealed the loss and pain she was still suffering. "What about our work could I possibly tell you, Mr. Mitchell?"

"Please, Joshua."

"If you like. We might be more comfortable speaking over there," she said, gesturing toward an empty bench that sat along the museum's west wall.

Josh helped her gather her few things and then joined her on the long wooden settee not far from the kneeling soldier. She wore a crisply starched powder-blue oxford-cloth blouse fully buttoned but for the collar and a pair of pleated black slacks. Her shoes were simple black loafers, no socks or stockings that he could see, and her thick black hair was pulled back and worn short. She looked comfortable and professional, and Josh felt immediately at ease with her.

She spoke as they sat. "So tell me, Joshua, how can I help you? Are you in the field?" She set her sketchpad on the bench between them, her box of charcoals on top of it.

"About as close as I've ever come is an art appreciation course in college."

"What do you do then?"

"I work . . . worked . . . for a technology supplier in Sacramento."

The truth, Joshua, he reminded himself. Always the truth.

"I take it you've had a recent change in employment."

Josh nodded and she was kind enough not to press.

"Did Mrs. Lane's work entail many trips to China?" he asked.

"She was the curator of the most extensive collection of Chinese art outside Mainland China." It had been a polite way of answering an obvious question.

Josh nodded. "How often did you accompany her on such trips?"

"Never," she said.

The answer surprised him.

"But, I thought you were—"

"It was the way she and Mr. Richmond wanted it. Someone needed to run the store while they were away, as he put it. Dianne secretly assured me that I would one day be curator, and as such would get all the traveling I wanted." She moved a tentative hand to her lips. "I never thought . . ."

Her voice tapered off, but Josh knew the guilt she felt at having inherited the scepter in this way. He placed his hand on her shoulder briefly, and nodded his understanding.

"I'm sorry," she said.

"No need. I knew her, too, remember?"

"First Mr. Richmond and now Dianne . . . but you didn't come for this." She dabbed her eyes with a tissue she took from her purse. "You were asking about our work."

Josh didn't even know what questions might yield the answers he wanted. Perhaps microfilm with the locations of secret military installations had been concealed in the skull of a jade figurine, but that seemed ridiculous. He had no more realistic idea how spies plied their trade than he'd learned from the black-and-white movies of his childhood. Still, it was the only question that came to mind. "What kind of pieces did Dianne and Mr. Richmond bring back from a typical trip?"

"Look around you. There was no such thing as a 'typical' trip, really. Once they returned with that magnificent piece." She indicated the kneeling soldier. "We really celebrated that night. The eight of us who regularly worked on exhibits went through a case of champagne."

The image of Dianne with a well-deserved hangover made Josh smile. How could she have been so disloyal to the country that had given her so much? The conflicting images and feelings tore at him.

"The last trip, in December, they returned with fourteen crates of things they'd collected over a sixty-day period, the largest of which was small enough to fit in your hand."

"More celebrating?" he said.

Carol Chang made a sour face. "No. Despite the quantity of the pieces they'd brought, many of which were magnificent, a key piece was not among them as hoped. It kept an entire new collection from being completed and put on display, as it had for two years. I didn't understand the importance of the piece that they'd failed to locate, and when I asked about it, it seemed to be a touchy subject with both Dianne and Lloyd."

"Couldn't you just display the collection without it?" It seemed so simple to him.

"Since I don't know exactly what was missing, is still missing, I can't say for sure, but in concept, it would be like showing a new car line to the public without a driver's door."

He appreciated the simplistic example.

As he was about to speak, she shrugged her shoulders. "But that's why Dianne dubbed the collection 'Casper.' She knew how elusive the key piece would remain. And she was so certain she would finally locate it during her upcoming trip in April."

Josh was stunned.

*Casper?* he repeated in his head. *Oh, my sweet Jesus!*

"To China?" he asked. He wanted the answer to be no.

"Of course, silly," she said.

Josh now knew that his worst fears were real, that Morris Goldman had spoken honestly. "Did she always give nicknames to collections in the making?" he asked.

"As long as I knew her she did."

Josh's heart raced. "What was the name of the collection you were working on prior to Casper?"

"That would have been Cheshire Cat. You know, the one who kept making himself invisible in *Alice in Wonderland*. We almost never found the key pieces for that exhibit. You want to see it? It's wonderful." Her pride was evident, but did little to infect Josh.

He felt only betrayal, fear, anger. Cheshire Cat had been the closely guarded nickname of their previous stealth development project at Barnett Air. Only a handful of people in the world knew this.

Or so he'd believed.

"I don't suppose the one before that was called Canterbury?" he asked in a whisper. His and Kenny's original project, the one which had gained Barnett's attention and funding, had been named for the Canterbury Ghost, after the Earl of Canterbury who, according to legend, had been imprisoned in his castle's walls for four hundred years, awaiting release. At times, it had seemed to the two starving programmers that it would take as long to free their dream from the drawing board.

"Yes," she said. "How did you know that?"

Josh stood and touched her on the cheek with his fingertips. "It's not important, really."

He turned and walked sluggishly toward the front door.

"Mr. Mitchell?" she called after him. "Joshua!"—but there was no answer.

# 19

*Hunger is insolent, and will be fed.*

—Homer (9th-8th? century B.C.)

Kenny's phone rang just three times before he felt it safe to pick up, but it seemed to him like thirty. The Caller-I.D. had already told him it was the one call he'd been waiting for, but the device he'd installed to detect phone taps had delayed in flashing green, the sign the line was free of bugs.

"Josh?" he answered quickly when he finally snatched the portable phone from its base and pressed Talk. He paced the wide expanse of the great room in his home on Auburn-Folsom Road, as he had almost without respite since he'd returned from the successful Navy demo on Saturday.

Though he hadn't heard from his friend since pleading with him to flee to another country, he'd known that Josh would never run.

"I gotta see you, Kenny. Now," Josh said flatly.

The red Turbo had been treating Interstate 80 like a Formula One course for the last twenty minutes, and already the gap between San Francisco and the state capital had been narrowed by thirty-five miles. At this rate, if he survived his reckless driving, Josh would be on Kenny's doorstep in another half hour. He hadn't wanted to consider the consequences of the punishing pace he'd demanded of himself and the car, his reflexes barely able to keep him from running under the rear axle of an eighteen-wheeler.

"Sure, Josh. Where are you?"

"I'll be at your place in thirty, thirty-five minutes. You alone?"

Kenny's oldest friend had never asked him such a question, but then, the week had held a lot of firsts for Josh Mitchell. "Yeah, always, you know that."

"Don't tell anyone I'm coming, Kenny, especially Hightower."

"Why the hell would I talk to him on weekends? I can barely stand talking to him during the week."

Kenny's attempt at humor had reached ears deaf to such light-heartedness. The thoughts that stirred within Josh's brain were as insidious as the human imagination was capable of spawning. He heard only what he needed to hear, and if it had nothing to do with survival, it passed without notice.

The first fat drops of rain struck the Porsche like stones and, unlike the cars going half its speed, exploded off the paint and glass in a fine mist.

In the distance, above the mountains that rose from the horizon line like a jagged rip in the fabric of heaven, clouds the color of coal had begun to form, scarred with yellow-and-white striae, eager to vent their electrical rage on the ground below.

If Josh slowed any as the road began to darken with moisture, the speedometer didn't register it.

The surveillance van had not been able to keep up with the nimble red car and had lost sight of it in Oakland traffic more than thirty minutes earlier. Brad Munford had little choice now but to follow the blinking dot on Tommy's monitor and stay as close as the lumbering Ford would permit. Sacramento was the most likely destination of their man, it was assumed, and the GPS tracker they'd planted at the impound lot appeared to verify that hunch, but where Mitchell would go once there could be a problem, though they had at least two probable destinations in mind. The possibility of his changing cars en route and losing them prompted a heavier foot on the accelerator than Munford felt comfortable with. His driving was also making his fellow agent in the rear of the long van carsick.

With the game escalating rapidly since Saturday morning—driven by Detective Fachini's unanticipated apprehension of Josh Mitchell—Karl Hetzler had pressed for, and ultimately gotten, taps on several phones in the Sacramento area, hoping one of them would yield a dividend.

Because of the extreme sensitivity of the information they were seeking, as well as Kanazawa's extensive knowledge of computers and his likely familiarity with electronic eavesdropping, it had been decided that the tap on his phone could not be done at the phone company's central switching office, or by means of a local transmitting tap that emitted an RF signal that could be detected up to a mile away. A far more sophisticated unit whose signal was optically isolated from the line—greatly reducing its electronic signature—had been concealed outside his home. The unit had only recently become available, and Hetzler hoped the head of Barnett software development hadn't yet learned of it. As was often the case in the covert world, the detector had reached the market ahead of the bug.

Their work paid off at 11:17 Sunday morning.

"He's heading for Kanazawa's home," Higgins announced when he'd hung up with their agent in Sacramento.

"Just like the old man thought," Munford said to the windshield. "How long, Tommy?"

Higgins used an electronic pen to touch a point on the computer screen that represented Kenny's address; the stats displayed at the bottom of the screen changed accordingly. "We're forty-three minutes out at our present speed"—he anticipated his partner's next move—"and I'm not interested in decreasing that number to forty, Brad, goddammit!"

He cursed again as he felt the van accelerate.


Kenny's home sat centered in the sixty rural acres he'd bought after Aero-Tech's acquisition, at the end of a long, winding, brick-lined drive that ran north off Auburn-Folsom Road. The balance of his money from the sale had allowed the construction of a boldly designed 6,500 square-foot multilevel house that had been built atop the property's highest point, a bulging hill that provided a commanding view not only of Kenny's own land, but of the other homes dotting the surrounding hills as well.

The front yard—all thirty acres of it—had been thickly seeded and was kept well-watered and closely cut, giving the impression that when one stepped from the front door, a golf cart should be waiting. By contrast, the back half, beyond the fence that bordered the pool, had been allowed to remain as close to its natural state as possible, the ground covered in waist-high pampas and fountain grasses and heavily sprinkled with California redbuds, white birches, and cotoneasters that ran all the way to the property line.

The late-winter storm still threatened, the inky clouds adding ominously to the view, and though it had sprinkled off and on over the last forty minutes, the rain had not yet begun to fall in earnest. Lightning danced and flashed in the eerie gloom.

From his front door, Kenny had seen Josh approaching for more than a mile. He tried to appear normal, even casual, when the Porsche stopped a few yards away, and raised a beer bottle to salute the wayward traveler.

"Knew you were too damned stupid to run," he called out as Josh closed the car door. "Want a cold one?"

Josh's face told him that he wasn't in the mood for a beer.

Kenny stood silently in the doorway as his friend neared him.

"We've got a problem," Josh said, walking past him and disappearing into the house.

Kenny followed at once, his mind fixed on Josh's words.

"I gathered that from your call," he said to Josh's back as they made their way toward the den. "What was that paranoid shit about Hightower? You no longer work for him, he poses no threat to you."

Josh's eyes hardened as he turned to face his friend.

That was dumb, Kenny thought. "Sure you don't want a drink?"

"Do you have any idea what the hell's going on here, Kenny?" Josh said, standing tensely by the fireplace. He appeared to be a man about to snap.

Kenny shrugged his shoulders. "It's been a crazy week, Josh. You're gonna need to be a little more specific than that." He sat on the arm of a fat leather chair nearby, motioning for Josh to sit.

Josh remained standing, his eyes closed and his fingertips lightly rubbing his forehead where his stitches felt like screws being turned into his skull.

"Want something for your head?" Kenny asked.

Josh looked up finally, taking a moment to focus on Kenny's face. "We've been sold out. That no-good son of a bitch sold us out, sold our software to the Red Chinese. All of it, everything you and I developed."

Kenny stood and moved slowly toward his oldest friend. He didn't like what he was hearing. "What the hell are you talking about, Josh?"

"Hightower. The bastard's a traitor, a fucking spy."

He put a hand on Josh's shoulder. "What kind of stuff did the doctor give you after your accident in Mississippi?"

Josh pushed his hand away. "Jesus! Kenny, aren't you listening to me!? This isn't about bumping my head or some pain pill I took three days ago, it's about the CEO of our company selling technology to enemies of the United States. Don't you get it? Hightower is a spy, just like that Navy bastard who sold secrets to the Russians a few years back."

Kenny knew it was vital he and Richard Hightower find out how Josh had come by such information—their very freedom depended on it. He was glad now that he'd warned Hightower after Josh's call. Though he'd initially believed he could convince his friend to leave the country before he got in any deeper with the law, he knew that such an escape was no longer an option.

Kenny only hoped that the old man would arrive before he had to make any decisions. He didn't care at all for the way things were turning out, but knew what he had to do.

"Sit down, Josh," he said. "Tell me what it is you suspect."

"I don't suspect, dammit, I know!"

"Fine, then tell me what you know. All of it."

Josh dropped into the chair near him, confused and angry. Kenny sat on an ottoman, less than three feet from him.

Josh seemed in a daze as he spoke. "It all started when I met Dianne Lane. She worked for Lloyd Richmond, the man who owned the Richmond Gallery and Museum in San Francisco—"

"They deal in all those expensive Chinese vases and stuff, right?"

"They didn't just deal in them, Kenny, they controlled the most extensive collection of Chinese treasures in this hemisphere. I believe Dianne Lane was Richmond's mistress. I also think a woman named Pamela Morrow had been his mistress a decade earlier."

"Never heard of her."

"She lived in Jackson, Mississippi, and died in a hit-and-run accident in 1989, though no one was ever charged with the crime."

"That's hardly unusual," Kenny said, stalling for time.

"Wait. Dianne came into the picture at almost exactly the time Pamela died, taking over her duties and eventually becoming curator of the gallery and museum, not just an art historian. She traveled with Richmond to China, helping him move huge sums of cash, and art objects of incredible value, between both countries."

Kenny had a questioning look on his face, as if trying to understand what any of this had to do with Richard Hightower.

Josh continued: "I think Richmond had Pamela killed in order to make room for his new love." The words hurt, but they had to be spoken.

"You're not making a lot of sense here, Josh."

Josh knew his thoughts were fractured and out of order, but it all made perfect sense to him, and would to Kenny, if only he could be made to see.

"I think that Dianne suspected her predecessor's death was not a simple accident, and probably feared the same fate awaited her. It was only a question of time."

"Why not just go to the cops?" Kenny asked.

"Lloyd Richmond was a spy but also part of one of the richest and most influential families in California. Dianne had to know that he was dealing with Barnett, though she might not have known with whom, but she was still part of that espionage loop, for Christ's sake, if only by association. If she'd said anything, he'd simply have denied it and shifted all the guilt to her, and who would have believed her over Richmond?"

"An outsider?" Kenny offered, knowing it was the answer Josh sought.

"Right! Apparently she'd decided to confide in someone at Barnett, someone she knew, or hoped, was outside the espionage ring, but someone with enough knowledge of the information in question to verify her story if given the proper evidence. That's why she picked me, I understood the technology and she knew I wasn't involved."

"She picked you?" Kenny said. He shook his head, as if doing his best to follow. "The woman whose death you're accused of causing picked you to help her expose a spy ring? Nice lady."

Josh was annoyed by his sarcasm. "She wasn't planning on dying, Kenny. She didn't intend to get me into such a jam, I know that."

"Then what happened? Why didn't she just give you this so-called evidence when the two of you were together all day?"

Josh threw his hands up. "Maybe she was making sure she could trust me. I think she was going to give me what she had at breakfast, probably some documentation or photos or tapes or something. Hell, I don't know, but she was murdered before we had the chance to meet again."

"Great, so far you've managed to thoroughly confuse me, Josh. How on earth does Hightower enter—"

"He was Richmond's contact at Barnett."

"That's bullshit. This man has been like a father—"

"Trust me, Kenny, please. I gotta have you with me on this. My life may depend on it."

Kenny slapped Josh's knee in a gesture of solidarity. "All right, assuming for a second that you're correct about Richmond, what did he hope to gain by all this? Money? He's richer than God."

"His wife is. Her family. Who knows how much money he has in his own right, or how much he wanted. Besides, I don't think it had anything to do with money."

"Things like this are always about money."

"Not in this case," Josh went on. "It's a wacko Don Quixote kind of thing driven by what happened during World War II. Richmond, who grew up in China, and his friend Morris Goldman, a German

Jew, had an intense fear of countries with excessive military might. Richmond thought it his duty to cut the balls off the U.S. in whatever way he could, thereby keeping our military in check and restoring some balance in world power. It was their way of preventing a third world war."

Josh could tell that Kenny was still not convinced. "When I went to the Richmond Museum this morning, I learned that he and Dianne used to give nicknames to their projects, just like we do. Guess what they called their latest project, the one they were working on when the old man died last month?"

Kenny shrugged.

"Casper," Josh said dramatically.

The news didn't earn the expression Josh had anticipated; in fact, Kenny suddenly seemed bored with the whole conversation.

"Coincidence," Kenny said, standing again. "It was, after all, a big movie. Lots of people saw it, Josh. That hardly proves a thing." He strolled toward the kitchen, his mind racing. Where the hell was Hightower?

An icy chill of suspicion descended over Josh.

He stood and followed Kenny, praying that he was wrong. "Oh yeah? Well, the previous one was called Cheshire Cat, and the one before that, Canterbury. How the hell can you dismiss something like that?" He stopped at the breakfast bar and rested his palms on the tiled surface, his body shivering, but it was not from fear.

Kenny dropped his empty beer bottle in the trash and opened the drawer beside the sink. He quickly withdrew a compact .38 Special five-shot revolver and pointed it nervously at Josh.

"Have a seat, Josh," he ordered, his hand unsteady. "The old man will be here shortly, and I'm sure he'll want you to repeat everything you've just told me." Kenny waved Josh into one of the stools with the barrel of the gun.

"You no-good worthless bastard," Josh said in a hushed anger that thawed the chill within him like the noon sun. "You were my best friend."

"That's right, so spare me that 'oh, I've been betrayed' song. I begged you to get your dumb ass out of the country, but no, you had to stay and pick at things, stir this mess until you'd created a black hole. All you had to do was walk away from it, but you just couldn't quit being the fucking hero quarterback, could you?"

"I trusted you more than anyone in my life, Kenny. How could you betray us like this?"

"Like I said before, it's always about the money." Josh said. "How much money? What'd it take to turn you into a traitor?" He wanted to strangle him, to put his hands around his throat and squeeze the life out of him.

"More than I'd have seen from programming in my lifetime," Kenny sneered.

Josh glared at him. "And Hightower? How much more money did he need, for God's sake?"

"You'll have to ask him that."

"Believe me, I will."

Kenny pulled another beer from the refrigerator and finished a third of it in a swallow, his eyes and the gun always on Josh. He chuckled as he remembered a conversation he'd had with Richard Hightower. "The old man always figured you for a Boy Scout, but I swear, you dumb bastard, neither of us had any idea you'd go after this Dianne Lane thing like you did. What the hell were you thinking? She was just another piece of ass, man, some pussy, not your damn wife of twenty years."

Josh rose from his seat, the anger in him beyond containment.

"Sit back down, dammit! Listen, Josh, I have no illusion about beating you in a fair fight, so don't think I'll hesitate to shoot."

Kenny dropped onto the stool at the opposite end of the bar, his tone softening a bit. "Dammit . . . why didn't you just leave the country while you still could? You'd have had a pretty good life in some postcard Scandinavian country—"

"It's not my home," Josh said.

"It'd sure beat the hell out of prison, though, wouldn't it? Besides, what choice do you have?"

"None, it appears. I'm sure either you or Hightower will be more than willing to put a bullet in me."

"That's not my style, you should know that."

"I don't know a thing about you. What I thought I knew went straight to hell when you decided to sell out my country."

"Oh, Jesus! Josh, get off this patriotic soapbox. Who gives a shit about countries and governments anymore? It's all about the individual these days, what you can get for yourself. You've seen the way things have changed."

"Yeah, I've seen, but it doesn't mean I've got to be part of it. I don't cheat on my taxes either. How can you sleep knowing you're going down in history as a traitor?" Josh glanced around him as he spoke, hoping to find something that might aid him in his escape. He saw nothing.

"Fuck history! I'll sleep just fine, thanks. Ten million bucks makes a pretty soft bed. But I suppose money doesn't really matter to someone who's always had it, huh?"

"I've never had any money, Kenny, I was raised—"

"I know, on an estate with a nanny and a governess. I've heard it all before—"

"No!" Josh snapped. "I grew up on a small farm in McNairy County. My folks still live there in the same house where I was born."

Kenny took another drink of his beer. "Bullshit. What is this, a game? Your folks live in the south of France."

"My dad raised corn and soybeans and my mother taught public school when I was growing up." He added proudly, "They still do."

"But you always told me—"

"I told everyone more bullshit than I'll be able to undo in my lifetime, but it was nothing more than that. I rarely had more than ten dollars in my pocket until you and I finished our work in that crummy apartment in Venice, but the thought of betraying my country for a buck never entered my mind."

Kenny threw his bottle across the room, narrowly missing Josh's head, foam spraying from its brown neck like a fire extinguisher. "Well, that's you, not me! I never had shit growing up and I'm in debt up to my eyes now! They want to take my house and put me on the street. My house, dammit!" His voice lowered. "Hightower gave me the chance to have everything I ever dreamed of, don't you see?

If you hadn't been such a fucking hero, he'd have cut you in, too."

"Sounds like he's an old pro at being a traitor."

"He's a pro at making money, you've got to admit that. He's been doing this kind of thing for years, long before he came to Barnett—"

"Before Barnett, while he was still president of Martin Aerospace?" Josh said, knowing well the sensitive military technology they had developed for years before falling on hard times. He wondered angrily if Hightower had been the reason for their seemingly inexplicable streak of bad luck.

"Even before Martin. Richmond approached him when Hightower was first in a position that gave him access to things of enormous international value, and our old buddy jumped at the chance. There's no telling how much money he's got in a Swiss bank by now."

"Or how much damage he's done to the U.S.," Josh said, with no attempt to hide his loathing. "How long have you been involved, Kenny?" Josh's eyes continually scanned the area for anything that might aid him in his break. He knew time was a heartless antagonist.

"I'm tired of talking. Just shut the hell up and sit there."

"We were friends—"

"And we could have stayed friends, goddammit!" Kenny snapped. "Now, I've got to kill you. Why couldn't you have just gone away like you were supposed to, you dumb fuck!?"

"You gonna kill me, Kenny? I thought it wasn't your style."

"Shut the hell up, I said! I'm tired of this shit," Kenny said, his hands trembling noticeably. He pulled back the hammer on the revolver.

Josh leaned back in his seat, angry but unafraid. His mind was too filled with thoughts of survival to allow fear to take seed.

He knew when Hightower got there, whatever indecision Kenny might have felt now would be erased. He spotted a shot glass lying in the sink, just within reach. He knew he'd get only one chance.

He had to keep Kenny talking, to get his mind off pulling the trigger. He could imagine the pressure he must be under from Hightower, and pressure of that nature always erupts suddenly—and violently. "How do you and Hightower plan to get away with all this? The FBI is already involved, Kenny. I now know why they got me out of jail in Carmel; they thought I might lead them to the person at Barnett who was dealing with Richmond."

"Doesn't matter," Kenny said. "After I called the old man this morning, he put in place a paper trail between your desk and Richmond's office in San Francisco that goes back to your first day at Barnett. When the cops add what they'll find with Hightower's cooperation to what they already have on you in Dianne Lane's murder, they'll have everything they need to convict. You're screwed, dead or alive."

Kenny cocked his head as if he'd just heard a sound outside. He rose to investigate; he could see out the front windows if he moved a few feet from his present spot. "Don't move a muscle," he warned, waving the barrel at Josh's head, then turned his back for only a second.

It was all Josh needed.

He snatched the shot glass from the sink and sent it flying across the breakfast bar. It had been thrown as straight and as hard as any pass he'd ever delivered, and it struck Kenny in the head just above the left temple.

Kenny dropped to one knee, a burning in his scalp and blood oozing down the side of his face.

Josh was around the bar and on top of Kenny just as the pistol was raised defensively in his direction. The sound from the muzzle blast barely registered in Josh's ears, but he felt a sensation like a whitehot iron touching him as the bullet ripped through the flesh of his right side.

With his momentum unchecked, he managed to grab Kenny's arm and the gun in both hands and direct the barrel away from his head as a second shot made a hole in the kitchen ceiling, the explosion echoing off the tile and stone. Kenny struggled for control of the weapon, trying to put the barrel squarely in his attacker's face.

They fell to the stone floor, kicking and cursing, striking each other in the face repeatedly as the gun refused to yield fully to either.

Josh felt his lip split when the barrel struck him hard across the mouth, and was surprised it hadn't fired. He was amazed at Kenny's strength, and found it impossible to simply overpower him. They rolled against the cabinets, banging into them with such fury that the door of one which housed pots and pans was split loose from its hinges and the contents of the cluttered cabinet spilled out onto the floor.

Finally, with a surge of strength, Josh was able to maneuver the pistol away from himself and direct it toward Kenny, the barrel now at the other man's throat, just under his jaw.

He let go of the hammer he'd been holding back with his right hand, Kenny's index finger still depressing the trigger. The flash from the explosion sent a blistering spatter of burning powder into Josh's eyes, tears clouding his vision.

He knew that if he wasn't able to restore his sight, he'd be dead.

As he blinked repeatedly to regain some vision, he realized that Kenny was no longer resisting him, that instead his body had gone into violent spasms.

He wrenched the revolver from Kenny's grip and fell back against a row of cabinets, Kenny on the floor beside him. With the backs of his hands, he cleared the tears from his eyes. Next to him, his oldest and closest friend twitched and jerked, like a snake that had been run over on the highway. Beside him on the stone floor, flecks of hair and bone, the back of Kenny's head, floated in a growing pool of dark red blood.

Josh could not keep down the vomit that rose in his throat.


The white van had driven past the sprawling house on Auburn-Folsom Road several minutes earlier, had noted the red Porsche in the drive, and now sat in the shaded cover of a small clump of trees where Kanazawa's street met an intersecting road from the south.

Munford had come over the hill on Auburn-Folsom at speed before he realized the lay of the land and, to avoid attracting attention, rather than turning suspiciously around, had chosen to drive on, pretending to be a repair service making a routine call in the neighborhood.

He and Higgins had been ordered to await specific instructions before making a move toward the house, but heard loud cracks from the house that sounded like gunshots.

As Higgins grabbed the cell phone to report what they'd heard, the phone rang in his hands. He answered it at once, the adrenaline already pumping.

"Yes," he said quickly.

"Goldman's dead," Karl Hetzler announced, his tone hard.

"Where?" the agent asked.

"His cabin."

"When?"

"From the crime scene report, death appears to have occurred about thirty minutes before Mitchell left the cabin."

"While we were watching him?" Higgins asked.

"Apparently so, Tommy," Hetzler said.

"Son of a bitch!" the agent cursed.

Higgins had been one of the men who'd watched the cabin from the fire road last night and cursed himself for not doing a walk up. He knew his orders were to remain in the car, but blamed himself now for the old man's death. He repeated his anger.

"Let it go, Tommy. This kind of thing happens," Hetzler assured him, doing little to lessen the agent's remorse. "Where's Mitchell now?"

Brad Munford had been able to tell from the one-sided conversation the gist of what had happened, and pulled a pair of 9mm Uzis from the weapons locker.

"He's inside Kanazawa's home north of town. Probably been in no more than a quarter of an hour. We heard what sounded like a couple of shots a few seconds ago, but wanted to check with you before we took any action. I was just about to call when—"

"Dammit to hell!" Hetzler shouted. "Get your asses in there and put that crazy bastard in custody before he kills every player in the game!"

"And if he resists?" Higgins said, assuming Mitchell would not come with them willingly.

"I want him alive, you hear me! Protect yourselves, but you damn well better be bleeding if you take Mitchell out! Understand!? Backup's on the way."

"Understand," Higgins said, ending the call.

He joined Munford in the front seats and checked his weapon.

"Let's get that fucker," he said.

Munford threw the Ford into gear and sped toward the house at the top of the hill.

# 20

Josh pressed the cold towel against his face, his eyes still watering heavily from the muzzle blast. His ears rang like a phone unanswered and he'd yet to examine the hole in his side, though a cursory look had given no cause for immediate alarm. Right now, he needed to see again; he felt vulnerable with his sight impaired, like a pilot without his instruments in a storm.

The chill water from the tap in the huge master bath—in Kenny's bedroom on the ground floor at the opposite end of the house from the kitchen—finally brought some relief to the fire in his eyes. He blinked repeatedly, his vision alternating between staring at the world through a window smeared with Vaseline and one which was almost clean.

When he could hold them open for several seconds, he turned his attention to the pain in his ribcage. As he removed his blood-stained MIT sweatshirt, he could see a dark hole the size of a pencil eraser between the third and fourth ribs, the bright red blood weeping steadily from it. Turning to put his right side toward the mirror, he found a matching hole where the slug had exited, about the size of his little finger. Like the entrance wound five inches away, the blood oozed steadily from it.

"At least it didn't puncture a lung," he mumbled gratefully as he began wrapping the Ace-bandage that he'd found below Kenny's vanity around his chest. It had taken him less than a minute to position a pair of gauze pads from the medicine cabinet over the oozing holes and secure them in place with the makeshift bandage. He'd treated each pad with a generous squeeze of Neosporin, though he knew it was not the care he needed. He could tell that at least one rib had been broken and he knew he needed stitches, if not some kind of surgery.

He was surprised it didn't hurt worse than it did, and attributed the numbness to the shock that had not yet fully registered. Regardless of the justification, he'd just blown his best friend's brains out, and knew he'd pay a dear emotional price for it one day, one day soon. He tried to force the thought away, but when he pulled on the clean Golden State Warriors sweatshirt he'd taken from Kenny's dresser, he was unable to repress the horror of what he'd done.

He vomited again, then found his mouth as dry as a dirt road in August. He pressed the cold rag to his forehead, his mind yelling at him to get a grip on himself.

When he started back toward the kitchen—where Kenny's bloody corpse now lay in a heap beneath an afghan Josh had taken from the den couch—he passed the entrance hall and glass front door in time to see a white van speeding up the driveway toward the house. "Dammit!" he said, darting from the doorway. He assumed the men were some of Hetzler's boys—or worse, connected with the guy who'd slammed him to the floor in his hotel room.

He knew, in either case, he wouldn't be able to explain away having just killed his friend; they'd laugh at his plea of self-defense before they cuffed him, or shoot him for resisting arrest, depending upon their mood.

Or their orders.

Without it being a purely conscious act, he grabbed the .38 Special he'd left on the breakfast bar and bolted for the back door, reaching it as he heard one of the men shout: "FBI, Mitchell—we have the place surrounded. Come out with your hands up. Do it now!"

Praying that wasn't yet the case, he sprinted across the decking that lay between the house and the pool. As he glanced behind him, he slammed into one of the deck chairs, sending it and his pain-wracked body sprawling across the washed-gravel surface.

The frantic noise of someone running was unmistakable to the two agents, and Munford and Higgins dashed for the rear of the house in response, weapons drawn. Despite Hetzler's warning, neither intended to join Dianne Lane or Morris Goldman, regardless of what Mitchell had to tell; Hetzler could get his answers elsewhere.

Josh arose at once and was now sprinting toward the fence that bordered the untended portion of Kenny's land. With his right hand gripping the pistol and his left on the top rail, he cleared the four-foot fence in a leap, though he fell again on the other side when his tennis shoes met the damp grass. Barely touching down before he was at full speed again, he reached the density of the wooded section before the agents had spotted him.

With the pulse pounding in his ears, he lay in the grass and stared back at the rear of the house. He could clearly see two men in suits, assault rifles in their hands, trying desperately to determine his direction of flight without being shot in the process, in case he was lying in wait behind the pool house or one of the sago palms that had been planted near the fence.

Content that he had a few minutes' head start, though aware a search helicopter was probably only minutes away, Josh stood again and raced down the back slope of the hill toward the tiny stream and dirt road that separated Kenny's land from the property behind him. He'd walked the land with his former partner when Kenny had first bought it, before construction on the sprawling house had begun, and recalled seeing the road. Kenny had told him it was an access road that meandered between the residential property and the working farms in the fertile valley, though, with the encroachment of wealthy executives seeking a more placid country existence in recent years, there were fewer and fewer farms being actively worked anymore. It was more profitable, and a hell of a lot less work, to sell to a developer wishing to carve yet another subdivision from America's fertile soil.

Agent Higgins returned to the van and grabbed his cell phone, placing a secured call to San Francisco.

He got his boss on the first ring.

"Kanazawa's dead," he announced matter-of-factly, still winded, though his pulse was more from the adrenaline rush than the exercise he'd gotten. Munford was still at the back of the house trying to find Mitchell, or the direction he'd fled. Higgins moved to rejoin him.

"That's not the news I wanted to hear," Hetzler said in an angered whisper. "And Mitchell?"

"Ran. Headed on foot into the woods behind the house. From what we can see, there's nothing but forest for miles in that direction."

"Goddammit!" Hetzler said. "You got any good news for me?" he barked sarcastically.

"A little. Mitchell's probably wounded. Can't tell how bad, but a sweatshirt in the bathroom is covered with blood, and it's my guess it isn't Kanazawa's. He's on the kitchen floor, still fully dressed."

"Kanazawa shoot him?"

Higgins's breath had almost returned to normal as he passed the kitchen. Through the den windows, he could see that his partner was heading back, alone. Higgins walked back toward the front of the house and peered down at the body of Kenny Kanazawa, the afghan now tossed to the side. "That'd be my guess, sir. I imagine Mitchell came in with a gun, making threats or demands, and Kanazawa tried to defend himself. This guy needs to be stopped."

"He will be, I promise you. He'll spend the rest of his life in a cage. Your chopper should be there any minute, along with half a dozen more men. You and Munford are in charge, Higgins; keep me posted. I want this man found—today!"

"Right, we'll find him," the agent said.

"And when we do," he vowed—knowing that since he'd sprung Mitchell from the Carmel Police in the hope that he would point the way to members of the espionage ring, Kanazawa's blood was indirectly on his hands—"you'll wish like hell you hadn't made a fool of me."

He also understood only too well how easily a criminal could slip past true justice using the plea bargaining farce preferred by spineless prosecutors.

Hetzler swore that was not going to occur this time.


Josh stumbled headlong into the shallow creek at the edge of Kenny's land, soaking himself. It had appeared without warning as he'd burst through a wall of tall grasses, and he'd slid down the rocky slope on his knees and palms. He struck the opposite bank with the side of his face, barely turning his head before his nose and chin took the full force of the fall.

He looked like a clumsy toddler and let out a muffled cry as he came to an abrupt stop, cursing under his breath.

It was turning out to be a really bad day, he thought.

When he'd retrieved the pistol from the stony creek bottom, he scooted up the bank toward the dirt road. He realized he couldn't be seen brandishing a weapon, especially if he hoped to get a ride, and tucked it in his jeans, pulling the sweatshirt over the small bulge. He noted how much room he had in the waistband of his pants, having eaten only one good meal in nearly a week, breakfast this morning at the Fairmont.

That it had only been a few hours ago seemed impossible.

A sudden noise down the road, beyond a curve to the left, forced him to seek cover in the tall scrub at the shoulder, certain it had been made by a vehicle pursuing him. It seemed hard to believe, he thought, clutching the gun's butt in his right hand—it hadn't been long enough for the feds to have found an access to this back road, even if they knew which way he ran.

Then another thought struck him: What the hell was he going to do with the pistol even if it were the cops . . . shoot it out? He had two bullets left and didn't intend either of them to be responsible for another death.

Except my own, he swore, knowing he could never endure a life behind bars for crimes he hadn't committed. The absolute insanity of the week was wearing at him, clouding his thinking. He pulled the sweatshirt back over the gun butt, afraid to toss it away.

He watched for the vehicle he could now hear clearly. It sounded like a car with a faulty muffler.

When the farm truck came into view, still in the curve where it was unlikely he could be seen, Josh stood and brushed the grass from his clothes. Half soaked, his face spattered with mud, he looked a mess, but begged silently for the driver to give him a ride anyway; he knew this might well be his only chance to get free of the area before the manhunt began in earnest. He'd seen *Cops* a hundred times; there would be no escaping the helicopters.

For the first time since he was a child, he prayed aloud: "Please, God, if You have any pity left for me, I need Your help; I know I don't deserve it, but if You'll help me, just this once, I'll never ask nothing of You again."

He'd never been more frightened or more sincere, and had to struggle to find a pleasant smile for the driver, hoping the terror he was feeling wouldn't be evident in his expression.

The decrepit powder-blue-and-white '55 Chevy pickup slowed as it passed—the driver and both front seat passengers studying the oddly out-of-place hitchhiker—but it failed to stop.

Then the rain began to pour like the clouds had just been squeezed dry, and Josh felt what little hope he had left slipping from him.

When the truck had traveled twenty or so yards beyond his position, its one working taillight suddenly illuminated, the road not sheltered by its rusty body quickly becoming a brown goo. In the rear, beneath a ramshackle plywood topper that ran the full length of the long bed, a dozen pairs of eyes stared back in the darkness, like a pack of cave-dwelling creatures wary of a strange animal lurking outside their den.

Josh returned the stare beneath a hand raised to protect his eyes, the rain plastering his hair to his head and dripping from the end of his nose. His body began to shiver from the damp cold that had already saturated his sweatshirt.

"Apúrate, mi amigo," a voice called out, a lone arm waving in the rain for Josh to hurry if he wanted a lift.

• • •

Brad Munford cursed when the helicopter pilot, having set down in the front yard of the ranch house, announced without room for argument that the rain and lightning had not only become too intense for a successful aerial search, but would likely ground him and his craft, right where they sat, for the duration of the storm.

The three agents who'd come by chopper—heavily armed and dressed for the potentially dangerous work that lay ahead—were immediately dispatched to pick up Mitchell's trail, amid the downpour, and fanned out from the rear fence, heading north into the woods.

In the van, Tommy Higgins studied the digital maps of the immediate area, searching desperately for a road, or egress of any kind, that might aid in Mitchell's escape. Despite the sophistication of the software, and the accuracy of its massive database, apparently none of the cartographers had thought the farm access road significant enough to include in their surveys. Hence, the thin blue line that should have represented it was missing from the agent's screen.

According to the computer, it didn't exist.

"There's nothing behind the house but woods and more woods," Higgins announced to his partner. "He's still out there, waiting for us to grab him. I sure wish I knew how bad he was hurt."

"Not bad enough, he's still on the move," Munford said as he sought shelter in the van. "I want you to pinpoint any place where he can catch a ride, Tommy." He checked his watch: "He's been gone eleven minutes now . . . that's maybe a mile at most in those thick trees and razor-edge grasses. How soon can he flag a ride?"

Tommy Higgins studied the computer screen and touched three or four points on the glass with the electronic stylus. "If he's fit, not seriously hurt, runs like hell, and keeps on the straightest path possible, he's still twenty-plus minutes from the closest indicated road north of the house, the direction he's headed."

"Twenty minutes," Munford repeated. He seemed pleased. "Show me."

Higgins indicated the most expedient and logical point of escape with the stylus, a small paved road two and a half miles north of Kanazawa's home.

"Print it!" Munford ordered. When Higgins had handed him three color copies of the map page currently displayed on the screen, Munford left the van. "Let's go, Rusty," he called out to the driver of the Hummer that had arrived with a trio of agents at the same time as the chopper team.

Pointing to the map, Munford said, "Rusty, we can pick up a road west of here that will lead us to the most likely point where Mitchell can catch a ride. If we hurry, we can cut him off."

In less than a minute, the four men had covered more than a third of the distance to the county road three miles to the west that would take them to the point indicated on the map. As they moved at the Hummer's top speed, the radio mounted beneath the dash crackled.

"This is Domingo," the voice announced. The agent, along with his two confederates from the chopper, had crossed the woods behind Kanazawa's house and had reached an unmarked farm road at the north end of his property. Only one set of unidentifiable tire tracks scarred the mud and they were fresh, though the rain was doing its best to erase them. "Put Munford on."

"You got him," Munford said impatiently. "What do you have?"

"You're not going to like this, Brad," Domingo said, "but it looks like Mitchell's already found some wheels."

Munford hammered the mike against his thigh. "Dammit!" he said. "Where?"

"There's a dirt road running along a small creek about three hundred yards north of the house. I doubt it's on your map."

"It's not!" Munford grumbled.

Domingo added: "One set of tire tracks. Can't tell anything for sure about the vehicle. My guess is that it's headed west."

"Then you'd better be heading west, too. We'll pick you up."

"Roger that."

Munford considered the best way to intercept Mitchell before he could put too much distance between them, because he knew every mile decreased the likelihood of reacquiring him. He indicated for the driver to turn the Hummer around and head back to the chopper as he radioed the van. "Come in, Tommy."

"This is Higgins," his partner answered.

"Tommy," Munford barked, his patience thin, "tell that pilot, whatever his name is, to get ready to put it in the air."

"What about the storm?" Higgins asked.

"The hell with the storm," Munford said through clenched teeth.

The old truck rattled and backfired along the access road, moving as if it would expire at any minute. In actuality, it was traveling at what would have been the speed limit had one been indicated, but to Josh—riding impatiently in the back—anything less than ninety felt fatally slow.

He'd squeezed in as best he could among the other men already beneath the topper, his knees pulled up against him. Including himself and the three in the cab, there were now sixteen in the antique truck.

It's a miracle it hasn't just died on the side of the road, he considered as it sputtered and popped going over one pronounced rut. He begged silently for one more hour of life in the anemic engine.

After a bout of laughter among the men that Josh neither understood nor attempted to join, the man to his left offered him a chew of tobacco. Josh couldn't identify the brand.

"No thanks," he said with a smile.

More laughter from the men prompted another to offer one of his remaining Camels. Again Josh politely declined.

Finally, a stinky cigar, as fat as Josh's thumb, followed the cigarettes, and the laughter reached a pinnacle.

Josh just shook his head this time, content to be the punch line of whatever joke the men were sharing. He awaited the pipe which didn't come.

"How the hell do you say 'I don't smoke' in Spanish," he wondered, running the French he'd taken for two semesters in high school through his mind and trying to make a parallel.

A pain seared his side as the man to his right shifted positions, jamming a knee into his injured ribs.

Josh adjusted his weight, moving away from the knee pressing against him. The pain was excruciating, but as he moved, he managed a smile at the man who had no idea his innocent movement had caused such discomfort.

As it had for ten minutes, a flurry of rapidly spoken Spanish passed between the men. One of them again began laughing robustly, compelling the others to join in. Josh, not wanting to appear too out of place, laughed along with them this time—mostly out of release of tension—adding to their merriment. He was sure the new joke had something to do with him, but it mattered little. They had saved his life, let them laugh.

His prayer had been answered, but he became increasingly worried when the muddy road on which they were traveling met no other roads; not so much as a fork or an intersection. If it was discovered that he'd taken this route, it wouldn't take a genius to follow it directly to him.

The physical pain tormenting his body, the cluttered din of a dozen strangers chattering and laughing around him, the pungent smell of exhaust fumes seeping into the bed, and the hammering of rain on the plywood cover, began to take a maddening toll.

When the hills gradually yielded to the flat farmland that stretched to the horizon north and west, Josh was relieved to see numerous roads similar to the one on which they'd been traveling meeting and crossing at regular intervals.

As the chances for capture by the cops decreased with this new terrain, some of the torment in his head began to subside.

There was no lessening of the physical pain, however.

Finally, they reached a farm six miles northwest of Kenny's house. The truck immediately emptied as the men, all fifteen of them, hurried into the large frame building just beyond the cab, leaving Josh to climb clumsily over the tailgate and onto the soggy ground.

"Tarjeta verde, por favor," a husky woman's voice said from behind him.

Josh turned to find a short, stocky woman in muddy boots, jeans, and a blue flannel shirt standing beside a neatly painted four-rail fence, clipboard in hand.

She appeared to be about fifty, perhaps a bit more, and she reminded him immediately of his mother.

He wondered what she'd think of him now, bruised, cut, shot, and running from the police like a common criminal.

"Pardon me?" he said, resisting the temptation to hold his throbbing side. He passed a hand casually and without attracting attention across his stomach to make certain the pistol butt wasn't protruding.

It was still tucked safely in his waistband.

"Don't speak Spanish, huh?" the woman laughed. "Sorry, most of the workers I get around here are from a bit south, if you know what I mean. I asked you for your green card . . . but I guess that won't be necessary." She noticed the pain that twisted Josh's face, despite his best effort to conceal it. "You okay?" she asked sympathetically, coming toward him. "Those boys didn't get rough with you, did they?"

"No, they couldn't have been nicer," he assured her. He found a smile. "Especially if I'd been having a nicotine fit."

They both laughed.

She liked Josh immediately.

"I take it you're not here for a job," she said.

"No," Josh said. His eyes wandered around the property, looking for an escape route. "Just hitched a ride." He knew the time he'd managed to buy was being quickly consumed. A sense of the world closing in around him was so intense that he felt like he was breathing under water.

The woman couldn't help noticing. "You want to come inside for a minute?" she asked, stepping closer to him and touching his arm. The need to mother him was strong from a woman who'd made a lifetime of mothering stray cats, dogs, and migrant farm workers. "Got a fresh pot of coffee on."

Josh looked to the heavens; the sky was still thick with clouds that threatened new downpours, but for the moment, it was not raining; hadn't been for five minutes. He cursed the break in the weather. He was a pilot and knew the chopper he'd heard approaching as the rain began would have been grounded during the storm, but he also knew that it would be able to lift off now. Searching. Hunting him down like an eagle hunts its dinner—without mercy.

Josh nodded, knowing that, since he had not seen another vehicle in twenty minutes, a second ride was not going to be easy to find. He also imagined that all the major roads within miles had already been sealed. "Thanks. I'd like that." Suddenly, just being inside, out from beneath stalking eyes, seemed to lessen the feeling of suffocation.

When they'd entered the main house, thirty yards up from the bunkhouse where the men from the truck had disappeared, the woman said, "I'm Micki Hatcher. And you?"

Josh hesitated, then chose the truth. "I'm Josh Mitchell. Nice to meet you." He closed the door behind him after allowing her to pass.

When he paused for a moment and looked back toward the road, Micki Hatcher's eyes caught it.

"So, Josh Mitchell, who's after you, the police?" She stood just inside the room, her hands on her wide hips, her manner cautious.

Josh turned and lowered his head, like a child in trouble. "Is it that obvious?" he asked.

"Well, I'd say you weren't a pro at running from the law. That's encouraging, at least."

He looked at her. "No. I'm not. How'd you know?"

"Hell, half the folks I get around here at planting time are running from something or someone. You get where you can tell." She turned and walked toward the kitchen, to the right of the front door. "Want to tell me why on earth I shouldn't turn you in right now, or at least send you packing? I love a good story."

The woman's words were troubling, but within them, his years of selling told him he might have an ally.

Josh dropped heavily into a chair in the kitchen, his side burning more with each minute. He wanted to take a look at it, and was glad he'd chosen a black sweatshirt; he could feel the blood soaking the fabric. It wouldn't show as long as it didn't drip on the floor.

Micki put a cup of black coffee in front of him and sat beside him at the kitchen table, sipping on a mug.

"It's a long story," he said wearily.

"That's why I went ahead and sat down," she said without a trace of condemnation or fear in her voice.

Josh knew she wanted, though probably didn't expect, to hear the whole story. There wasn't time, he thought, as the feeling of being caged increased.

Never had his life been so out of control, so void of hope. The sense of desperation that all criminals on the run must feel seized him. He half expected the ground to open up and swallow him, like in the Old Testament stories of his youth. He dug deep within him and summoned the charm and sales ability that had been his greatest assets all his life. He needed her help, whatever she could give, and he would get only one shot at securing it. "I don't know where to begin, Mrs. Hatcher."

"Micki," she insisted. "Try the beginning. I find it always works out best that way."

He nodded, though her pleasant manner did little to lessen the dread that festered behind his best smile.

Within ten minutes, Josh had given Micki Hatcher a condensed version of his life of late, up to the point where he'd fought with and killed his best friend. He'd even told her about how he'd loved his job and how flying had always made him feel free, like the wind that danced among the tall corn stalks in September. The imagery was warm, homespun, and completely sincere—he could have easily been her own prodigal son (though he had no idea whether she had children of her own) and soon saw that she was exhibiting all the right "buying signals." Not once did she turn her eyes away or show the slightest hint of censure. He might as well have been telling her about an episode of a soap opera that she'd missed, instead of recalling the real events that had changed so many real lives.

When he held up his sweatshirt to reveal his bloody right side, to lend authenticity to the whole bizarre tale, the butt of Kenny's small blue-steel .38 Special showed with alarming presence in his jeans waistband.

He withdrew the gun and laid it softly on the table, the barrel toward him and the butt within easy reach of her, gambling that the ultimate gesture of trust by him would invoke a similar sense of faith on her part.

She seemed surprised by the action, but still showed no fear.

"Take it," he said, pushing it even closer. "I don't know why I grabbed it anyway. I couldn't actually shoot anyone, except maybe myself."

"Now, that's crazy talk, Joshua. It is Joshua, isn't it, not Josh?"

"Yes, ma'am. That's what my mama always called me." He found a smile for the first time in the ten minutes he'd talked. "So did Pamela . . . I mean Dianne," he corrected himself.

"I can see how you'd get them confused."

"Not really them, just their names," he said softly. "I never had the pleasure of meeting Pamela Morrow."

"I'm sorry your friend, Kenny, turned out to be a . . . well . . . let's just say, not the person you believed he was."

It had been put as nicely as Josh could have imagined, though it did little to help. "Thanks," he said, his heart full of warmth for the woman he'd met less than a quarter of an hour earlier. He knew now that she would help him if she could, and was pleased that he'd been able to summon some of the old charm. Under different circumstances, he might have been ashamed of having intentionally "played" the woman, but these were the circumstances under which he now lived—and under which he could just as easily die. There would be no remorse, or if there was, it would come some day when this was all far behind him.

Though the hope was still there, the possibility of it ever ending seemed too alien, too improbable.

Micki looked seriously at him, forming her words carefully. "Let me ask you something, Joshua, and I warn you, I want a straight answer."

"Sure," he said, certain that nothing she could ask him would be worse than what he'd already revealed.

"Did you love her?" Her eyes didn't move.

Josh thought for only a moment. "I don't know if you'll understand this, Micki, but I've loved Dianne all my life, long before I'd ever laid eyes on her. It was as if a void had existed all these years and was suddenly filled when she sat down beside me. It's not like I knew her for only eighteen hours, but for years." He took a sip of his coffee. "Does that make any sense at all?"

"More than you might know," she said, nodding gently.

Josh touched her hand.

Micki scooted her spindle-back chair away from the table and stood, satisfied that what she was about to do was right. She said, "Now, let's get that done up properly, get you something to eat, and then get you on your way. They'll be coming before long, I suspect. You'll need as much of a head start as we can give you, Joshua"—she looked deep into his eyes, like a mother helping her child regardless of the consequences to her—"if you're going to finish what you've begun."

Josh was incredulous. What the heck was she talking about, all the head start "they" could give him? His eyes asked the question for him.

"You do want to put your boss in his place, don't you? If what you've told me is correct, I'd say he deserves it."

Josh nodded.

"Good! I was hoping you'd still say that, Joshua, but you're not gonna get the job done sitting there bleeding on my floor."

He looked down and noticed that he'd been dripping on the linoleum, the crimson pool at his right foot as large as a silver dollar.

"But . . . how can I?" he asked, looking for a paper towel.

She gave him a sign with her hand not to worry about it. "As I see it," she said, "there're three steps to this plan. I'll take care of the first one right now." With that, the stocky woman pressed an intercom button on the kitchen wall and shouted something in Spanish. She didn't bother to translate for Josh, knowing he'd understand in a minute.

When she released the button, she walked to the back door, four or five steps from where Josh sat, and opened it, waiting impatiently. The man who'd been driving the pickup hurried from the bunkhouse and up the back steps, wiping his feet as he entered the kitchen.

He took off his well-worn hat and held it in front of his chest, but before he could speak, she said in English, "Juan, there may be some men from the FBI or the local police snooping around here in a little while. They're after this man here. They want him for murder and a number of other things he didn't do." Josh was floored by Micki's candor, and his expression probably said so to the man in the doorway. Still, he couldn't help admiring her simple honesty. She continued with barely a breath: "His name is Joshua Mitchell and he's a friend of mine, a dear friend. Would you ask your boys to forget that they ever saw him? It would mean a great deal to me."

Juan leaned around the corner of the door jamb to get a better look at the man he'd given a lift to, studying Josh's face carefully, but especially his eyes. Then he stood proudly erect. "What man are you talking about, señora? I see no one. Also, I'm sure my men have seen no strangers today." His understanding smile seemed to divide his leathery face.

"Muchísimas gracias, Juan," she said affectionately, squeezing his shoulder. "Now, you and the boys get Old Yeller ready to go. And I mean pronto, mi amigo!"

"Ya me voy," he said and disappeared.

She slammed the door and started across the kitchen. "Old Yeller?" Josh said.

She held up a hand to silence him as she vanished from the room. In fifteen seconds she'd returned with a large first-aid kit, far more elaborate than Josh had expected to find in a home.

"Lots of cuts and bruises around here during planting and harvest," she explained opening it on the table. "I'm pretty good at fixing most things that don't go too deep. Now, let's have a look at that hole in your chest."

Josh took off his sweatshirt and dropped it to the floor rather than setting the bloody thing on the table. Before he could undo the two silver clasps that secured the Ace-bandage, Micki had cut it off. She was surprised at the bruising from the auto accident in Mississippi. His whole left side was a dull yellow with purple blotches.

"When the car flipped?" she said.

He nodded.

She observed the nearly black gauze pads that had stuck to his ribcage. When she yanked them away, Josh grimaced.

"Sorry," she said. "No time to kiss it and make it feel better."

"I know," he said sincerely.

The two finger-sized holes were still oozing blood, though some crusty clotting had begun around the edges of the wounds. She took a generous helping of Collastat—a coagulation agent—and covered a double-thick gauze pad with it, pressing against the rear hole. Josh held it in place. When she'd repeated the procedure for the front hole, she wrapped his chest in clean gauze, circling him half a dozen times. A couple of strips of wide surgical tape over the pads—to prevent blood from showing through on his clothes—completed the procedure. It had taken less than three minutes.

She shook out six Advils in his hand from a plastic bottle and told him to take them, they wouldn't make him sleepy like a pain pill might, though she had some of them, too.

Josh did as he was told, washing them down with what was left of his coffee.

Micki crammed the rest of the bottle in his hand, wrapping his fingers around it. "Take them when you need them, Joshua. If it hurts, acknowledge it."

He nodded. "You've done this before," he said admiringly.

"Not the first bullet wound I've seen . . . nor the last, I suspect. Boys get pretty rowdy on payday sometimes. Someone always sneaks in a handgun no matter how close you watch things, usually a short-nosed twenty-two. Haven't had anyone die on me yet, knock wood," she smiled, pleased with her quick patch job. She handed him a clean sweatshirt she'd brought from the back of the house along with the first-aid kit. It bore a bold logo from an agrochemical company he'd seen a hundred times but had not thought about since helping his dad plant corn back in Tennessee.

He hoped he'd get the chance to help him with one more crop, before time or circumstance made it just a part of their common past. Though farming hadn't been the life he'd wanted to live, he'd never really minded putting in the long hours in the field alongside his father. There had been a soulful reward for the work that trying to coax six million bucks out of a chief financial officer had never quite offered.

He remembered what Micki had said before Juan left. "Old Yeller?" he repeated.

"You'd better not have been just bragging about being able to fly, Joshua. Were you?" She stood squarely before him, her gaze firm.

"Call it bragging if you like, Micki," he smiled, "but I'm the best damn pilot you ever saw."

"Now, that'd take some doing. Good, that's step two in this plan of mine. Help me a minute, will you?" She moved to the refrigerator.

Josh held out his hands while she filled them with two of the largest chicken legs he'd ever seen, fried a deep golden brown with batter as thick as cake frosting. She stuck a small plastic squeeze bottle of Evian under his left arm.

"Best I can do under the circumstances," she said apologetically. "We gotta scoot if you're gonna get away from here before we have visitors." She practically pulled him toward the back door, grabbing his pistol on the way and stuffing it in the back pocket of her jeans.

Nothing surprised him anymore.



Brad Munford strapped himself in the passenger seat of the Bell Jet Ranger, an M16 with a long barrel and 4.5 x 15 sniper scope across his lap. In the back seat, two of the best shots in the Bureau's western region sat comparably outfitted, eager to place a crosshair on Mitchell's forehead. The chopper lifted off just as the rain began to abate. The pilot let out a silent sigh of relief.

"The last thing the team on the road said was that the tracks were heading west," he shouted into his mouthpiece as they gained some altitude. The other three men in the helicopter nodded that they'd heard him. "That's where we'll head. I want to be low enough to spot him if he's still on foot, and fast enough to catch whatever he's riding in. Understand?"

The pilot nodded.

Munford chambered a round as the helicopter began to move, staying just fifty feet above tree level. Regardless of what kind of vehicle Mitchell may have found to give him a lift, or how fast he was traveling on the ground, Munford knew the Jet Ranger could overtake it easily.

The biggest question at the moment was Mitchell's direction: which road he'd chosen. Though the choices were initially limited, with only one air search unit, a decision had to be made. Munford looked at the map and let his instinct guide his choice.

"Here," he said to the pilot. In a minute, they were over the three agents still on the tiny mud road. "Domingo?" he called into the mike.

"This is Domingo."

"Talk to me, buddy."

The man talked into his handset as he jogged along the road. His two buddies behind, noting every broken twig, crushed blade of grass, or sign of a footprint in the brown goo. The rain had lessened and the tracks had become increasingly defined. "Nothing we've found so far indicates that Mitchell has abandoned his ride, and the vehicle is definitely headed west."

"You found some tracks?"

"Yeah, a couple of footprints on a slippery bank at the edge of Kanazawa's property, and then a couple more nearby that led to the center of the vehicle's tracks, then disappeared," Domingo said.

"Roger that," Munford radioed back. "Any idea what kind of ride he got?"

"Got one pretty clean tire print about four hundred yards back. Can't be sure, Brad, but it looks like a truck tire to me. At least, it's got that kind of aggressive tread on it, though it's pretty bald from what little I can tell. If I had to guess, I'd say he caught a ride in an old farm truck that just happened to be passing by. The lucky bastard," the agent on the ground added.

He was tired of jogging after a vehicle he would never catch on foot.

"The Hummer should pick you up as soon as we can direct it to an intersecting road. It doesn't help that this damned dirt road isn't on the map."

"I'm the one up to my butt in mud chasing this guy, remember?"

"Roger that. Sorry for the delay, Domingo. Stay with your ground search and keep your eyes open for anything suspicious—anything."

As the rotors beat the air overhead, and the steady vibration of the airframe numbed his feet where they touched the floor and the backs of his thighs where they made contact with the seat, Munford got the strangest feeling Mitchell wasn't merely running, blindly racing down the first road that presented itself.

He knew well that felons in flight were either wildly erratic or coldly calculating, and his instinct told him that Mitchell understood that his life depended upon a level head. And luck.

Brad Munford couldn't have known how right he was.

# 21

Old yeller sat in a clearing beside a tin shed, a hundred yards from the east side of the main house. Juan and two of his men were pouring gasoline from a five-gallon can into a fitting in its side, a dozen empty five-gallon cans already at their feet. Four more men stood beside the plane, two at each wing, in case the plane needed to be repositioned for takeoff. The rest from the truck were eradicating the wheel tracks where the plane had been moved from the shed by brushing the area with small branches cut from a nearby tree. Juan had ordered that no sign of recent activity remain behind, and waved enthusiastically as his boss and her invisible new friend approached.

Micki waved back and called out in Spanish to her foreman of more than twenty years, but Josh was too amazed at the frantic activity that was unfolding before him to do much more than stare with an ever-widening smile.

"Isn't she a beauty?" Micki said proudly.

"That she is," he said.

Twenty-five yards ahead sat a bright yellow Air Tractor biplane, its lightweight aluminum frame, covered in fabric and paint, an anachronism in an age of carbon fiber and Kevlar swept-wing jets. Its six-hundred-horsepower Pratt & Whitney radial engine would have been, in the right airframe, capable of speeds greater than three hundred miles per hour, but in this dinosaur, a third of that was more likely.

It was the quintessential crop duster, and one of the best-handling aircraft of its kind ever built.

More importantly, it was identical to the one Josh had flown as a boy.

His spirits lifted and his shoulders seemed to pull back on their own, his mind on something positive, something he could control, for the first time in nearly a week.

"Thank you, God," he said quietly, making a celebratory fist with his left hand and taking a huge bite of the fried chicken in his right. He'd finished the other piece before they'd cleared the bunkhouse.

Micki patted the tail of the plane lovingly as they reached it. "My husband, Dell, God rest his soul, used to do all the crop dusting for our farm and the neighbors to the north. Took most of his waking hours some weeks, but how he loved to fly around in that old Air Tractor. If the cancer hadn't taken him in '86, I reckon he'd be flying her to this day." She looked again at Josh. "You ever seen an old biplane like this before?"

He took another bite of chicken, his stomach wonderfully full, and gave her a huge grin. "Ma'am, I used to buzz my neighbor's hogs in an old 301 Air Tractor just like this whenever I got the chance and he wasn't around. Cost them fifty pounds apiece. He never could figure out why they wouldn't fatten up like others he'd had." The two of them laughed together for a moment, as much from the release of tension as Josh's story. He added: "The question is not whether I can fly her, but whether you're really sure you want to do this. I can't promise you a thing about where I'm gonna end up, or if I can get her back to you. You might have to come get it halfway across the state. Perhaps you ought to reconsider."

Something told him she wouldn't.

"If you can fly her, Joshua, then you'd better get your butt in and go; I reckon we've eaten up just about any lead you may have had. Don't you worry about Old Yeller. She'll find her way home okay."

His face showed his continued concern. "What will you tell the FBI when they get here, ma'am, because they'll be here, as sure as the morning's going to come?"

Micki Hatcher told Juan to have his men move the gas cans and then hurry back to the bunkhouse, to keep an eye out for company. When they'd left, she stepped up to Josh. "Listen, son, I don't want you to think that I've got no regard for the law, because I do. So did my Dell. We always believed in obeying the law, faithfully, when it was fairly applied. When someone's wrong, anyone, no matter what kind of right they think they've got on their side, they're still wrong. Simple as that. I may be an idiot, and you may be lying your fool head off to me, but I don't believe it's so." She reached in her back pocket and handed him the pistol he'd given her earlier. "You get that son of a bitch that hurt Miss Lane and let me worry about the law. Deal?"

"Deal," Josh said.

He grabbed the huge propeller and gave the radial engine a full counterclockwise turn, to force any oil that had accumulated in the cylinders out the exhaust ports. He'd been taught long ago that old radial engines, especially one with as many hours on it as this one surely had, were bad about leaking oil into the lower cylinders when they'd sat for a while, and not performing this ritual could result in a bent rod when the engine fired. With the leakage cleared, Josh picked up the pistol he'd set at his feet, stuffed it back in his belt, and climbed into the cockpit. He gave Micki a smile as he threw the master switch; the woman stepped away from the plane.

After Josh had primed the cylinders with fuel, and advanced and set the throttle and mixture, he pressed the start button, holding it in while the highly geared electric starter whined and whirled the massive Pratt & Whitney engine to life. The nine bucket-sized pistons gulped in huge volumes of air and aviation gas, sputtering and coughing like a giant unexpectedly awakened from a deep sleep. Finally, as the battery began to weaken, the radial fired, belching fingers of fire and oily, black smoke from its bank of exhausts.

It felt like a piece of heaven to Josh, a part of his past that existed outside the lunacy and horror of the week, a part that no one could take away as long as he could stay in flight. Perhaps he'd just seek some point high above the city and then send the biplane headlong into Richard Hightower's house, wrapping up all pieces of the puzzle in one massive fireball.

But he knew there was no way to ensure the man would be there; hadn't Kenny said that he was even now at Barnett, guaranteeing that the trail of espionage and death would lead straight to Josh? Why not then fly into the sixth floor, and burn the place to the ground?

His own thoughts seemed as deranged as the world around him.

He pulled on the old goggles that were hanging from the instrument panel and revved the engine, now that the oil temperature needle had indicated movement. With an affectionate and grateful salute to the woman standing beside the shed, her thumbs pointing skyward in front of her, he moved the plane easily down the grass strip.

In a few seconds, he was airborne, doing a barrel-roll fifty feet above the ground for his benefactor.

Micki Hatcher could see Josh's arm extended high outside the cockpit, waving what was left of the chicken leg enthusiastically.

She waved back, though she knew his mind was now on the air ahead and what he had to do.

"Well, I'll be," she grinned broadly. "That boy can fly. He reminds me of my Dell."


As the biplane sped southwest toward the lower Napa Valley, at just over a hundred miles an hour and three hundred feet off the ground, Josh considered the soundness of his hastily laid plan and then reconsidered it, just as he'd done a dozen times over the last fifty miles. One moment, it all made perfect sense, the most logical step in an illogical game of death that held at least some ray of hope for him; the next, it seemed a ludicrous string of idiotic thoughts that would probably mean his certain recapture and possible execution.

He shouted his arguments over the thunderous exhaust of the engine, the wind stealing his voice as it passed his lips.

"Why the hell should she help me," he yelled—certain he should be flying toward any other spot on the globe but where he was headed—"especially after I confront her with the information I've got? I've lost my mind entirely . . . she'll call the cops the second she lays eyes on me."

He shook his head, closing his eyes for a moment as he did. "You're really dumb, you know it?" he shouted. "She already thinks you're responsible for Dianne's death. She's not the answer to your problems."

He forced his protective voice to be silent, knowing full well that this woman represented his only chance, regardless of the risk involved.

"I've got to make her see that it wasn't me who took Dianne Lane's life, that none of this lunacy has anything to do with me," he whispered into the chill air that beat against his face, yet he knew, in some strange way, this hellish week had everything to do with him.

When the impulse to change his mind had vanished, despite knowing that his plan was risky, Josh turned his thoughts to where he could land the bright yellow crop duster.

He checked his gas gauge. He had enough fuel for seventy-five more minutes of flying, even at his current pace—more if he slowed to the craft's normal cruising speed. With the ocean now only twenty minutes west of him, and the ground becoming increasingly littered with homes and businesses, he'd have to touch down before he ran out of opportunities, soon in fact. Basic navigating had kept Interstate 80 on his far left since leaving the farm, and with few exceptions, he'd traveled over scantly populated farmland, vineyards, and rural towns, attracting little attention and, thankfully, no unwanted company. For the first fifteen minutes he'd been in the air, Josh had looked behind him nearly as much as ahead, certain the helicopter he'd heard earlier would pop out of the ominous clouds at any minute and begin firing on him like an enemy fighter.

As always when he was behind the controls of an airplane—any kind of plane—he'd relaxed, falling in love with flying all over again;

and not just because it had delivered him from his pursuers, but more because it had reminded him of his youth, of a time before the lies had ensnared him. In truth, he hadn't warranted the horrors that had been visited upon him since Tuesday morning, but Josh knew deception always found a way of returning to you. He called it the "Karma Credit Plan," though he'd never expected such payment would be exacted for crimes he'd thought of as petty. With the exception, he reconsidered, of turning his back on those who loved him most.

He skimmed the treetops, watching closely for power lines, sure no radar could pick him up, even if the feds had learned of his method of escape. He doubted that Micki had said anything—knew she hadn't—and wondered how he could repay her kindness.

He'd find a way. Someday.

Ahead, beneath the left wing, as the Bay Area skyline began to fill the western horizon, Josh spotted a small airport a couple of miles north of Vallejo. He knew it had to be the Napa County Airport off State Route 29; he'd flown over it years before while getting his jet rating. Though too small for jet traffic, it was perfect for his needs.

He'd flown into numerous similar airports in his life, and knew that while not expected, he would nonetheless be welcome if he observed all FAA guidelines and endangered no one—he had no intention of drawing unwanted attention to himself.

Following the book exactly, he made a wide right turn to bring him north of the runway, watching closely for any other aircraft in an approach pattern, then swung back to the south to put the biplane squarely in line with the narrow asphalt strip. With the storm having only just passed, and still promising to unleash another bout of rain, the airport appeared deserted. He touched down without incident—a landing that made him grin with satisfaction—and taxied to a spot not far from the main hangar, where he hoped he wouldn't be taking anyone's assigned space.

"Just like riding a horse," he whispered when he switched off the engine.

Within fifteen minutes, Josh had made arrangements to leave the plane for the afternoon while he conducted some business in town.

The mechanic had assumed the unknown pilot meant Vallejo, five miles down 29, and Josh had not corrected him.

He then called for a cab and waited, searching the road through a window in the hangar like a prisoner waiting to catch a glimpse of the hangman. He tried to tell himself he was only watching for the cab, that he was safe for the moment, but he knew differently.

Madeline Richmond's home was thirty-five miles southwest of the small airport, in the heart of San Francisco, and while it would certainly have been more economical to have rented a car, Josh knew he couldn't risk having his name suddenly appear in a computer in the Bay Area. With any luck, the cops had no idea how he'd vanished, and would probably consider many other places before turning their attention to San Francisco. He imagined they were even now conducting an extensive manhunt of the hills and woods north of Kenny's home.

As he waited the ten minutes for his ride, he fished in his pocket for enough change for the Coke machine. He found only a single quarter and a few pennies, not enough to relieve the dryness in his mouth that the hundred-mile-an-hour wind had exacerbated.

As a thought struck him, he felt a fresh pang of anxiety. He pulled his wallet from his hip pocket and stared at the emptiness that laughed back at him like a crooked clown's mouth. "Dammit!" he said aloud, then turned around to see if the mechanic working on the Cessna nearby had heard him. He gave no indication he had.

*What the hell am I going to do for money?* he wondered, knowing that the FBI would be closely monitoring his every credit card charge and ATM transaction, ready to pounce. He'd been halfway to Kennedy on Monday before he'd realized that Monica had been in his wallet—again—and had left him with only fifty dollars, which had disappeared during the course of the week. He'd meant to stop a dozen times at an ATM, and cursed himself now for having not remembered to do so.

When he checked his watch to see how long it had been since he'd called for the cab, a smile spread across his face.

"You know of a pawn shop open today?" he asked of the driver when he'd plopped into the back seat of the Veteran Cab.

"I think Joe's Gun and Pawn is open on Sundays," the driver said, helpful but obviously eager to be on his way. The man was short and chisel-faced, with a piece of gum in his mouth being chewed as fast as his jaws could move. Josh guessed him to be about sixty, with the thin, gaunt build of one who drinks more than he eats.

"How far?" Josh said.

"Nine-hundred block of Tennessee Street, just off Sonoma. That's the road we're on now, except it's called State Route 29 out here. It's only about eight miles. Want me to head there?"

*Tennessee Street,* Josh repeated. The irony suited his mood.

"Please," he said.

Within twenty minutes, Josh walked out of the small brick-and-iron-bar structure with his nine-thousand-dollar Rolex President no longer on his wrist but with five crisp hundred-dollar bills in his pocket.

No questions. No paperwork.

An hour later, Josh was standing on Pacific Avenue, before the huge wrought-iron gates of the Kennerly family estate.


Josh spent the afternoon at a deli on Broadway, around the corner from the mansion, eating biscotti, drinking espresso, and trying to appear ordinary. His scruffy whiskers weren't out of place, nor were his jeans and sweatshirt, yet he felt as if every eye in the bustling place was on him; scrutinizing his anxious expression; watching his darting, nervous eyes. There was no way to conceal the pain that tormented his haggard body and he felt as if he must appear to all like the crazed killer he was thought to be. The crushing reality that he no longer had a place of sanctuary—anywhere—corroded his spirit like an acid, slowly trying to consume what spirit he had left. He fought the feeling, determined to have the answers he needed, the answers to which he was entitled.

Maybe, he thought, that was the reason criminals on the run so often gave themselves up: the experience of having no place to lay your head without having to keep one eye open was the most exhausting thing a person could experience. Certainly the most grueling ordeal he'd ever endured, and still he could see no positive end to it.

As the afternoon slowly ticked by, sleep came for him repeatedly, calling out his name in the stillness between thoughts, whispering for him to relax and just rest his head on the table. One hour, the voices insisted, sixty insignificant minutes, is all it would take to feel all right again.

Josh could feel himself growing disoriented—from loss of blood, he suspected—his thoughts becoming animated and comical, as if reality had been temporarily suspended.

To try and fight it off, he worked and reworked his speech in his mind, the one he was determined to deliver, without interruption, to Madeline Richmond as she sat patiently in the library of her estate, listening attentively and eager to be of assistance.

The absurdity of that imagined scene made him chuckle out loud, and the two young women at the table near him laughed under their breath in response.

"Sorry," he said softly in their direction without making full eye contact. One of the women smiled warmly at him but the other gave him an odd look before reengaging her friend in conversation.

Josh gulped the hot, tart coffee and forced his mind to Lloyd Richmond's widow, the bitter, diminutive woman with the death cough. He'd have only one opportunity to get her attention—and her help. The billionairess hadn't struck him as a woman known for her patience or mercy. As he rehashed his plan, he realized he couldn't just walk up to the front door and plead for her help. She wouldn't answer the door herself, and when the butler or the hulk announced who it was, the cops would be there before the door chimes had finished echoing in the foyer.

He'd wait until dark and then scale the high stone wall surrounding the estate.

*Jesus Christ, Josh,* he thought. *There's got to be something else you can do.*

He knew, however, that there wasn't. All of his options had run out.


By dark, the search radius around Kenny Kanazawa's home had reached the ten-mile mark, and the number of FBI agents, local

police, and volunteer trackers involved numbered sixty. Brad
Munford and Tommy Higgins knew that if they hadn't found
Mitchell by now, he'd managed to elude them, and was probably
beyond their perimeter. Well beyond.

Karl Hetzler knew this as well, and it made him furious. He no
longer cared to bring Mitchell in to face a jury. He'd decided, having been made a fool, that facing a coroner would be preferable.

When he'd announced his decision over a secure cell line to
Munford and Higgins, he'd gotten no argument.

The search team had checked Micki Hatcher's farm just before
two P.M., with Munford and the helicopter setting down in the large
clearing near the old tin shed up from the main house. Domingo and
the other men who'd originally been on the road had been picked up
by one of the four Hummers now scouring the area, and had joined
Munford at the house. The search of her home, bunkhouse, and out-
buildings had been thorough but routine, just as with the other
dozen or so farms in the area. They'd found nothing but a cluster of
farm hands who (Munford learned from Spanish-speaking Domingo)
had not seen a single stranger all day.

Of course, Munford thought, not entirely believing it but unable
to find any evidence of Mitchell having been there.

Roadblocks had been established on all roads, paved or otherwise,
within ten minutes of the suspect having disappeared into the
woods. He'd attempted to cross none of them.

It was as if Mitchell had been swallowed up by the muddy road on
which he'd run.

The tracks from the truck, which had been so promising at first, had
eventually disappeared in a quagmire of muck and other vehicle traffic.

Juan and Micki had grinned when the chopper finally lifted off.

"That was part three, Joshua," she'd said to the afternoon sky.


When Josh dropped from the ten-foot wall in back of the estate, he
found himself between a thick, prickly bush of some kind and the
wall itself. The fall had made more noise than he'd anticipated, and
for several minutes, he hugged the cool ground without movement,

watching the rear of the property for any sign of alarm or response.

When none came, he sat up with his back to the wall, a view of the home visible between a pair of the thorny bushes.

Where his need for sleep had gone, Josh had no idea, for he was now fully alert, his senses heightened to the point of pain. Breaking and entering was not something Josh thought he'd ever add to his resume of job skills—especially into the home of one of the wealthiest women in California. Compounding his fear was the belief that Derek DiAmo, the old woman's chauffeur and bodyguard, would most likely shoot him the moment he laid eyes on him, for criminal trespass if for no other reason.

He checked his waistband to ensure that the pistol hadn't been lost as he scrambled up the tree that had allowed him access to the back of the estate. It was still there, with its two remaining bullets. Why it mattered, he wasn't sure, but it provided a sense of security.

Josh knew that whatever evidence Richard Hightower had planted against him was damning, but he knew he had to convince someone of his innocence, someone powerful, someone who could protect him. Madeline Richmond was the logical choice—his only choice—and though she might consider the very thought of helping him preposterous, he was determined to have his say.

The lack of alternatives, something he'd always taken for granted, hardened his conviction and forced aside the thought that what he was doing was wrong. If he was to save himself, as Morris Goldman suggested, he must stick to his plan.

*She said she had no choice,* he remembered, thinking back to the lifeguard's words on Carmel Beach. *Is this what you meant, Dianne?* he wondered. *Being driven to your death?*

As he watched the rear of the house, through the massive twelve-foot windows that ran from floor to ceiling across the back, Josh could make out separate movement in at least two ground-floor rooms, though a clear view of the activity within was prevented by thin lace curtains. He couldn't tell if the figures were those of DiAmo and Madeline Richmond, or simply two of the house staff. He didn't even know if the woman was home.

He'd have to wait to be sure.

Finally, a light came on in an upstairs room—a room on the west end of the structure opening onto a terrace nearly as large as Josh's entire apartment. Before the sheers were released by the housekeeper and allowed to fall together, Josh had seen Madeline Richmond pass, a long cigarette holder between her fingers.

Her bedroom, he felt sure.

He doubted DiAmo was a regular visitor to her private chambers, and knew that if he was to talk with Mrs. Richmond, he had to make his move before the house became so still that any sound might be detected.

Or worse: the alarm had been activated for the night.

Josh stood and crept carefully toward the west end of the house, keeping in the shadows created by the interior light spilling across the generous landscaping. He was relieved and surprised that no motion-sensitive floods came on, alerting the household to the presence of an intruder.

When he reached the corner of the mansion, he found huge square quoins carved from single blocks of granite adorning the edge, spaced two feet apart and protruding a full inch and a half from the sandstone walls. It was a simple matter to climb them like a widely spaced ladder. A minute after he'd locked his fingertips onto the first cornerstone, he was standing on the terrace outside Madeline Richmond's bedroom.

The terrace where Josh now found himself had a railing three feet high, with elaborately carved sandstone balusters capped by ten-inch-thick slabs of round-edge granite; a pair of eight-foot French doors led to the bedroom. On either side of the doors was a matching window, and all were covered in the same white lace sheers found downstairs.

With no light behind him, Josh knew he couldn't be easily seen from within the room unless he ventured too close to the glass and the interior lights painted his outline, but just standing there in the dark made him nervous. A few deep breaths helped, and for the first time, he realized how much the temperature had dropped with the setting sun.

Between the tiny loops in the curtains, he was able to watch as the woman he now believed to be a nurse rather than a housekeeper

shook her finger at the old woman and attempted to get her to sur-
render her cigarette. Madeline Richmond would have none of it, he
could tell, though he couldn't hear anything more than muffled
sounds coming from the room. After a few more seconds of this, the
nurse retreated, pulling the door tightly closed behind her. Madeline
disappeared into her adjoining bathroom, also closing the door.

*It's now, Josh,* he thought, moving toward the French doors. He
pulled the pistol from his pocket and wrapped a rag around the butt
that he'd taken from a dumpster outside the deli, prepared to break
the glass as quietly as he could. Before he struck the pane that would
allow him to release the inner latch, he tried the knob, just in case.

It turned.

He couldn't believe it, and imagined that DiAmo's presence had
given everyone in the house a false sense of security.

Careful not to be heard, his eyes darting nervously between the
bathroom door and the hall door, Josh stepped quietly inside. He was
sure his pounding heart would signal his arrival.

The bedroom was at least thirty by forty, with walnut paneling
from floor to ceiling, exposed beams, and thick wool carpeting. The
bed was a massive and ornately carved canopy, its mattress covered
by a heavily textured silk duvet, a half-dozen overstuffed pillows and
decorative throws at the headboard. On the wall opposite the bed,
within a carved Italian-marble mantel, fat logs crackled, filling the
room with the rich warmth that can only come from an open flame.
Before the hearth sat an antique brocade chaise and a small
mahogany butler's tray.

Beside the bed, sitting at floor level, he spotted two machines: an
oxygen concentrator about the size of a large humidifier, and a
machine that resembled a small air compressor that delivered medication in nebulized form. Both hummed quietly in the shadow of an
expensive wheelchair that he imagined had not seen much use, considering the sense of hard determination he'd gotten from the
woman during their one meeting at the cemetery. On the left bedside chest sat at least a dozen prescription bottles of various sizes, all
with names he didn't recognize and couldn't pronounce.

Josh tried to discover the method by which the grandame of the manor summoned the nurse, DiAmo, or other members of the staff. A cursory examination revealed no tasseled pull beside the bed, no obvious buttons or switches in the wall or fashioned into the night-stands, no intercom or closed-circuit monitoring, yet he was positive there had to be something.

He crossed the room, still puzzled and knowing he had to find the answer, then spotted a tiny remote control lying on the coffee table beside an orderly stack of magazines. He'd seen similar units offered in security magazines that floated around the development lab at Barnett Air. One press of the black button would bring a meal or a cup of hot tea, depending upon the time of day; one press of the red would bring the nurse or DiAmo—or both.

Josh heard the toilet flush in the bathroom and snatched the remote from the table, then moved quickly to put his back against the hall door, opposite its handle, where he would be concealed until Madeline had moved to the center of the room. There, he was also ready for anyone who might enter unannounced.

Mrs. Richmond reentered the room, having changed into a rose-colored cashmere, shawl-collar robe and matching house slippers, her petite form appearing all the more frail with the absence of the two-inch heels which she'd worn when he'd seen her at the ceme-tery. In the pocket of her robe, fed by a trio of probes attached to her chest, a remote telemetry transmitter sent her heart rate to a receiver in the nurse's room down the hall. The old woman was coughing badly as she crossed the room, the latest issue of *George* in her left hand, the long cigarette holder still in her right.

She reached the chaise, leaned back comfortably, covered her legs with a chenille lap robe, and was stuffing a small, silk pillow beneath her knees when she noticed the strange man standing in the shad-ows in the corner of her bedroom.

Josh was amazed that she didn't appear the least bit afraid, or even startled. He didn't try to understand it; he was feeling enough anxi-ety for the both of them.

As Josh was about to speak to let Madeline Richmond know that she shouldn't be alarmed, she said in her raspy voice, "Good evening, Mr. Mitchell. Nowhere left to run?"

# 22

Karl Hetzler stood at the window in his office in downtown San Francisco, agents Munford and Higgins sitting quietly on the couch behind him. The verbal report of Mitchell's murder of Kenny Kanazawa, as well as his subsequent escape and disappearance, had been delivered in full earlier in the day. The added detail that had been provided in the written report that he now held in his hand had done nothing to calm the man who had personally freed Mitchell from the Carmel Police. Hetzler knew such decisions gone wrong were career-ending, and swore, as he watched with disdain the traffic moving freely below him, that wasn't going to happen to him.

Mitchell was not going to take him down—quite the opposite.

"You said he appeared to have been shot. How bad do you think he was hurt?" Hetzler turned to face his men.

Munford responded; Higgins was lost in his paperwork. "Hard to say, really. Lab boys found a lot of blood at the scene. Most was from the victim, the rest, undoubtedly from Mitchell. There was blood on the kitchen floor, down the hall, and all over the master bedroom and bath. The white sweatshirt he was wearing was soaked in blood and had an entry and exit hole in the right side" —he indicated the approximate positions on his own shirt—"about four or five inches apart. Small amount of blood at the exit hole, but no visible tissue or bone fragments. He was apparently shot clean through, but I don't believe the bullet caught a lung."

"Think he'll try for a hospital or one of the all-night clinics?"

"Doubt it. It'd be too easy to intercept him there and he knows it. If the wound doesn't infect, he'll probably just keep treating it himself."

"You think it will infect?"

"You can bet on it."

"Meaning?"

"That he'll be sick as a dog in five or six days; dead in ten."

Hetzler pondered this, hoping for a more immediate solution to his problem. "Blood loss?" he asked.

"A lot, but again not life-threatening. From the way he ran out of the house and into the woods, I'd say he was actually in good shape for a guy who'd just been shot," Munford added.

Hetzler turned back to the window, his mind darting between thoughts. "Where would he go?" he said aloud, though it had been asked as much of himself as the other agents.

Higgins continued to study the file he'd been compiling on the suspect, his mind groping for some small piece of information that had been missed.

"If he tries for home, we've got him," Munford assured his boss. A team from the TBI had been dispatched to Selmer, Tennessee, by three P.M., and taps had been put on both his parents' home phone on Highway 64 and the phone at Selmer Middle School where Josh's mother taught math and science. Other agents, as many as the Bureau could spare on short notice, were shadowing friends and relatives that had been hurriedly identified. "I really don't think he'll—"

"He can fly!" Higgins chimed in. "Hell, I should have thought of that sooner." From the other men's expressions, he realized that some explanation for his outburst was required. He stood, Mitchell's file in hand. "I'm not saying I have a clue where he's headed, mind you, I'm still working on that, but wherever it is, I'll bet my ass he'll go there in the air."

Munford shook his head, amused. "Not exactly an inspired thought, Tommy. We've got all the airports within two hundred miles covered—"

"Not all of them," Higgins interrupted, holding a hand up to still his impatient friend. "The son of a bitch has a pilot's license. We all know he's not likely to walk up and buy a ticket at the American counter, but he just might rent a small plane from one of the private airports that are scattered all across the state."

Hetzler put his hand to his chin, rubbing the rough stubble that had accumulated since morning. He nodded slowly. "It's sure as hell worth a try, Higgins. Get on it."

"Right away," Higgins said, disappearing from the office.

"That's not a bad lead," Munford said. "Think Tommy's got something?"

"Could be. Nothing about Mitchell would surprise me anymore."

"Want me to give him a hand?"

"No, not right now. There's a long shot I want you to check out first."

"Sure. What have you got"

"It may be nothing, Brad, but something Mitchell said when I was talking with him in Carmel has been bugging me. I don't think the boy realized he'd even said it."

"What is it, sir?"

Hetzler said, "It's the kind of crazy idea that would fit Mitchell's way of thinking." He moved to his computer screen and began tapping keys.

Munford looked over his boss's shoulder at the database he'd summoned. "What are you after?"

Hetzler held up an open hand indicating for Munford to be patient, then returned to his keyboard. When he'd entered the necessary search criteria and the answer had come back to him, he said, "This is what I'm looking for, Brad. Write it down and get over there right away."

The agent took out a small pad and pen and jotted down Lloyd

Richmond's address. Taking Larkin Street north, and then right on Pacific Avenue to Hyde, the mansion was little more than a mile from their location.

He checked his watch trying to decide if he had time to grab a cup of coffee en route.


Madeline Richmond glanced around her and noticed for the first time that the remote control was not on the coffee table where she'd left it. When her eyes returned to the intruder's, Josh's left hand was outstretched, the tiny electronic "bodyguard" in his open palm.

"Looking for this?" he asked. He thought he detected a trace of fear in her expression.

Or was it controlled rage?

"How clever of you. And now, what do you plan to do, kill me?" She leaned back comfortably, the magazine across her lap. If she had felt any fear, it no longer showed on her well-lined face.

"Why would I do that?" Josh asked. "What on earth could I possibly gain by harming you in any way?"

"Then, why are you here? You've obviously gone to some great lengths to see me again. Is it money you want?"

Josh shook his head in disbelief. "No, dammit, I don't want money." His obvious anger made her jump. "I'm sorry, Mrs. Richmond," he apologized, "but it's been a hell of a week."

"So I've been told," she said flatly.

He said, "You have no idea why I'm here, do you?"

She shook her head, partially muffling a severe coughing spasm with a linen handkerchief. "I suppose it has something to do with Dianne."

Josh listened at the door for a moment, in case the nurse had heard the woman's terrible coughing. He detected no sound of footsteps.

"How well do you remember your husband's assistant from eight or ten years ago, Pamela Morrow?"

Madeline Richmond's coughing stopped as suddenly as it had begun, and she said fraility, "Quite well. Why do you ask?"

*Just go on and tell her,* he chided himself for his hesitation. *If you can't convince her, and gain her help, you're screwed.* Despite his belief in the evidence he'd uncovered, calling Dianne Lane a traitor came harder than he'd imagined. He took a breath, looking away for a moment.

When he turned back to the woman, he said, "I believe Pamela Morrow and Dianne Lane were both using the Richmond Gallery and Museum to sell United States Military secrets to the Chinese, and I think that's why they were killed. There's more. I'm afraid your husband was behind it all, ma'am."

Madeline Richmond looked incredulous. "Is this some ludicrous attempt to divert suspicion from yourself, Mr. Mitchell, and into the laps of three who cannot possibly defend themselves?"

Josh moved closer to the loveseat. "I know how loony this must sound to you, Mrs. Richmond, but bear with me for a moment, please."

"Why should I? You've just accused one of the most honorable men this state has ever produced of treason, and now you want me to listen to your rationalization. I think it's time you left." She started to rise.

"Please don't get up, ma'am." He instinctively touched the butt of the pistol, and wished he hadn't as soon as he'd done it.

Madeline Richmond noticed the gesture and then saw the blood on the right hip of his jeans. She nodded as she leaned back in the loveseat again. "So, you're not above killing me, after all, I see."

"Please forgive me, Mrs. Richmond. I know this is all very shocking to you, but if you'll just give me a few minutes, I believe you'll begin to see that I'm not as crazy as I sound."

"It would appear I've been left little choice. As miserable as my health is at the moment, and as inevitable the end, I'm not ready to hurry it along. You may attempt to prove to me that you're not the lunatic you appear to be."

"Thank you," Josh said, dropping to his good knee at the side of the coffee table. The hall door was now ten feet behind him, and no longer able to be seen without turning around.

Over the course of the next fifteen minutes, Josh laid out everything he'd learned during the week, embellishing nothing, and leaving out only the part about Lloyd Richmond's affairs with the two women. It gave him no pleasure whatever to paint a picture of the woman he loved as a traitor to her country, and nothing further would be gained by alluding to the personal relationship she shared with Madeline's husband.

When he'd finished, the woman puzzled with his words for a painfully long minute before speaking. "You think my husband was buying military technology from your company and then reselling it to the Communists. Technology you and your former partner developed."

"Yes, ma'am, I know he was. Kenny Kanazawa confirmed my suspicions before he died."

This piece of information, Kanazawa's death, seemed to register heavily in her eyes. She looked at Josh with a new wary regard. "How did he die?" she asked.

Josh couldn't believe his stupidity at having let the words slip. He knew she'd never believe Kenny had been killed in self-defense. He'd lie.

As he considered some hurried story about stumbling upon Kenny's body after someone else had shot him, the words refused to form. "I killed him during a struggle at his home earlier today. I assure you, it was not intentional, Mrs. Richmond, and it was not what I wanted. I'm no killer."

A sudden knock on the door sent a stab of fear through Josh.

"Mrs. Richmond?" the voice from the other side of the hall door called. "Will you be needing anything from the kitchen before I dismiss the cook?" It was one of the staff, a male voice; Josh imagined that was why the door had remained closed.

He turned his stare from the door back to Madeline Richmond, who seemed to instinctively understand that she mustn't call out in any way. "No, thank you, Robert. Tell Frances to have a pleasant evening," she said, her frail voice barely carrying beyond the heavy door.

"Mrs. Madison said she'd be up to administer your medicine in fifteen minutes. Will that be convenient?"

"My nurse," the woman whispered to Josh. "Yes, thank you, Robert. That will be all."

Josh began to breathe again. *Fifteen minutes*, he considered. He looked to his watch, but it was no longer on his wrist. "Great!" he groaned, then spotted a clock on the nightstand. He made a mental note of the time: he either had to have won this woman over or be well on his way by ten minutes before the hour.

"Before we were interrupted, Mr. Mitchell, I believe you were trying to persuade me you're not a murderer."

"I know that sounds asinine considering what I've just told you, but I swear I've never murdered anyone in my life. And I had nothing to do with Dianne's death, nothing at all."

"But you were lovers."

Josh was not surprised by her words. "No. We never . . ." He didn't know how to put it.

"Oh, come now, we're both adults here. Nothing you could say would shock me more than what you've already said. After all, she was in your hotel room an hour before her death, wasn't she?" The woman's eyes were probing, angry.

"Yes, she was in my room, but we only talked—"

"My husband tried that one on me, too. Honestly, you men must think we women lose our minds completely when we become wives. How naïve do you think I am, Mitchell?" Her voice was excited, and a new bout of coughing began.

Josh could feel his only chance at freedom slipping quickly away. He tried again, as sincerely as he could. "Ma'am, no matter what you think, I didn't sleep with Dianne Lane. And I didn't kill her."

"I know you didn't kill her," the woman said in a voice wracked with pain that originated not only in her lungs but also in her soul. "I did."

Josh was on his feet. "What did you say?" he mumbled, the words tripping over disbelieving lips.

The coughing abated momentarily, but it had obviously weakened the frail little woman. She passed the handkerchief across her mouth slowly, not speaking.

"What the hell do you mean?" he said dumbfounded, his voice

louder than he'd intended. He moved toward the door, putting his back to it. He couldn't have heard what he'd just heard; his mind had to be playing tricks on him.

The slender arms dropped wearily to Madeline Richmond's lap, her face drawn. "You heard me correctly. I killed Dianne Lane. Or, to be more precise, I paid to have it done."

"Why?" was all Josh could say.

"My dear boy, you really are a babe in the woods. No one killed Dianne Lane because she was selling secrets to the Red Chinese. She was a whore, plain and simple. She and my husband had been having an affair that went back more than fifteen years. Of course, back in those days, she was called Pamela Morrow. She only took the name Dianne Lane after her convenient fatal accident in Jackson, Mississippi in 1989 necessitated the change in identity. Not a bad plan, I must admit, and it worked for a while. It allowed them to go on seeing each other for another eight years or so before I found out she was back. Well, she never actually left though, did she? And to think, I invited the harlot into my home for dinner . . . treated her as a friend."

Josh put his fingers to his temples and pressed hard, certain his skull was going to explode. "You're telling me that Dianne Lane and Pamela Morrow are one and the same?"

"I believe that should be 'were,' Mr. Mitchell . . . were one and the same." There was a note of pride in the gravelly voice.

Though the simple explanation seemed to completely satisfy Madeline Richmond, Josh could see only anger and loathing in the murky darkness that enveloped him. He touched the pistol butt, stroking its cold, lethal hardness between his fingers.

His logical side fought for control. "Then it was you who sent the men after me in Natchez."

"Damned incompetent fools. Though, I must admit it has worked out better this way. I prefer the idea of you spending the rest of your long life in prison for Dianne Lane and Morris Goldman's murders to a quick death. I never did care for that man, you know, although you apparently found him interesting enough." The pride had now become loathing, hatred for the man across from her, a man whose crime was that he had found Dianne Lane attractive and desirable, as her husband had.

Josh was about to speak when the door burst open, slamming him against the wall. DiAmo rounded the door, his huge chrome automatic already drawn.

If Josh had not already had the pistol in his grip, he would not have had the time to draw it before the bodyguard fired a well-aimed shot. When he'd been thrown against the wall, the impact had nearly knocked the .38 Special from his hand, though Josh had somehow maintained his hold. As DiAmo yanked back the door, Josh raised his arm and fired defensively toward the space that formed, neither aiming intentionally at DiAmo nor purposely missing him, simply firing in response to the surprise of being knocked half conscious by the heavy wooden door.

An erratic shot from DiAmo's weapon sent a round past his head into the paneling behind him. As Josh moved a hand protectively to his face, he saw the hulk stagger, and then fall onto his back.

*Oh, Jesus Christ! I've killed him!* he thought as his mind began to clear from the blow. He heard screaming coming from downstairs and someone shouting for the police to be called. None of the staff entered the bedroom, though several of them yelled out for Mrs. Richmond to respond.

Josh looked at the old woman who was sitting erect on the loveseat, one hand to her heart, the other holding the handkerchief against her lips. She appeared frozen in place.

Before he could pull himself away from the wall, the nurse burst into the room.

"Are you all right, madam?" she called out, noticing DiAmo's limp form beside the bed. Then she spun around, her eyes fixing first on Josh, then on the pistol. "Oh, Lord!" she cried, stepping toward Madeline Richmond. "Please don't kill us," she pleaded.

"I'm not going to kill anyone," Josh said, his ears still ringing. "See how badly he's hurt." He waved his weapon at the bodyguard, remembering Kenny and hoping that he hadn't blown the back of DiAmo's head off as well. The image that tried to form was vile, and he forced it away.

The nurse knelt beside the big man and hurriedly examined the gash that ran for four inches across the right side of his head just above the ear. It was bleeding, but not terribly; the concussion from the shot had knocked him out.

The nurse took a clean towel from one of the equipment stands and pressed it against the wound. Josh picked up the .45 Automatic DiAmo had dropped.

"You could have killed him, you bastard," she barked with little regard for the fact that he now held a weapon in each hand.

Josh squeezed his eyes shut and said a silent prayer of thanks.

"Thank heaven he's not seriously hurt," Madeline Richmond echoed aloud. Her anger of moments before was now simply fear. "What are you going to do with us?" she asked, maintaining her composure.

"Nothing," Josh said. "I'm not going to harm any of you. I'm sorry about what happened. I didn't mean to . . ." He didn't bother finishing; he could tell his words were unheard. He knew the police were on the way; they wouldn't take long responding to a break-in and shooting on Pacific Avenue.

He considered the last round in the chamber, knowing that it represented little defense, and stuck the small pistol in his back pocket, the heavy automatic still in his right hand. When he'd made his way to the terrace doors, he turned back to the old woman, wanting to put a bullet in her brain. Her back was to him, defiant even in her moment of greatest fear.

"I'll tell them everything, you know. They will believe me, eventually," he said. "You and the great house of Richmond will be ruined, destroyed."

She turned to him with a sneer. "I was never a Richmond except in name. I'm Madeline Beaumont Kennerly. I was born a Kennerly and I'll die a Kennerly, and your anemic threats mean less than nothing to me, you pathetic little man. I'm dying in case you haven't noticed, though not as quickly as you'd prefer, I suspect. I have more money and lawyers than you've ever dreamed of, and won't spend a second in custody, even if you can convince them to listen to your desperate babbling before they execute you. They won't believe you, of course, and you know it."

She was right, and he did know it. If he sold everything he owned, he couldn't afford the legal muscle it would take to stay out of the gas chamber, to say nothing of prison.

He'd played his trump card and had lost.

There was nothing to do now but run.

He raised the .45 and pointed it squarely at the old woman's forehead, remembering the joy and beauty Dianne Lane had brought to his life, the same joy and beauty she'd doubtless brought to Lloyd Richmond. His eyes closed as he imagined the bullet passing through her skull, rightfully ending the life that had taken away the only woman he'd ever truly wanted.

He felt the serrated trigger beneath his index finger and tried to convince himself that he would be correct, even justified, in pulling it, but no matter how many people she'd hurt, no matter how much she had stolen from him, this evil, bitter woman could not make him something he wasn't—a killer.

Josh lowered the gun and disappeared over the terrace ledge just as Brad Munford knocked on the front door.

# 23

Marie Edwards finished for the day and headed for her car, taking care to securely lock the nearly restored antebellum mansion behind her. She was proud of the work she'd done and looked forward to the ribbon cutting ceremony on Saturday before the Historical Preservation Society. They would be finished by Friday evening, twenty-four hours from now, she'd warned her staff with a stern smile during the lunch that she'd hand-delivered at noon. There was no time to spare, even for normal meal breaks, if the finishing touches were all to be completed before the festivities and formal tour on Saturday morning.

She checked her watch as she skipped down the steps: ten P.M. She'd be back on the job by six A.M., as would they all.

Marie was ready for a glass of wine and a hot bubble bath.

"Ms. Edwards?" Josh called out from the hedgerow at the far edge of what used to be the carriage drive, beside her silver BMW. He would have preferred to have met her inside, away from prying eyes, but had been forced to remain outside and out of sight until the last workman, the electrician, had left. His truck had pulled from the curb only a minute before Marie had appeared on the porch.

The unfamiliar voice that seemed to come out of thin air startled her, and she stopped short of reaching her car. She looked for the source of the sound, but didn't answer.

Josh stepped into the faint light that spilled from the front-porch lamp, revealing himself. "Marie, I'm sorry. It's Josh Mitchell."

"Joshua?" she said, straining for a better look. She barely recognized him with his four days' growth of beard, scruffy hair, and clothes as dirty as a tramp's. "My Lord, what's happened to you, Joshua? You look awful."

He stepped closer, confident that she would neither scream out nor run. "I imagine I do look a sight," he said with no smile, barely able to keep his eyes open. "I need your help, Marie."

"Of course, Joshua. Some men from the FBI came by on Monday asking all kinds of questions about you."

"What did you tell them?" The news didn't surprise him, though it worried him that Marie might still be under surveillance. Probably not, he thought, realizing that if the feds were still shadowing her, they would have been on him like a duck on a June bug by now. At this point, Marie Edwards was likely nothing more than one of many people he'd talked with in the week following Pamela's death.

"Nothing," she assured him. "Just that you'd come around asking some questions about Pamela. They seemed satisfied and left after fifteen or twenty minutes."

Josh could feel the fever stirring within him, deep, like the gradual but certain onset of the flu. His face felt on fire.

Marie said with obvious concern, "Are you in serious trouble, Joshua?" She moved to him, putting her hand reassuringly on his forearm.

He lowered his head, his shoulders slumped, no longer able to be held erect. "Yes, ma'am. I'm afraid I am."


The three principal agents on the thirteenth floor of the FBI Headquarters in San Francisco, as well as a couple dozen more agents in New York, Tennessee, Mississippi, and Washington, DC had spent the last four days—and nights—poring over every bit and byte of data their staggering resources had been able to amass on the man who now sat unofficially atop of their Ten Most Wanted list. Every possible place Mitchell might have chosen for sanctuary—from childhood friends to college roommates; from ex-girlfriends to fourth cousins—had been checked, rechecked, and then staked out.

The suspect would have to show up somewhere. They always did.

Special Agent Hetzler meant to have Mitchell, whatever the cost, and he had the full support of the Director in his quest. The Bureau had been following the theft of military secrets for four years, and wasn't about to be outwitted by the missing link they had identified only last week.

As Munford and Higgins dug through mounds of obscure and useless data, searching for the one secret in Mitchell's past that might show them the light, Hetzler stood before the huge window in his office, his mind processing everything he'd read over the course of the week.

"Tell me again about that trip he made to Mississippi last week," he said pensively.

Higgins sighed. He'd gone over this in depth three days ago and had found nothing worth their time. "We've been over it all before," he said wearily.

Hetzler turned slowly, saying nothing.

Higgins rethought his position, pulling a page of notes marked with a flag from the stack. "Flight 754 from San Francisco International arrived in Jackson, Mississippi at ten-thirty-two P.M. Wednesday with Mitchell on board. After he landed, the suspect drove his rented Pontiac to Natchez, arriving at the Day's Inn on Highway 61 just before two A.M. Checked into Room 224.

"The next morning, he visited a mom and pop pharmacy across from Braden High School on Homocitto Street, spending at least twenty minutes with the owner, a Mrs. Betty Price and her husband, Robert. We talked with the woman and her husband; all Mitchell wanted was some information about one of Lloyd Richmond's former employees, a former Natchez resident named Pamela Morrow."

"Tell me again what we know about this Morrow woman," Hetzler said returning to the window. He thought better with the ocean in view.

"Graduated Ole Miss in '77, worked as an art historian for Richmond for several years before being killed by a hit-and-run driver at the end of '89. A real babe according to her picture."

Hetzler pondered the information. "Where was Mitchell at the time of her death?"

"In Boston. Confirmed. He was in the middle of a computer seminar that he was co-hosting. No chance he had a direct hand in it," Higgins said.

The senior agent was still sure there was some connection there, even if it wasn't clear to him yet. "Go on," he said.

"After leaving the pharmacy, Mitchell visited Marie Edwards. You remember, boss, the black woman who oversees the restoration of those big old Civil War homes along the Mississippi."

"Why?" Hetzler asked.

"More questions about Morrow," Higgins said.

"Why the preoccupation with a woman dead ten years?" Munford asked, hoping his boss could enlighten him.

"Other than the fact that they both worked for Richmond, I don't know," Hetzler said, chewing on Higgins's words. "But Pamela Morrow worked for the old man long before Mitchell came into the picture. He was only a kid then, and couldn't have known her." The tenuous connection refused to yield to logic. Hetzler sensed that something existed they hadn't yet uncovered. Finally he said, "Brad, I think you and I need to talk with Marie Edwards. I've got a hunch she's a much larger piece in this puzzle than we've thought."

Higgins said with a trace of skepticism in his tone, "You think Mitchell will head back to Natchez? Seems pretty thin to me."

"Perhaps. But I'm beginning to understand the way Mitchell thinks. It's just the kind of move he'd make."

"More hunches, sir?" Munford said.

"It's more than that, Brad. He's revisited everyone he's come in contact with since Lane's death, everyone except Edwards. If I were going to put my money on his next destination, that'd be my bet."

"But why her?" Higgins asked.

"Maybe we'll find that out when we get there," Hetzler said.

"When are we leaving?" Munford asked.

Hetzler looked out at the sun setting over the Bay. "On the next flight to Jackson. But first, get the attorney general on the phone. I want roadblocks, television, the works, and I want it yesterday. If he's headed halfway across the country, let's make it as tough a trip as we can."

Josh had spent the balance of Sunday, all day Monday, and a portion of Tuesday running, hiding, and sleeping in the storm sewers beneath San Francisco—beginning with the one just beyond the rear wall of the Kennerly mansion. He'd managed to elude the dragnet that had been thrown around the Pacific Heights estate within minutes of his departure, though he saw and heard dozens of police vehicles passing right overhead, lights and sirens blaring, for most of the first night.

Early Tuesday morning, through the iron grates of a sewer perhaps two miles from Madeline Richmond's home, he spotted a panel truck with the name of a Bakersfield bottling business emblazoned on the sides. While the sliding side doors were open, the driver making the last delivery of his route, Josh concealed himself in a dark corner of one of the empty container compartments.

At a truck stop in Bakersfield, like a gift from Heaven, he'd found a hopper-bottom eighteen-wheeler filled with California barley bound for the Jack Daniel Brewery in Lynchburg, Tennessee, less than two hours from his home. While he would have given his life's savings to have ridden in the cab with the driver, he'd wisely opted to make the 2,150-mile journey on top of thirteen hundred bushels of grain, beneath the thick, red vinyl tarp.

Once, when the giant Kenworth diesel had been stopped at a roadblock along I-40 near Topock, on the California-Arizona border, where the state police and the FBI were conducting one of the most thorough searches in recent memory, Josh had had to completely bury himself within the fine, dry grain, deriving what little air he could manage from a large paper grocery bag pulled over his head and held tight at the neck. He was thankful for the many times he'd played hide-and-seek in the grain bins on his own farm, always the last one to be found. He'd never imagined such boyhood pranks would one day help secure his freedom.

As he'd waited for the truck to begin moving again, the carbon dioxide level within the grocery bag had gotten so high from having to reinhale his own breath, that he'd almost given in to the need for fresh air. The truck had finally, mercifully, been allowed to leave.

During the journey, Josh had survived on chips, candy bars, and warm soft drinks bought from a vending machine at the truck stop where he'd first spotted the grain truck. It was the last food available to him. By the time he'd hitched a ride from Little Rock to Natchez—aware that going directly home would surely mean being apprehended—Josh was exhausted, and he knew that his fever had worsened.

He wanted to sleep, perhaps to die, but he did not want to remain awake and alert for even one more hour.

The only part of the story he'd omitted, as Marie drove him through the quiet streets of Natchez—away from the mansion and, from what he could tell, away from the city as well—was the part about Pamela Morrow having faked the accident that had supposedly claimed her life. He saw nothing to be gained by telling the woman who was trying to help him that her best friend had not died in 1989, but a mere twelve days ago.

"I know a place where you'll be safe," Marie said when he finished the harrowing tale, his last words barely above a labored whisper. "You can rest, take a shower. I'll bring you a change of clothes and some hot food. It's going to be all right, Joshua. I promise."

Marie was surprised that he didn't respond to her offer, then heard the sound of gentle snoring over the rhythm of the engine.

She looked at her car phone and thought about the call she had to make, but decided it would keep until she was safely away from the cabin.

She knew, once there, Joshua wasn't going anywhere for a while.

• • •

The late afternoon light crept in through a narrow slit in the faded cotton curtains, slowly inching its way up the bed, from Josh's feet to his head, like the scanning beam of a copy machine moving in slow motion. When it reached his face, his eyes began to stir behind closed lids, dancing back and forth in search of a familiar image from a forgotten past. Only demons from the last twelve days revealed themselves, but it was the sight of Pamela's limp body lying on the beach in Carmel that awakened him from a fitful sleep.

"Oh, Jesus," Josh muttered in a low, guttural voice as he sat up in bed, his eyes and mind trying to come to terms with a world that was instantly alien. He remembered little after he finished telling Marie his story in the car, and this bed and this room were not among the images. Without the benefit of a thermometer, he could tell that his fever had not lessened.

He was in a room no larger than ten by ten, with a low ceiling and bare wooden walls of cedar planks, tightly fitted but without insulation. The floor was also wooden, and well worn. A single six-pane window had been cut in one wall, with little attention to trim or detail. The bed was narrow and lumpy, with a low spot in the center that seemed to want to swallow him.

When he threw back the sheet and heavy cotton spread, he realized that he was naked but for his boxers, neither his clothes nor his sneakers anywhere in sight. He swung his legs off the bed and felt a small round throw rug lying between the cold floor and his feet. Without insulation, the room was quite cool, but he could smell the scent of a heating fire coming from beyond the closed door. He took another whiff: he could have sworn he smelled coffee brewing.

A painful catch in his chest caused him to drop back to the mattress and grab his side when he tried to stand. The clean white bandages that Micki Hatcher had put in place on—when was it, he wondered, Monday? No it had to have been Sunday, he reconsidered—were now dingy and gray with large, irregular circles of dried blood darkening their centers.

He understood too well that his increased fever was likely the result of infection, but knew that he couldn't treat himself for any-thing as serious as that. He also knew that to leave his wounds untreated would ultimately mean death.

He recalled the stench and filth of the storm sewer system beneath San Francisco, where street runoff and stagnant rainwater mingled in the darkness, and remembered his bandage having been soaked more than once when he'd tripped over some unseen obstacle. He didn't want to think about that now, drawn to the aroma of coffee brewing and the hope that there might be a bottle of aspirin some-where in the cabin.

Josh stood and stumbled painfully toward the unpainted door, turning the old glass knob slowly. The outer room was empty except for a few pieces of cheap furniture along the walls and a large wood-burning heater in the middle of the floor. He didn't care about the furnishings: the room was deliciously warm, in sharp contrast to the bedroom. The coffee aroma was much stronger in this room, and mingled with the scent of burning oak. It reminded him of his home in Selmer, before his parents had installed central heat and air con-ditioning during his first year of high school.

He looked about for his clothes, but they were nowhere to be seen.

In the tiny kitchen, adjoining the room with the wood heater, Josh discovered the origin of the heavenly aroma: an inexpensive West Bend Quick-Drip, its warmer still on though the brewing, according to the timer, had finished a quarter hour earlier, at four P.M.

"Four-fifteen," Josh repeated aloud, looking for something for his mounting headache. He was pleased to know the time, but won-dered what day of the week it was. He was sure he had been capable of sleeping for days on end, and tried to decide if it was Friday, or if Saturday or even Sunday had slipped by him.

In the narrow cabinet beside the small, white porcelain sink, he found a half bottle of generic-brand aspirin and popped four into his mouth. They tasted like slices of chalk.

He opened three more cabinets searching for a glass but found only a box of Zesta Saltines, a stack of paper plates, and a few odds and ends. Though there were six small cabinets in the diminutive kitchen, their entire contents could have been put in a shoe box.

He turned toward the table opposite the sink. The note lay beneath the closest of two mismatched coffee cups:

Joshua,

I've set the coffeemaker to come on at four o'clock. If you get up before that, just flick the switch from Auto to On. I'm afraid there's nothing to eat but some old crackers and some really stale sugar cookies in a Mason jar in the cupboard; I only come here when I want to get away from the city.

Help yourself to whatever you find, but I'll be bringing you something hot and filling when I finish work at the house tonight. I'll try not to be too late.

Sorry about your clothes, but it was the only way I could think to get things that would be sure to fit you. If you don't mind, I'll be tossing them out when I'm through. They really stink.

See you soon,

Marie

P.S.: I lit the pilot light on the water heater. Feel free to use the shower.

Josh found himself grinning for the first time in recent memory. "I can take a hint," he said as he filled one of the cups with steaming black coffee.

"So, it's still Friday," he said to his cup, savoring the warmth and flavor of his first sip. He hadn't slept as long as he had imagined.

Perhaps, after his shower, he'd climb back into bed and nap while he waited for Marie to return with hot food and clothes.

Hot food! God, what a wonderful pair of words.

With cup in hand, his aspirin washed down, Josh wandered back into the main room, studying the foliage that lay beyond the one large window. He'd already determined that wherever he was, it was in the woods away from the city. How far away, he had no idea. It didn't really matter, he thought. For the first time in days, he felt a warm sense of security that almost resembled normal life.

"It's probably just the coffee," he said cynically, remembering that he was standing almost naked in a hideout about which he knew nothing, including its location, his body tormented with pain.

He tried to hold on to the pleasant thoughts and dispel the pessimism that wanted to take seed. It wasn't easy, but the image of Pamela, sitting across the table from him at Scomas, helped a bit.

Sometime after leaving Madeline Richmond's home, in the emptiness and quiet of the storm sewers, he'd decided to always think of the woman he'd come to love as Pamela Morrow, the name she'd been born with, and not as Dianne Lane, though he knew it was a lie. He'd permit this one. Dianne was a name that had been taken in a moment of desperation in order to hang on to a relationship that had mattered to Pamela. He knew well how elusive such relationships were, and would not fault her for the choices she'd made. He wanted to always remember her as close to her roots as he could take her memory—to Natchez, before whatever drove her to the life that had doomed her.

He opened the front door and stepped out onto the narrow wooden porch, the corrugated tin of the rain roof only a few inches above his head now. He ran the back of his left hand along the ridges, the washboard music created by his fingertips resonating in his ears. The porch could have passed for the one over his grandparents' home in Bethel Springs, eight miles from his parents.

The sound of a vehicle approaching tore the silence, yanking Joshua from his melancholy. He slammed the cabin door behind him and stood beside the window, struggled to locate the origin of the familiar but threatening sound.

The badly kept drive that ended at the front porch quickly disappeared into the thickness of the pine woods. He knew the vehicle would be upon him before he could determine who was driving it.

It's got to be Marie, he reasoned. Please let it be Marie.

Fifteen agonizing seconds later, his uncertainty was answered when her BMW stopped just beyond the porch and Marie Edwards sprang from the driver's seat, a grocery bag in one hand, a large

Wal-Mart sack in the other. She closed the car door with her hip, giving it an animated shove. He was relieved to find her alone.

Josh fell back against the adjacent wall, exhausted, but suddenly became self-conscious standing there in nothing but his underwear.

Even as he thought of darting for the bedroom, he could hear Marie struggling with the lock. "Oh, the hell with it," he said. "She undressed you, remember?"

When he pulled the door open, Marie let out a startled yelp, almost dropping the grocery bag.

"You scared the heck out of me," she said, picking up the Wal-Mart sack she'd set at her feet.

"Sorry," Josh said.

"That's okay. I figured you'd still be asleep." She looked him over quickly as she passed in the doorway. "I hope you just got up," she said with a wrinkled nose.

"Don't worry, I'm heading for the shower right now. You won't recognize me in half an hour."

"Good. Your new clothes are in the white sack there. Sorry, Wal-Mart was the best I could do under the circumstances. It's on the way from work."

"Anything's fine. Heck, I was practically raised at Wally World."

She smiled broadly at his comment, and found the simple admission endearing. "I thought your family always had money," she said as she set the grocery sack on the narrow kitchen counter.

"Nope, but that's a part of the story you haven't heard yet. Perhaps after I clean up."

Marie pressed her palm against his forehead. She was surprised at how battered he looked in the light. "You're still hot. I've got some aspirin"

"Already took four," he said, though they'd done little to relieve his headache.

"Good. They'll lower your fever. I'll doctor you proper when you get out."

Josh was touched by her compassion and generosity. "Thanks, Marie," he said, his voice shaky. "I can't thank you enough."

"It's nothing."

"Don't kid yourself. It's everything."

She pinched her nose playfully. "Off to the shower and don't take too long, your food will get cold. How does vegetable beef soup and some hot tea sound to you?"

He nodded that it sounded fine, though his hunger was mixed with an uneasiness that caused him to wonder whether it would stay with him.

She noticed his ebbing energy and placed a hand against his forehead: he was too hot for her liking. "Make it a cold shower," she said as he grabbed his clothes and moved toward the bathroom.


Night surrounded the remote cabin in a velvet blackness as Josh sat before the fire in the big room finishing the last of the thick, dark brown soup. After a large bowl, slowly consumed, he was not surprised to find himself nauseated, though he was determined to keep the soup down. Only the hot tea, some type of herbal concoction Marie's mother used to swear by for all types of ailments, had a settling effect.

"How was it?" she asked.

"It was wonderful," he said, sipping the hot brew. He didn't tell her about his queasy stomach.

It had taken Josh the better part of an hour to scrub the stench from his body and then scrape the stubborn whiskers from his face. His hunger and the smell of the soup warming on the stove had convinced his empty stomach that it wanted every drop of it. He kept sipping the tea, hoping it would quiet the discomfort.

When she'd put the bowl in the kitchen sink, Marie announced that it was time to have a look beneath his bandage. The gauze wrapping had not improved in appearance with the addition of soap and hot water and now looked worse, taking on a sickening crimson hue where the dried black blood had been softened and then diluted.

"Do we have to?" Josh asked half-seriously. He was sitting cross-legged on the floor in his new Wal-Mart jeans, his chest and feet bare.

She remembered how attractive he was. "I don't know if I bought the right stuff, but I grabbed a handful of things from the pharmacy: gauze, peroxide, tape, Neosporin—you know, enough to make the lady at the checkout counter think I was heading for a knife fight." She pulled the items from a bag in the same sack that had held Josh's new wardrobe.

Josh smiled, but did not want to remove the bandages. It wasn't the fear of pain that caused his hesitation, but fear of the unknown. If the wound was as badly infected as he imagined it would be after living in a sewer for two days, capture was only a question of time.

"Maybe it would be better if we didn't disturb it. I've heard that some injuries heal better if—"

"Now!" she ordered. "And I don't want to hear another word."

"Yes, ma'am," he said, inching closer to her.

Marie tenderly cut away the damp wrapping, being careful not to remove the gauze pads from the holes over which they'd been placed. She stuffed the discarded bandage into the grocery bag that held the Styrofoam plate and plastic utensils from Josh's dinner; all that remained now were two pink squares that stuck to his right ribcage.

"Ready?" she asked.

Josh nodded, then clenched his teeth and put his mind on the yellow flames dancing within the wood-burning heater.

Marie gave the square in front, below his breast, a gentle tug. It moved but didn't release. When a bit more pressure was applied, it pulled away from the skin. The shower had done its part.

She said nothing but let out a short gasp, putting her fingers to her mouth as she did.

Josh closed his eyes and cursed silently before looking. A circle nearly as large as the four-inch square of gauze was now a disgusting fusion of bright red and violet. The wound itself, though no longer oozing blood, was still gaping and as black as tar, with a yellowish-white ring of pus encircling it. It was more infected than he'd feared.

When the rear bandage was removed, though it had been more stubborn and took some painful persuasion, the same threatening sight lay beneath it, and the shivering that she'd noticed since he came out of the shower seemed to be worse.

"You've got to get to the hospital," Marie said, realizing that she had neither the supplies nor the skill to treat such an injury. In the poor neighborhood in which she'd spent her youth—where the police came only when pursuing a suspect and proper medical care was a concept reserved for whites—she'd seen knife slashes and bullet wounds no more serious than this claim a life in a few days. "I mean it, Joshua," she said, her voice troubled. "There can be no argument about this."

"I can't go to the hospital, Marie. You know—"

"Joshua, you'll die if you don't! You must believe what I'm telling you." She had to force her eyes from the injury, as if looking away would somehow permit the poison to spread through his bloodstream unchecked. "Please," she pleaded, looking him directly into the eyes.

He touched her arm gratefully. "Do what you can for me, Marie. That's all I can ask."

"Joshua—"

"Listen to me, Marie. I realize I haven't lived as long as I might have under different circumstances, but this is the hand I was dealt. My parents always taught me to take life as it came and not complain. I don't want to die, but if I do, so be it. I will not go to prison, understand? I won't."

Marie attempted another argument, but he silenced her with an open palm. "I've lived a great life and I've met and lost the most incredible woman I've ever known. I know there won't ever be another like her in my life."

Marie's eyes began to fill with tears.

"It's okay, really," Josh said, forcing a smile. "Hell, most people go a lifetime never meeting the right person."

"What will you do?" she asked.

Josh took a shaky breath. "I just want to rest for a day or so more and then try to figure out some way to see my folks. It'll probably be the only chance I get. I'm not going to die without seeing them."

"No, Joshua, you can't. That's the first place they'll be looking for you."

"Probably. I might get lucky, though." He wiped the sweat from his forehead with an index finger. "I never told you they used to call me 'Lucky,' did I?"

She shook her head no, her voice frozen.

"Now, show me what you've got in that medicine bag of yours."


When the plane landed in Jackson at five P.M. Friday evening, Karl Hetzler and Brad Munford were met by a four-man team from the U.S. Marshal Service. They had already been informed by the senior FBI agent that the man they were seeking was wanted for espionage, income tax evasion, criminal trespass, assault with intent to kill, at least a trio of murders, and interstate flight to avoid prosecution. He was to be considered armed and extremely dangerous—if Hetzler could have added any more charges, he would have gladly done so.

"We have two cars waiting outside, sir," one of the marshals announced. "A Suburban for the assault team and a nondescript four-door for the tail car."

"What kind?" Munford asked.

"A Saturn, sir," the agent said.

Munford nodded his approval. He didn't want to attract attention while he shadowed Marie Edwards. He would be in constant communication with the team vehicle, always less than a minute away; if the suspect was spotted, there would be little chance of his escape. Mitchell would die before he would be allowed to elude them a second time.

During the flight to Mississippi, Munford had come to agree with his boss's belief that if Mitchell had not contacted Edwards yet, he soon would, assuming he was still alive. Why his boss believed this so profoundly was based more on intuition than logic, but gut hunches had always been good to the odd little man in the front passenger seat of the Suburban heading at maximum speed for Natchez, and he knew Karl Hetzler wasn't about to ignore the one that had been eating at him since shortly after Mitchell's miraculous disappearance from Kanazawa's neighborhood.

By seven-fifteen in the evening, the six federal agents had grabbed a quick dinner-to-go at a McDonald's on the outskirts of Natchez and had located both Marie Edwards's residence on Arlington Avenue at State Street as well as the mansion on Canal Street at Washington. It pleased the senior agent that the two locations were only three quarters of a mile apart.

"Convenient," Hetzler had said when they'd been identified on the map, "for her and for us."

There was no sign of her car at either location, however, a fact that caused considerable concern for Karl Hetzler. They didn't want to question any of her staff at the mansion, for fear of spooking her if she learned of it. The mansion appeared closed for the evening, early for the first time in a week, but according to what they'd been able to discover, would be reopened at six in the morning as the caterers and volunteers began preparation for the grand opening. Hetzler believed it was unlikely Edwards would return tonight.

It was now a question of finding her. And waiting.

None of the men were strangers to stakeouts, and quickly decided who would take the first, second, and third watch. Mr. Hetzler would not be required to take a watch, of course.

One of the marshals joined Brad Munford in the black Saturn and the vehicle then sped away.

Hetzler and his three associates took up a position not far from Marie Edwards's home, in a cove a short block away that provided a clear view of her front porch and driveway, believing that to be the best chance of spotting her. Munford and the remaining marshal began cruising the restaurants and night spots of Natchez, in case she'd gone out to dinner. Unlike in San Francisco, they assumed the silver BMW 318i wouldn't be difficult to find in the sleepy Mississippi River town.

At half past one on Saturday morning, the car they'd been looking for pulled into Marie Edwards's driveway. Hetzler was awakened at once.

"When the woman's inside, I want her car examined thoroughly. Every inch of it, you understand?" he said. "If there's something there, I want it."

"I'll take care of it," the marshal directly behind him responded with the confidence of one who'd searched suspect vehicles many times, locked or not.

Hetzler radioed Munford. "The woman just got home, Brad. What's your position?"

"We're at Union and Oak Street, less than a mile from her home," he said into his portable radio. "Be there in a couple of minutes. She gonna stay for the night?"

Hetzler watched as the front porch light was extinguished, and then the living room lamp. When the bedroom light came on, he said, "Looks like it. We're in a short cove, Fine Avenue, just northwest of her driveway. Go up to Rankin, come in from our right, and then pull in behind us with your lights off."

"Ten-four," Munford said.

The driver of the Suburban said, "How do you see tomorrow playing out, sir?"

Hetzler thought for a moment. "She's not going to miss her moment in front of the cameras; she's worked too long on that old house for that. If she's gonna lead us to Mitchell, it won't be until after the open house and all the pats on the back have been exchanged."

"You're assuming Mitchell's in Natchez, sir. Isn't that quite a long shot?"

Hetzler stared out the windshield at the neat brick home across the street. It was a long shot, but there hadn't been so much as a supposed sighting of Mitchell since Sunday evening. It was a reasonable gamble, he felt. He said in a low voice, "Long shots are better than no shots."

"Yes, sir, I suppose they are," the marshal said, unconvinced.

The agent leaned back against the passenger door, his arms folded across his chest. As he lowered his head and closed his eyes, he said, "I don't expect her to leave again tonight, but we can't take any chances, so stay sharp. Wake me at first light if I'm not already up. I have a feeling tomorrow's gonna be a big day."

Marie Edwards awoke early Saturday morning with a feeling of joyful anticipation—it was her day, and, after six hard and long months, was well-deserved. But, just below the surface, a dull sense of dread tempered the excitement.

She knew she had done the right thing by calling them . . . about Joshua.

He would die if she hadn't, and she didn't want his death on her conscience. Following his half-thought-out plan to see his parents wasn't as important as getting the help he desperately needed.

He would see that it was all for the best . . . in the end. She just prayed that he'd been honest with her last night. Everything she'd planned was dependent upon that fact.

As she hurriedly dressed, choosing her best navy suit and just the right amount of jewelry, she tried to put the wounded man off her mind and concentrate on the opening ceremony that was, for all intents and purposes, in her honor. After all these years, she'd finally arrived. It had been a long and hard road, and one that she'd not willingly walk again, but she was at last a respected member of the community that had shunned her since birth.

A wide grin spanned her face as she backed her car out of the driveway. With her mind on the last minute details of the open house, the black Saturn that fell in behind her could have been a red Ferrari—it would still not have been noticed.


Josh had slept fitfully, his fever still mounting despite having taken three of the six Keflex that Marie had left for him. The antibiotics had been left over from a bout with strep throat she'd successfully fought at Christmas. At nine A.M., he sat up in bed and realized that the chills still had him in their icy grip.

A headache thundered in his skull, driving him toward the kitchen and the aspirin. The note under his coffee cup this morning informed him that his generous benefactor would be bringing him some lunch—actually a plate she'd fix from the buffet at the open house—as soon as the ceremony was over, a little after noon.

Though his stomach growled, the thought of actually eating anything was now nauseating. Relief from the pain was all he wanted.

He popped another Keflex into his mouth along with four aspirin and washed them down with water from the sink. Though the coffee pot had been set to come on automatically, he'd arisen three hours before its scheduled start time. He looked at the On switch and decided to pass on coffee as well.

When he fell back into bed, the pain in his right side was much worse, making him realize that without hospitalization, loss of consciousness, and finally death, would be coming sooner rather than later. He knew there would not be the chance to see his mom and dad, and the thought saddened him, though the feelings that soon replaced it were regret and anger.

Regret that he'd not seen them when he'd had ample chance, and anger that his last chance had been stolen from him.


Brad Munford joined the masses of dignitaries and curious townsfolk who'd come to celebrate the perfectly restored masterpieces of architecture from their collective past. Some wandered through the home, giving curious grandchildren lessons in history, painting vivid images of the contrasting worlds of slave and slave owner. Others had come to be transported back to a time they'd never known except from paragraphs in history books, a world that had vanished but which had once thrived in splendor on this very spot. Still others had come to simply admire the woodwork or furnishings, considering how they might incorporate some touch of the antebellum period in their own homes.

Only one at the party had come with no interest in the home whatsoever, and he stood with his glass of punch and his finger sandwich less than six feet from the guest of honor.

When the last handshake had been exchanged and the last official photo had been snapped, Marie Edwards stood in the parlor, happy and pleased. It had been an even more spectacular morning than she'd imagined. By Monday, her face would be on the front page of the newspaper which had ignored her existence for thirty-eight years, despite her many accomplishments in high school, college, and the state capital.

It was a sweet victory, indeed, and she savored it for a minute longer before taking a Styrofoam plate and stacking it with as many items as she could carry. Satisfied that she'd grabbed enough to satisfy him if he was again hungry, she covered the plate with a thick paper napkin bearing a likeness of the front of the mansion, and slipped out the side door.

Munford had already left through the front, and was now once again in the passenger seat of the Saturn. He radioed Hetzler.

"Unless she's got one hell of an appetite, I'd say she's bringing a doggy bag to someone, boss."

The marshal behind the wheel of the Suburban said, "When you add that to the Wal-Mart receipt we found wadded up in the ashtray in her car, I'd say your hunch was divinely inspired, sir."

Hetzler didn't mind the compliment, but his chief pleasure came from the knowledge that Mitchell was only minutes away from being taken into custody. "I hope the son of a bitch resists," he whispered to the side glass, knowing the broad range of grievances for which one could be legally shot.

With the law-conscious marshals in tow, however, he and Munford would have to play this one by the book or face a formal hearing. Prison, with the gas chamber waiting in its wings, he reconsidered, would serve Mitchell as well as a bullet in the brain. "Not divinely inspired, just damn lucky," he said to the man.

"Brad," he radioed.

"Sir."

"You lose the woman and I'll see you get the duty station on Guam."

"She's all mine, boss, don't worry," Munford said as he stayed exactly two cars behind the BMW.

"I wonder," Hetzler said in a whisper, the mike on his lap.

"Sir?" the driver asked.

The agent shook his head. "Nothing," he mumbled, and yet for some unknown reason he wasn't so sure Mitchell would be as easy to grab as they thought.

# 24

Marie Edwards drove anxiously down Lower Woodville Road toward the south side of town. In another five minutes at her current speed, she would be on Carthage Point Road, the two-lane highway that led to the cabin cutoff. The old wooden fishing shack that had once belonged to her mother's only brother was less than two minutes from that point. Josh would be waiting for his lunch and she hoped that he was well enough to eat it. She'd seen the ravages of infection and fever more than once in her lifetime and knew that Josh could be anywhere from merely sick to half-dead by now. If only she'd had a way of contacting him, at least she'd know if he was still okay.

She checked her watch: twelve-twenty P.M.

Her call should be bringing Joshua the relief he so desperately needed within the hour. She wanted to be there first, though, to explain.

Marie added speed as the road left the last populated area and changed from a forty to a fifty-five zone, and felt the engine willingly respond to her command. She noticed in her rearview mirror that a car was behind her. She studied it for a second, wondering if it could be following her.

Using a pair of small, powerful binoculars, Brad Munford had seen the woman's head turn toward her mirror, and directed the marshal to widen the gap between the two cars. They were fifty yards back; a hundred wouldn't hurt, and might even provide a measure of relaxation for Edwards that closer shadowing might inhibit.

"Son of a bitch!" Munford shouted as the Saturn seemed to jump ten feet to the left with a shuddering crash.

Neither had seen the car that struck the Saturn in the right rear at a blind intersection just before a small grade. By the time the noise and confusion had ended, the Saturn sideways in the road, Edwards had disappeared over the hill and had vanished from sight.

Brad Munford leaped from the passenger seat and shouted into his hand unit. "This is Munford. We've been in an accident. We've lost the woman."

"Goddammit!" Hetzler shouted, knowing that their vehicle was two minutes behind the Saturn. That meant a two-mile lead for the woman. "What the hell happened?" he barked, realizing that he'd allowed the lead to get too great.

Munford studied the goofy-looking teenager climbing out of the rusted green Ford pickup and shook his head. The kid seemed dazed, but unhurt.

"Whoa, dude," the kid said, his tone one of amazement. "Where the hell did you come from, man?"

The marshal who'd been driving the Saturn shoved the boy up against the truck, patting him down quickly. No weapons, and no apparent smell of alcohol.

"Some dumb kid ran a stop sign and slammed into us broadside," Munford said into the mike.

"Dammit to hell," Hetzler grumbled. "Step on it, will you!?" he snapped at the driver of the Suburban.

"Yes, sir," the marshal said, calling on every horsepower under the massive hood.

Marie studied her mirror as she sped down the back side of the grade, and was pleased to find the black car no longer behind her. She guessed they'd tuned off at one of the side roads, just as she was going to do in another minute.

At twelve-thirty-five, Marie stopped in front of the cabin and switched off the engine. It tinkled softly as she stepped past the grill, and as she stared down the roofline, toward the road she'd just driven. She was grateful that the others had not yet arrived.

But she was alarmed by Josh's failure to meet her, and hurried inside, leaving the food plate on the front seat.

The sight that met her eyes was worse than she'd feared.

"Joshua," she called, sitting beside him on the bed and placing a hand on each shoulder. She shook gently, but he didn't respond.

"Joshua!" she yelled, shaking him harder.

His skin was as ghastly pallid as Pamela's had been on the sand in Carmel, his breathing imperceptible. The sheet beneath him was damp all around his fervid body, his exposed skin covered in droplets of sweat.

"Joshua!" she shouted, shaking him harder still.

One eye opened slightly, followed by the other. A smile began to add animation to his lifeless lips.

"Hi," he said weakly.

"Oh, my God. You scared the hell out of me. I'll be right back." With that, Marie raced into the kitchen and filled a pan with the coldest water the tap would deliver. Ten seconds later, she was pressing a cold rag against his forehead.

Josh managed a couple of deep breaths and tried to shake the cobwebs from his brain. It took a minute or two for him to realize that he had not yet died, as he'd dreamed, but was still in the cabin in the woods, only waiting to die.

He smiled generously at the woman who was doing her best to keep him alive. "You bring me something to eat," he said, his voice a little stronger.

"You feel like eating?" she said incredulously.

"No, but I wanted to know if you remembered me."

"Of course I remembered you."

"Even with all the excitement of the morning?" he said, trying to raise his head.

"Yes," she said, rewetting the towel. A little color had come back into his face. "Have you had anything to drink lately?"

He shook his head.

She returned to the kitchen and brought both cups filled with cool tap water, the bottle of aspirin in her suit pocket. "How about aspirin? When was the last time you took some?"

"About nine," he said.

She put four in his mouth and handed him a cup of water, which he quickly drank. He finished the second one more slowly, but managed to get it all down.

After fifteen minutes of Marie's care, Josh began to feel almost like living again, though his side felt like a horse had kicked him.

As he was about to thank her for all she'd done for him, the unmistakable sound of several vehicles pulling up outside invaded the stillness of the tiny room. His eyes went to Marie's, but she only looked away.

He knew she'd summoned the help that would save his life, but would cost him his freedom. With her head still turned toward the back wall, her eyes shut, Josh touched her arm.

"It's okay, Marie. Really. Perhaps you should let them in."

Marie looked back at him, her eyes tearing. "It will be okay, Joshua. I promise it will."

Josh nodded, and Marie rose to open the front door.

When she'd left the bedroom, Josh fished beneath the pillow and pulled out Kenny's small .38 Special. He drew back the hammer, putting the last round in the top chamber, and pointed it toward the room.

"Is this what it felt like, Pamela," he said, trying to sit as erect and defiant as possible, "when there was nowhere left to run?"

As the bedroom door opened, Josh aimed the pistol at the opening. The man from the hotel room in Sacramento ducked quickly then made a diving leap toward the bed, grabbing the gun and taking it from Josh before it could be discharged.

Josh had been surprised by the speed and strength of the man and released his grip on the gun without a fight. The second gun, DiAmo's chrome automatic, was quickly located beside the pillow and taken as well.

As the large room just beyond the bedroom seemed to fill with strange men, Josh gave in to despair. At least he'd get to see his mother again, even if it would be in prison. The image of her loving and trusting face under such circumstances was as disturbing as any he could imagine.

A second man joined the man from the hotel and then a third, each looking down at him with curious interest. None spoke. One of the latter took the weapons from the man who'd collected them and then left the room. A few seconds later, both of the other men followed him, leaving Josh in the bedroom alone.

Josh rose again on his elbows and called out: "Marie!"

She came to him quickly, but she was not alone. On her right was another woman, dressed in jeans and a large flannel shirt, a Yankees baseball cap covering her head. Despite the attempt to conceal her identity, he recognized her immediately—or believed he did—though he was sure the fever was responsible for the hallucination. He squeezed his eyes shut, certain Marie would be alone with him in the room when he reopened them.

The second woman was still there, though standing beside the bed now.

"Dianne?" he whispered in disbelief.

"Hello, Joshua," the woman said. "It's so good to see you again."

The second woman pulled the cap from her head, allowing her sandy-blonde hair to fall into place. She was even more beautiful in person than she'd become in his dreams of her, a vision. She leaned across the bed and kissed him softly on the lips.

Josh looked at Marie Edwards. "I don't understand," he said.

Marie smiled. "Joshua, I'd like you to meet my very best friend, Pamela Anne Morrow. Pamela, this is Joshua Mitchell. I'm sure the two of you have a lot to talk about." With that, she crossed the room, stopping in the doorway. "Ten minutes, Pamela. Then you'll have to be leaving."

Pamela smiled at her friend. "Thanks, Marie."

Marie closed the door behind her.

When the senior FBI agent reached the scene of the accident, ninety seconds after it had occurred, a small crowd of passersby had already begun to form, including an officer from the Mississippi Highway Patrol. Hetzler joined the junior agent at the rear of the Saturn, where the old green Ford seemed to be trying to mate with it. The vehicles were locked together by the tangle that used to be their bumpers.

"You okay?" he asked.

"Fine," Munford assured him.

"Good, you and the marshal get in the other car." He turned to the cop, displaying his Bureau credentials. "I assume you were heading north, officer."

"Yeah, that's right." It seemed an odd statement to the patrolman, but then, the FBI often seemed odd.

"How long you been on this road?"

"Ten minutes, maybe fifteen."

"Always heading north?"

"Yeah. Why?"

"Do you remember passing a silver BMW heading south?" Hetzler crossed his fingers.

The man was resolute: "Didn't pass one."

"You sure?" Hetzler asked, but the man's expression said no mistake had been made. The agent celebrated silently, knowing the choices of alternate roads Marie Edwards could have taken had just been diminished significantly. He gave a quick signal and one of the marshals spread a detailed map of the immediate area on the hood of the patrolman's car. "All right, assuming she didn't continue south for long, from this point what's the most likely road the car I'm after would have taken?"

The patrolman studied the map. He touched two roads that both headed west from the highway. "Either River Terminal Road or

Carthage Point Road, assuming this person you're talking about is headed for the river. One's about three miles ahead, the other a little more than a mile past that."

In thirty seconds, the Suburban, with all six men on board, was speeding toward the first turnoff. The cop could handle the juvenile driver who'd failed to stop.

According to the map, River Terminal Road was more than three miles long itself, but unlike their second choice, showed no outlet on the far side. The Mississippi River prevented that, an obstacle that not even the slippery Mr. Mitchell could defy. It wasn't likely that Edwards could have reached him, fed him, and left by now.

He prayed she hadn't taken the second turnoff, though, with a little manpower within the next five or ten minutes, it could be effectively blocked at the far end.

"Have the state police block off the south end of Carthage Point Road, where it meets Butler Lake Road," Hetzler ordered the marshal behind the wheel when he handed him the mike. He continued to study the map. His instructions were relayed and they were assured a car could be at that location in less than a quarter hour.

"Gotcha, you bastard," Hetzler said with confidence when River Terminal Road came into view. The marshals checked their weapons as the man in the center of the back seat reached into the rear compartment for the vests.

It was a moment Hetzler had waited for since first photographing Mitchell on the beach in Carmel.


Pamela Morrow sat on the bed next to Josh, rubbing the side of his face tenderly with her fingertips. "Marie told me everything when she called yesterday. I can't believe what you've been through, Joshua. I had no idea."

"I saw your body on the beach, Dianne . . . Pamela . . . God, what am I supposed to call you?"

"What do you want to call me?"

"I could use a little help here."

She nodded sympathetically. "Well, you met me as Pamela Morrow. Let's keep things simple for now."

"Simple?" he said incredulously.

"Pamela Morrow is my real name, Joshua. I only took the name Dianne Lane in 1989, after Pamela had been well . . . killed."

"But I saw your body in Carmel. You can't fake something like that. You were dead." He knew it was impossible, and yet he had seen it with his own eyes.

"It's true, the woman you saw was dead, but it wasn't me, Joshua, any more than it was my real body on that street in Jackson in 1989. As then, it was a Jane Doe, only this time a woman who had drowned somewhere else along the coast. She had no family and no one to claim her. When my people learned of her, and the striking resemblance between us, they put everything together."

"I can't believe I'm hearing this. I actually considered the possibility that you might have had something to do with Pamela Morrow's death back then . . ."

"Why on earth would?"

"To allow you access to Lloyd Richmond and all his connections," Josh said.

Pamela smiled. She understood why he would have made such an assumption and didn't fault him for it. "This has been awful for you, hasn't it?"

His eyes responded for him.

She touched his face gently. "I'm so sorry for the pain it has caused you. I didn't know."

"How could you not have known?" he asked. "It was all over the news." His expression registering the hurt he felt.

"As soon as the exchange was made in Carmel, as well as swapping my fingerprints at FBI headquarters in Washington, I was hurried out of the country and out of Madeline Richmond's reach. By the time you saw the woman on the beach, I was in Canada. By that Tuesday night, I was in England. I knew nothing of what was going on back in California, I swear, Joshua. I only learned about it when Marie phoned yesterday. If I had known, I would have come at once." She pulled the sheet down to his waist, studying his damaged body. The sight made her angry and sad at the same time. She laid the palm of her left hand against his chest, surprised at how hot he felt.

"Marie knew all the time?"

"She's known since 1989. I know it violated every rule my people operate by, but Marie was the closest friend I'd ever had. I couldn't let her go on thinking I'd been killed. She's kept the secret all these years."

Josh's mind reeled. "You said 'your people.' You mean the people you work for?"

"Yes. They're the ones who found out about Madeline Richmond's intent to have me killed, and one of them quickly and convincingly posed as a hit man willing to accept the contract. To keep her from trying again, something she would have attempted until she finally succeeded, I had to die for the second time in eight years. She's an extremely powerful woman, you know, and utterly ruthless."

"How well I know."

"Of course you do," she said sympathetically.

Josh couldn't get out of his mind the damage she'd done to her country, and despite his desire to hold her and forget everything he'd learned, couldn't let it go unsaid. "You're a spy, aren't you, Pamela? You sold my technology to the Chinese."

Pamela smiled. "Yes, I'm a spy, Joshua, and a damn good one, I'm told." As the horror registered in Josh's eyes, she elaborated: "I work for the United States Government, Joshua, not against it. My friends, my people, are the CIA, and nothing of yours ever left the country. My father tried to correct the ills of the world following the Second World War single-handedly, but soon came to realize that he had neither the means nor the global understanding to accomplish his goals. His lifetime of connections proved invaluable in the Cold War years, however, and he was more than willing to help the country he'd come to love and think of as his home accomplish its objectives. He was a great man, Joshua, with noble ideals and lofty dreams for mankind, most of which were never realized. It didn't keep him from trying though, and I was proud to help any way I could.

"But the business of trying to maintain a balance in world power, and how I got involved in it all, is a complex and lengthy story, one I'm afraid we don't have time for now." She ran a hand gently down his chest. "Just trust me, my love, I'm one of the good guys."

Whether it was the last two words she'd spoken, or the mention of the Central Intelligence Agency, his mind was reeling. "I don't understand any of this," he said.

"I know. It's very confusing at first, but in the end, it's all pretty simple. Some people want things, others are willing to do anything to provide them. Neither seem to worry about the cost in terms of lives or world stability. Since it's impossible to stop such things, it's our job to see that such exchanges, if you will, are done with our country's long-term interests in mind. Some, like Iran-Contra, don't go according to plan. Many others do. It all works out as long as some are willing to work for causes and beliefs." She lifted one of his scratched and scuffed hands and held its palm against her face. "We can have a long philosophical discussion about it one day. It was the favorite topic of debate between Lloyd and me when no one else was around."

He hadn't wanted to think about that aspect of her life, but there was no avoiding it now. He said, "What was your relationship with Lloyd Richmond?" not really wanting an answer, but knowing he had to have one.

For the first time, Pamela looked away, and when she turned back to Josh, her eyes were sad. "He was my father, Joshua. I was the child of another woman he could never find the courage to tell Madeline about. I guess he was afraid of what she might do to him, or me. He secretly provided for me and my mother all my life, with the one stipulation that my mother never reveal his identity. She never did, he came to me after her death. Lloyd left me the gallery and museum when he died, as well as the money it had made that Madeline never knew about. She always believed, and never cared to learn otherwise, that the gallery and museum were a break-even proposition, a toy of her husband. When she learned after Lloyd's death that there was still more than thirty million dollars in post-tax profits left after probate, and that I was sole beneficiary, I think that's when she decided to have me killed." Her gray eyes became the softest he'd seen. "I know he loved me, Joshua, even if he didn't have the nerve to face that witch."

"I can understand the way he felt," Josh said sincerely. He wanted to hold this remarkable woman, to keep her safe for the rest of her life, but sensed something remained unsaid. "You're leaving soon, aren't you?"

"Yes. I have to."

Josh nodded as the pain of her leaving took a bite out of his soul. He didn't think he could bear to say goodbye to her again. "What about us? How can you just walk away again?"

She leaned to him and kissed him passionately. "I know you went through all this for me. That's why I made them take me to you. They didn't want to, said it was too dangerous, but I convinced them it was what I wanted more than anything in the world."

"What are you saying?" he asked.

"I came back for you, Joshua. You're going away with me."

"Away? Where? What about the police?"

"By this time next week, your buddy Richard Hightower will discover that all his carefully laid plans have backfired, and that video and audio evidence on him and your ex-partner is in the hands of the attorney general. Madeline will be shocked to find that the trail leading to the man she hired to kill me, as well as Mr. Jack Farris of Mobile, is far more damning than even her lawyers can explain away."

"Jack Farris?" he asked. It was all he could do to keep up with her.

"The man she hired to kill you. Sorry, we didn't expect she'd do anything remotely like that, especially to you."

Josh nodded. He believed her.

Pamela continued. "As far as the police and the Bureau boys, it will all work out in a few weeks, or months at most, and your good name will be restored. We'll see to it. We can be pretty clever when we set our minds to it." There was more than a touch of pride in her voice.

Nothing would amaze him anymore.

"In the meantime, we'll have to disappear, I'm afraid. Madeline is still wealthy and she still wants us both dead, especially now; her power is not to be underestimated. I think it's also fair to say that Jack Farris is out there, still hoping to earn his fee. I don't know him, but I know his type. He'll have to be dealt with carefully, and quickly. It will happen, though, believe me."

He sat up fully, his fever still haunting him, though his headache had lessened. He did believe her and knew that the CIA was more than capable of handling a man like Jack Farris. He turned his attention to the thought of spending time with the beautiful woman beside him.

"Where will we go?" he asked, though it mattered little.

"I hear the south of France is nice this time of year. We could say hello to your parents while we're there." She gave him an impish wink.

"Seriously," he said.

"Okay, seriously. First, we're going to get you to a hospital in Canada where you can be cared for properly; we'll be there in a few hours. In the meantime, just to make sure you don't do anything dumb like die on me, there's a doctor waiting at a private airport a few miles from here where our plane is waiting.

"Then, when you're all better, we'll arrange for your parents to join us in Canada. I'm sure they will be glad to see their baby boy again, especially since he's grown up to be such a fine, handsome man." She leaned against him again, and this time, he returned her kiss.

As she grabbed his shirt from the chair back she said, "We can spend a week or so with your folks there, probably around Lake Louise. It's spectacular in the spring; you'll love it and I'm looking forward to meeting them."

Despite his still-fuzzy mind trying hard to process all that had just occurred, Josh couldn't hold back the smile that formed.

"Finally, you and I are going to disappear to a romantic island in the South Pacific where we'll live on pineapple and shrimp and run around naked all day." She buttoned his last button as he sat dumbfounded. "We can finally finish what we started at the Sandpiper Inn."

"It's time to go, Pamela," the big man from the hotel announced as he poked his head through the door. "Our juvenile delinquent driver won't keep the Bureau boys at bay forever. Boat's waiting."

"Thanks, Mark. We're coming now." She turned back to Josh. "Ready, sweetheart?"

"Boat?"

"A little safety net, that's all. We'll cross the Mississippi back into Louisiana, just like we arrived. It's unlikely they've anticipated such a move, though I suspect the roads around here are already swarming with cops and FBI guys. This kind of stuff really makes them crazy."

"I can see that you love irritating the FBI."

"It's mutual, Joshua, I assure you," she grinned.

"Pamela," he said, his mind trying to assimilate a thousand different thoughts, "I love you. I've loved you since I was a boy. You know that, don't you?"

Marie joined them and the two women helped him stand, his weight supported in part by each. Pamela was careful not to hurt him as she wrapped her arm around his waist.

"I know," she said as they walked slowly toward the front door. "When we spent that wonderful Monday together, I was amazed by all the things I had begun to feel about you, but realized I had to force them aside because I knew it was going to be impossible for us to see each other again. I was a little afraid, too; I thought I would be just another one-night stand for you. It was hard to accept that you felt the same way about me as I did about you, after such a short time." She gave him a gentle squeeze. "That's the real reason I came back for you, Joshua. I've never met anyone who loved me no matter what I did or who I was, and I'm never going to let you go again."

"After all he's been through on your behalf, Pamela, I don't think he's going anywhere," Marie said, her heart full of love for her best friend and her newest friend. They deserved each other, she felt.

Josh could only grin.

He thought about all the tragedy and horror of the last twelve days, and realized that through it all, he'd somehow managed to find not only the part of him he'd lost ten years ago, but the woman he'd dreamed of all his life.

Perhaps it had all been fate.

For whatever reason, he regretted not one second of it.

Maybe, he thought with a smile whose origin went back to a plane bound for San Francisco, "Lucky" wasn't such a bad nickname after all.

# Acknowledgments

As the years now number more on the spent side of my life than on the available side, I have become far more appreciative of so many things of which I was only partially aware when the balance tipped heavily in the other direction. For that reason, if no other, I would not ask to reclaim one day from my past.

Many kind and talented people have generously added their own special spice to my life along the way, some with suggestions or work, some with help or in need of help, some with room and board, some with warm hugs, still others with plates of home-made cookies. This book is the direct result of a collective commitment to bringing dreams to life, a dedication to the synergy of love and effort.

I would like to extend my heartfelt thanks to each of these fine folks for his or her immeasurable contribution to my work and to my life: to Herbert and Linnie for proof that true love lives eternal; to my mom and dad for fifty years of shared dreams and creating dreamers; to Joan and Bob for the support only family can give; to Chuck and Stacia for Shelbey and Brooks; to Micki for continuing to become a fine young woman in a world filled with mediocrity; to Sybil for her God-given voice and the courage to use it; to Casey for always making his mama smile; to Brian for his saintly patience; to Arnie V. and Louise for the countless Sunday dinners; to Terry Pahn (occasionally pronounced: ter-u-don) for the unwavering belief; to Dusky Norsworthy and Charlie Holbrook for, among many other things, Fishbones; to Lane Anderson for his considerable programming expertise; to Dr. Michael Smelser, a fine physician, a fine friend, and a generous tutor; and to his wife, Judy, for taking Pamela and Joshua to the beach; to Don and Debbie Reid for the red carpet and the call at nearly midnight; to Tim and Julie Craig for reminding me that play is as vital to life as work; to Debbie Stanford and Cindy Cain for being the kinds of fans every writer hopes for, whether or not they are worthy of them; to Bill Adler at Adler & Robin Books for being a fan; to Suzanne Schwalb and the rest of the team at Whitebridge Communications, Nashville, for polishing the star so well; to Ingram Books and a sales staff which takes a back seat to none; to Tom and Kathie Sims for the music, the shelter, and the inspiration; to Rob and Julie (Mrs. Tennessee America, 1997) Tallman for so many things; to Lieutenant Joe Grebmeier, Commander of the Monterey County Coroner's Office, for the assistance; to Carmel-by-the-Sea firefighter, Todd Hutchings, for his willing help; to Dennis Meloni of San Francisco for allowing me to disrupt his Tuesday morning; to Dan at Century 21 in Sacramento for the information; to Steve Smith, Ron Wilburn, and Dave Robbins at McNairy County Airport for the many helpful bits of trivia; to Bridget Walker at the Day's Inn in Natchez for taking time to talk with a stranger; to Terry Abernathy, Esq., for keeping my legalese accurate; to Pat Sweat for keeping me accurate south of the border; to Pat Knight and Judy at Pat's Diner in Selmer, Tennessee for the good burgers, sweet tea, lousy jokes, and the occasional credit; to Adam Dunn at Carroll & Graf Publishers, Inc. for the kind attention to so many aspects involved in the production of this book; to my loyal and dear friend Kent Carroll for his unparalleled interest and involvement in each of my stories—I cannot imagine having been blessed with a more caring, knowledgeable, and unselfish publisher at this point in my writing career . . .

. . . and especially to Anita, the love of my life, for not waking me from this dream.